Carp

By Chris Cawood
Magnolia Hill Press
Kingston, Tennessee

This is a work of fiction.

Front and back cover design by Anne Powers.

Printed in the United States.

Library of Congress Catalog Card Number 97-93523

ISBN 0-9642231-4-7

5 4 3 2 1

Carp

By
Chris Cawood

Book Number: _1334_/3000

(author signature)

Author Autograph

Other Books By Chris Cawood

1998: THE YEAR OF THE BEAST

Tennessee's Coal Creek War

How To Live To 100 (and enjoy it!)

Legacy Of The Swamp Rat

The Spring of '68
(To be published in 1998)

This book is the second in a series of mystery and general fiction by Chris Cawood. A selected number of each edition are autographed and numbered. If your book is autographed and numbered and you would like to receive the next in the series with the same number and autographed, please phone the publisher and reserve your copy at no extra expense:
1-800-946-1967

This is dedicated to my son, Shannon, and my grandson, Jacob.

Also, over the past four years in researching the river travel portion of this story, my best friend, Jerry Seale, and I took my 24-foot pontoon boat down the Tennessee, Ohio, and Mississippi rivers from near Knoxville to New Orleans.

I dedicate the spirit of this story to all the "river rats" who helped us along the way. We found that the folks along the river are willing to help. In places like Saltillo, Tennessee; Paducah, Kentucky; Cairo, Illinois; Osceola and West Helena, Arkansas; Memphis, Tennessee; Greenville, Vicksburg, and Natchez, Mississippi, we found people who aided us on our river odyssey. A big thanks goes to the guys in the sheriff's office of Iberville Parish at Plaquemine, Louisiana, and to Wally of Wally's Outboards who rescued us from an island in the Mississippi River when our engine went out and fixed it late one evening.

The Mississippi is a powerful, wild, tempestuous, and ruthless Old Man who is unforgiving to those who take him lightly.

Acknowledgments

This book would never have been completed without the help of several people who read drafts, made comments, and encouraged. I want to thank my fine editor, Gaynell Seale, who worked tirelessly to make this a readable manuscript. She has been my editor on all my books, and she adds a special touch to each project.

Another friend, Anne Powers, designed the cover which I really like. From past experience, I know a book is often judged by its cover. If this one is, it will be found worthy.

Author's Note

I began this book in 1991 when I didn't know how to write as well as I do now. I liked the story, but the finished product was about seventy pages longer than this. It rambled a bit. Over the last six years, I have refined *Carp* to where I hope the reader finds it an interesting story.

I would point out to the reader that there are two or three scenes of R-rated sexual explicitness and a few instances of coarse language. They are used to show character development, realism, and to move the plot.

Hope you enjoy.

Chris Cawood

Prologue

He glanced down at the lighted dial of his watch—3:45 a.m. February 14—Valentine's day. Another holiday he would have to make up to his girlfriend.

The steady hum of the Piper Navajo's twin engines and their soothing vibration were almost hypnotic. Sleep would have come easily except for the cold wind rushing in through the open cockpit door.

His gaze returned to the earth. Ahead and a thousand feet below, the confluence of the Alabama and Tombigbee rivers in rural, southern Alabama shone in the bright moonlight like fingers of molten lead.

He kneeled at the open door, adjusted his night-vision goggles and aimed the hand-held laser toward a reflective target on the ground. A patch of fluorescent green sparkled to life.

As the plane continued in its pre-set slow circling, he kicked bulging burlap bags out the open door. He timed the drops at thirty-second intervals to ring the target on the ground. Five bags thudded to the opening in the pine forest before he moved back to the control panel.

He took the plane off the pre-set pattern and brought it on one last circuit of the area. There were no house or car lights on the ground below. The moonlight only reflected weakly off the rivers. He studied the maps by the red glow of the panel lights and calibrated his wrist altimeter with the one on the panel.

The plane climbed to 5500 feet. The fuel gauges showed enough left, by his calculations, to take the craft due south to Mobile and then into the Gulf of Mexico.

Once the plane leveled off and was aimed toward the drop point, he stepped out of the pilot's seat, squatted, and duck-walked to the open door. He felt for his pistol, knife, packet of food, and cash. He strapped on the parachute and steeled his courage for the push out of the plane.

He edged backward until he was in the doorway. Both gloved hands gripped the door facing until he felt the cold of the metal. He went down his mental checklist and renewed his resolve for his first jump.

To his left, the joining rivers appeared below him. He made his coiled legs push him into the cold, rushing air and away from the plane. Momentarily, he saw the bright strobe light of the plane becoming ever smaller and ever farther away. The plane continued southward against the inky backdrop of the starry sky.

He rotated his body toward the ground, pulled the rip-cord, and waited for the jerk of the parachute.

One

Wispy tentacles of fog reached skyward and the sound of the morning was silence.

Green clothed the Tennessee River banks with varying shades from the bright new-leafed tulip poplars to the emerald of kudzu.

The shoreline bathed in the warm sun of the first day of May with only one house in sight from as far as the eye could see in either direction.

Joe Chapman had planned it that way. A house–a home –perched on the limestone outcroppings, had been ten years in the building. And the dock where he sat now, rubbing his bare back against the warm support post. In his hand he loosely held a fishing pole. Beside him his .357 magnum pistol lay loaded. Beside it a six-pack beer carton, half empty. Down the dock another ten feet, his big yellow dog, J. R., sprawled on the graying boards and slept with his head pointed toward Joe.

Joe jerked his head around at the sound of a splash and saw a blue heron emerge from the river a hundred yards away with its breakfast. This was the pristine side of life that he desired and envied.

He glanced at his watch. The first day of May. Where had the first four months of the year gone?

A year before, May Day had been a day of celebration. Law Day. He was chosen by the bar association to speak at the local high school's civic classes about the Constitution and Declaration of Independence.

"When in the course of human events it becomes necessary for one people to dissolve the political bonds which have connected them with another, and to assume among the powers of the Earth, the separate and equal station to which the Laws of Nature and of Nature's God entitle them, a decent respect to the opinions of mankind requires that they should declare the causes which impel them to the separation,"—he could still quote them. Only they didn't mean as much now.

Life had tumbled from May Day–a day of celebration–to mayday–a time of desperation. Divorced, bankrupt, and suspended from the practice of law, he wondered how it had all slipped away so swiftly.

"We hold these truths to be self-evident, that all men are created equal, that they are endowed by their Creator with certain unalienable Rights, that among these are Life, Liberty, and the pursuit of happiness," he whispered the treasured words.

"We the People of the United States, in order to form a more perfect union, establish Justice, ensure domestic Tranquility, provide for the common defence, promote the general Welfare, and secure the Blessings of Liberty to ourselves and our posterity . . ."

Then his thoughts settled on the phrase—*the pursuit of happiness*.

He had gone to law school to *establish justice*, but over the last ten years he had been reminded that his life tended toward the *pursuit of happiness*. He was "out of control," his ex-wife had told him. "Living on the edge" was another term she used. Grow up, settle down, drink less, party less—all good admonitions. He hadn't listened.

Large, dark shadowy figures swam in the shallows near the dock.

Joe Chapman grabbed his pistol, stood, and blasted away, stopping only to reload. His dog slunk away to the farthest point of the dock.

"Carp, damned carp. That's all there is in here anymore. Damn TVA and damn the wildlife resources people. This river should be free-flowing and full of trout." He fired off another volley in the direction of the nearest Tennessee Valley Authority dam, although it was forty miles down stream. To him the symbol and principle were important.

When the water settled to near stillness, Joe Chapman bent over the wood boards and looked at his reflection in the water. He was certain that some of the river water coursed through his veins. He remembered reading that scientists thought the content of blood matched in some way the content of sea water from which they said life came.

If that were the case, he was sure some of the water from the Powell, Clinch, Holston, French Broad, Emory, and Tennessee flowed through him. Chapmans had lived along those rivers in Tennessee for more than two hundred years. They had been born, married, and died within view of those arteries of commerce and waterers of agriculture. And when they took a notion, they pissed in them.

When he focused again on his image, he saw on his head the results of the excesses of the night before. His head was hairless, shaved by a barmaid after he had lost a drunken bet.

That was the way he was. People would just have to accept him that way. He was not going to make himself over to please a wife or society. He got to his feet and walked to the post. He bent his head over and rubbed his scalp against the warm wood. Hair would grow back. The sun would rise. He would overcome. Time would heal the wounds that society and an unforgiving wife had inflicted upon him. He looked down at both bare arms. Scars of other wounds ran from his wrist to his elbow on each. The rays of the sun felt good to his left arm but lit a torch in his right.

He turned and threw an empty beer bottle into the water. He aimed and fired off three more rounds—the last hitting the floating brown bottle. He moved his sights to the other side of the dock and fired the remaining rounds at more carp.

"Carp! Carp!" he shouted with an echo rebounding from the rocky cliff of the far bank two seconds later.

"J. R., did you know that *carp* is a verb and a noun?" He looked at the large dog whose ears had perked up at the mention of his name. "No, no, I guess you didn't know that. I've been carped at, carped on, and carped into. So much, that I think I'm turning into one. The bottom eating shitfish of society."

The sound of tires sliding in loose gravel pulled his attention to the driveway and the Jeep that was descending in a dusty cloud. He grabbed his Oakland Raiders cap and slid it over his slick scalp. It sat loosely above his ears. He hurriedly pulled on a long-sleeved shirt.

Joe walked toward the now-stopped vehicle.

"How's the Honorable Charles Palk, district attorney general, today?" he shouted in a formal salutation to his long time friend.

"Good. And you, Joe?" Palk stood with one hand on the roll bar of his open Jeep.

"Great. Couldn't be better," Joe said and adjusted his cap.

"What's with the hair? You got cancer on top of everything else, Joe?"

"No. I just wanted to look like you."

"Mine's just receding," Palk said and rubbed his hand over a polished scalp that was hairless to ear level.

"Yeah. It's receded or retreated on all sides. You have more hair under your nose than on your head."

Palk stroked his mustache while his blue eyes shot Joe a sharp look. "There's nothing I do that requires hair."

"Mine will grow back, and when all those women are running their fingers through my hair, I'll be thinking about you."

"Really. What happened?"

"A waitress shaved it last night. I either lost a bet or she wanted my hair as a trophy."

"Yeah, I could have figured that. I mean what really *happened*? Why are you like this? What were you shooting at? What's going to happen to you?"

"Wait a minute. What is this, *Twenty Questions*? We go back a long way. Come down and sit on the boat with me and have a beer."

They walked down the driveway to the dock. Palk looked at his watch.

"It's nine in the morning. Anybody drinking beer at this time of day should be hospitalized. I'll sit with you for a minute though. You got any coffee? A Coke?"

They stepped onto Joe's houseboat. Joe offered Palk a Dr. Pepper and pulled another bottle of beer out of a case for himself. He slid two wooden chairs around for them to sit on and faced away from the sun.

"How do you like my home?" Joe asked and gestured toward the boat's cabin. "A twenty-year-old 34-foot boat. A six cylinder Ford engine and a propane stove."

"What about that home?" Palk asked and pointed back to the house looming over them near his Jeep.

"Charlie, you know that's gone. The new owners take over Monday. Ten years of work and building. Paying and redoing. Adding on and remodeling. Gone. Foreclosed.

"Bankruptcy and no job prospects will do that to you. I'm worse off than when you and I started that little law practice twelve years ago. Now you're the attorney general for the county, and I'm the laughing stock."

"What do you have left?"

Joe stood, went to the rail of the boat and spit into the river. "This is it. I convinced the bankruptcy judge that the boat was my homestead. I got to keep it. I have my '72 Harley, clothes, a few law books, a couple of thousand dollars, and my old dog."

Charles Palk shook his head and then took a long swallow from the Dr. Pepper.

"Yeah, I see it in your eyes, Charlie. It's a long way down from having two Corvettes. a Dodge Ram pickup, a Bonanza airplane, a speedboat with twin 150 Mercurys, and a . . ."

"Wife?"

"Yeah."

"You shouldn't name her when you're listing your possessions, Joe. Women aren't chattel. Or have you missed the last thirty years?"

"She didn't understand."

"She understood perfectly. Wives don't like for their husbands to have girlfriends."

Joe took his cap off and rubbed his head. "She always forgave me before. Why not this time?"

"There comes a time when it's just not worth it, when there's no hope of a change, of improvement. That's all. That's why she left."

"But you can turn your life around. You're young. Thirty-nine? You could law clerk for someone until your suspension runs out. A year, right?"

"No, hell no!" Joe threw the bottle into the water. "I can't even clean the toilets in a law office for a year. Our law board saw to that. I can't be around a law office."

"Well, it was a pretty serious offense. You have to look at it from the board's view."

"That's what's wrong with you. Ever since you became attorney general, you look at everything from *society's* viewpoint instead of the individual's rights. I should have a right to the *pursuit of happiness.*"

Joe reached over, picked up his pistol, and aimed it at the bay window of the house.

"Don't do that. You have the attorney general for an eye witness."

Joe laid the pistol down and sat back down beside his friend.

"If you've been pursuing happiness, I believe your dog has lost the scent. You might should look up the definition of happiness."

Palk reached over and picked up the pistol from where Joe had placed it. "You aren't thinking about suicide?"

Joe spit over the railing. "Suicide, no. Murder, yes. If I died now, they'd have to hire pallbearers. When I was flying up to the Derby or down to Bimini, I had all kinds of friends. You're the only one who's been by since the divorce and bankruptcy. What kind of friends is that?"

"Some people don't know what to think about you now, Joe. They're bewildered, befuddled. They think you've lost it."

Joe stood back up and looked at his house.

"What I've lost that I want back, I'll get back. Those kinds of friends I don't want back."

Palk looked at his watch.

"I've got to go. Stop by the office. I'll see what I can do for you. A job somewhere. Not in law."

"Not right now. I'm just going to cruise around on the river for the summer. Dock here and there. Think things over. By fall, I'll be out of money and ready to look for something to do. It's just going to be me and J. R. on the boat for now. Maybe a girl every now and then." He smiled.

Palk shook his head. "Think things over. You don't need anymore women problems though. They have a drug now that will decrease your sex drive."

"How do you know? You been taking it?"

"No. Marriage and children will also do it for you."

Palk turned from the dock and eyed the boat. "What do you call this old tub. Every boat has a name, doesn't it? Did you have a christening ceremony?"

"It's called *THE ESCAPE.*"

Palk paused. "Yeah, maybe that's a good name. You need to escape. Call any time."

BETWEEN CARRYING LOADS OF his meager possessions on board from the basement of the house, Joe continued his target practice with the elusive carp. He lined the walls of the cabin with assorted boxes—food, a manual typewriter, a shotgun, an antique Bowie knife, law books, and clothing, including a folded black, pin-striped suit that he once wore to court. A case of Jack Daniel's, two cases of Classic Coke, and three cases of beer were stacked on each other near the door.

He looked around at his living quarters for the summer. A bed, small breakfast table, and the captain's chair pretty well consumed the area. The two-burner stove and small stainless steel sink occupied one side of the cabin wall. *THE ESCAPE* was fun for a weekend, but how would it be for the summer?

He walked back outside. J.R. would have to share the cabin with him. He called the dog, picked up a stick, and held it out. "Get it, J. R. Jump. Jump."

The dog began a trot down the dock and then broke into a full run. He left his feet two strides from Joe and flew by, snatching the offering from his hand and landing a few feet beyond.

"Good dog, J. R." Joe threw the stick into the water. "Go get it!"

J.R. just sat on his haunches and looked toward the water.

"I know. You won't go in unless I do. You're totally untrainable for retrieving anything in the water. That must be from your father's side, you mongrel," Joe said and patted the dog under his chin. A cross between a Golden Retriever and a Samoyed, J.R. had always been reluctant to enter the water except to play with someone already there. Joe figured there must have been a third set of genes, maybe from a pit bull, that canceled out the retriever in his dog.

He walked to the back of the boat and looked at the name. "I'm not escaping. It's time for a new name and a new christening." He sat down on the planks and thought. J. R. came and sat beside him.

"Stay here, J. R. I'll be right back."

He sprinted to the basement of his house and reappeared momentarily with a can of paint and a brush. He stirred as he walked toward the stern. He set the paint and brush on the dock and jumped into the waist-deep water still wearing his jeans and sneakers. He took the brush and began the revision of the name.

He blacked out the *E* and the *S*, changed the *P* to an *R* and the last *E* to a *P*.

It wasn't the work of an artist, but it mirrored his sentiments. *THE CARP*.

"Perfect. We now have us a new home, J. R." He reached onto the dock, took a bottle of beer, and smashed it into the prop. "I christen thee *THE CARP*. May you have many happy voyages."

He felt something brush against his thigh and looked down. "Carp. Damn carp have attacked me!" He grabbed the dock and swung out of the water. "Where's my gun?"

He retrieved his pistol and fired into the water until it clicked to empty. He glanced around for the box of cartridges. When he looked back up, he noticed a gray-skinned object floating near the stern of the boat.

"I got one! I shot me a carp. I knew I could do it." He looked closer and saw what he thought was a hook on the floating object.

"Aw, shit. It's just a carp that some fisherman threw back." When it floated closer, Joe wasn't sure what he was seeing. Maybe it wasn't a fish.

He reached for a broom from the deck of the boat and waited for the object to float in close enough to sweep to him. He lay on the dock and stretched as far as he could until the bristles of the broom stroked the smooth-skinned object toward him.

A woman's purse. He plopped it down on the dry boards and watched as the water-logged bag slowly drained. J. R. gave a halting bark toward it and sniffed the leather.

"Get back, J. R." Joe pried the top of the purse apart and worked with the rusted zipper until it moved a couple of inches. More water drained away when he turned it on its side. He prodded the zipper farther open and dumped the contents onto the boards of the dock.

A comb and brush. Compact and mirror. A package of Salem Lights. Two key chains with keys. A change pocket. A small spiral note pad and a pocket calendar book.

He brought a box out from the boat and placed the purse and its contents in it and set the collection on the boat in the sun.

He looked up the river toward the county seat of London. "Bet some lady missed her car keys when she got back from her boat ride," he said and then turned back toward the house.

"I've got to get everything else loaded before dark. We're taking off in the morning, J. R., for a long boat ride." J. R. wagged his tail. He loved to ride the boat. He would plant himself like a hood ornament on the bow of the boat and bark at any passing craft.

BY DARK ALL WAS loaded except for the Harley. Joe and his dog sat on the boat and had a hamburger dinner. "Too much fat in that for you, J. R. The humane society will be after me in addition to the lawyers' board and my creditors." He threw the dog piece after piece and watched him catch the morsels in the air.

The cool night air made Joe fetch his shirt that he put on again but left unbuttoned. He put his feet up and listened to the sounds of the night flow in from the woods above and across the river.

"Where were they?" he would always ask when the thousands of crickets, cicadas, and frogs came alive. He never saw them during the day, but at night their thousands of stringed instruments played an interminable chorus of chaotic verse. They needed a conductor to keep them together in harmony.   But then their harmony and peacefulness were actually in their discordant melody. Their soothing stroke was that one took up where the other left off. It was as though a million tiny violins were tuning up, but the tuning up was their song.

He leaned back and took in the aroma of locust blossoms and honeysuckle.

In recent years, he had heard the preaching about simplifying lifestyles. His had been simplified for him involuntarily. No wife, no home, no job. What he had left was a boat, a Harley, and a dog. Yes, this was the simple life.

TWO

B y midnight Joe Chapman had finished three more beers and two cigars. Clouds started to roll in and masked the stars first. He watched as the first fuzzy lumps of gauze-like mist blew across the river and brushed the face of the moon like a black veil on a widow. It was time.

He walked to his Harley and checked for the coiled rope that he had already placed in the saddlebag. He reached for his helmet on the seat and put it over his shaved head. Then he grabbed the smaller one.

"Here, J. R. You want to ride?"

The dog bounded off the boat and ran to him. J. R. liked all kinds of travel. He had ridden in Joe's airplane, the speedboat, the pickup truck, and the houseboat. But the motorcycle was the most exciting and the most challenging.

Joe had a friend who made horse harnesses to fashion a special apparatus that allowed J. R. to sit up behind him with his front paws on Joe's back.

Most of their rides were on the back roads. Occasionally, they would venture onto I-75. There, with J. R. behind him dressed in a leather jacket and helmet, Joe would observe passing motorists' children point to the odd couple. J. R. looked very much like a blond lady in the get up until he turned his head to show his canine nose to astonished tourists.

Joe strapped the dog into the harness and snapped the helmet into place. He straddled the cherry-red machine and kick started it. It roared to life with a soothing vibration and the unmistakable rhythm and sound of a Harley.

It was about five miles to London by way of Highway 11 and

the narrow bridge into town.

Out of the driveway and onto the country road, Joe saw no other traffic. What he was going to do needed the cloak of anonymity.

He gunned the cycle across the two-lane bridge and circled the courthouse just to the south. The county seat town with its oak sentried courthouse was deserted at this hour.

He stopped near a ditch, dismounted, grabbed the rope from the saddlebag, and, in the darkness, searched in the dewy grass for the three old tires he had left there the day before. He kept an eye on the street while he looped the rope around the tires and tied the other end to a support arm of the motorcycle.

Back on the chugging machine, he pulled the tires through the courthouse yard to beneath the stone statue of Lady Justice. He poured a quart bottle of gasoline into one tire, got back onto the cycle, and flipped a lit match into the lone tire. An instant torch of fire reached upward as far as the scales of justice.

He gunned the cycle and headed back toward the bridge. With no traffic visible in either direction, he released the second tire at midspan. Another quart of gasoline and his second match lit the bridge's center up like a hand carrying the Olympic torch.

The last tire bounced along behind him. The motorcycle lurched down the highway, turned into a subdivision road, and continued on to an exclusive home at the end of a cul-de-sac.

Joe killed the engine. He ran with the last tire and last quart of gasoline to the white concrete birdbath that sat in the middle of the yard. He set the tire on top and did his business for the last time. By the time he kicked his cycle to life and reached the end of the subdivision road, flames were licking skyward and gobs of burning rubber cascaded over the edge of the white pedestal onto the grass below.

A mile away at the top of a ridge, he pulled into an overlook that in the day time provided a view of the bend of the Tennessee River as it snaked through London. At this hour, Joe could see in the distance his three works of arson.

Courthouse workers would talk in hushed whispers on Monday about their ideas as to who did it. Bridge traffic would have to be detoured for five miles to replace the burned-through pavement. Judge Harkness would fume about the vandal who forever marred his beautiful birdbath.

Mission accomplished. Joe despised them all. Lady Justice had turned her back on him when he needed her. The bridge was more a hindrance to traffic than a conduit. And the judge needed a taste of his own medicine.

In the distance the triangle of orange flames licked silently at the black night. Then the soft noises of the night were overcome by the sound of sirens wailing as fire engines, police cars, and rescue units responded.

The blue, red, and white flashing emergency lights blended with the orange of the fires. They reflected off the river and bounced back from the low clouds moving in.

Joe leaned back and patted J. R.'s head. He pulled a cigar from his pocket, lit it, and took in a deep draw. It was better than the Fourth of July.

Three

T he blare of the siren startled Joe awake. He pulled the curtain back beside his bed on the houseboat. The sun was already bright. He looked at his watch. Almost noon.

He looked back out and saw the county cruiser. The blue lights were hardly visible in the glare of sunlight.

"Joe Chapman, you in there?" the voice over the loudspeaker asked.

Joe slipped on his Raiders cap, a pair of shorts, and shirt and edged toward the door. He looked back at J. R. who clung to the floor.

"How in the hell could they catch me this quick?" he whispered.

Joe stepped onto the warm deck of the boat, and a youthful, pudgy officer walked toward him. It was Tom Trotter. Joe had known him and his father for years.

"Mr. Chapman. They're saying you're fixing to go away on the river. I just wanted to come by and tell you I really appreciate you helping me get the job with the sheriff." He looked at Joe and smiled a broad and toothy grin. "I don't believe all the bad stuff some folks are saying about you. I just wanted you to know. I thought you always kept things lively. We're gonna miss you."

"Thanks, Tom. I'm glad you came by." Joe looked over at his Harley and saw the last quart jar that had carried gasoline the night before was propping up the cover of the saddlebag. He edged over and pushed it down.

"What happened to your hair? Get it caught in a lawnmower?"

"No. Just shaved my head. Thought it would be a lot neater. Not much to keep up with. What's happening, Tom? Thought I heard a lot of sirens real early this morning."

"Yeah, couple of teenagers on a cycle were starting fires all over town last night. It was worse than Halloween. The courthouse yard, the bridge, and Judge Harkness's yard. We figured it was some juveniles that had it in for the judge."

"Did you catch them already?"

"No, not yet. We got a pretty good I.D. Somebody saw a guy and a blond girl on a cycle gunning it through town. A janitor in a downtown building."

Joe put his hand on the engine of his Harley. "Boy, I'm glad my motor isn't warm. Somebody might accuse me of setting those fires."

"Naw, Mr. Chapman. Nobody would think you'd do such a thing."

The crackle of the radio from Tom's cruiser interrupted. He walked back up the driveway, grabbed the handset through the window, and spoke into it. He put it back inside and waved at Joe.

"I've gotta go, Mr. Chapman. Dispatcher says there's a lead on those fires. There're a couple of boys over toward Kinton riding a cycle that matches the description. Good luck on the river."

Joe shook his head. Poor kids. They'll probably arrest and convict them, knowing the justice system around here. He whistled for J. R. "Come here, Blondie."

Joe began a walking inspection of *THE CARP*. He paced along the narrow passageway on the portside of the boat to the stern deck to check the engine and gas tanks. He took the cover off and felt for the connections on the wires to the sparkplugs. They were tight. The propane tanks registered full for his stove and lights.

Next, he made a circuit to check his docking ropes and anchors. Then he went inside the cabin area and turned on the switch for the running lights and strobe. He went back outside and cupped his hands over the green and red covers. They were burning.

Back inside, Joe inventoried his food and cooking supplies. He tapped on the tank that held his wash water and looked in the corner for his gallons of drinking water. All was well. It was time for his departure.

He went back out and strapped his Harley to the outside wall of the cabin. The cycle was too valuable to chance losing to a big wave tossing it overboard. He turned to go back into the cabin.

"Joe Chapman, is that you?" He heard the scratchy voice descend from behind him.

He turned and looked at the bent old lady walking down the driveway. A black shawl over a flowered dress and a small black hat adorned Joe's first client, Mattie Hensley. She walked with a shuffling, bow-legged gait and stabbed her walking cane into the loose gravel. She watched where she walked while carrying a bowl under her left arm like a loaf of bread.

"Brung you something. A going away present. I remembered how you liked my peach cobbler. Here's a whole bowl. You keep the bowl. Don't worry about returning it."

"Thanks."

"Is that what you're going off in? That old tub. Will it float?"

"Yes, very well."

She squinted at his head. "What happened to your hair? Delilah shave your head, or you got cancer?"

"You never were very subtle, Miss Mattie. More the former than the latter."

She scrunched up her brow and looked at Joe for a minute. "Oh, I get it. You know it takes me longer to process words with just half a brain."

"Miss Mattie, you have a whole brain and you know it. That accident just injured your brain a little. I think you're well now. It's been ten years."

"We don't need to tell anybody, Joe. Just as well they think I have only half a brain. I also pretend to be deaf. I hear more gossip that way.

"By the way, everybody says you've been disbarred. Is my will still good with you being disbarred?"

"Yes, it's still good. And I haven't been disbarred. Just suspended. A year off. I can go back then, if I want to."

"So, it's still good. I don't need a new one?"

"No. It's good as gold."

"Gold, huh? I wish I had gold."

Joe stepped closer to her and whispered. "I think the last time you and I calculated your wealth, you had over a million in assets."

She smiled. "Not bad for a retired school teacher with half a brain, huh?"

"Not bad at all."

"Joe, you be careful on the river. You're my favorite lawyer, bar none . . . or disbar none. Ha ha."

"Thanks."

"I gotta go." She took a few steps toward her old black Ford, then stopped and turned. "Joe, I'm dating a young fellow now—he's seventy-five—and we might be getting married."

"Great, I'll come to your wedding."

"Never mind that. I may need one of those pre-nutshell agreements if we do. Can you do that?"

"If you wait a year, or if you get married before, go see Charlie Palk. He can put you onto someone who can do one."

She waved a weak goodbye. Joe shook his head. She had outlived three husbands and was thinking of a fourth at eighty years of age. He watched her get into the 1953 Ford that she had purchased new. The black widow rode again.

He turned and looked at the blue and white boat. This would be an adventure and a relief. He was actually looking forward to getting away on the river. His depression would be stroked away by the rocking of the boat and the freedom of the water.

There would be no schedule, no telephone, no clients. On the other hand, there would be no money coming in, no companionship, and no news.

He stepped onto the deck of the boat and almost into the box where he had placed the contents of the purse. He pulled a chair up and picked up the items one by one.

Two key chains, one with car keys he recognized as being to a Ford product. That key chain holder had an image of a vintage Ford Mustang on one side and the zodiac sign Libra on the other. The second key chain holder was a black, rectangular piece of soft plastic which said "Cathy" on one side and "Deb's Balloonery, Baton Rouge" on the other. A St. Christopher's medal lay beside a few coins. The note pad and pocket calendar book were still soaked. He peeled a few pages apart and stared at the writing.

He looked up. He should have given the purse to Deputy Tom Trotter so they could have tracked the owner. He shook his head. The purse would have probably gone into the sheriff's vault never to be seen again.

Only a few pages of the pad and calendar contained any writing. He tore those out and put them inside the cabin to dry out more slowly on the table. He would have plenty of time to see if he could come up with a name and address. Maybe this Cathy was still on the river and he could return the purse in person. He imagined a slender beauty but knew his luck would probably produce someone who looked more like Roseanne Barr. He liked puzzles. He would decipher the writing on the river.

He had time. Time to reflect. Time to look forward. He could sort out his past problems and contemplate a future occupation—a future life. What would he be if he shed the cloak of the legal profession?

JOE EASED INTO THE captain's chair, turned the engine key to on, pulled out the choke, and pushed the starter button. He listened. The old Ford engine turned over and caught. He pushed the choke back in to where the motor would idle.

He walked outside, loosed the mooring ropes, and nudged the rear of the boat away from the dock with his foot. Back inside, he put it into reverse until he cleared the dock area.

After one last glance at his former house on the hill, he pressed the throttle forward and felt the comforting movement. He reached forward and slid the glass away from the front window. Spring air moved through the screen and across his face. He leaned his head over and felt the cool breeze on his bristly scalp.

He aimed *THE CARP* downstream toward Kinton and Chattanooga, away from London, his problems, and his late night episodes of arson.

Joe knew this part of the river well. Without his navigation maps, he could pinpoint where the sand bars and other hazards were hidden just a few feet below the surface. Here, he could go outside the green and red Corps of Engineers buoys that marked the nine-foot channel for tugboats and barges. His boat only needed a couple of feet of water to float freely. In past years he had pressed his luck and scraped across old silo foundations that the TVA lakes of the Tennessee River had covered.

Where he floated now once was farm land until the river was dammed and the water flooded the banks. A hundred years before, farmers had tilled the ground just a few feet below. Two hundred years before, Cherokees had fished, hunted, and piled up heaping mounds of mussel shells along the shores. It was one wave of possession after another.

Yet, the river was still here, although in a tamer and fatter form. He had walked the shores at low water in the winter and found relics of past generations. Pottery shards, arrow and spear heads from the Cherokee; rusty nails and blue glass from the more recent migration—he had a collection of it all.

Power paved the way for progress along the Tennessee. Those who had power moved those who did not. It had ever been so. His own ancestors had been moved from two farms along the Clinch and Tennessee as TVA moved its construction down the Tennessee Valley. They gave up their homeplaces in the name of progress—the individual sacrificed for the good of the larger society.

WITH NO SCHEDULE AND no need to be anywhere in particular, Joe put *THE CARP* to anchor an hour before sundown near Kinton. Twenty miles of river lay behind him to his past home. This would be a good place for his first night—a bleak indention in the limestone of the riverbank to his east with the sun soon to drop behind the ridges to the west. He was out of the line of travel of barges and there were no houses in sight. He and J. R. were free.

"Here, J. R." Joe held a tennis ball high above his head in his right hand. J. R. stood on his hind legs and begged for the ball.

"We're going swimming." Joe looked up and down the river, quickly stripped to his underwear, and dove into the water, still holding the yellow ball. J. R. followed.

Together beside the boat, both swam. Joe would toss the ball a few feet away and race the dog to it. In a few minutes, J. R. tired of the retrieving and swam toward the back of the boat. Joe hoisted the dog onto the deck, looked around again, stripped his shorts off, and tossed them onto the boat. J. R. stood, shook the water off, then lay down to watch Joe.

"I've got to get some laps in, J. R. I'm getting flabby."

He began circling the boat in measured strokes. The cool water flowed around the contours of his body. He put his head beneath the surface and swam for a full minute underwater. The sensation of the river water over his shaved head where days before there had been an abundance of hair gave him a feeling of freedom that he had not known lately. He spewed out bubbles of air and felt them pelt his face like droplets of rain.

The massage of the water slowly eased his mind and relaxed his muscles. The baptism of fire he had bestowed the night before and this immersion of water today cleansed him of the soil he had felt for the past year.

Joe broke the surface and looked for his dog. He turned onto his back and watched his wake as he swam around the boat. This was going to be all right. The river, him, and his dog. His breathing steadied. His thoughts drifted away from the past and forged ahead to the summer.

Back on the boat, Joe dried, dressed, and prepared for dinner.

With his limited funds, this would not be a gourmet cruise. Instead, he reached back into his stock of recipes where he had won an honorable mention at a Spam cooking contest. He turned the gas stove's front burner to low, chopped up a can of Spam, a fresh onion, and a green pepper, and sauteed them in a shallow iron skillet.

In five minutes it was ready. He drained the drippings of grease and water into J. R.'s dog food pan and poured the remains onto a plate. He took his plate, two pieces of bread, and a Coke to the deck. He sat back in his chair and enjoyed his first meal on the boat away from his dock.

In the distance, the sun dipped below the foothills of the Cumberlands. The nearer ridges turned from their bright green of spring to pastels of deep blue as the light faded. Occasionally, a fish jumped near the boat. Swallows played touch and go with the water's surface as they skimmed Mayflies for their dinner. Down river a hundred yards, a squadron of ducks came in low, wingtips almost kissing the water, fanned their tail feathers and slid rear first into the water.

The sweetness of honeysuckle mixed with the aroma of Spam, onions, and pepper to complete the assault on his senses.

Before the curtain of darkness enveloped Joe and the boat, he mixed a glass of Jack Daniel's and Coke and put a match to a cigar. He knew he didn't deserve such a good life.

AFTER TWO HOURS AND two glasses of Jack and Coke, Joe

moved inside. His cabin would have to be prepared for sleeping. He moved a few boxes around until he had them arranged in what he thought would be a good order.

A box of law books tumbled over and spilled its contents onto the floor. He placed them back in the box and noticed the Bible storybook his mother had given him and read to him from when he was a child. He put it on the table next to the box that held the contents of the found purse.

He moved the dim gas lantern to the table, poured himself another drink, and sat down with the storybook. He fanned through the pages looking for his favorite Old Testament character—Samson—the strong man with the ironic sense of humor. He found it. His mother had read him the story at bedtime hundreds of times. The artist had illustrated the story with four color drawings.

Joe consumed each drawing. Samson killing the lion with his bare hands. Samson tying the tails of foxes together and turning them loose in the Philistines' fields with firebrands strung between them.

Then there was Delilah with Samson lying in her lap as she sheared his head. Finally, the drawing of Samson after his hair had grown back pushing the pillars of the Philistine temple apart and killing more in his death than in his life.

He stared at Delilah with Samson in her lap. She was lovely. Lithe, long hair, a silky dress that clung to the contours of her body. He had always wanted to be like Samson. Strong and a judge of his people. His hand slipped to his scalp and he remembered the words of Miss Mattie, "Delilah shave your head?" It was hard to take the good parts without including the bad.

He pushed the book aside and brought the box with the contents of the purse nearer. Who was the owner of this purse? The key chain indicated Cathy was from Baton Rouge. She smoked and owned a Mustang. A Libra, she must at least occasionally check the signs of the zodiac.

How had the purse found its way to the river and then to Joe's dock? Had she lost it as a wave crashed over a boat? Had it been stolen and tossed into the river by a driver going across one of the many bridges? Had she fallen asleep at the wheel and her car crashed through a bank into the depths of the river? Was she alive or dead? Married or unmarried? Young or old? Pretty or ugly?

Why should he care? He could just toss it back into the river. But he was a lawyer, trained to put pieces of evidence together and get the whole story. He took another swallow of his drink.

He opened the purse wider. There was no driver's license, no credit cards, no photos,—nothing to give a last name to this "Cathy." He took a legal pad and began to write what he knew about the

purse's owner. "First name: 'Cathy.' Zodiac sign: 'Libra.' Drives: Ford
Mustang. Smokes: Salem Lights. Gives gifts from or works at: Deb's
Balloonery. City and state connected to: Baton Rouge, Louisiana."

He stood and went to the cabinet where he kept his navigation
maps. Buried beneath those of the Tennessee, were the Corps of Engineers maps of the Ohio and Mississippi. He flipped open the Mississippi set and let his finger trace down to Baton Rouge.

If she came by river it was a long upstream ride. More likely
she came by Interstate Highway. Two of them, 40 and 75 crossed at
the northern edge of the county not far from a bridge that spanned the
Tennessee. Both highways were loaded with drug runners with 40
being a main East-West highway and 75 running from Michigan to
Florida.

He put the maps away, propped the door to the cabin open, and
lay down on his bed. He emptied his last glass of Jack and Coke and
put the empty on the floor beside him. He blew out the gas lantern
and lay in the dark.

A soft breeze, carrying the scents of the riverbank and the
sounds of the night creatures, drifted in and caused him to pull his
blanket closer and to sink down into the mattress.

His mind traveled to Baton Rouge.

He had gone there twice to football games. Tennessee against
Louisiana State. Both times he had flown his plane with three friends.
One was Charlie Palk.

Baton Rouge—Red Stick. He remembered the legend. The city
derived its name from the tradition that a large red rod stood at the
boundary line between Indian nations—red from the blood of animals
that had been impaled on it. It had been a half dozen years since he
had been to Baton Rouge, but now the imaginations of Cathy were
pulling him back.

He felt his obsession growing in his mind like a cancer. It had
happened times before. A woman—a Delilah—would beckon him to
come, to follow. She wanted his head on a charger like John the Baptist. His mind drifted in and out of a fitful sleep. Minutes became
hours. He turned from stomach to back.

Then he saw her.

Dressed in a white, flowing gown that came all the way to the
floor, she stood before him at the open cabin door. Silent but with the
slightest Mona Lisa smile, her pale green eyes brightened with what
appeared to be glowing coals when they turned their gaze toward him.

The white gown hung loosely from her right shoulder, off her
left, and barely covering her left breast with the clinging fabric. In her
left hand she held a replica of the scales of justice. Her hair was
straight, bright, glistening—the color changing from gold to lustrous

red as though the sun hid beneath it. She turned like on a pedestal, and with each rotation the sun became brighter through her hair. A single white ribbon adorned her head at the crown.

She then moved slightly toward Joe and stood at the foot of his bed. Her head continued to rotate and grow brighter. She extended the scales of justice and spoke one word. "See."

She began to raise her right arm, and Joe saw that she held a red, elongated piece of carved wood. She brought the phallic-shaped piece of wood to her mouth, gave it a kiss, and then pointed it toward him. "See," she said and pressed it closer until the wood and her head burst into light like a thousand suns.

Joe brought his hands up to cover his eyes and sat bolt upright in the bed. Then he heard the horn of the tugboat and saw the brilliant rays of the light from the barge that was searching the night for obstacles on the river.

He jumped out of his bed, closed the cabin door, and fell back into a more peaceful sleep.

Four

The next morning District Attorney General Charles Edward Palk and his wife slept peacefully in their suburban brick home on the outskirts of London. Their house, too, overlooked the Tennessee River. Pre-dawn light was just beginning to filter above the eastern horizon.

Palk could number many friends and a few enemies. Because of the enemies, some of whom he had put in the state prison system, he had installed a security system in and around his house, complete with motion detectors, cameras, and infrared sensors. There was a phone on his side of the bed and one on his wife's.

Emergency numbers were programmed into both. But only ten people had the number to his phone. Among those were the governor, sheriff, coroner, police chiefs of all the towns in his district, and Joe Chapman. Joe was the only non-law enforcement person to possess it.

He and Joe had been through law school, their own law practice, and a few elections together. Joe had been his campaign manager in his election to D. A. Joe was the practical joker of the two, saving his best for election shenanigans.

Palk tossed to half awake. He looked at the clock beside his bed and then wondered about Joe. Was he going to spend the spring and summer on the river? Would Joe recover? Except for his wife, Palk was closest to Joe.

He turned back over. He had a strange premonition. Something bad was about to happen. To him? To Joe? He tossed over again. It was five-thirty. He needed another hour's sleep. Bad things could wait until daylight.

At six his phone rang him out of his sleepy concern.

"I'll get it. Who could it be?"

"Get it and see, honey. What time is it anyway?"

"Six. Go back to sleep."

Palk reached for the phone. He had left strict orders with the sheriff and his chief assistant that he was not to be disturbed for routine crimes. However, he wanted to be notified about every homicide from the first moment the body was discovered. These times demanded that an elected official be somewhat of a publicity hound even at tragic occurrences. He wanted to be there before the body was moved. Numerous newspaper photographs showed him standing near a sheet-draped body, trying his best to appear solemn and caring.

This had better be important. By the fourth ring he had the receiver in his hand and to his ear.

"Palk here. Who's calling?"

"General Palk? This is Chief Deputy Sheriff Osborn Ratliff."

"What's the matter?"

"I'm sorry to bother you, General Palk, but the sheriff said you wanted to be notified immediately of any homicide . . . and we have a body here."

"What do you mean you have a body? Is it murder or not?"

Palk flipped on the lamp near the phone as though that light would help him understand.

"We don't rightly know yet. A fisherman found this body floating in the river about two miles from downtown."

"Shit." Palk thought of Joe and his gun. Joe's house was about two miles from town by river. Surely he didn't commit suicide.

"We thought you should come down, General."

"You can't tell whether it's murder, suicide, or a drowning? You know I don't come out for drownings."

"Yes, I know that. This body has a rope around part of its leg. So I suspect foul play. But I can't say for sure."

"What is this *its* stuff? Can't you tell whether it's a man or a woman?"

"Not exactly, sir. It's been in the water a long time. The turtles and carp have had a time with it."

"Well, Ozzie, you are sure it's homosapien, aren't you? I don't need another orangutan."

"Yes, sir, I would bet my life on it being human."

"Okay, I'll dress and meet you there. Don't move the body. Where are you?"

Palk had developed a finely tuned sensitivity to the classification of unidentifiable death victims five years before. Then, Palk had made a big deal about the suspicious death of a female who was trapped in a burning car that had burst into flames after hitting the guardrail of I-75 just a mile outside of town.

His photo was made at the scene with the rescue squad removing the body from the vehicle.

Witnesses had reported that the driver had run from the car as soon as it struck the metal beam. The driver could not be found, and Palk vowed before television cameras that he would not rest until the culprit had been apprehended and accounted for his abandonment of the auburn-haired female in the car.

The body was so badly burned that only a little hair was left on the head with most of the skin seared from the body. After a search of the area by numerous officers, the driver was located in a nearby motel—drunk. Palk again insisted the driver would be prosecuted under the vehicular homicide statutes for reckless endangerment while intoxicated.

As soon as the autopsy began on the victim, it was discovered the body was that of a large orangutan. The driver turned out to be a migrant carnival worker who had run off with his orangutan friend and a case of beer. He had driven from north Georgia up I-75 and wrecked in Palk's district. The driver ran because he had stolen the orangutan and was afraid to face the consequences. The blood-alcohol tests on the driver came back with a .20 result, but the orangutan's was .25. By Tennessee standards both were more than twice over the limit where intoxication is presumed.

Since the theft of the orangutan occurred in Georgia, Palk was forced to send the driver back there for prosecution.

From that time, his political enemies, and some close friends, referred to him as "Monkey" Palk.

Palk grabbed a cup of coffee from the kitchen, pulled on his work pants and boots, and headed for the door. There was no need to wear good clothes to a messy scene at the river.

BY WAY OF THE winding road he had to take, it was five miles from his house to where deputy Ratliff was. The sun wasn't up, but the sky was turning from pink to orange in the east. The old jeep bumped down the gravel road. Palk finished his cup of coffee.

Flashing blue and red lights of squad cars and ambulances lighted the dark cove where fishermen launched their boats into the river. Palk pulled around the vehicles and parked near a huge oak whose limbs hung over the river. He looked at those already there—deputy Ratliff, other deputies, ambulance attendants, and a news photographer. He did the circuit shaking everyone's hand until he got back to the deputy.

"Where's the body?"

Ratliff nodded toward the sandy river bank. A white sheet covered a contorted hulk.

"Where's Jesse?" Palk asked the deputy.

Ratliff pointed toward a nearby sycamore where the county

coroner, Jesse Putnam, leaned against the tree and puffed on a cigarette. Putnam was dressed in his normal attire for an assistant funeral home director—black suit, black wing-tip shoes, and an overcoat pulled tightly around him to ward off the cool morning air.

Elected by the county commission to the office, Putnam served the county well. He was distinguished looking with white hair and a short clipped mustache. He was tall and gaunt. His job was not to say exactly how a person died but to make a basic decision of whether it appeared natural or a homicide. The expert pathologists, forensic anthropologists, and such would then delve into the hows and whys. No one had ever seen him when he wasn't dressed in suit and tie.

Palk motioned for Putnam to approach.

"Jesse, have you taken a look at the body yet?"

"Why no, General Palk. I would never encroach upon the authority of your office and perhaps rearrange evidence or something. I knew the body would still be here until your arrival."

Palk looked over his glasses at Putnam who stood five inches taller. "Thanks."

Palk motioned Ozzie to join them.

"Ozzie, is there anything else besides the fisherman just pulling the body from the river? Any other evidence? You mentioned a rope. Was the body tied to something? It wasn't a lynching, was it?"

"No, sir. I don't believe so. I was waiting for you before questioning him anymore. It's old Jake Rathborn. He's about dead himself. Want me to get him?"

Palk nodded and motioned for Putnam to follow him toward the body. Rathborn's small fishing boat was tied to a tree root nearby.

Past the body and at the river's edge, Palk gazed over the water as though he might catch a glimpse of another body or a piece of evidence that might be floating away. Where the water lapped up at the shore, he kneeled, pulled a weed from the bank, and chewed on it. Camera flashes lighted the contemplative attorney general.

Palk knew Rathborn as he knew most of the older generation in London County. He was a retired clothing mill worker who now spent his days farming and fishing. He owned a hundred acres on the far side of the river. It was said his health was failing. He glanced back. Rathborn was walking slowly toward him. He had gone down faster than Palk realized. He was now rail thin with sunken jaws and a pale, jaundiced tint to his skin. He wore the uniform of farmers—bib overalls and a flannel shirt. Palk got to his feet.

"Caught a big one didn't you, Jake?"

Rathborn nodded. His eyes were downcast and his mouth drawn.

"Jake, where were you when you first saw the body?"

Rathborn looked up the river and pointed a bony finger to the other shore.

"Well, sir, I was fishing from my boat here just about a hunnert yards up river and over toward my place."

"Was it tied to anything? Or was anything around it?"

"No. I'd been fishing all night. Had a lantern. At first I thought it was a log or a big loggerhead turtle that had died and was floating by. It was all doubled over, and just a little of the back was visible. Everything else was underwater. But it was floating right by my boat, and I just stuck my walking cane out and snatched it over toward the boat.

"That's when I seen it was a body. It partly turned over. So's, I hooked my cane under an arm and pulled it over here to this landing. Then I walked up to the convenience store and called the sheriff's office."

"Nothing else?"

"No. Course, I wasn't looking for anything else. A body floats up to you at five in the morning, you ain't looking for anything else except a way out of there."

"Yeah, I guess so."

Palk turned and looked back over the river. The sun had now risen above the ridge to the east. Down stream another mile was Joe Chapman's former house. Mist was coming from the water's surface, and a heavy dew dripped from leaves overhead. It was an ironic scene of death and beauty. He turned back to the dazed old farmer.

"Thanks, Jake. Well, Jesse, you and me and Ozzie better go take a look before we send it off to Johnson City for an autopsy."

The body had been pulled ten feet from the water's edge. The ambulance attendants, sheriff's photographer, and a couple of reporters had gathered now and waited for the uncovering.

Palk stood near the body and motioned for the sheet to be pulled back. Then the full impact hit him. He grabbed his stomach and turned away. It was the worse he had seen. Putnam took a long draw on his cigarette and spewed smoke toward the leaves.

"Those carp and turtles did do a job on this one," Putnam said and kneeled near the body. "There's no way I can give an opinion. Send it on up to Dr. Trout."

Palk recovered a bit and turned toward the carcass again.

Only ragged edges remained where ears and lips had once been. Empty eye sockets stared back at the attorney general. Finger bones protruded through rotting flesh. Much of the abdomen had been eaten away. Shreds of shirt and pants clung to what was left of the body. One foot still wore a cowboy boot with a length of rope tied just above.

Palk and Putnam bent nearer the body to see if there was any recognizable feature. A patch of medium length hair was rooted to skin barely attached to the skull. What was left of the body was bloated and every opening was filled with grime and sand. As Ozzie had indicated on the phone, gender could not be determined. The chest and genital area had been carved away by the scavengers of the deep. Skin color would not determine race.

"At least a month and probably two," Putnam said to indicate his estimation of the time the body had been in the water. "They aren't pretty after that long a time."

Palk nodded. He directed the photographer to make numerous pictures of the body. He then made a brief statement to the two reporters present. Palk turned back to Putnam.

"Jesse, you accompany the body to Johnson City. Tell Dr. Trout to be sure to do a blood screen for alcohol and drugs. Save the rope, boot, and clothes. Maybe we can get an I. D. through dental records if anyone comes forward with a missing person. I also want to know how long he thinks the body's been in the river and how long it's been dead. Got it?"

"Yeah," Putnam said, flipped his cigarette to the ground, and put it out with the sole of his shiny black shoe.

Five

R ising at dawn on the river was traditional for Joe Chapman. In years past, when he had taken his houseboat on weekend cruises around the lakes of the Tennessee River, he enjoyed most the sunrises and sunsets.

It was like watching an artist at work. Gray turned to pink, then orange, then red as the sun rose. Ridges and coves took on shape and color. They moved from skeletal hulks to full-fleshed richness as their clothing took on brightness and form.

He had become a man of routine—a comforting routine that allowed his mind to flow like the river. Cooking breakfast was one of the things he enjoyed more on the river than at home. At his house he scarcely ever ate breakfast, but on the river it was an event.

He laid the slices of bacon into the cold iron skillet and then lit the gas flame beneath. Water for grits started to boil in a pan. On the third burner, he cooked his coffee an old-fashioned way. Ground coffee beans were scooped directly into an old pot. There was no filter, no dripper, no separation. It boiled, and then he would cut it down to a simmering temperature to allow the grounds to settle to the bottom. In a minute, he could pour from the top and have the darkest, heartiest coffee he could stand. When he got as low as the grounds, it was time for a fresh pot.

Joe looked outside where J. R. had already swam to shore and was chasing a flock of geese who had been feeding in the morning dew. Nearby, a gathering of ducks and terns—lake gulls as they were known locally—walked in feathered convention. Each group minded its own business with no show of territorial selfishness. Off to the right, a blue heron stood on a piece of driftwood at the river's edge. One spindly leg was tucked into its body—still, silent, and blending in as though it was an extension of the log. The animals, too, had their routine.

The shiny coat of the heron brought Joe to reconsider the vision of the night before. It could be explained logically. He looked over at the Bible storybook. The image of Delilah had been in his mind when he fell asleep. He had also pictured a red stick in thinking of Baton Rouge. From the statue in the courthouse yard, came the scales of justice. In addition, three glasses of Jack and Coke would tend to confuse the images. The stinging light had been from the tug pushing a barge up river.

There was one thing different and unexplainable though. The drawing of Delilah showed a beauty with black hair; his image had golden red. And what did she mean when she spoke? "See."

Was this the Cathy of the lost purse? He much preferred that thought. He would rather face her than confront Lady Justice.

AFTER BREAKFAST, JOE READIED *THE CARP* for another day on the river. He walked a complete circuit of the boat, whistled for J. R., started the engine, and hoisted the anchors.

The river here was less than a half mile wide. With no boat traffic, the calm water reflected the sun off the river's surface like golden broken glass.

For early May, the warmth was unusual. The day drew on and Joe traveled farther south and west. Fishermen, sunbathers, and swimmers began to sprinkle the shoreline. He scanned the borders through his binoculars for the mile markers that would tell him how many miles he was from the mouth of the Tennessee. Along both sides, magnificent homes crowned the riverbanks and precipices of the limestone bluffs.

When TVA finished the Watts Bar Dam in the 1940s and began to hold back the flowing Tennessee, it created many small islands where before there had been arms of land reaching out. These islands, for the most part, remained government land and either became wildlife refuges or recreational oases where people could camp, swim, and fish. Some were named—like Thief Neck, Sand, and Dead Gut—while other smaller ones remained nameless.

The larger islands flourished with vegetation and could measure over a square mile in size. *THE CARP* could have circled the smaller ones in five minutes or less. They provided hideaways and breeding and nesting grounds for egrets, geese, hawks, groundhogs, and raccoons. The larger ones supported populations of deer.

Other types of wildlife enjoyed a refuge on some of the islands. The isolation of these points of protruding landscape made for excellent dropoff points for planes flying marijuana or cocaine into the area from Mexico or Central America. These specks on a map were near the limit of the flight miles before the planes would have to refuel. The nighttime deliveries were retrieved by runners with high-powered boats who snagged the booty from the dark water and distributed it throughout Tennessee, Kentucky, Georgia, and the Carolinas.

Other wildlife infesting these peaceful islands included parties where drugs and alcohol were plentiful. There also were rumors of experiments with rites of Satanism and old-fashioned orgies. Joe had heard stories along through the years about these odd occurrences and had found some evidence to confirm them.

One day a few years back while camping on a medium-sized island, he explored and found a campfire still smoldering from the previous night. Less than twenty yards away, the severed head of a dog was hoisted on a metal spike, driven into the ground but extending ten feet into the air—the standard of a cult. There were strange symbols scraped into the earth surrounding the campfire. His retreat was swift.

Another time, he was camping with his wife on the boat, anchored off a small island. He had listened in the dark of night to a plane flying low—not more than a hundred feet from the surface of the water. The plane passed, a splash broke the moonlit surface of the river upstream, and two boats left the other side of the island and roared to the point of the drop. There was enough substance to the stories to keep them going.

The dark on these islands was reserved for the criminal, occult, and sinful element of society, but daylight bought out the families with picnic baskets. Young people with boomboxes, six-packs, and jet skis would find an island for a daytime outing. Uncles and aunts would have at their annual attempt to catch a fish. Recreation of all kinds reigned supreme along the Tennessee.

THE CARP glided smoothly downstream at a determined but deliberate pace toward Watts Bar Dam where it would have to be locked through if Joe didn't turn back toward London. To the left, he was approaching one of the many islands. As he came nearer, he first heard the sounds of music and then the bark of a dog on one end of the island. J. R., planted as usual on the bow, perked up his ears at the sound.

Joe picked up his binoculars and scanned the shore of the island. He saw what he first thought was a family and its dog. There were two figures on a blanket sunbathing. The boat approached slowly. Joe turned up the power of the binoculars and pressed them harder against the bridge of his nose.

He couldn't believe his fortune. The figures were two young women, lying on their backs in nude sun worship. They were oblivious to the approach of the boat and to the barking of their dog. Joe looked up and down the shore of the island but saw no other boat or person.

He pulled back on the throttle and edged *THE CARP* ever closer. If they were exhibitionists, he would play the voyeur.

One of the women raised a bottle of suntan oil and dribbled the liquid onto her stomach. She stroked it over her breasts and neck. The other one turned onto her stomach and propped up on her elbows. She yelled at the dog but didn't look toward the water. The one with the suntan oil sat up and rubbed more oil onto her legs. At this distance, Joe could distinguish no tan line, if one existed, but he could feel the oil on his fingertips. Their dog quieted but continued to stare toward the boat.

It didn't take much water to float *THE CARP*, so Joe brought it nearer the island. He had not removed the binoculars from their position.

When he saw their dog again, he noticed it had been joined by another dog who could have been a brother to J. R. He put the binoculars down and looked onto the deck for his dog. He wasn't there. He focused in on the two dogs on shore. That dog *was* J. R. The dogs were running up and down the shoreline, stopping just long enough to smell each other.

He had to put ashore to retrieve his dog. He pulled back on the throttle to neutral and let the boat glide into the shallow water. The women still hadn't noticed. He should blow the horn. He waited until the last moment possible and then sounded a blast. The women looked toward the boat and pulled towels around their bodies.

He dropped two anchors and waded to shore.

"I'm sorry, ladies!" he yelled as soon as his feet were on solid ground. "My dog saw your dog and jumped off the boat." He nodded toward J. R. and the other golden dog. "My dog isn't well-trained."

All three looked toward the two dogs who now were running toward the edge of the island's woods. J. R. caught up with the big yellow retriever who slunk to the ground, rolled over, and then stood. J. R. mounted the other dog.

"Oh, no." He looked at the women. "Your dog's a female, I suppose?"

They nodded their heads.

"I'm sorry. My dog's been on the boat for a long time. I'll get him." Joe started to walk toward the woods.

"Might as well wait. Can't get two dogs apart once they's started. We don't care. She needs to have pups anyway." They tied their towels closer around them. "What's your name anyway? And where'd you come from?"

Joe thought for a minute. He didn't want to give his name and address to just anyone—not that he had an address any longer. They might sue him for J. R. screwing their dog. Lawyers were targets for all kinds of malicious lawsuits. He looked at the name on his boat.

"I'm Carp. That's home," he said and pointed to the nearby craft that hardly looked like a home.

"Carp? What kind of name is that? You mean like the fish?" the one who had rubbed suntan lotion into her smooth body asked.

"My mother had an odd sense of humor. What's your name and where're you girls from?"

"I'm Kellie. This is Rose. We're sisters."

"How did you get here on this island? You have a boat?"

"Yeah, our boyfriends are out fishing," Kellie said. "They'll be gone till dark."

"Boyfriends?" Rose said and scrunched up her nose.

Joe's heart began to pound. He looked down at his shirt and saw the cloth flutter. All he needed was to be caught on the island with two nude young women by their boyfriends. He turned and looked back for J. R.

"They're still doing it," Kellie said. "Your dog don't believe in a long courtship, does he? What about you, Carp?"

"A little longer than that."

"No, I mean what do you do and where do you live? Are you married?"

"No, I'm not married," Joe said and looked down at the sand. "I used to live in London, but now that's home. Just me, the boat, and my . . . my sex-crazed dog." Joe pulled his cap off and swatted at a fly.

"What happened to your hair?" Rose asked.

"Leave him alone, Rose, I think that's neat. A lot of the guys are getting their heads shaved now," Kellie said. She rubbed her hand over the bristle of his head. "That feels weird. A good weird. You know like, 'hurt me so good.' That's a *good weird*."

"It wasn't on purpose. If I'm neat, I'm accidentally neat . . . and accidentally good weird."

Joe looked at the girls while they turned to check out the dogs again. He knew the kind. They were pretty . . . country . . . and rough. Now, they were as seductive as any, but in fifteen years—after three babies, ten years working in the sock or hosiery mills, and moving from mobile home to apartment—they would be coarse, scruffy, and as crude as the men they knew and worked with. Their breasts would sag, their hair would be brittle, and their faces would reflect the forlornness of the recognition of being where there was no way out. He wasn't much better off. He sat and talked with them for a few more minutes, glancing over his shoulder for his dog and any approaching boyfriends in a boat.

"Watching those dogs made me hot, Carp," Kellie said.

"What?" Joe asked.

"You got anything to drink on that boat? Some beer?"

"Water, Coke, coffee, . . . and beer," Joe said. "Take your pick."

"I feel like a beer," Kellie said. "You want one too, don't you, Rose? Let's go check out Carp's boat."

The girls picked up their bags of lotion and clothes and walked through the shallow water toward the boat. J. R. ran up to Joe.

"You finished having a good time, boy?" Kellie asked.

J. R. stayed at Joe's side while the other dog sat near the blankets.

"Come on, J. R., get back on the boat. We're going to be leaving in a bit."

The girls persuaded him to start the boat up and circle the island. He then killed the engine and let the boat sit in the still water. He joined Kellie and Rose on the deck with a beer.

"You didn't see us naked, did you, Carp?" Rose asked.

Joe shook his head. "I just saw my dog go to the island. We were cruising by real slow."

"Yeah," Kellie said and readjusted the towel that was tied loosely at her breasts. "We know your kind."

They watched the fish jump in the river, talked, and had two more beers.

"So what do you do, Carp? For a living?" Rose asked.

"I'm a lawyer. But I'm taking some time off. Just got divorced. Going to relax and think things over this summer on the boat."

"On this boat for the whole summer?" Kellie asked and looked around at the boat. "I'll probably need a lawyer some day, Carp. You lawyer over in this area?"

"I have a little. You have good judges." Joe noticed the alcohol was having an effect on Kellie. Her syllables were prolonged and her enunciation— bad to start with—was getting worse.

"Why'd your wife and you split? She get a boyfriend?" Kellie asked.

"No, nothing like that. More my fault than hers."

"You have a girlfriend now, Carp?"

"No."

"You're cute, with that shaved head and all. Not a bad body either," Kellie said and rubbed her hand down Joe's chest and stomach and then onto his thigh.

Rose glanced over. "O. K., Kellie, that's enough. Don't get Carp all worked up like his dog."

Joe took a long drink of his beer.

Kellie got up and stretched. "What does this look like inside? Mind if I go in?"

Joe shook his head and remained seated. "Not much in there

in the way of luxuries. Take a look."

"You better stay out here, Kellie, in case the guys come back."

"Don't worry about them. I like the way this boat feels. It makes me sleepy. I could take a nap." She left Joe and Rose with their beers on the deck.

"Who's older, you or Kellie?" Joe asked Rose.

She turned in her chair and squinted at him. "You kidding? Hell, she's three years older than me. She's an old lady. She's twenty-four. She has the hots for you. Can't you tell? Don't let it go to your head though. She gets the hots for a lot of men."

Joe felt his face grow even warmer in the sunshine. His hands began to sweat. "Not for me, Rose. She's just being friendly. I need to drop you girls off and be on my way," he said and stretched his arms above his head.

"Carp, Carp, would you come here for a minute," the whiny voice came through the screen door to the cabin.

Joe slumped down.

"See. What did I tell you? Better go. Don't miss your chance. Today's your lucky day. I'll watch your dog," Rose said and nodded toward the cabin.

"Well, I'll just see what she wants."

"I know what she wants," Rose said while Joe moved toward the cabin.

It took Joe's eyes a minute to adjust to the darkness of the cabin. He closed the cabin door and looked at the bed.

Kellie lay face down with the towel still around her. She reached over and turned the radio to where it was playing some music with a rhythm she liked. She never looked at Joe. She pulled her knees up nearer her breasts and let the towel fall off.

The slight film of suntan oil was the only thing covering Kellie's body. Her hips began to sway in harmony with the music. She parted her knees and raised herself up on her elbows so that her breasts would join in the slow dance with her hips. She still didn't speak or look back. In Joe's view, she didn't have to.

He got onto the bed behind her and let the contours of his clothed body blend with hers. He rubbed her shoulders and leaned his head onto the back of her neck. Her rhythm continued. He reached under her and rubbed the remnants of oil into her breasts. With the thumb and forefinger of each hand, he felt her nipples come alive and accept the oil.

She moved her buttocks against his clothed groin. He thought she could grasp him through his shorts. And she did.

"Oh, that feels so good," he said, closed his eyes, and let his body sink farther onto hers. His hands left her breasts and measured her stomach inch by inch.

He raised slightly, pulled his shirt off, and threw it to the floor. He leaned back into her, and from his navel to his neck felt her warm body grow in movement. The cleft of her buttocks alternated in holding and releasing him through the thin cloth of his shorts.

He kissed the back of her neck and nibbled on her earlobes. His hands continued their exploration beneath. Where oil and moisture met, his fingers found a warm and welcoming reception. He parted her and rubbed his finger on its target until her movement became more frenetic.

"Dammit, Carp. Your dog has more sense than you do. Take off your damn shorts and give me a better shot at milking that thing!"

He scooted off the bed, quickly obeyed her command, and let his shorts fall to the floor.

She turned her head and looked back at his penis, already red from the friction of the cloth.

"Looks like it needs something softer and smoother," she said and parted her knees farther.

Joe looked and needed no further invitation. He got back onto the bed, leaned into her, and felt the comforting hotness envelop him. He hardly had to move. Kellie moved her bottom in circles, plunges and bumps until Joe dug his fingernails into her breasts and bit into the back of her neck. She wasn't perfection, but she would do today. Perfection could wait until tomorrow.

"KELLIE! YOU BETTER GET your ass out here! The guys are back," Rose shouted five minutes later. J. R. began to bark from his position on the deck. The bass boat was just a half mile away and closing on them quickly.

Joe stumbled to his feet and searched for his shorts and shirt. Rose burst through the door. Kellie rolled off the bed and wrapped the towel around her. All three huddled on the floor of *THE CARP*.

"You got to hide us, Carp. They're both jealous as hell," Rose said and faced Kellie, "as though they would have anything to be jealous about."

"Why don't you just jump off and go back to the island? I'll pull out and be gone by the time they talk to you," Joe said and started the engine.

"No, no, just go. They wouldn't understand."

Joe pushed the throttle to half speed and turned away from the island. Within a minute the bass boat was alongside and the two men were beating on the rail of *THE CARP* with wooden paddles.

"Stop! Stop! We want our women!" they shouted over the whine of both engines.

It was no use. Joe eased the power back and idled. He would reason with the men. They hadn't seen anything. He walked out to the railing.

"What do you two want?"

"Our women. Rose and Kellie. We know they're in there. We saw Rose run in when we came around the island."

"There's nobody here but my dog and me."

"The hell you say. How about if I just come on board and look around?"

Joe shook his head. But before he could make any further explanation, THE CARP lurched forward, sending him falling to the deck, and knocking the bass boat away and turning it around. THE CARP was at full throttle with Kellie at the wheel when he got back into the cabin.

The bass boat and its two irate occupants started back up in pursuit.

"We can't outrun them in this, Kellie. You might as well just get on board with them," Joe said.

"They'll kill us—or worse," Kellie said and pressed harder on the throttle control.

The bass boat pulled alongside again. The men shouted. Kellie looked straight ahead and pressed even harder on the throttle control.

One of the small circular windows in the cabin exploded and a lead fishing sinker fell to the floor. Splinters of glass showered over Rose who was hugging the carpet.

Joe looked at the broken window and then at the speeding boat and its cursing men. "Shit. That's enough. Nobody attacks my boat and gets away with it." He slid open the drawer where his pistol rested, grabbed it, and started outside.

"Don't shoot them, Carp. A window's not worth it!" Rose shouted.

Joe held on to the railing and kept the gun beside his leg until he was even with the engine of the bass boat. He aimed the .357 magnum and squeezed off three rounds into the housing of the 150 horsepower Mercury in quick succession.

The boat spun to a stop in the midst of smoke and the smell of gunpowder and oil. The cursing men dove for the floor and covered themselves with fishing gear.

Back inside the cabin, Joe pushed Kellie out of the captain's chair and took control of THE CARP. He eased the throttle back and turned the boat a bit to where he could see the occupants of the bass boat. They were using the paddles to go back to the island where the blankets and other dog remained.

"I thought you said your boyfriends wouldn't be back till dark," Joe said.

"Well, they got back earlier than we thought. They're going to be mad as hell for a few days. You've got to keep us on the boat, Carp," Kellie said.

"Why can't I just drop you off at a road and you go on home. Boyfriends don't own you. If they come over, call the police."

"No, you don't understand. Just take us with you. We have some relatives in Chattanooga who'll hide us out for a while."

"You'd better tell him the truth, Kellie," Rose said, "or I will." Rose and Kellie stared at each other for a minute.

"Those weren't our boyfriends, Carp," Rose finally said. "They were our husbands."

Joe looked back toward the island. "Oh, shit."

Six

E arly the next morning in Baton Rouge, Carol Sent sat at her desk with her second cup of coffee of the day.

Soon, she would start the normal schedule of six appointments with men, women, or couples who needed the aid of her counseling in marriage and family problems. Six hours—fifty minutes for talking and listening and crying—and ten minutes for wrapping it up with notes for the file. But she always set aside the first half hour of the day for herself. Here she would steel herself against the little agonies to follow.

She liked what she did, but there was always too much crying. At three strategic locations around the room, sat boxes of tissue, easily accessible to hands of clients sitting in any of the three comfortable chairs.

She had plenty she could have cried about herself. She was still getting over a divorce two years before. She learned just a year before that her long lost father had died on a ranch in Wyoming. And now her sister was missing.

Three photographs sat on the little corner shelf next to her desk. She studied them and drank her coffee. One was an old black and white of her sister and her sitting on the back porch steps of their small farmhouse in western Louisiana. She was then nine and her sister four. They both stared into the camera while a chicken perched on the porch behind them.

Then she looked at the one of her beaming toward the camera in her graduation gown. She had conquered education and was ready for the world.

In the most prominent place, though, stood the photo of her beautiful sister, Cathy. It was the same shot they had used for the poster for the ballet performance at the local theatre three years before. Her long golden red hair was pulled into a bun on the crown of her head. One leg was held almost parallel to the floor. She stood on the toes of her other foot in the shiny ballerina slipper.

Now, Cathy was missing. But that wasn't unusual. Although they were only separated by five years of age and a few miles of downtown Baton Rouge, the rift between them had enlarged over the years. When they could have grown closer and become best of friends, they had drawn apart and barely spoke.

Carol glanced down at her schedule. With her own family failings, she wondered why she had chosen such a profession. But then she knew that was the answer. The problems of her own family gave her insight into the root problems of families everywhere.

She was an advocate of counseling. All counselors received counseling and supervision. They had to. But she understood the need. What appeared to be her family failures were no more than a doctor coming down with the flu, a coach losing a game, or a race driver having a wreck. You just get up, get well, win some more, and race again with a deeper determination to do better.

This time, though, it had been longer than normal since she had heard from Cathy. She broke down and punched in Cathy's phone number and listened to the receiver. The musical tones played the numbers. Then the recording: "The number you have dialed is no longer in service." She dialed again to be sure there was no mistake. There was none.

The office intercom buzzed. "Yes?"

"Carol, your first appointment for the day just called and canceled."

"O.K." She looked at her schedule and then her watch. She had time to drive over to Cathy's house and see if she was there before her next appointment.

She put her shoes back on, walked across her carpeted office and onto the wooden hallway floor. She grabbed a cup of coffee in the kitchen and walked briskly out the door into the bright sunlight of what promised to be another humid day. Spanish moss hung near head high in the live oak trees she passed going to the parking lot.

Across town she turned into the narrow street where, just behind the streetside businesses, squatted five small brick houses in a semi-circle. They were probably nicely appointed for the 1950s, but looked out of place in the modern Baton Rouge. She pulled as close as she could to the house where her sister lived. She took the key from her purse that Cathy had entrusted to her for emergencies when they were on better terms.

The key still fit. Inside, Carol glanced around and felt for the light switches. The room became barely illuminated with pale blue light. "Cathy? Cathy?" There was no answer.

One bedroom, one bath, a small living room, and a combination kitchen-dining area made up the house. Cathy didn't need much and couldn't afford much on her modest income.

She stepped down the hallway to the bedroom and knocked. Again, no answer. She turned the doorknob and pushed the door open. Darkness struck her. Black blinds over the two small windows and heavy drapes covering them kept all sunlight out. She reached around the doorfacing for a light switch. She clicked it on and watched a red fluorescent bulb buzz on to cast an eerie glow on the sparse furnishings of the room.

She shook her head in disgust. Beside the bed lay several magazines and books on the occult—witchcraft, voodoo, and numerology. How many times had she urged her sister not to read such trash—all to no avail.

Back in the living room, she picked up the phone. It was dead. She held down the disconnect button for a few seconds but there still was no dial tone.

She turned to leave and came face to face with the landlady.

"What are you doing here?" the landlady asked her.

"Looking for my sister."

"Well, she ain't here. Gone. Probably six, maybe eight, weeks ago. Don't rightly remember. Took off in her Mustang with that Bartley fellow."

Carol's mind was a whirlwind of activity. She had met Cathy's new boyfriend just once. He was a con man—a charmer. He was Cathy's project for the year. She was always rescuing some no good creep. Bartley dressed better than some scum, but he was a low-life anyway.

"She didn't say where she was going or when she would be back?" Carol asked.

"No. Just like always. Said she'd be back. Gave me some money to keep the power on but not enough to pay the phone bill. I'm about out of that now."

"Thanks." Carol handed the landlady a business card and walked out the door toward her car. Why should she worry? Care? If Cathy wanted her to know where she was going or where she was now, she knew her phone number. She had an answering service, a mailbox, a fax, and E-mail. She was ready to receive if Cathy was ready to send.

She wasn't her sister's keeper. Cathy made sure of that. But what if something had happened to her? Bartley . . . she couldn't trust Bartley.

Seven

In the brief two days that Kellie and Rose had been aboard *THE CARP*, Joe had grown to like their presence.

They took turns fixing meals and cleaning up afterwards. Both of the young women learned how to captain the craft and steer it between the buoys marking the main channel. At their insistence, Joe was headed toward Chattanooga and farther away from his home town of London.

The night before, he had slept alone beneath the stars on the front of the boat and left the cabin and bed for the women to share. He had not been confronted with the vision of the young goddess on the second night as he had on the first. Perhaps the apparition was a product of too much whiskey and stress.

J. R. was a good judge of people, and he seemed to like the women. Kellie had found an old captain's cap and was now wearing it at the wheel. Rose was a bit more sullen and concerned with the situation. She lay on the bed and stared at the ceiling.

Joe sat cross-legged on the deck at the bow and would occasionally motion for Kellie to turn the boat more starboard or to port. In front of him, he spread the navigation map books of the Tennessee, Ohio, and Mississippi. He had never been on the Ohio or Mississippi in any kind of boat. If he went as far as Chattanooga, he might as well continue toward Baton Rouge.

He traced the course with his finger and wrote down the number of dams he would have to lock through. He calculated the mileage. Five, maybe six, weeks at a leisurely pace with no bad luck would put him near Baton Rouge. He could look up this Cathy of the lost purse. If he found her and she was receptive, he could spend the summer there. If not, there was always New Orleans just another day or so on the river from Baton Rouge.

He brought the box with the purse and its contents from the cabin and set it in the sunshine. He took the spiral notepad that had the pages stuck together by water and looked for any other notes. It was still damp. With great care he pried one page from another.

He opened the address book and noticed that the front page where the owner's information would have been was torn out. Other pages were torn in half as though someone had ripped them out in anger or haste. There were a few partial numbers and names left on pages he had not seen before. He tore those pages out and laid them with the others he had already taken.

He looked at the small scattering of evidence. He was not that good a detective at all. On television, a cop could have found the owner or told a great deal about her by these items—a comb, a hairbrush, two key chains, a change purse, the notepad and pocket calendar. But he was at a loss. The key chains told him the most—libra, a Mustang, and balloons. The owner was a little different.

He looked at the keys on the second chain. He recognized the imprint on one. "Do not duplicate. U. S. Postal Service." A post office box key. Then there were a couple of other keys that could be door keys. They lacked very much distinction. He got up and took the box and his maps back inside.

"What about the dog?" he asked and sat down beside Kellie.

"What dog?"

"Your dog. The one J. R. got romantically involved with. The one we left on the island."

"Oh, don't worry about her. The guys will take care of Sheba. My husband cares more about that dog than he does me. If we both had been on this boat and you would've asked him to make a choice, he would've taken the dog. He'd have told us to have a good time."

"I don't think so, Kellie. Not the way they were yelling and throwing things."

"No. They'll go home, cool down in a couple of days, write a check out of my account to fix the motor, and that'll be that. We'll spend a week in Chattanooga and go home. They'll be glad to see us. I hope."

"Where do you live?"

"Just outside of Harriman toward Oakdale. If you ever come through, just stop at any of the bars and ask for Kellie and Rose. We live side by side. Married brothers."

"Two sisters marrying two brothers. That's odd."

"They're not *our* brothers."

"Oh, I know. I was just thinking," Joe said. "Do you think they'll report you missing? Say I kidnapped you or something?"

"No, Carp. You're safe. Everything'll be O.K."

The first bridge across the river on the northern fringes of Chattanooga was coming into sight. Joe took his binoculars and looked in the distance at the smoky colored Lookout Mountain. The sun had already gone behind the high ridges but its rays still shone on the peak of the mountain.

He looked down-river for a landing area. Somewhere along here he could park *THE CARP* for the night and get the girls to the bus line. They would visit an aunt and then go home. He had already determined to give them money for the trip home and to repair the motor on the bass boat.

He looked at the bridge they were nearing and noticed two men staring back. They were standing near the abutment on the left dressed in nice business suits. One had a pair of binoculars and the other held a radio or telephone to his ear.

"They've turned us in, girls. There's a couple of cops eyeing us from the bridge. Your men probably reported you kidnapped and said I shot at them."

Joe focused in on the two while the boat went beneath the bridge. They got into a car and drove away.

"It won't be long now. They'll have the sheriff to send his boat out to arrest me. You girls have got to back me up. O.K.?"

"Rape," Kellie said and didn't smile. "It would be better for me if I said you kidnapped and raped me." Then she thought and looked closer at Joe. "Naw, our men would think we were damaged goods either way. I'll just tell the truth, Carp. What is the truth anyway?"

"Those weren't your husbands, were they?"

"No," Kellie said. "You said coats and ties. If our husbands died tomorrow, we'd have to go to Wal-Mart to buy ties and jackets to bury them in. They both work in a lumber mill."

At the foot of the city aquarium, Joe pulled the boat into a city owned dock and tied up for the night. He thought he might as well make it easy for the cops if they wanted to arrest him. At least his boat would be secure.

He lodged the gangplank he used for taking his Harley on and off the boat onto the walkway next to the dock. He cranked the cycle up and roared off the boat and up the steep drive. In a minute he was back.

"You girls get your clothes together and I'll take you to the Choo Choo for dinner. You can catch the bus there to your aunt's."

"Do we have to go, Carp? I like it on the boat. I like you."

"You're married, Kellie. You've got to go. And Rose too."

"I can't take you both at once. Not enough helmets and not enough room. Who's first?"

Rose nudged Kellie toward the Harley. J.R. barked a jealous litany and let out a mournful howl when Joe took off with Kellie behind him instead of the dog.

They zigzagged through the unfamiliar streets toward the brightly lit downtown. Few people were on the streets. Kellie squeezed her arms around Joe's stomach and dug her fingernails into his skin. "You won't forget me and the ride we had, will you, Carp?" she yelled into his ear above the roar.

Joe turned his head slightly while Kellie leaned forward. "Which ride?" he said and smiled.

At the restaurant, Joe made sure Kellie was safely inside. "You wait at a table and have a cup of coffee. I'll get Rose and be right back."

The headlight of the Harley streaked across THE CARP, the only boat docked at the landing when Joe got back. He gunned the engine and yelled for Rose. There was no response. He cut the engine and walked onto the boat. Neither Rose nor J. R. were outside.

"Where are you?" Joe yelled and opened the cabin door.

Rose sat cross-legged on the bed, rubbing J. R.'s head. He lay asleep at her feet. Joe blinked in the near darkness. Only the filtered glow of the security light through the window of the boat illuminated the nude Rose.

"You can't go to the Choo Choo that way, Rose." Joe turned and looked back out the door and then again to Rose. "What are you doing sitting here naked as a jaybird?"

"Just waiting for you, Carp," she whispered and continued to stroke the dog's head. "I'm not going anywhere until I get what my sister got. My old man's gonna think I done it anyway. Might as well. It's my little stud fee for J. R. here having at our Sheba."

Joe felt his heart start thumping. Why was he always faced with these temptations? Didn't he signal them last night by sleeping outside that he wanted to leave these married women alone? He felt his resolve melting.

"I can't, Rose."

She sat up straighter. "Why not? You think I'm not pretty? My teeth not nice enough? My tits not full enough?"

"No, Rose. You're plenty pretty," Joe said and looked closer at her teeth while she sat there with her lower lip puffed out. She did have two overlapping teeth on the bottom row, but he had never let imperfect teeth stand between him and a romp before.

"Why then?"

He knew he couldn't say it was his moral upbringing after what she knew he had done with Kellie. "I can't . . . not with J. R. in here."

Rose got up and led the dog onto the deck, returned and closed the door behind her. "Take your clothes off, Carp, and lie down. I've only read one book during the last five years, and it was *Women on Top*. I want to show you what I can do on top."

He quickly dropped his clothes to the floor and climbed into the middle of the bed. She straddled him and sat her soft bottom onto his abdomen.

She looked at his bare arms. "What happened to your arms? Were you in a bad wreck or something?"

Joe pulled his arms up and covered them with pillows. "Don't look at them."

"You want to talk first, Carp?" she asked. She reached behind her and grasped Joe with a cool hand. She leaned forward until a nipple was at his lips. "Lick it. Kiss it." She looked back to where her hand was doing some work.

"No."

"No, what?"

"No, I don't want to talk first."

"I didn't think so." She lifted her body up and moved backwards a bit. She brought her hand down lower and replaced it with something warmer. Joe groaned and closed his eyes. Rose began a slow, circling movement. She controlled the tempo. She would raise and lower herself as she felt the waves building.

Joe opened his eyes once. This Rose had no thorns.

BY THE TIME THE Harley pulled into the parking area of the Choo Choo, Kellie had drunk five cups of coffee.

"What the hell kept you two?"

Joe shook his head and Rose lowered hers.

"That's what I thought. My little sister can't let me get ahead of her. At least you're here in time to pay for this."

KELLIE AND ROSE GAVE Joe their phone numbers before they boarded the city bus for their aunt's. The diesel smoke was still strong in his nostrils as he strapped on his helmet and gunned the Harley toward *THE CARP* and the solitary life of the river.

Eight

T he same two men peered from the next bridge downriver when *THE CARP* chugged out the next morning. Joe looked back. He hadn't been arrested or shot at. He would go his own way. Maybe they were tourists who had never seen a Harley strapped to a wall of a dinky houseboat.

He didn't care. His sleep had been fitful. The vision had visited again.

She had repeated the imploring, "See, see." Except this time it sounded more like, "Seek, seek." In appearance, though, she was the same—white gown, and tumbling, bright red hair. She held out the scales of justice and her hair formed an iridescent halo around the carved ivory of her face and neck. She appeared as though in a mist. Dawn had brought Joe back to the reality of his journey on the Tennessee.

He found himself pushing the throttle to a bit faster position than the days before. There was more urgency in his quest for Baton Rouge. He had swam his laps around the boat and done his push-ups before breakfast. He would be in shape by the time he came face to face with the real Cathy. She would want him as much as he wanted her.

West of Chattanooga, the Tennessee cut its way between the mountains. This was the narrows—the boat threatening catapult of two hundred years before. Here, Indians would wait for riverboat captains who were unwise enough to tempt the whirlpools and sucks of the turbulent water. If the boats survived nature's tests, dugouts with bands of Indians would challenge the resolve of the settlers who ventured through their hunting grounds.

Joe had never been farther south on the Tennessee than Chattanooga. Here, he paid close attention to the buoys and navigated a conservative course.

His mind kept going back to the thought that, perhaps, he was going farther and farther away from Cathy. If her purse showed up near his home in London, why did he suppose she was back in Baton Rouge? Maybe she was back at the courthouse waiting for him. He would have to speak to the vision the next time it appeared and ask a few questions.

Past Nickajack Dam, *THE CARP* followed the river as it entered northern Alabama. From northeast corner to northwest corner, the river had sought an easier route to the Gulf until it was repulsed by geography and turned back northward to cut across Tennessee once again.

FOR THE NEXT THREE days Joe kept his boat on course. He motored past Scottsboro, Guntersville, Huntsville, and Decatur. He only stopped for gas and to replenish his supplies.

In the mornings and evenings he would exercise and swim. J. R. would leap at a stick he held out and snap it from his hand. When he ran out of sticks, Joe held out his pistol and made it a target for the dog's assaults. He put on a heavy glove as J. R. sometimes missed the gun and latched down on his wrist. He was proud of his dog-training ability. J. R. could be a police attack dog.

Each evening after dinner, Joe turned his attention to the contents of the purse. He pored over the scraps of paper and the jumble of words that were, for the most part, unconnected. He pulled a few stray hairs from the hairbrush. They were covered with mud. He tried to wash them clean and then laid them out to where he could see the color. Was she really a redhead like the vision?

He couldn't decide. He held them against a white piece of paper. Blond or red? What he had seen on the goddess who appeared to him was hair that seemed spun from highly polished bronze, the texture of silk, and flaming like the sun hid beneath the tresses.

The phrases he had been able to decipher from the bits of paper did not reassure him. The words spoke of "dinner at Kent's" or "to Kent's place after work." There were no full phone numbers or addresses in the paper from the pocket calendar book. And the only name anywhere was Kent. Was Cathy married, engaged, or spoken for? That would have to change. Kent would have to move aside.

IF IT HAD BEEN Jack and Coke that enticed Cathy to visit him on the first night, Joe determined he would try it again. He sat on the deck of the anchored boat at midnight and sipped from his supply. He turned all lights off and left the cabin door open. She would be free to come and go as she pleased.

The moon hung on the western horizon like a clipped fingernail tossed on black velvet. A meteor streaked from south to north. The sounds of the creatures of the night regained dominion of the blackened landscape.

He sat, drank, and listened to the cacophony of grating sounds.

Barking dogs in the distance. Screeching owls returning to their nests with harvests of mice. The song of the cicadas. And the low throaty croaking of frogs on logs near the shore.

In a couple of hours, he had consumed half of a fifth of whiskey and three bottles of Coke. He stumbled through the cabin door, grabbed a blanket from the bed, and returned to lie beneath the clear sky on the deck of the boat. His last sight before drifting off to sleep was another shooting star piercing the Big Dipper.

A short time later, she stood over him. Her eyes radiated like sparklers when she looked down at him. Joe had some questions. He tried to speak, but his voice had left him. He could not utter a word in her presence. She walked to the edge of the boat and turned her back to him. She bent over and reached for water from the river. Still, her hair glowed and flowed down over her gown.

She turned back and held out the scales of justice.

"Joe, you must hurry. See. Seek."

She stepped toward him and held out the hand that she had dipped in the water. She touched him on the cheek with her cool, wet hand.

Joe blinked awake. J. R. was standing above him, licking him on the face.

AT DAYBREAK JOE AND J. R. swam to shore. They both ran up and down the sandy bank for a mile and back. Joe's head ached, but he would work it out. He found a tree with a limb he could reach and did pullups. He ran some more until they were back even with the boat. Joe dove into the water and the dog followed.

He had to get to Baton Rouge. "Hurry, see, seek." The words rang in his ears and prodded him on. Cathy needed him.

Here the river was as wide as he had ever seen. For five and ten minutes at a time, he could aim THE CARP at a point on the horizon and then go and sun himself on the deck. It was almost as though the boat was on auto-pilot. He would be tanned and fit when he found his goddess. He put his hand to his scalp. His hair had started a regrowth—with little result to date.

He flipped from stomach to back. He would readjust the steering and then take some more time in the sun. There were no other boats and nobody along either shore for as far as he could see.

By late afternoon, THE CARP had passed Florence and Sheffield, Alabama. The sun beat down hot on Joe's skin. He walked to the front of the boat and sat where he could put his toes into the current and splash water back onto himself.

The water was wide and smooth. The boat skimmed along at a moderate speed while it drifted nearer the left shore. Ahead and to the left, an old black fisherman sat on a rock outcropping and dipped his pole to the water. He was the first human Joe had seen in hours. He waved. Joe waved back. Joe took his binoculars and fine-tuned in on the gray-haired, stout fisherman. He was still a quarter mile away.

The fisherman laid down his pole, stood, and waved some more. Joe stood, smiled, and returned the wave, still pressing the field glasses to his eyes. The old man's hand gestures became more frenzied.

Joe laid his binoculars down. *THE CARP* was almost parallel with the man. Was he afraid that the boat's wake would ruin his fishing? Joe looked back and saw that the boat's course was taking them too near the bank.

Before he could take a step toward the cabin, Joe heard the grinding sound of boat bottom against sand. *THE CARP* came to a sudden stop but Joe didn't. Inertia threw him off the boat into the water in front.

He was still fifty yards from the bank. By reflex, he began to swim.

"Stand up! You can stand up there. You're on a sandbar!" the fisherman shouted.

Joe stood in thigh-high water. His feet sank into the sand as he walked in exaggerated steps back toward the boat. The water there was less than knee deep. J. R. stood at the bow and barked.

"Your captain didn't see the sandbar!" the old man shouted.

"I don't have a captain. I'm it!" Joe shouted back and swung himself onto the deck of the boat. He cut the power to the engine and walked around the deck of the boat from front to back and along both sides. He kicked a plastic bucket against the wall and into the river. He stormed past J. R.

"Get out of my way, you old dog." J. R. cowered into the cabin.

Water flowed around the boat. They were stuck tight on a sandbar. He started the engine and put it reverse. There was no movement. He looked along both shores with his field glasses.

The only sign of civilization was the old fisherman. He had resumed his position with pole in hand, hat pulled low against the sun, and sleeves rolled to mid-arm.

Joe sat and stewed in the captain's chair for a few minutes. Then he and J. R. walked and swam to the bank near the fisherman.

"Hi. I'm Joe Chapman."

"My name's Goose Collins. What happened to your hair?"

"Oh, I just cut it short for the summer. Catching many fish?" Joe asked and sat down as though nothing had happened.

"Not a one. But it keeps me away from the house. We got a whole passel of folks there today. Collins's sandbar catches more boats than I do fish. Most folks around here know where the bar is. The barge pilots do. It's on the navigational maps. You have any of those?"

"Yeah, I have them." Joe looked over at his boat. It hadn't moved an inch. "How do they get them off when they get stuck like that."

The old man looked up and down the river. "Tomorrow's my wife's birthday. She'll be sixty-seven if the Lord lets her live until then. How old you think I am?"

"Oh, about sixty-five."

"Lawsy, man, what do you think? I go for older women? I'm seventy. I've got my three score and ten in and I thank God for every extra day he gives me. You thank God for everything?"

"Not for getting caught on a sandbar."

"Why not? There's a purpose to everything. I believe it."

"Is there a purpose to me getting off that sandbar?" Joe asked.

The old man smiled. "I tried to warn you. I waved. I stood up. I waved. You just kept on coming. Kept your nose buried in those glasses and never paid it no mind. It's hard to tell young white men anything—or old white men either, for that matter."

"I just thought you were being friendly."

"Friendly? I don't even know you. I expect I will before you get off there though. There's only three ways to get off that bar. One, you catch a barge going upstream and hook a line to it. Second, you wait for the water to go up when a big storm comes through. Or thirdly, you get Goose here to pull you off with my old Oliver tractor."

"Mr. Collins, when can you do that?"

"Don't call me that *mister* stuff. Makes me sound old. You call me Goose, and I'll call you Joe. O. K.?"

Joe nodded his head. "Goose, when can we get your tractor?"

Goose began to wind up the line on his fishing pole. He looked to the west where the sun was dropping behind the sand-colored hills.

"It'll have to wait. I observe the Sabbath from sundown on Saturday until sundown Sunday. The Sabbath is just beginning. Tomorrow about this time we can bring the tractor down."

Joe shook his head but didn't say a word.

"Get you some clothes and bring your dog on back to the house with me. We'll feed you and bed you down for the night. You can go to church with us in the morning. It's Mother's Day."

Nine

Soybeans, cotton, pigs, and beef cattle. That's what Goose Collins raised on his tenant farm. He owned his house, barn, and outbuildings, but the surrounding acreage he tended for a percentage. His acres stretched from the river until they disappeared into a pine forest beyond a dirt road.

"How many acres you care for?" Joe asked.

"I don't *care* for much of it, but we tend nearly four hundred acres. It keeps a retiree like me real busy."

They walked from the river toward the cluster of buildings. As Joe neared the barn, he sniffed the unmistakable aroma of a pig pen. They turned the corner and he saw a huge sow who had rolled onto her side to allow a multitude of piglets to nurse from teat to teat. The white underbelly gave way to pink skin and nipples. There were not enough spigots for the number of piglets so they played a game of musical teats with each, in turn, knocking another away.

Joe and Goose leaned against the fence and watched the sow quietly acquiescing in the assault of piglet mouths against her body.

"There's a few things I never tire of." He turned toward Joe. "One is watching baby pigs nursing. Or a newborn Hereford calf."

"Me either, Goose. But that's just two things."

"Or a good woman in bed," Goose said and elbowed Joe.

Joe looked at the sow. "That's a lot of bacon."

"Bacon, nothing. There's more there than bacon. The hog is the most totally utilitarian animal that ever was made. We use every bit of the hog. Feet. Snout. Brains. There's nothing about a hog you can't eat. I guess you know about chitterlings or chitlins. Lard out of the fat. Soap. You come back in November when we have the hog killings if you want to see a sight. Not many folks still kill their own hogs. But we do."

Joe looked on in silence. Maybe this was where he belonged.

A cow and pig farmer in northwest Alabama. Fish a little. Watch the cows and pigs. Tend the cotton and soybeans. Forget courts and people fussing about money. Get back to nature. Back to the basics. Make your own soap and lard.

"Let's go have a cup of coffee before supper," Goose said and leaned his fishing pole beside the barn door.

In the almost dark now of evening, Joe saw what looked like the skeleton of a tractor. All the wheels were metal. There were no rubber tires. He walked around it. He had never seen one so old except at fairs. The name plate said Oliver.

"Is that your nickname for it or the brand name?"

"That's an Oliver make. Fine tractor. You start it by turning the flywheel. It'll cough and sputter and then come to life. I'll show you tomorrow evening."

"You're going to pull me off the sand with that?"

"Yep," Goose said and slapped his hand against the metal fender.

Yellow light poured from the windows of the house as they neared. The surrounding area wasn't lacking for motor vehicles. Joe counted five cars, three pick-up trucks, two motorcycles, a large farm truck, and two without wheels that sat on blocks—a 1955 Ford and a 1956 Chevrolet.

Children played all around the house, on a swing set, throwing a baseball, and chasing after a black and white speckled dog. J. R. growled but was restrained by Joe.

It looked like a typical farmhouse—faded white clapboard siding with green shutters beneath a green asphalt shingle roof. Red brick piers at the corners and intermittently spaced in between gave support. A screened porch stretched across the entire back.

"You can bring your dog onto the back porch. That way, that little pooch out front won't bother him."

Goose offered Joe a seat inside on a couch-like glider—metal arms and back with plastic covered cushions. Goose stepped off to the kitchen for coffee. A soft breeze filtered through the screen wire up from the river and past the barn. It brought the full aroma of the pig pen.

Joe reached over and picked up three magazines from a table—a *National Geographic*, an *Architectural Digest*, and a *Southern Living*. They weren't what he expected to see on the porch of a pig farmer. Then he remembered the words "totally utilitarian" that Goose had used in describing hogs. He hadn't expected that either. *Prejudice.* He was guilty of pre-judging someone by what he expected. He had fought racial and religious bias and prejudice in his law practice and now, on a mental level, he had done it himself.

He reached over and picked up a book from a stack. Horticul-
ture. Another was about animal husbandry. He turned to the back
and saw little pockets that could have held the old-fashioned library
cards.

"Sugar or cream?" Goose asked when he returned with coffee.

"Just black."

"You're in fine company then," Goose said and handed Joe a
cup.

A black girl of five or six burst through the screen door, pig-
tails bouncing, and ran to Goose's lap.

"The boys won't let me play ball with them." She looked up at
Goose and tears shined in streaks down her puffy cheeks.

"Aw, child, don't pay it no mind. They're just being crazy, not
wanting to let you play. In a few years, they'll want to play. That's
when your old grandpa will worry. Now go on back out and play with
the dog or something."

The girl ran back past Joe without the slightest hint that she
noticed him sitting there.

"Grandchildren. They're the greatest thing that can happen to
a man. Play with them . . . and send them home. I have eleven. You
got any?"

"No."

"You're too young now. But when you do, you'll love them."

They both sipped on their coffee and a procession of children
streamed in and out of the back porch to see Papaw Goose. Joe looked
at each one. Some were lighter skinned than others. All were more
brown than black. Goose was black. He noticed what he thought were
oriental features on some.

"What are you retired from, Goose?" Joe asked.

"The railroad. Thirty years on the Southern. Then it was
changed to the Norfolk-Southern. Rode the last passenger trains as a
conductor. Did different jobs on the freights. Rode the rails. Been all
over the South and most of the other states too. Still, when I hear
that whistle late at night, I'm ready to go. It's in my blood."

"You ever go through a little town called London? Forty miles
from Knoxville. That's where I'm from."

"Oh, yeah. Quiet little town. When the train went over the
Tennessee River on that trestle at London late at night, I would stand
on the outside of the caboose and piss in the river and say, 'Piss on
you, Tennessee. Bear Bryant's coming to town.' " Goose laughed. "Of
course that was a long time ago. Cabooses and Bear have been gone
a long time."

Goose leaned back and lit a pipe. "I got another one if you
want to smoke along. Only type of smoke that my wife allows around

here. And that's just out here on the porch. Won't be no smoking or drinking inside."

"She's a smart woman."

Goose smiled and closed his eyes. He listened to the sounds from the barn and river. "Smart and pretty. I knew that when I first met Millie."

"When was that?"

"I met her in San Francisco when I was shipping out to Korea. When I came back, we married. We'll have five children here with their husbands and wives, and the grandchildren. There'll be twenty-four altogether, counting you. She's a great cook. I told her to throw on an extra handful of meat and vegetables for you. They're all going to spend the night and go to church with her on Mother's Day tomorrow. You religious, Joe?"

Joe thought. He remembered his early childhood. The Bible storybook. Samson and Delilah. Mornings in Sunday school and church. He had drifted away during college. Education and the law became his gods.

"Yeah, I'm religious. But I'm not really a member of any organized church," he finally said.

Goose laughed. "That's me too. I'm a Baptist. You're what we call a backslider. We'll get you reintroduced to *real* religion in the morning. You just been going to white folks church. You'll see . . . and feel the difference."

"I didn't really bring any clothes for church."

"We'll take care of that."

The sound of women in the kitchen, pots banging against each other, oven and refrigerator doors closing, and the smell of baked and fried food came through the open door. Joe rubbed his stomach.

"What about Mother's Day, Joe? Where's your mother?"

"She's dead."

"Sorry to hear that."

"Well, I do have an old client who's like a mother to me. Miss Mattie, I call her. She has a son. But he went away in the seventies to New York to be an artist. Never heard from him again, except for a card at Christmas. So, she takes me to church every Mother's Day, except this one I guess.

"She says it does us both some good. I guess she's right, but I can't stand her preacher. He's an arrogant asshole with slicked back greasy hair. Has a little sickly handshake. More interested in passing the basket than anything else. But Miss Mattie thinks the world of him."

"We really like music at our church. You have a favorite hymn, Joe?"

Joe thought back to the PBS special he had watched years before that explored the origins and spread of the hymn "Amazing Grace."

" 'Amazing Grace' would have to be it."

"Oh, yes, praise the Lord. A great song. You know that was written by a slave trader?"

"Yes."

"The Lord can change the heart of a man. Amen. 'Out of the eater came forth meat, and out of the strong came forth sweetness.' "

"What? What did you say?"

"I was talking about John Newton, the slave trader who wrote 'Amazing Grace.' He sold captured men into slavery. He devoured us. He was strong and bound us. But in the end, God turned him around. He wrote a song that brought release to millions and the sweetness and smoothness of the words and melody are like the pulp of a cantaloupe."

"But wasn't that the riddle that Samson put to the Philistines at his wedding feast?"

"Yes. See, Joe, you know more Bible than you thought."

Joe looked into the distant darkness. "I know Samson."

THE TABLE LOOKED TWELVE feet long to Joe. It was loaded with bowls of vegetables, meats, and steaming rice. Eight chairs were arranged along each side. Five black women were busy carrying plates and utensils and finishing placement of the food.

Beyond, in what must have been the living room, small children were taking their places around another table.

When the hubbub settled a bit, Goose took Joe by an arm and tapped on a glass with a large metal spoon. "Ladies, this is my new friend, Joe Chapman, who had the misfortune of running his houseboat aground on the Collins's sand bar. He's to have dinner with us and spend the night. Going to church with us in the morning."

There were smiles and a bit of hushed talking among the women. Joe noticed one of the women was not black at all but was oriental.

"This is Millie," Goose said.

"So glad to have you as our guest," she said, bowed slightly, and reached out her hand.

"I'm sorry to mess up your birthday, Mother's Day, and such," Joe said.

"It's no bother. You're here for a purpose. I know it. Please have a seat," she said.

After all the sons and daughters and sons-in-law and daughters-in-law were introduced to Joe and seated, Goose said the blessing.

Joe looked around and marveled at the amount of food. Incessant chattering among everyone at the table showered him with family tales. He was glad he was sitting next to Goose.

It was a Chinese food feast. They handed him heaping bowls of steamed rice, stir-fried vegetables, platters of pork, beef, and chicken strips. Egg rolls, noodles, soy sauce, hot mustard, and hot tea capped off the abundant offering. Once again, it was not what he expected from an Alabama pig farmer.

Those at the table finally began to talk with Joe. From polite questions and small talk, he learned that all of Goose's children were college graduates. A son and a daughter were school teachers. Another daughter was a nurse. The youngest son was a beginning engineer with the state highway department. The oldest son was an agent for the Federal Drug Enforcement Administration.

The DEA agent sat across from Joe but did not speak directly to him. He was the only one wearing a suit and tie.

"Where are you located?" Joe asked.

"Mobile."

"How long you been with the agency?"

"Ten years."

"You ever been to East Tennessee?"

"Lots."

"Business or pleasure?"

"Business."

Joe turned to Goose who was smiling. The eldest son must have won a Calvin Coolidge closed mouth award from the agency.

"Joe, you ain't going to get much out of John John. He thinks everybody he meets is a potential drug dealer. He's not much a one to talk about his business."

"Oh, that's understandable. Drug runners are serious people. They might learn something that would compromise an investigation or put another agent in jeopardy."

"Joe here's a lawyer," Goose said to his eldest son.

John John looked up from his food and stared at Joe's head. "Yes, I could tell by his hair cut. How am I to know that he's not running drugs on that little houseboat out there on the Tennessee River?"

Joe looked at Goose who gave him no help. "The only drugs I have out there are aspirins, Jack Daniel's, and beer."

"Two out of three of those are illegal in parts of Alabama."

Goose laughed and so did the others at the table except for John John and Joe. John John favored Goose in appearance. He was large, athletic, and black. His neck muscles were barely contained by the collar of the white shirt. Deep set eyes stared out poker-like from beneath a broad, prominent brow.

"John John, tell Joe about that plane that went down out there in Mobile Bay a few months back," Goose said.

"I can't. It's still under investigation."

"Well, I can tell what I know because it's not confidential." He turned toward Joe. "Seems this plane was found that went down in the Gulf about fifteen miles out from Mobile. It broke into two large pieces. Landed near a fishing boat. Just a medium-size two engine job. No pilot, no passengers. But they found one package of cocaine. Isn't that right, John John?"

"Can't say. It's still under investigation." He picked up an egg roll and bit into the end. There was no hint of emotion on his face.

"I almost went with the DEA out of law school. I interviewed with all the agencies—DEA, FBI, and CIA. I had an electrical engineering undergraduate degree. I fooled with electronics—cameras, audio surveillance, and such. I still keep up with it as a hobby. You can get a lot of good stuff at Radio Shack. I installed a surveillance system for the attorney general in my county."

"Why didn't you sign on?" John John asked.

"My mother was dying of cancer. I didn't feel like I could leave the area then. Started a little law office with my friend who's the district attorney general now."

"What are you doing on the river?"

"Taking the summer off."

"I wish I could do that. I'm lucky to have two days off," John John said.

"Are you married, Joe?" Goose asked.

"No. Not now."

"I guess that's how you can afford to take the summer off. I sure couldn't when I was raising this bunch," Goose said and looked around the table.

Joe nodded.

THE ROOSTER ON THE fence post about twenty feet from the back porch crowed Joe awake the next morning before sunrise. He slipped on his shoes and pants and walked out the door with J. R. He caught the screen door and eased it closed, avoiding sound that would awaken anyone. He retraced his way to the river and viewed *THE CARP*, still suctioned to the sand bar. His worries that it had floated off on its own were disproved.

Back at Goose Collins's house, he took his shoes off and tip-toed into the kitchen. He needed a cup of coffee. Goose and Millie were already there.

"Have a good sleep?" Goose asked.

"Yes, very good. A lot better than some I've had lately."

"Oh, you don't sleep well on the river?"

"It's just the sounds, movement, and lights, I guess. Been having some funny dreams."

"Nightmares?"

Joe thought for a minute. "No, not nightmares. Just weird. About a young woman. She keeps following me."

"She following you or you following her?"

"Yeah, I don't know. She wasn't here on the back porch last night though."

For a half hour, just the three of them sat and drank coffee. Joe learned more about the Alabama black man who married a Chinese woman in San Francisco. They were just a handful of years short of fifty together.

"I bet you enjoy having all your children home. And grandchildren."

"Yeah. They're all here except Goose Junior. He was killed in Vietnam. A great football player. Bear Bryant wanted him. But he went to war. It's a pity. I still think about him."

"I guess it's hard to understand sometimes."

"Yeah, I went to Korea and he went to Vietnam. Protecting our country. I guess we did good though. Alabama hasn't been attacked by any Koreans or Vietnamese. We did our duty."

Grandchildren and children began to come one by one into the kitchen. Millie, her daughters, and daughters-in-law started cooking breakfast. Joe and Goose wandered out to the back porch.

"You better catch a bathroom now and wash up for church, Joe. Before all these kids take them over."

Joe looked at his watch.

"Do you mind if I use your phone to call Miss Mattie? I'll pay you. It's Mother's Day, and if I don't call, nobody will."

"Sure. Go ahead. Don't worry about paying. With all these children and grandchildren, I think I own the long distance company. It's in the hallway there past the kitchen."

A housekeeper answered the phone at Mattie Hensley's back in London, Tennessee. Mattie's son had been involved in a serious accident in New York. It was the first she had heard of him in a year. She had gone to see about him. She would tell Mattie when she returned that Joe had asked about her. Joe hung up the phone. Miss Mattie had finally gotten to be with her son on Mother's Day.

THE LITTLE CHURCH HOUSE sat squat in the middle of an opening of red clay surrounded by a pine forest two miles from the Collins's home. White boards faded to gray and a steeple from which a board hung loose enclosed the house of worship. Although the outside appearance was worn, the inside was one of warmth of solid wood pews, a dark hardwood floor, and freshly cut flowers in front of the pulpit.

There was the rustle of conversation, the occasional laugh, backslapping, and scuffle of shoes against wood as the worshippers slid into their familiar pews. Children looked for mothers. This was the matriarchal Sunday. There were more women than men. Most wore either a red rose or a white one to commemorate their mothers. All were black except for a young white couple near the rear.

"Yuppie do-gooders," Goose whispered to Joe.

Joe himself was the target of nods as he took his place on the Collins's pew.

At an old piano at the front sat an equally old black lady. She wore a black hat and veil, black dress, and black anklet boots. Her head was bowed in meditation above the ivory keys. She opened her eyes and looked over the congregation, her head giving a jerk when her eyes settled on Joe. Then there was a wink and a smile.

"Her husband passed on a month ago," Goose said.

After a deacon made a few announcements and welcoming remarks, congregational singing began. Joe did not recognize most of the songs. His eyes followed the lady at the piano while he lip-synched the words.

The songs progressed, the singers became more enthused, and the piano lady moved with the spirit. She banged down hard on the keys with her slender fingers and began to move her body with the rhythm. Her feet stomped the pedals and her bottom polished the wood bench like a shoe shine boy's rag on a pair of black wingtips. She began to sing too, her mouth opening wide.

Joe had never witnessed a piano being attacked like this before except when he saw Jerry Lee Lewis do "Great Balls of Fire" at a Tennessee governor's inaugural ball. He closed his eyes and let the movement take him back to his childhood.

The preacher was almost as active as the piano lady. He called for and received numerous "amens" while he condemned sin and thanked God for their blessings. His arms beat the air. He tilted his head until his voice echoed off the ceiling and back onto the pews. A towel was passed between the piano lady and the preacher. Both wiped sweat from their brows. This congregation needed a lot of preaching. They got an hour's worth. Joe welcomed the sound of the preacher's voice when he heard the words "Now in closing—" Then his heart began to pound.

"Now in closing, brethren, I'd like to say that we are especially blessed today," the preacher said and looked directly at Joe, "in having a fine young gentleman from Tennessee here with us who is a house guest of Goose Collins and Mrs. Goose. Millie, that is.

"Goose tells me that Mr. Chapman here is quite an accomplished singer," he said.

Joe's ears burned and he could feel perspiration popping out on his forehead. He turned toward Goose and was greeted by a broad, tooth-filled grin. The preacher continued his praise. The piano lady nodded her approval, and "amens" sprang up from distant points in the room like mushrooms after a rain.

"Now, make Joe Chapman welcome as he comes forward to lead us in one of his favorite hymns."

Amidst a chorus of "amens" and handclapping, Joe found himself standing and making his way to the front as though propelled by an unseen hand. He turned and faced the congregation. They were so silent that he wondered if they could here his heart beat. His eyes danced over the sanctuary and finally settled on the white couple in the rear. Their presence was like two lilies floating on a sea of India ink.

He wiped the sweat from his forehead and scalp with a nice white handkerchief while he struggled for thoughts and words. It would be impossible to match the beat and rhythm of the piano player on any song that he knew. He looked over his shoulder at her, and she smiled, hands on the ivory ready to go. Words and melody escaped him. Then he thought of the PBS program and the hymn he had mentioned to Goose.

"Thank you. You are most kind to ask me to lead you in song. However, I would like you to join me in an accappella version of one of my favorites. We'll start very slowly. 'Amazing Grace.'"

To another chorus of "amen," Joe began in a soft, low voice the words to the beloved hymn.

"Amaa—zing grace, how sweet the sound
tha—at saved a wretch like me—
I once wa—s lost, but now I'm found—
was blind, but now I see—"

As he neared the end of the first verse with the members joining in, the tempo began to increase and his voice was lost in the thunder of the others like an owl's hoot in a tornado. The piano player could no longer resist. Her hands and feet began pumping away an upbeat version that carried Joe and the others along like so many corks on an ocean wave.

Through six verses that he did not know the words to, Joe was swept along, letting the congregation lead. By the conclusion, everyone was standing. Joe felt a reprieve from his sentence. Now it was his turn.

"Now, ladies and gentlemen, you may not know it but today is
Goose's wife's birthday. Goose was telling me only last night about his
love for Millie and how they reared these wonderful children. So, this
being Mother's Day, I think it would be appropriate for Goose Collins
to come forward and give his testimony of love and devotion for Millie
and tell what Mother's Day means to him."

Goose was pushed forward by hands of relatives and friends
until he stood next to Joe. Joe reseated himself at his pew. He smiled
at Goose who was now the one sweating. In brief comments, Goose
related his observations on love, family, and Mother's Day.

Outside after the service, Goose led Joe to the side of the
building and the cemetery. He walked to where a pine shaded a grave.
Goose pointed to the head stone. "Hezekiah Ezekial Collins Jr." It
gave his birth date and date of death. Engraved on the stone was a
goose in flight and beneath in smaller letters—"Goose Junior."

"You see why I go by Goose now, don't you, Joe?"

JOE'S MASTERY OF GOOSE at church brought all of the
family closer to him. They admired someone who could get the best of
the patriarch of the family.

"If you're ever in Mobile, look me up," John John said and
handed Joe a business card.

Joe's attempt to persuade Goose to try an earlier pulling of
THE CARP from the sand bar fell on unresponsive ears. Instead,
Goose invited Joe on a tour of the outbuildings of the farm after lunch.

The walk among the buildings and animals brought to light
more of Goose's innovations and accomplishments. There was a
greenhouse for earlier vegetables. Inside the barn were stalled prize-
winning Hereford cattle, four horses, and six mules.

A 1955 Ford Fairlane and a 1956 Chevrolet, restored to
perfection, rested beneath coverlets. The two carcasses he had seen
earlier outside were used for parts on these, Goose explained.

But the most amazing discovery was made when Goose opened
the door to a twenty-by-forty-foot white concrete block building. It was
surrounded by a well-landscaped border. Above two polished oak doors
was a simple sign: "LIBRARY."

Goose opened the door and took Joe inside. Each wall was
covered with shelving that housed books from the floor to eight feet
high. Above the shelves were windows set high into the block walls.
Skylights in the roof gave a natural light easy for reading. Along one
end of the room were two computers with printers. Stacked at the
other end of the floor were boxes of books. Two large tables with
matching chairs occupied the center. There was seating for twelve.

"All of my children and practically all the neighborhood

children have used this library," Goose said. Joe took a book from the shelf, opened it to the back, and saw the library card pocket with the card that said at the top—"Goose's Library." He thumbed the card up and saw that it had been checked out several times. There were names and dates.

"How did you do this? And why?"

"The why is simple. We needed it years ago. This library has more volumes and equipment than the school had. They didn't do it. They didn't care. But I saw during all my years on the railroad that educated people read. My children read. They had no excuse not to.

"The how was a little harder, but not much. You'd be surprised how many publishing folks and organizations would give books when they were asked. I went to every library in towns where the trains laid over and got donations. I wrote to publishers and got seconds and remainders. I set up the card system in my spare time.

"John John helped me get the computers at a surplus government property sale. We're on the Internet. These boxes are full of books that I haven't catalogued yet. Don't have room for them on the shelves. I'm giving to other libraries now.

"It's here for the neighborhood kids and adults too. Anybody who wants to use it. Of course, there are some who don't want to, but that's up to them. My grandchildren love to come out here and read and use the computers."

Joe walked around the room while two of Goose's granddaughters came in and sat in front of the computers.

Goose opened the door and let the late afternoon sun slant in.

"Let's see if we can get old Oliver started up. We can ride it down to the river just sightseeing and not be in violation of the Sabbath."

They walked over to the barn where John John joined them still dressed in his suit.

Goose wiped the dust off the fenders and seat of the old hulking metal heap. He checked the gasoline and oil while Joe and John John looked on. He set the choke and ignition control and stepped to the flywheel. He leaned down and grabbed it at the bottom with both hands and with an upward thrust of his whole body gave it a great heave.

The Oliver spat out a puff of black smoke and sputtered for a second before it ground into silence. On the fourth attempt, it came to life with a weak putt, putt, putt, that sounded more like a sewing machine than a tractor.

It warmed up and gained strength and sound, like a giant waking from an afternoon's nap. After making a few adjustments to the choke and throttle, Goose was able to coax the tractor to shoot a

plume of dark exhaust toward the barn's roof. He climbed up to the
metal seat and pointed Joe to a looped length of cable on the far wall.
Joe, with Goose's instructions, secured it with a clamp to the rear hitch
of the tractor.

Goose aimed the behemoth toward the river and Joe, John
John, and J. R. walked behind like a procession out of "The Wizard of
Oz."

Goose parked the tractor a little ways upstream from *THE
CARP*. He handed Joe a bundle of rope that had been on the tractor.

"The metal cable's too heavy for you to swim with out to the
boat. Tie this rope to one end and swim with it to the boat. Then you
can pull the cable to you and clamp it to a support on the back of the
boat. Understand?"

Joe nodded agreement. He stripped down to his shorts. John
John took off his suit coat and walked down to the river's edge with
Joe. Joe bit down on one end of the rope and dove into the water. J.
R. followed while John John fed out the rope from the bank. When Joe
reached the boat, he threw the end of the rope onto the deck and
climbed aboard. He reached back and brought J. R. on deck too.

John John fed out the rope and cable while Joe pulled it to the
boat. Joe's arms strained against the cable and current, finally pulling
the metal end to him. He struggled with wrenches, pliers, and clamps
at the back of the boat until he secured the cable to a main support.
The boat would either be pulled free—or torn apart.

"Ready!" he shouted toward Goose.

Goose looked at the sun, still perched above the ridges to the
west. "I'm not. Still the Sabbath."

Joe sat on the deck and dried himself. John John smiled and
rejoined his father at the rear of the tractor.

Once the sun had settled behind the low ridges, Goose turned
up the power of the old Oliver and stretched the cable until it was taut
between him and the boat.

"When I signal, you give that old boat as much backward
thrust as you can, and I'll see what this old Oliver will do!" Goose
shouted at Joe.

Joe started the engine and let it idle until he saw Goose's
signal. He then pushed the throttle to full reverse. The Ford engine
roared and water washed around the boat from the prop's turbulence.
Goose stretched the cable tighter until it sang with the sound of steel
threads on the verge of shredding. *THE CARP* shuddered but did not
dislodge.

Goose signaled to Joe. They both eased off on their engines for
a minute. Then they tried again. Joe thought he felt the boat move
a bit to one side but not to the rear. Another attempt moved it the

other direction. He poked a stick in the sand at the very point of the bow so that he could measure any backward movement.

They thrust and released for fifteen minutes until Joe felt and heard at the same time *THE CARP* begin to slide loose from its captor. Once the movement began, it came easily.

Joe guided the boat into deeper water and dropped anchor. He loosened the cable and threw it into the water. On the lip of land at the river's edge, Goose and his son smiled and waved. Joe swam back to shore with the rope and J. R.

"That old tractor performs better than it looks," Joe said to Goose.

"A lot of us do."

Goose looked at Joe's bare arms. "Man, those are bad scars. What Happened?"

Joe rubbed both arms, knocking droplets of water off. "It's a long story." He reached out a hand to Goose and shook. "Thanks for your hospitality. I'm going to head toward Baton Rouge and see if I can find that young woman I was telling you about. I may stop on my way back. What do I owe you for the tow job?"

"Nothing, Joe. We're friends. Friends don't owe each other. They just help when they can. Pass it on."

Joe turned and shook hands with John John and then looked back at Goose.

"I better get on my way. Thanks, Goose. Tell Millie I really enjoyed it. Good to meet you, John John. I need to get down river a way before dark. And dry off."

"Be careful, Joe," Goose said. "The river will turn north in a little ways, but that's only temporary. No river worth anything, or man for that matter, turns north for very long. They all head south. Like the Mississippi."

Ten

C harlie Palk sat in his third floor office of the London County Courthouse turning pages in a notebook. He flipped through photos, lab reports, autopsy findings, and notes by investigators. There had been too many unsolved murders in his district. This was election year. It was driving him nuts. Unprosecuted homicides were the highest in five years. Higher than when he took office. That was the rub.

When he was campaigning, he had promised to try someone for every homicide. There would be a conclusion. Finality. Justice. Judgment.

Now his words would come back to haunt him. If he was his opponent, he would ask: "Are we better off now in prosecution of homicides than we were four years ago?" Then they could hang a picture of the orangutan and him next to the question and ask: "Who does Charlie Palk think he's monkeying around with?"

They would do it too. Politics was savage. They couldn't attack his personal reputation, just his professional one. Where was his campaign manager—Joe Chapman—when he needed him?

He turned and looked out the window, beyond the walkway lined by neat rows of marigolds and the full-leafed oaks that shaded Lady Justice below, to the Tennessee River that wound its way through town. When would Joe and his boat reappear?

The body they had fished out of the river just two weeks before was the third unidentified victim of the past two years. The remains of all three rested beneath the domed stadium of East Tennessee State University two hours away. There Dr. Linus Trout and his team of forensic pathologists and anthropologists tried to identify and give a cause of death for all murder victims in the eastern third of the state. Football fans did not know, or care, that beneath the thirty yard line in the catacombs of the basement, over a hundred unidentified bodies cooled until all hope of prosecution or I. D. was gone.

With Interstates 75 and 40 crossing in his district and with the Tennessee River meandering through, Palk was fast approaching the conclusion that this area was the dumping ground for every gangster, pimp, serial killer, or drug lord in the eastern United States. I-75 was already known as "Cocaine Alley" for the drugs and money passing through between Florida and Michigan.

Palk reserved a faint hope that the latest body would be identified. And if luck was with him, it would be an out of state fisherman who fell overboard.

The light on the phone console lit up before Luann buzzed him on the intercom.

"General Palk, Doctor Trout is on line one and says it's urgent that he speak with you . . . . And Mattie Hensley is here and says she needs to speak with you. I told her you were busy, but she says she'll wait."

Palk gritted his teeth. He wiped clear his desk with his forearm until he found a legal pad. He swiveled in his chair and faced the beauty of the outdoors before he answered the darkness of the phone.

"I'll take Dr. Trout's call, Luann. Tell Miss Hensley it'll be a while before I can see her."

"That's all right, Monkey, I ain't got nothing else to do," Palk heard Mattie Hensley say before he pushed the button to talk with Dr. Trout.

"Dr. Trout, how are you today? How's the dungeon at your university?"

"Fine, General Palk. Listen, I finished the preliminary stuff on this body you brought up that had been in the river. Got time to hear about it?"

"Sure. Shoot."

"My, what are you, prescient or something?"

"What do you mean?"

"Oh, nothing. You'll see in a minute. As they say, do you want to hear the good news or the bad news first?"

"Hell, Linus, quit playing games with me. Give me what you got."

"Okay. You're a bit testy this morning. Anyway, I'll give you

the good news first." He paused and shuffled some papers. "It's not
an orangutan." He shuffled some more papers. "The bad news is that
it's not a drowning. You got a homicide."

"Shit. How?"

"He was killed by a .22 caliber slug. Hollow point that
flattened out when it hit his skull. Tore a big hole in his brain. I've
got the slug, but it'll be hard to match up with ballistics."

"Well, I'll be shit."

"Only the next election will tell for sure."

"Cut the crap, Linus. Tell me everything else you know on the
body."

Palk leaned back and propped his feet on the window sill. He
pressed the receiver between his shoulder and ear and put the legal
pad in his lap.

Dr. Trout filled him in. The body had been in the water at
least a month, maybe two. It was dead hours or up to two days before
entering the water. There was no water infiltration into the lungs.
Blood and tissue exams indicated traces of marijuana and cocaine but
no alcohol. The male was between twenty-eight and thirty-six and of
Hispanic or Latino extraction.

"What about the rope around his leg?" Palk asked.

"Well, I'm not an expert in that field, Charlie, but I do travel
a lot. That rope looks more like what is used by ocean going fishermen
than what we normally see around here. I've seen such rope in South
Carolina, Florida, and the Gulf areas of Alabama, Louisiana, and
Texas."

"He may not have been killed in Tennessee at all?"

"Yes, the timing would make that possible. But don't bank on
it. Oh, by the way, the boot was especially interesting."

"Why's that?"

"You know I wear western boots all the time. And the one this
guy had on is a very expensive handmade boot. I saw a similar pair
in Mexico City for over six hundred dollars. This guy was not your
average hitchhiker."

"Thanks. Let me know when you get a final report."

Palk cradled the receiver back onto the unit on his desk. It
was a start. Money, drugs, and a .22 caliber slug. They went
together. The rope and boots, maybe not. He would tell the press just
enough that the killer or killers might think he knew more than he
did. He needed them to make a mistake. If they only disposed of the
body in Tennessee, he was out of luck.

LUANN COULD NOT AVOID talking to Mattie Hensley
despite the fact she had a desk full of work to do.

"Oh, I just love Joe Chapman to death. It's a shame he got disbarred."

"Mattie, he's not disbarred. He's just suspended for a while. Joe'll be back. You just wait."

"Was it about that girl in the accident? That's what I heard. It wasn't his fault. He's really down on himself. The last time I saw him, his dog looked better than he did. He'd lost all his hair and smelled like a beer joint."

"No, Mattie. Mr. Palk said he saw him too. He was going on a boat trip. He had his head shaved. You know Joe. It was just some crazy stunt."

"Well, I think he has cancer. He just wants to go off and die like those elephants do."

"Where do they go?"

"I don't know. I've never seen one around here." Mattie Hensley laughed into her handkerchief.

"I believe Mr. Palk is off the phone now. Let me see if he can talk with you."

Luann knocked on Charlie Palk's door before entering. She quietly closed the door behind her. She put her hands on her hips.

"You're going to have to see her. She'll sit out there until Hell freezes over if you don't."

Palk looked at all the papers on his desk, the notebook on the homicides, and the notes he just took from Dr. Trout. He was too busy to see one of Joe's old clients that he was not very fond of anyway.

"Oh, all right. Send her in. But interrupt me with an *important* call if she's not out in ten minutes."

Luann brought Mattie Hensley in. Mattie watched until Luann was out and the door closed.

"Monkey, you know that Joe Chapman is usually my lawyer. But he's gone. So I came to see you."

"He'll be back before long. Why don't you wait?"

"Maybe he will and maybe he won't. He made my will for me. I want you to take a look at it and re-do it. I'd hate to die and have my will thrown out because my lawyer was disbarred or suspended or whatever. Besides I want to make a few changes. You heard about my son?"

"I'm a full-time district attorney general, Mattie. I'm not supposed to be doing private work."

"Never you mind, Monkey. I voted for you last time and made a big contribution. Nobody has to know."

Palk thought back. She had made a sizeable donation. This was going to be a close election. He needed all the votes and contributions he could get.

"Oh, okay, Mattie. I'll do it, but I won't charge you for it. Just between friends."

"Whatever. Now this is what I want to do." She leaned closer and whispered instructions to Palk.

After the allotted ten minutes, Luann buzzed on the intercom. "General Palk, Ozzie Ratliff is on the phone. He says it's important."

Palk looked at his watch. "It's okay, Luann. I'm still talking to Mattie."

"No, General Palk. Ozzie is *really* on the phone. He says it's urgent."

"Excuse me, Mattie," Palk said and reached for the phone. "This is important." He hoped the deputy had come up with a lead on the identity of the body. Maybe a bulletin on a missing person had come in. A homicide investigation was always easier if he at least knew who the victim was and where he was from. "What do you have, Ozzie?"

"General Palk, you know that body we found with just one boot?"

"Sure."

"Well, we found another boot that looks a lot like that one."

"Great. Where did you find it?"

"About a mile down stream from where they found that body. Near Polecat Creek . . . . But there's a problem."

"Why? What?" Palk asked and removed his glasses.

"It was on another body."

Eleven

C arol Sent handed a tissue across to her last client of the day—a recently divorced woman who was now having problems with a teenage daughter.

"I know you feel that you're the one who has to be entirely responsible for her direction now. But sometimes, especially with girls, you just have to be patient. They have to go through some rebellion. They do that with their clothes, their hair, even with some of the friends they choose."

"But she's all I have left. I'm a failure at my marriage. I don't want to be a failure as a parent."

"You weren't a failure. Your husband was a jerk." Carol glanced at the clock on the wall behind her client. "Give your daughter a little space. Don't complain. We'll talk more about it next week."

"Okay. I guess that's all I can do right now. Thanks, Carol."

Carol closed the door behind her client and went back to her desk. She sat down and looked at her daily calendar. But the thoughts wouldn't leave her. She found that she was thinking more and more about her own problems when she was talking with clients. Was she talking to herself when she was giving them advice?

Her own husband was a jerk. She should have gotten over the divorce two years before by now. She had no children. But she had a kid sister who acted like a child. And as much as she tried, she couldn't put the thought of where Cathy was out of her mind.

If that lady thought her daughter dressed funny or had peculiar friends, she didn't know what Carol had seen with Cathy. A sister who had inherited all the physical beauty and musical and dance talent of the family was deficient in her emotional stability. Cathy wobbled between the beauty of ballet and the seaminess of a stripper. She could mingle with the elite society of the university set except for the fact that she was always finding hopeless cases to rescue. Her friends tended toward the bottom feeders of humanity.

And where was she now? Carol checked her mail daily hoping just for a card, a note, something to say where Cathy was. Before, when she had taken off cross-country with rodeo riders, bike clubbers, or rock groups, she had always sent word. But now nothing. She would report her missing. But as sure as she did, Cathy would show up the next day and complain about the concern.

Carol decided she was going to put aside the thoughts of a failed marriage and her relationship with her kid sister and do something for herself. The advice she had given to others, she was taking herself. Tonight was her second class of a creative writing course for the community at Louisiana State University. The assignment was to make a character come to life by *showing* and not *telling* about a prime component of the character.

She would mask Cathy in fiction.

She turned open her notebook. She already had a page of a two-page assignment. On the first page she showed Cathy as a talented ballerina. Now she would show her stripper side. She tapped her pencil against the desk. How do you show a stripper? Describe the movement and rhythm? Peel the layers of clothes off? What do they start off wearing anyway?

She glanced at her watch. She would have to drop by one of the clubs that Cathy frequented and see first hand. The instructor would know if she weren't accurate. She opened a drawer and went through a stack of business cards she had accumulated. Cathy had always been good to give her a card from each of the joints she had worked. It was sort of like she was rubbing in the fact that she was a stripper and her sister was a college graduate.

There it was. The Classy Kitty Cat. The card showed a drawing of a pink kitty with a black mask and g-string. Carol glanced at the address. It was close enough for her to drop by before class and still give her time to write another page.

AT SIX IN THE afternoon, it was still hot when Carol pulled into the parking lot behind the gaudy pink building. She had changed into black jeans and black pullover before she left her office. She wouldn't look too out of place. She wadded up some money, stuffed it into her pocket, and left her purse under a seat of the car.

When she entered the front door, she was greeted by a full-length mirror directly in front of her and a caged cashier to her left. She smoothed back her auburn hair, took a deep breath, and gazed at her image. She could have worked here if she wanted.

"It'll be five dollars, ma'am."

She heard the voice but did not see the source. Then the young black man stepped out into view behind the bars of the cage. He was talking on the phone, smoking, and counting money at the same time. He raised his eyebrows at her and smiled.

Carol reached into her pocket, took the wad of money out, and peeled off a five.

"Here. Am I too early? Are there any . . . dancers?"

"You're never too early at the Classy Kitty Cat." He pushed a button and a buzz sounded from the door in front of her. "Go on in." He motioned toward the door.

Inside the room, Carol stopped and let her eyes adjust to the darkness. Ahead of her was a semi-circular stage. There were flashing multicolored lights, and a glass sphere suspended from the ceiling rotated while a ray of light danced off it and reflected a thousand sparkles around the room.

She looked for a table to herself. There were just a handful of men in the place and they sat near the stage. Three topless waitresses stood at the bar and eyed her. Carol put her hand to her mouth and coughed. She took a chair away from everyone and near the side wall. She was having second thoughts about this adventure.

Shortly a waitress came over. "What can I get you?"

Carol averted her eyes from the bare breasts of the woman and looked her directly in the eyes. "I'll have a Diet Coke."

"A Diet Coke?"

Carol nodded. The waitress turned away. Carol reached for a pen. She didn't have one. Nor a piece of paper. What kind of writer was she going to be? She had forgotten the essentials. She looked around. A girl was taking the stage and music surrounded her. She would write it down when she went back to the car. Now she would just have to put it all to memory. She concentrated on the sounds, sights, lights, smells, and the movement of the girl.

"Welcome Cheyenne to the stage!" a voice shouted over the speaker system. Carol looked around and noticed an announcer who also played the music on a platform at one end of the room. No one clapped. The few men bent over their beers.

When the waitress came back with Carol's drink, she lingered after making change and receiving her tip.

"Didja come to try out?"

Carol shook her head. "No. Just to observe."

"You's got the body for it, you know. Good money, too. Boss says if ya interested, come on back to his office." She nodded toward a door just off stage that looked like a full-length mirror.

"Thanks. I just came to watch."

"Whatever," the waitress said, turned, and headed back to the bar.

Carol intently watched the dancer on stage. It wasn't the old time strippers that she had imagined. These girls didn't start with layers of clothing and peel them off to the bouncy music. They started with the bare essentials and were nude before the first chorus of the song was played. They spent their time on stage bending, stretching, embracing a bright stainless steel pole, and crawling on all fours. They would back up to one of the men near the stage, look backward, and wiggle their naked bottoms. Nothing was left to the imagination. Dollar bills were stuffed into their garters by the appreciative men who received a few extra seconds of up close viewing time for their money.

There was nothing classy about the Classy Kitty Cat, she concluded. These men and women had never seen a real stripper. For a little bit she would get on stage and give them an old-fashioned strip show.

Before she noticed, a man was in the chair next to her. He brought his beer with him.

"What's your name?" he asked and put his hand on her thigh.

"Excuse me!" Carol said loudly enough to be heard by the man. "I don't think I invited you over and I know I didn't invite you to put your hand on me. I rarely let my ex-husband do that," she said. She pushed his hand off. "Whatever you've got, I'm not interested. I just came to watch the girls. Please move on."

The man stood, turned the can of beer up to his mouth, and then looked back down at Carol. "I hate lesbians," he said and moved away.

Carol looked at her watch. This wasn't going well. It was still two hours until her writing class. She wouldn't be intimidated into leaving, but she wasn't going to stay any longer than necessary.

In a few minutes, the dancer who had been on stage came and sat next to Carol.

"We have some back rooms where you can watch me dance in private if that's your thing," the dancer said and leaned closer to Carol.

"No. You got the wrong idea. I'm just here on a project. I'm trying to get an idea of what a stripper does for a writing class I'm in. My sister works at these . . . clubs sometimes. I'm describing her."

"Oh. Your sister. Who is she?"

"Cathy. Cathy Pelton. She's not here now. She's out of town."

"I don't know no Cathy Pelton, and I know all the girls who've ever danced here."

"She probably goes by some other name."

"What does she look like?"

"Tall. Long hair. Reddish blond. They say she has a very attractive derriere. I wouldn't know."

The dancer was silent for a minute. She stood. "Come with me."

When they were in a long hallway where enlarged photos of the performers hung, the dancer pointed to one. "Is that her?"

Carol looked. It was Cathy. She was in a full white gown with a red long-stemmed rose in her right hand. The gown swooped down from her right shoulder to show a bare left shoulder almost to her breast. "Cat Red," the caption read.

Twelve

T he modified six-cylinder Ford engine continued to push *THE CARP* down the course of the Tennessee, not sputtering a time. Joe Chapman resumed his routine of river life. He swam, he fished, he did push-ups, he played with J. R. The dog would now assume an attack mode as soon as Joe held out a stick. He would run, leap, and grab the wood out of Joe's hand without command and be ready for another.

Joe watched the scenery flow by. This was new river to him. When he neared Shiloh Battle Field, he slowed the boat, anchored, and took J. R. and the Harley on a tour of one of the killing fields that turned the Civil War in favor of the North. He read inscriptions on monuments and wondered if any of his ancestors had fought for either side. At the museum he punched the Chapman name into a computer that printed out the names of all Chapmans who had fought at Shiloh. One had been wounded fighting for the North. Two who fought for the South had died of dysentery. What a heroic death, he thought. In one of the decisive battles of the war, his family members had died of diarrhea—the runs.

Back on the boat, he stopped for food and gas at Saltillo. Off the river and onto a wide creek, the dock's main building sat under the low-slung limbs of willows and oaks. Water ran off the tin roof in sheets fed by a piping system that was meant to cool the heat from the rays of the sun. Men sat beneath an open porch, watching Joe approach and taking drinks from their bottles of beer. No one moved in the late afternoon sun. Joe looked back toward the river to be sure he had not entered the Twi-light Zone and been cast into a scene from a Faulkner novel.

The men were friendly and helpful. One offered to sell him the dock and adjoining country store. Joe declined but appreciated their kindness. He figured they recognized a kindred soul in him and his rough looks. With food and fuel to last him to Paducah, he cast off from Saltillo.

For the next three days, he focused his binoculars on eagles, deer, and other wildlife along this vast stretch of the Tennessee. He watched with fascination the small boats with canopies that the mussel divers used. They would go down to the bottom of the Tennessee and dredge up buckets of the mollusks to sell for their shells. Buttons, ornaments, and jewelry were fashioned from the shiny, hard material. On a good day, a diver could scrape up six hundred dollars' worth, one told him.

From Shiloh, past Interstate 40 west of Nashville, along the banks of the Land Between the Lakes, and finally to Kentucky Dam, he was not slowed by mishap or another dam. He was speeding toward what he hoped would be his rendezvous with the one he now termed The Lady of the River. Malory could have his Lady of the Lake. The Lady of the River had a much more attractive body.

She had appeared again on his first night back on the boat. It was the same silky red hair flowing down a white gown. She had provided no new clues, no more information, no revelations that aided him in his quest. But she had turned and allowed him a view of a very attractive derriere, firm, compact, uplifted and covered tightly by the clinging gown. She was just as alluring aft as fore.

Perhaps her return meant he was on the right track. He would keep going as long as she appeared.

He pored over the contents of the purse. Again and again. There must be more. Something he had missed. The paper was now dried and brittle. A key showed signs of rust.

While he waited to be locked through Kentucky Dam, he studied the maps of the Ohio and Mississippi. Just a few miles ahead the Tennessee would end when it ran into the Ohio. Another forty miles and the Ohio would end when it hit the Mississippi at Cairo, Illinois. This would be the test. Would the apparition appear when he entered these new waters? Or was she just a Tennessee River woman?

IT WAS TO THE side of the first bridge as he neared Paducah that Joe, for the third time now, noticed the two men with business suits peering at him through binoculars. Why were these Chattanooga men following him? Then they were joined by what looked like a police car. He thought back to Kellie and Rose. It had to be his shooting into the engine of their husbands' boat. They were going to arrest him for assault with a deadly weapon.

When binocular stare met binocular stare, the men joined the uniformed officer in the car and drove off. Joe filed the occurrence away. He couldn't run. If they wanted him, they would have to arrest him. Maybe the Ohio and Mississippi were considered international waters and he could not be arrested.

The current grew stronger where the Tennessee merged with the Ohio, and the water turned brown from the spring rains. Joe felt *THE CARP* waiver a bit in the current. It took a stronger hand and more fixed attention to guide the boat on a straight line. It was dwarfed by the mighty Ohio.

He had passed beneath many bridges on his odyssey, and he viewed them from different angles. There was a singleness of purpose—to traverse the water—but a multitude of designs. The architectural form varied. Ribbons of steel gilded the river as though they were bows tied by a giant hand.

From afar, the bridges appeared to be great wonders, rooted to the banks and stretching long arms across to embrace the other side. There were great arches, steel cables, beams with rivets, and a roadway of asphalt or concrete. They grew up out of the mist and twilight to take on lives of their own. The designers must have thought they would be judged not only for their utility but also by their style and grace.

One thing they forgot. Bridges were like people. From beneath, all the flaws, pock marks, rough edges, pigeon nests, and graffiti could be viewed. There was no way to pretty up the underside of a bridge. It was best not seen. But to boatmen, the bridge all too often displayed its human side of scars, waste, discoloring, and decay.

As he neared the riverside city park at Paducah, Joe's eyes swept the shoreline for a place to dock for the night. Somewhere here he could gas up and replenish his food and water supply. J. R. sat and looked shoreward too.

Just beyond the park, Joe spotted a deserted warehouse with a barge dock that was not in use. He pulled back on the throttle and slid *THE CARP* to the side and toward the bank. J. R. paced along the side of the boat. Joe readied the mooring ropes he would have to secure quickly before the current took him back out into the Ohio. With the gentle bump of the side of the boat flush against the wood pilings of the dock, Joe jumped onto the deck of the unused dock and wrapped the bow rope first, then the stern, and finally the one at mid-boat. He looked at the boat with pride in his speedy work. He was becoming an old hand as a solitary sailor. J. R. jumped off the boat and stood beside him.

Blue lights flashed on the street to his right and reflected off the white skin of *THE CARP*.

"Just stay where you are!" Joe turned his attention to the two squad cars and the voice from the speaker. He put a hand on J. R. who had begun barking.

"It's okay, boy. They're going to arrest me, not you."

Two uniformed officers and the two men he had only seen through his binoculars since Chattanooga walked down the asphalt ramp toward him.

"Can't I dock here? I thought it was unused," Joe said.

"We don't care about that. Are you Joe Chapman?" one of the officers asked.

"Yes."

"Is this your boat?"

"Yes."

"We're here to seize it for these creditors," the officer said and handed Joe a set of court papers.

"What?" Joe said. He unfolded the papers from the McCracken County Circuit Court. They gave the officers power to take and sell his boat for a payment of debt established by a Tennessee court owed to Family Thrift.

"I don't understand," Joe said. "I took care of this debt through my bankruptcy. It's wiped out. My boat is my homestead. That was established and allowed by the bankruptcy judge in Tennessee."

"Mr. Chapman, this is Kentucky," one of the suited men said. "We've been following you all through Tennessee, Alabama, and now here. We missed you in Alabama when you left on that Sunday. You're not in Tennessee. Your homestead was in Tennessee. It's just a boat here. We'll probably get enough from it to pay about half what you owe us."

"The court was a *federal* bankruptcy court. Kentucky is still a state of the Union, isn't it?"

"Well, we prefer to call it a commonwealth," one of the officers said.

Joe saw he was getting nowhere with the officers or creditors. He looked toward the boat. All he had was on it. He read the papers again.

"It just says the boat. Not anything else. Is that right, officers?"

"Yeah, get everything else off that's yours. We're going to secure it, put the notices of sale up, and auction it off in ten days. What's not off by then will go with the boat."

"It will take me more than one trip to get everything off," Joe said.

"Just don't mess with the boat," the officer said. "I'm going to post the notice on the boat and put tape around it. The creditor here has a chain and lock to secure it to the dock."

The men in the suits walked toward *THE CARP* with the chain rattling between them.

"Stay here, J. R.," Joe said and walked back to the boat.

He gathered some papers from the cabin along with his cache of money. He found a large jacket and stuffed his .357 magnum pistol and his Bowie knife into inside pockets. He hid his shotgun beneath the mattress of the bed.

He wrapped three fifths of Jack Daniel's in some newspaper and put it in the saddlebags of his Harley. He looked at the box that contained the contents of the purse, took it, and put it in the saddlebag alongside the whiskey. Clothes, J. R.'s leashes, and finally the one pin-striped lawyer's suit.

Joe cranked the Harley and rode up the gangplank to where the officers and creditors were standing. J. R. growled at one of the creditors when he held out a rolled up paper to give to Joe. The dog took off from a sitting position and in two bounds left his feet and snatched the papers from the terrified creditor's hand.

"Don't bite him, J. R. You've had your shots. I'm not sure about him."

Joe lifted his dog onto the back of the Harley, put him in the harness, and fastened it. He strapped the smaller helmet around the dog's head and kicked the cycle back to life.

He pointed a finger toward the creditors. "I'll see you in court." He throttled the Harley toward downtown Paducah.

Thirteen

I t's a hundred dollars for a week. Seven days."

Joe looked away from the tattooed forearms of the boarding house clerk and tried to remember how much money he had left after a month on the river. A year before, a hundred dollars wouldn't have caused him to blink. He had spent that much on drinks for him and any lady of the night. He had spent twice that for a room for a night at the Derby. Now, though, his money would have to last him longer—all summer.

His spending on the river had been meager—food, gas, bus tickets for Kellie and Rose, and the money to repair their husbands' boat motor. His mental calculations told him he had nearly thirty-five hundred left from the four thousand he started with. That would last a long time on *THE CARP*, but without the boat, he'd be broke before he got back to London.

"Well, son, you want a room or not?" the old man asked and blew cigarette smoke past Joe.

"I have a dog and a Harley. Where could I put them?"

The clerk didn't look up. "No dogs are allowed in the rooms. You could tie him in the courtyard if he won't bark. You can park your cycle there too."

Joe walked toward where the clerk had pointed. He glanced out the door to the courtyard and toward the alley that led to it. He turned and looked back at the lobby of the hotel that had been made into a boarding house. A hundred years before, it was probably the grandest hotel in Paducah. An open courtyard was encased by a quadrangle of rooms. Paint hung in strips from the decorative woodcuts near the ceiling, pieces of tile flooring were missing, and bare hardwood showed darkening deterioration. Its time had passed.

"Do you have anything on the ground floor where I could be close to my dog?"

The clerk took another draw on his cigarette and examined his yellowed chart of the building.

"Son, most of the people here are long-term residents. They get the lower floors by seniority if they want them. We only have one elevator." His finger moved around the sheet. "You're in luck. I have something on the second floor that overlooks the courtyard. It hasn't been taken yet. The guy who did have it died a couple of weeks ago. Chenault was his name. Regis Chenault. An artist. We scrubbed it with soap and bleach. Shouldn't be any of the smell left. How's that?"

"All right, I guess." Joe handed the clerk a hundred dollar bill. "What did he die of?"

"Who?" the clerk asked and quickly stuffed the hundred in the cash drawer. He began to write a receipt.

"That Chenault fellow."

"Oh, I don't know. Tuberculosis or AIDS or something. I don't keep up with that sort of thing." He grinned and handed Joe his receipt.

Joe started to ask for his money back but realized the futility of it. He wasn't homophobic. Whatever the guy died of went with him. A room's a room. A bed's a bed. At least he would be near J. R. and his Harley.

"Here's your key. The bathroom is at the end of the hall. No women in the room. No loud music. No fires or cooking. If you puke, clean it up. And no pissing in the hallway. Any questions?"

Joe thought for a minute. This wasn't the Peabody, Hyatt Regency, Maxwell House, or Opryland Hotel.

"No. Those were the same rules my mother always gave me. Sounds a lot like home."

Joe took the key, went outside, and brought J. R. and his Harley down the alley and into the courtyard. He tied his dog on a rope to the handlebars of his cycle. He patted J. R.'s head and talked to him until the dog lay down next to the cycle. Joe took his possessions from the saddlebags of the cycle and walked inside and to his room.

He looked around. It would do. It would have to do. Bare wood floor that had escaped sanding or polishing through at least four Presidential terms. A bed, dresser, one straight back chair, and a small bedside nightstand were the furnishings. A single light bulb hung from the twelve-foot ceiling on a frayed electrical cord. There was also a small lamp on the nightstand with a twenty-watt bulb. One window did open onto the courtyard. He could stand there and see two of his three prized possessions. His boat was a different matter. He had no view of the river.

He put his meager possessions away except for what he wanted to look at. He took a copy of his bankruptcy papers and a legal pad, pulled a chair to the window for light, and began a study of law for the first time in months. He had hoped he never would have to look at them again. They chronicled the tale of his downfall. On page after page he looked at creditors' names and remembered the reasons.

Family Thrift was just a minor creditor compared to some of the others. He owed them less than twenty thousand. He owed the girl's estate over two million. If he had been more diligent, it never would have come to this.

Joe thought about Charlie Palk and their partnership. If Charlie Palk had not been elected, it would not have come to this. Palk was the detail man of the two in the firm. He watched out for deadlines, statutes of limitation, for anything that would have forecast trouble on the horizon.

They were the perfect two-man law office. Joe was the rainmaker, the extrovert, the trial lawyer. Charlie was the brief writer, the researcher, the clock watcher, and the accounts receivable policeman.

His finger ran down the list of items he was allowed to keep even though he filed bankruptcy. It stopped on his boat. He valued it at five thousand dollars—the limit for a single homestead in Tennessee. Some creditors—including Family Thrift—had filed an objection to him being allowed to keep it. But there it was in black and white. The bankruptcy judge ruled that the boat could be considered his homestead even though it was not attached to any land.

Joe took a pen and began to write in a strong and deliberate manner on the yellow pad. He pressed hard to keep his hand from shaking. Rage flowed through his fingers and onto the pages. "These assholes are going to pay for this," he said to the bare walls.

By dark he had filled half the legal pad with legal arguments and venomous side comments for Family Thrift. J. R. barked, and Joe looked out the window. He laid the legal pad aside and picked up the two motorcycle helmets.

"You want to go for another ride?" he asked J. R. when he reached the cycle. When the dog was in place, Joe pushed the cycle down the alley toward the street. He passed an old man sitting, hunched against the wall of the building in the alley, drinking from a brown paper bag encased bottle of wine. The man looked up and saw the dog on the rear of the cycle. When Joe and J. R. were to the street, the man stood, turned the bottle up for one last drink, threw it at a trash can, and walked past Joe shaking his head.

Down at the river, THE CARP was entwined in yellow police line tape. Joe parked the Harley and stepped onto the boat. He eased under the tape and opened the cabin door without disturbing either the tape or the notice of seizure. He retrieved two law books, a couple of sheets, several bottles of Coke, and some cans of Spam.

Back at the hotel, Joe slipped J. R. through a back entrance and into his room. He stripped the bed of its present sheets and replaced them with his own.

BY MIDNIGHT J. R. WAS asleep, and Joe lay stiffly between the clean sheets and tried not to come into contact with any other part of the bed that might have been touched by Regis Chenault. The right side of his brain told him that nothing there could infect him, but his left side told him not to take any chances.

Since he had departed from Alabama and Goose Collins, he had not drunk any Jack Daniel's—until this evening. The desperation drove him back to the bottle—three glasses of Jack and Coke. He hoped it would make him drift off to a better sleep. Now, though, he could still feel the gentle rolling of THE CARP. He had been on the boat so long that his sense of balance had assumed the flow and sway of the river.

Long after midnight, Joe opened his eyes from a fitful sleep and saw before him once again the Lady of the River. Her form was a bit different. She stood at the foot of his bed backlit by the glow from the open door of his room to the hallway. Her features were dark and shadowy. She still had long red hair, but her gown was wrinkled and soiled. Joe rubbed his eyes with the back of his hand when he heard the first words.

"Regis, is that you?"

His mind whirled. Who was she asking for? Regis? How did she know Regis? Joe stared at the face of the lady. The hair was not as long as before. He saw a beard. His left hand reached for his nightstand light and for his pistol. He clicked the light on and the figure did not disappear. The dim rays shadowed a man who looked more like Willie Nelson in a nightgown than a beauty queen.

"Who the hell are you?" Joe asked. He aimed the magnum at the chest of the bearded, red-haired intruder. The man had a key in his hand and on his face the expression of a burglar caught in the act.

"I'm Keith. What are you doing in Regis's room? Where's Regis?"

"Regis died two weeks ago according to the man downstairs."

Joe sat up in his bed but kept the gun aimed at the trembling target. "What're you doing in my room?"

The man managed a wan smile. " 'According to the man downstairs.' That's good. It could've been, 'According to the Man *upstairs*,' " Keith said and lifted his eyes and face toward the ceiling.

He backed away slowly while Joe swiveled around and sat on the edge of the bed.

"I'm Regis's friend. I've been gone for a few months. I had a key to his room. We shared . . . conversation. I knew he was ill. But I didn't know the end was so near."

Joe eased the pistol down and laid it on the nightstand. He stayed seated on the side of the bed and motioned to Keith to take the only chair in the room. A few uneasy moments passed between them while Keith sat and arranged himself. He looked around the room.

"You know," Keith said, "Regis always said I could have first grabs on this room if anything ever happened to him. I wonder what they did with all his work. He was quite an artist."

Since he was already startled awake, Joe sat and talked with Regis's friend. Keith was a fellow artist who traveled a great deal. He would go to all the river towns, to the public parks along the waterways, and paint portraits of tourists. They might never hang on the walls of museums, but they would grace the mantel places of many homes. And it was a living. What did Joe do?

Joe briefly explained his situation and why he was in Regis's room for a week. Keith gave Joe directions to the county courthouse and the federal building. In addition, he gave him the name of a law firm that would let him use their library and word processors. "They've represented my father's family for years. I'm the 'black sheep' of the family. That's not my term—it's theirs. I think it's politically incorrect."

"All things work together," Joe mumbled after Keith left. He locked the door and went back to bed.

AFTER BREAKFAST ON SUNDAY morning, Keith took Joe on a walking tour of the historic Paducah downtown. He saw the great floodgates and the wall that serpentined along the river. Keith pointed to a watercolor hanging in a shop along a brick-lined sidewalk.

"Mine."

Joe nodded. "That's good work."

Joe pointed to *THE CARP* that floated nearby, festooned with yellow ribbon and black print.

"Nice boat," Keith said. "I hope you get it back."

"It's my home."

"The sooner you do, the sooner I get Regis's room."

ON MONDAY MORNING JOE donned his Raiders cap and prepared himself for the hustle and bustle of people on the streets going to their jobs. At least they had jobs. He left J. R. in Keith's care, put the law book and legal pad under his arm, and walked the eight blocks to the law office of Bertran, Caylor, and Stran. Behind the lone desk in the foyer sat an attractive brunette who was talking on a telephone headset and typing at the same time.

"May I help you?" she asked when she clicked off the phone conversation.

"I'm Joe Chapman—"

"Oh, yes. You're Keith's friend. He's already called. He talked with Mr. Caylor and made arrangements for you to use our facilities. He said you're a Tennessee lawyer," she said with a bit of skepticism in her voice as she eyed Joe.

Joe took his Raiders cap off and held it to his chest in front of the Statler Brothers T-shirt logo. His hair was not yet long enough to lie down on his head but stood up in furrowed heaps.

"Yes, I just need to borrow a typewriter or word processor and a legal directory to prepare some papers for filing with the local bankruptcy court."

"Certainly. We could type it for you or you could use one of our para-legals to help draft the documents."

"No. I don't want to be a bother. I can do it."

"As you wish. But a friend of Keith's is a friend of ours."

Another young lady appeared and showed Joe to a second-floor office where he sat at a desk in front of a word processor and telephone. There, for the next two hours, Joe busied himself typing papers and calling clerks of court. He found out the schedule of hearings and judges' names. He typed the language he needed saying that he demanded an expedited hearing because of the possibility of suffering "irreparable damage." He smiled at being able to use the legal terminology once again. He did enjoy adversarial matters.

When he was done, he pressed a button on the processor, and out spewed a five-page legal document that was neat, crisp, and ready for filing. He requested that his boat be released and that Family Thrift be penalized for violating an order of another bankruptcy court. He proofread it three times and then walked back to the reception area. He needed five copies.

"Tell Keith that Vickie said 'Hello'," the receptionist said as Joe prepared to leave. "If you need anything else, feel free to come back by."

Joe walked to the federal building and to the bankruptcy court clerk's office. He filed the original and a set of his past bankruptcy papers, had the clerk to stamp the other copies as filed, and placed the matter on the hearing docket for Thursday. He walked another copy to the local courthouse to the office of the clerk who had issued the seizure. Then he took a final copy to the law office of Family Thrift's attorney.

He returned to his boarding house and found Keith and J. R. lounging on the grass near the Harley. Keith had his easel set up.

"Would you do me a favor, Joe?"

"What's that?"

"I'd like to do a sketch of you, J. R., and your Harley."

"Sure. I have plenty of time. I have to wait until Thursday to have a hearing about my boat."

"You sit on the cycle first. We'll add J. R. after I get everything else roughed in."

For the next two hours, Keith labored away with colored chalk on a portrait of Joe, his dog, and his cycle. He then painted their names on the motorcycle helmets.

FROM MONDAY THROUGH WEDNESDAY Joe and J. R. walked with Keith along the streets of Paducah. Flowers were at full bloom and the grass was green from all the rain that had taken the Ohio River to almost flood stage. Everywhere they went, people would speak to Keith, smile, and compliment him on his works. The city was vibrant and alive with the resurrection of spring. Joe knew he would have to spend more time here if the judge postponed his case or dismissed it altogether.

"Don't worry about it, Joe," Keith said. "I've spoken to the judge."

"You've what? You know the judge? You can't speak to a judge about a pending case."

"I'm not a lawyer. I'm not a party to the lawsuit. I just told Judge Olive that a nice young man would be in court on Thursday to try to retrieve his boat. I hoped he would be there and give you a fair hearing."

When he wasn't walking with Keith, Joe spent the days holed up in his room studying the contents of his lady's purse. He longed for the river. Baton Rouge beckoned him but he was only halfway there. His obsession grew when she did not appear. She had deserted him during his days in Paducah. He tried everything. He slept with the contents of the purse on his chest. He tasted the metallic surface of the keys. If only he could find the Mustang or the post office box that the keys fit, he could find Cathy. But there were probably a thousand Ford Mustangs and ten thousand post office boxes in Baton Rouge. He wanted, he desired, he lusted after the owner—the red-haired beauty with piercing eyes and the captivating body.

JOE WAS UP EARLY Thursday morning. He shaved, brushed his hair back as much as he could, and put on the suit he hadn't worn for a year. He took extra time and smoothed J. R.'s coat. The dog turned over and let Joe rub his belly.

A knock at his door startled Joe. He pushed the dog beneath the bed and told him to stay there.

"There's a phone call for you at the desk," the tattooed man said. He paused and caught his breath. "It's a hard walk up those stairs." He took a draw on his cigarette. "You know I ain't no messenger service, don't you?"

"Who is it?"

"Said he was a lawyer. Otherwise I wouldn't have walked up the stairs to get you. I'm not a healthy man, you know. Now get your butt down there. Keep it short. That phone's my business."

Joe walked down to the lobby with the clerk.

"This is Joe Chapman," he said into the phone.

Family Thrift's lawyer was on the other end of the line. Joe listened. The creditor made an offer. They would release the boat for two thousand dollars and Joe would dismiss the case that was set for the hearing this morning.

"No. Not a chance," Joe said.

"How about a thousand dollars?"

"I pay you or you pay me?" Joe asked.

"You pay us."

"No way. I'm not paying one cent. They should pay me. They took my home. I've had a lot of expense finding suitable quarters here in Paducah," Joe said and looked around at the decrepit lobby. "I've been delayed on my trip. Tell them to stick their offer up their collective ass! And have a nice day," Joe said and handed the receiver back to the clerk. "I'm through with your phone."

"What was that all about?" the clerk asked.

"Just some negotiating," Joe said. He ran up the stairs and back to his room. Adrenaline was flowing. They were scared. He could tell. They knew they were in the wrong. He couldn't wait to see them in court. He took J. R. out to the courtyard and passed Keith in the lobby.

"I'll look after the dog. You have a good day in court," Keith said.

PRECISELY AT NINE O'CLOCK, Judge James B. Olive entered the bankruptcy courtroom along with his clerk who called the court to order. About twenty lawyers and a few clients were seated in the eight rows of benches in the courtroom. Thursdays were reserved

for hearing motions and urgent matters. The judge called out each
case to determine whether it was still for hearing. The lawyers
answered as their cases were announced.

Judge Olive brought each file near his face when the clerk
called the name. He was an older man with a full, jowly face and
pinkish skin. Thinning white hair was combed straight back. His
double chin was slightly obscured by a goatee. In his black robe,
Judge Olive looked to Joe like Colonel Sanders preparing to give orders
to kill the chickens.

When the clerk reached Joe's case, Judge Olive motioned to the
clerk and he called the case out himself.

"In Re Joe Chapman versus Family Thrift. What is this case
about?"

Both Joe and the lawyer for Family Thrift stood to address the
judge from where they were only four spaces apart.

"Your Honor," Joe began, "this is an action to hold in contempt
Family Thrift Corporation for violation of the permanent injunction
that was entered in this matter in the Eastern District of Tennessee
because of their execution upon the exempt property of the debtor."

"Are you the party or the attorney for the party?" the judge
asked.

"Your Honor, I am the debtor and I am representing myself."

"Very well. Thank you, Mr. Chapman. Now what do you say
about it, Mr. Williams, for your client?"

"Your Honor, first of all, Mr. Chapman was a lawyer but his
license has been suspended, so he can not stand here as a lawyer
and—"

"What does that have to do with anything, Mr. Williams? You
don't have to be a lawyer to represent yourself. *Pro Se* is the term for
it, am I not correct?"

"Of course, Your Honor, you are correct—"

"Yes. Well, thank you. Now what is your side?"

"We say that our client did not violate any order of this court
or any other court in that our client executed on property that was not
exempt."

"I'll get back to you in a minute. I hope you are correct. I have
little tolerance for a violation of any bankruptcy court ruling."

It felt good to be in court again. Joe sat back and crossed his
arms while Williams shuffled in his place. He motioned Joe to step
outside to discuss a settlement.

Outside in the hallway, Williams leaned near Joe and
whispered, "My clients never ask my advice before they do fucking
dumb things. Can we give your boat back to you and let you be on
your way?"

"I need to be made financially whole. How about five thousand?"

"No. My client won't agree to pay you anything. I can barely persuade them that they were wrong to take your boat. Judge may ream them out good, but I don't think he'll make them pay anything."

"Can't do. I'd just as soon wait for the court's decision," Joe said and turned away.

In an hour, Judge Olive had finished disposing of six different motions in quick order and returned to Joe's case.

"I've read the pleadings, Mr. Chapman and Mr. Williams. Mr. Chapman has filed a copy of his Tennessee bankruptcy case in which his boat, *THE ESCAPE*, was allowed to him as his homestead exemption under Tennessee law. That order was not appealed and is now final. Mr. Williams, why should a Federal Bankruptcy Court in Kentucky not recognize a decision of a sister court in Tennessee?"

"Well, first of all, Your Honor, a boat is not your ordinary homestead exemption even in Tennessee."

"That's so, Mr. Williams. Your client objected in Tennessee. The judge ruled on it and granted Mr. Chapman a homestead in it. The order was not appealed. So why the seizure?"

"Well, sir, when the boat entered the waters of the Ohio River and came into Kentucky, it lost its protection as a Tennessee homestead and reassumed its status as a plain old boat in Kentucky."

The judge's skin went from pink to a deeper shade of red. His jaws puffed out, and he gritted his teeth before he spoke.

"Mr. Williams, is that the kind of logic they teach you at Yale? I suppose if a turtle from Tennessee perchance swam into the waters of the Ohio in Kentucky, that you would strip that poor creature of its shell and send it back to Tennessee naked and homeless—and give the shell to your finance company client to sell."

"Your Honor, this is not a turtle."

"No, but it was an order of a sister bankruptcy court. Once it was determined, the homestead follows the property regardless. Mr. Williams, I am surprised that you would do this to a fellow member of the bar who has fallen on some hard times." The judge turned toward Joe. "Mr. Chapman, what do you have in the way of damages?"

Joe approached the lectern. "Your Honor, while I dearly love this historic city, the defendant forced me to stay here against my will for almost a week. I was locked out of my home. My trip was delayed. I had more expense for a hotel and meals. I had to board my dog. I've been embarrassed by having my home swathed with yellow police tape. And this was a gross violation of a federal court's order."

"Very well, Mr. Chapman. I regret that your stay in Paducah was involuntary. It is the decision of this court that the petitioner, Joe

Chapman, receive one thousand dollars from the defendant if paid by sunset tonight or two thousand dollars if there is any further delay. Anything else?"

"Thank you, Your Honor," Joe said.

"No, Your Honor," Mr. Williams said and pulled his client toward the door.

THE YELLOW TAPE WAS off *THE CARP* before Joe reached the river, and at the boarding house, the thousand dollars waited in an envelope held by the clerk.

"A Mr. Williams said to give you this," the clerk said.

"I'm going to be leaving in the morning," Joe told the clerk. "A day early."

"There's no refund," the clerk said.

"I didn't expect one. Oh, by the way, you're invited to a party this evening. Just come as you are."

THE RAGTAG PARTY GROUP was made up of Joe, J. R., Keith, and the tattooed clerk. Keith knew a restaurant that had a garden patio area. Joe donned dark glasses, kept his pin-stripe suit on, and placed a special harness and leash on J. R. to make it appear he was a lead dog. Joe ordered steaks for them all.

"I'm a rich man," Joe said. "James B. Olive is a brilliant judge. You should have heard him comparing me to a naked turtle. Williams just cringed when the judge flushed and ate out his client. You should have been there, Keith."

"I thought Judge Olive would be fair with you."

"This is my kind of party," the clerk said and poured him another drink from Joe's bottle. He held his glass in one hand and his cigarette in the other.

Joe looked around and then tossed J. R. a piece of steak. "We all celebrate," he said.

EARLY THE NEXT MORNING, Joe repacked his possessions on the boat, lashed the Harley to the wall, and said goodbye to Keith.

"Here, hang this in the cabin so you'll have something to remember me by. You know where to find me if you pass this way again."

Joe took the colored portrait of him and two of his prized possessions and hung it in the cabin of the third. He pushed off with thoughts of Baton Rouge and radiant Cathy.

Fourteen

T he large black man slowly fingered the pencil. He laid it down
and reached for the cup of coffee. John Collins was an accomplished doodler. He had taken it up as a child when his father
emphasized to his brood of children that all of them should not speak
at one time. While he waited his turn, he doodled.

Doodling now had become a part of the waiting in his
occupation. Waiting on the telephone. Waiting for a lab report.
Waiting to testify against some drug dealer. Waiting for pieces of the
puzzle to fall into place.

He was particularly accomplished with hard lead pen-
cils—airplanes, star-shaped patterns, or tic tac toe against himself.
Time had made him an expert.

Now he sat waiting in his office of the DEA suite. From his
window he could see Mobile Bay. That was where the latest puzzle
had begun. Ten miles out in the Gulf, a pilotless plane had gone
down. One kilo of coke was recovered in the wreckage. For over three
and a half months he had been searching for the other pieces and been
frustrated.

Except for a fishing boat being nearby when the plane hit, he
might never have known about the one kilo of coke or the plane. Also,
the plane had not sunk immediately. The fuselage had broken apart
like a huge egg shell. The Piper Navajo now sat in a warehouse where
the DEA stored evidence and confiscated property.

Why was no one on board? Why just one package of coke?
Where was its occupant or occupants?

If the plane had flown just a few more miles, John Collins
might never have had to deal with the whole mess. It would have
sunk to the bottom of the Gulf and not been a problem to his agency.
It could have gone quietly away, but it didn't.

The plane was a type that could make the trip from Central
America to the States on one tank of gas and play hide and seek with
radar by flying near the water's surface.

Solemn John was his nickname. Few saw him smile. He

practiced a sullen tight-lipped expression to remind himself how dangerous it was to talk about anything his agency was involved in. It was a job requirement for any good agent. If not, they could end up dead or fired. He even regretted mentioning the plane to his father, Goose Collins. The press had carried stories about the plane, but there was no need for him to mention it. In this business you could not trust anyone fully. Your neighbor—or your brother—might be a drug runner.

The doodling this time was in anticipation of a call from the sheriff of Clarke County, Alabama, fifty miles due north. There was a report of a body found near a package of cocaine. In the piney woods in the sparsely populated area between the Alabama and Tombigbee rivers, the body had decomposed past recognition.

A month earlier, a hiker ten miles from where the body was found stumbled across another package of cocaine. The markings on the package linked it with the one found on the plane. It was as though someone had salted the Alabama landscape with packages of the white powdered drug.

Collins quit his doodling. He took a straight-edged ruler and drew a line on a map from the place the hiker found the package to the point in Mobile Bay where the plane was found. The line passed through Clarke County. How close was it to the body? Maybe they were all connected or maybe it was just coincidence.

There was a knock on his door before it swung wide. His younger co-agent wore a broad smile and fanned a piece of paper in front of him.

"This is it, John. The sheriff faxed us the location of the body. Another package of cocaine. And guess what?"

"What?"

"There was an unopened parachute with the body."

Collins took the piece of paper that showed the location of the body in Clarke County and aligned it with his own map. He put his pencil to the location on his map. It was on or very near the line that he had just connected.

"George, call the sheriff. Tell him we are on the way and not to move the body or anything until we get there. Tell him this might be connected with the other coke that was found up there last month."

Collins grabbed his jacket and checked out through the agency's switchboard. He would be gone the remainder of the day to Clarke County and he would need a four-wheel drive off road vehicle to drive to the site of the body.

He let the younger agent drive the Jeep up U.S. 43 to Jackson and down county road 15 to Carlton. From there it was old farm roads and hunting trails into the triangle formed by the Alabama and

Tombigbee. It was thick scrub pine, dense brush, and undergrowth. He couldn't imagine anyone finding anything in this type of terrain. It just went to prove that there wasn't one square foot of the world that hadn't been walked over by someone.

After an hour of following the trail left by other police cars, they came to an opening in the trees where a delegation of law enforcement had gathered. Fifteen or so men and women officers looked toward them as they bumped to a stop.

George Stephens followed his older colleague toward the center of attention. Collins had dealt with dead bodies before. Stephens hadn't. The heap of the remains was now covered with black plastic sheeting.

Collins shook hands with the sheriff and thanked him for waiting until he got there. He took his own camera and began recording the scene. One of the sheriff's people was videotaping the location.

"I'll need a copy of your video, sheriff. I'm glad you brought it," Collins said. He looked around and it struck him. He was the only black man in the group. Times were changing. He couldn't imagine a white sheriff waiting for a black agent twenty years before, maybe not even ten. This sheriff was a good one. Some weren't. Some were in cahoots with the drug dealers and looked the other way when loads of coke passed through their counties.

"There's not much left, Agent Collins," the sheriff said. He motioned for a deputy to pull the plastic back.

The sheriff was right. What was left of the body was lying on its back. Its face had been eaten away by wild dogs or some kind of animals. They had come early and often. A hand and foot were gone. Maggots were feasting on a small amount of what was left of the abdomen. Flies buzzed around in the hot afternoon sun.

"How long you think, Sheriff?" Collins asked.

"Three to five months." He pointed to a limb above in a pine tree. "Looks like he broke that when he fell. We had a cool spring. If it had been warmer, there wouldn't have been anything left. The sap and resin on the pine tree limb tell me that too."

Collins nodded as though he knew what the sheriff was talking about.

"There's a lot of stuff here, Sheriff. Looks like this fellow expected to walk out of here if his parachute had opened."

Scattered near the body were a pair of night-vision goggles, two knives, a .45 caliber automatic pistol, bottled water, and small military type canned food containers.

"Yeah, his chute never opened. Carried a kilo of coke and all this modern technical stuff and his chute never opened. Wonder what he was thinking when he came down the last few hundred feet?" the sheriff asked. He smiled and tilted his head upward.

The parachute case protruded to the side of the skeletal remains. The package of coke lay nearby. Collins could see the similarity of markings on this package with those found on the plane and farther north by the hiker. Each exporter had almost a signature way of identifying shipments. There were codes of the place of manufacture, export city, and number of packages in the bundle. The DEA knew most of the codes.

"Have your people turn him over and make pictures from all angles. We want to get everything. Scrape it all up. Probably need to do at least a half mile radius search. I'll send some men up here to help with it. We might find another body. They usually don't fly alone. Too afraid that someone's going to fly off with a load," Collins said. He turned and looked as far as he could see in all directions. "Those are the Alabama and Tombigbee, aren't they?"

"Yes. Used to be good fishing in the Alabama. I don't know now," the sheriff said.

ON THE DRIVE BACK to Mobile, Stephens sat under the wheel while Collins mulled the puzzle. He hoped for an I.D. on the body. It might be someone they already had a file on. It was worth having a reconstruction artist to do a sketch. This could have been a big load that was dropped off.

"What do you think happened?" Stephens asked.

"The problem with this kind of case is that you don't want to draw conclusions too early. If you do, you'll be looking for evidence to support your conclusions rather than to find out what really happened. Let's go with what we have. A downed plane in the Bay. A bag of coke there. One north of here. One near the body. Careless. That's the only conclusion I have so far . . . and that's not really a conclusion because it could have been done that way on purpose. To mislead us.

"I've been at this office for ten years and have seen all kinds of drug deals. Some go bad by accident. Some go bad when one dealer is trying to create problems for a rival. And sometimes we get lucky and catch someone.

"I haven't come to any real conclusions on this one. It's weird. They all are. We're dealing with weird people. A lot of them are real smart. Smarter than us. But it's when they start *thinking* they're smarter that we catch them."

"What do we know about the origin of the plane?" Stephens asked. A light rain began to fall and dusk settled in on the road to Mobile.

"Not much. It was leased out of Jackson, Mississippi, on forged papers. We found the pilot whose name was on the documents. He's clean. Has an air-tight alibi. He was piloting a business group in Denver that day."

"Did the pilot of the leased plane file a flight plan?"

"Yeah. Was supposed to fly from Jackson to Daytona for a week and then back. Never did get to Daytona. Probably detoured to Colombia, picked up a load, and then flew back to the states.

"The coast guard picked up an unidentified on its radar the day of the crash coming in near the Texas-Louisiana border. Lost it before they could make contact or force it down. Could be the same one or completely different."

"You think that body we just saw was the pilot?"

"Could be. We'll check with the guy at the airport who leased the plane out to see if he recognizes him when we get the sketch. Could be that he was scattering the load where he could go back and find it. Send the plane into the Gulf. Trick his bosses into thinking that he was part of an unfortunate mishap."

"We've only recovered three packages of coke. There had to be more. Right, John? No one would risk going to Colombia or wherever for three packages."

Collins glanced over at the younger agent and then toward the road ahead. "At least you're starting to think like an agent. No, nobody would fly a plane in for three packages. There's more. Somewhere there's more." He leaned back, crossed his arms, and dozed off to the sound of the windshield wipers' steady rhythm and the splashing of water against the underside of the Jeep.

IN AN HOUR THEY were back to the office building in Mobile. Collins told Stephens to turn in the Jeep and go home while he checked by the office. "We'll get back on it in the morning."

As soon as Collins walked into his office, he saw the yellow Post-It note stuck to the console of his phone. It was short. "Call the sheriff of Clarke County."

"Sheriff, this is Agent Collins. What's up?"

"Agent Collins, I thought you'd like to know about the body."

"What do you have already?"

"That guy must have been sorely disappointed when he jumped and pulled the cord on that parachute."

"Why do you say that?"

"It wasn't a parachute at all. Just a parachute casing holding a pillow. He didn't have a chance."

Collins hung up the phone and pulled his chair near the window. He leaned back and laced his fingers behind his head. He looked toward Mobile Bay. "What a horrible last half minute," he said.

Fifteen

They lay among the pile of mail that Carol Sent sorted through. Two picture postcards. One had a scene of a horse in a pasture behind white-planked fencing. The other was a sky-line view of Birmingham, Alabama. Carol recognized the writing. She looked at the postmarks. They were dated a week apart.

They probably weren't written on those dates. Cathy was playing a game again. There was no telling when she gave them to some trucker and told him to mail them. The Birmingham scene bore a Pensacola postmark while the horse card was mailed in Denver.

The messages were brief—as they always were. "I'm okay. Water my flower bed if you get a chance. See you soon—Cathy." The other said, "We're traveling north. Don't know exactly where I'll be in a week. See you soon—Cathy."

Carol opened her desk drawer and tossed them inside. Irresponsible. Immature. Inconsiderate. Imbecilic. She gritted her teeth and thought of all the "I" words that described her sister. She had been worrying for weeks. Now she gets two cards with no idea of where her sister actually is. Didn't Cathy know she would worry? Had they drifted that far apart?

They didn't have the same father, but they had the same mother. That must be the difference. Cathy got her recklessness from the genes of her rodeo following father while Carol retained the responsibility of the farmer's daughter. Maybe it was her mother's fault for letting two men who were so different father her daughters.

Carol shook her head. No, she wasn't going to blame it on her mother. That was too simplified an answer. Cathy was searching for something. Was guilt driving her or passion? The desire to reform or a self-imposed spiral toward destruction?

She opened the drawer and took the postcards back out. She reread them. There was no word about any companion. Nothing about when she would return. And absent were any words of affection or love toward her sister. Cathy was a victim of her own talent and desire.

Carol looked closer at the card with the horse. All was not lost. Her assignment for this week's creative writing course was to describe a setting. The instructor had given her good marks for her two-page description of her character as a ballerina and a stripper.

Now they were moving on to the importance of setting to a short story or novel. "You have to give readers enough to let them see your main setting as a place they would be interested in and would enjoy visiting. You don't have to describe every detail or else you will cheat your readers from using their own vivid imaginations to fill in and flesh out what they see. The problem is the balance," the teacher had told the class.

Carol took a pencil and began to write. She thought better with the silence of the pencil rather than the clickety-click of her word processor. Once she had it written out, then she would put it on the machine. She saw the horse. She heard it breathe and snort. She felt it nuzzle a sugar cube from her hand. She tasted the spring breeze that came over its body and smelled the musky aroma. She put her hand on the rough boards of the fence and almost lodged a splinter in her palm.

She was there with the horse. But she didn't see Cathy.

Sixteen

Charlie Palk slammed his fist down on his desk. The cup of coffee toppled over pouring a brown stream among the documents and the June 5 edition of the *London County News*.

"Damn!"

He flipped the switch on the intercom, pushed back from the desk, and avoided the dripping coffee.

"Luann, I just knocked over my coffee. Bring me something to clean it up."

Luann was through the door with a whole roll of paper towels almost before he turned off the intercom. She handed him several, tore more off, and began to blot up the mess.

"What happened?" she asked and picked up the soaked documents. She tried to dry each one and laid them on the nearby conference table.

"Did you read the story that Mike gave the paper? That S. O. B." Palk walked to his window. Beyond the glass and past the oak trees that shaded the courthouse yard, and beyond the neatly rowed marigolds, was Main Street. A block down Main was the office of the newspaper. Next door to it was the campaign headquarters of Mike Garrison—his opponent for district attorney general. The blue and white banner was over twenty yards long. It proclaimed the candidacy of Mike Garrison in letters too large for anyone to miss. Palk thought it was put in his view to goad him.

His former assistant was waging a dirty campaign. They both were unopposed for their parties' nominations in the July primary and were certain to face each other in the September general election.

Mike Garrison was ten years younger. He stood six feet three inches tall and had wavy black hair. He had a strong, jutting jaw and a boyish smile. A bike rider and marathon runner, he was in appearance everything that Charlie Palk was not.

Garrison was a local football hero and hailed from a large and established family. In the courtroom, he displayed his intellect and thoroughness. He was quick-witted. Palk had handpicked him to prosecute some of the big-name cases during the past four years. He was an excellent prosecutor.

Now, Palk was engaged in the political battle of his life. Palk had believed Garrison would keep the contest clean and above board. But the Garrison supporter's words in the newspaper had to have been planted by Garrison himself.

"You didn't read that?" Palk asked Luann.

"Well, I read it, but I guess I didn't take it as personal as you apparently did."

"Not take it personal? How could I do anything else?" Palk picked the newspaper up and peeled the pages apart.

"Let me read you this. 'Mike Garrison, candidate for district attorney general, would not deny today that unsolved murders and unidentified bodies would be issues in his upcoming campaign to unseat District Attorney General Charles Palk.

" 'Garrison's campaign manager, Shane Andrews, stated earlier at a campaign appearance that London County was becoming the laughing stock of Tennessee for its unsolved murder cases. He went on to say that the county was becoming known nation-wide as a safe place to dump bodies.

" 'He said the people would have to decide what kind of *primate* they wanted to have as the prosecuting attorney. The comment brought roars of laughter from the approximately one hundred supporters of Garrison.' "

Palk looked up at Luann. "How can I not take that personally?" He laid the paper down, took a handkerchief from his pocket, and wiped beads of sweat that had popped up on his head like droplets on a glass of ice water.

"Well, you know how politics can be. A lot of things are said that people don't really mean. And I bet half the people in the county don't even read the newspaper anyway," Luann said and kept wiping the desk with paper towel after paper towel.

"You're right that half the people don't read the newspaper. Half of them can't read. And half of them don't vote. But it's the other half who do that worries me.

"Mike's supporters are starting on a campaign of making me look like a clown. That damn orangutan is going to be the end of me. And now we have two bodies that we can't even identify, let alone prosecute someone for killing them."

Luann opened the door to go back to the reception area and then paused. "You know what you need, Mr. Palk?"

"Yeah, I know what I need," Palk said and threw his handkerchief on the table. "I need a couple of arrests to make these people forget that monkey. I need a hundred thousand dollars to run my campaign. And I need Garrison and the newspaper to move their places farther down the street so I don't have to see them every time I look out my window."

"That might help. But what you really need is for Joe to be here to run your campaign. Remember last time you were all concerned too until Joe took over for you. He wrote some really nice ads, made a speech or two for you, and that old fart of an opponent just sunk into the slime. Joe Chapman is what you need." Luann closed the door behind her.

Palk turned and rubbed his head. He walked back to the window. Beyond main street a few blocks was the river. She was right. He was surprised by Luann's coarse words. She had probably worked around his office too long until the language began to rub off. But Joe did have a way of getting rid of "old farts."

He thought back to their campaigns of the past. It had been a reversal of roles. Joe Chapman had been elected first. A young legislator. Palk was his campaign manager. Joe won the seat when his opponent died four days before the election. Those were the days. Nashville. Parties at the governor's mansion. Printers Alley and the Opryland Hotel. After two drinks, Joe would get lost in the maze of hallways in the hotel. He didn't recognize that they were color coded to help him to find his way back to the right room. Palk laughed.

After Joe lost interest in the legislature, Palk ran for attorney general and Joe managed the campaign. That was where Joe shined. He seemed to relish being in the background. Strategy, arm twisting, and below the belt antics were his strong points. Nixon's cronies were pikers in dirty tricks compared to Joe.

Palk sat next to the window and remembered the opponent who "just sunk into the slime."

A body, badly burned, had been found near a trash dumpster. It went months without identification. The opponent called a news conference for the site of the dumpster where he was going to say how he would have proceeded if he were the prosecuting attorney. His talk was typed up and his positions in relation to the dumpster were choreographed for the cameras. Joe somehow got a copy of the speech and the directions that told the opponent to "step right three steps" then "go back two steps" and "put right hand on dumpster and look into camera."

It was beautiful. Without telling Palk, Joe and a cohort, on the night before the news conference, went to the dumpster. They dug a trench four feet deep, filled it with a mixture of sand and water, and then scattered dry dirt and a little straw on top to make it appear normal.

The next morning, in the presence of television cameras and

reporters, the opponent took his directed three steps to the right, back two steps, put his hand on the dumpster—and began to sink up to his armpits in the miry mess. The video of him being sucked into the hole while saying how bad a job Palk had done in preparation and prosecution sunk his campaign. The people could not take him seriously.

Joe's campaign strategy was to make the public laugh at an opponent. "A candidate can take anything except being laughed at," he often said.

Perception. That was the whole of politics. Perception is reality when it comes to voters. Palk never had to utter a word about his opponent.

Now, he knew he was in the same position. If Mike Garrison had people laughing at him, it was over. He moved to his desk and opened the drawer. There facing him was a picture of him standing next to a sheet-draped orangutan. Joe Chapman had it framed and presented to him. He slammed the drawer. He had to beat the monkey. He had to identify these bodies and work on having someone arrested.

LUANN'S VOICE CAME OVER the intercom. "Mr. Palk, Dr. Trout is on the line."

Palk reached for the phone. This could be good news. An identification. Something. Anything.

"Good morning, Dr. Trout. Do you have news?"

"Monkey, these are the strangest ones we've had in some time. It's difficult to make much out of it so far. I do definitely believe there's a connection between the two bodies. They both appear to have been in the water about the same length of time. They were both dead and well into rigor mortis before they ever hit the water."

"How can you tell that?"

"Well, I'm speculating to an extent since the bodies would tend to loosen up after a time, especially in the water. But it's like they were placed in a box or something, doubled over, and then carried to the river a day or so later and thrown in with some kind of weight tied to them to hold them toward the bottom. I believe that's what that rope went to.

"You see, I can tell they were in a contorted position when they entered the water because there's less debris, dirt, leaves, and stuff in those areas where parts of their bodies were pressed together and stayed that way. Sort of like if you close your arm at the elbow and hold it tight, nothing will get into that area."

Palk leaned back in his chair and put his feet up on his desk. "How was the second one killed?"

"The same way. A .22 slug to the head."

"What about dental work?"

"Yeah, they both had some. But you know as well as I do that until we have a missing person to match dental records with they're useless. There's no national clearing house of dental records. If you have some families who've reported missing people and they can provide me those records, we can check it out. These two had pretty bad teeth. Expensive boots but poorly kept teeth."

"Well, what about the boots?"

"Similar. Very good quality, as I said before. Good leather belts too. . . . And that reminds me. The other thing that ties these two bodies together is the belts. I haven't seen anything like it before, and I don't have the foggiest idea what it means. But on the inside of each belt there is sort of a brand or stencil with some numbers and letters. It's the same on both belts. Could've been that they bought their belts at the same store and this is an identification of some kind."

"What does it look like, or say?"

"Wait a minute. I have it written down here some place. Hold on."

Palk could hear the shuffling of papers while the doctor tried to locate the belts' inscriptions.

"Here it is. It says '1918,' then there's a dash mark and 'ZZZ'."

Palk wrote it down on a sheet of a legal pad and read it back to Dr. Trout. "I ought to take a look at that."

"Yeah. What you want me to do next?"

"I'm going to send a reconstruction artist up to look at the bodies. He can draw what they looked like when they were in better shape and alive. We'll send the drawings around the country to other police jurisdictions for missing persons. Go public if we have to. It's okay to show him everything you have."

"Will do."

Palk hung up and put his feet down. He looked at the legal pad. The numbers and the letters. Did they mean anything? Nothing to him. He threw the pad on his desk. "Shit."

He knew the sequence of events—identity, motive, connections, arrests, convictions. He had to have the first to start the ball rolling. Otherwise it was no identity, no motive, no connections, no arrests, no convictions, no win, no Attorney General Palk.

He decided to take a drive.

"Luann, you can reach me on the car phone or page me if there're any emergencies. I'm taking your advice. I'm going to drive along the river and look for Joe."

"Good. Now, let's see. I believe that's the first time you've taken my advice. I'm noting it on my calendar."

THE WARM MID-MORNING air refreshed him. He walked down the brick path past the marigolds toward his Jeep. He now parked on the side of the courthouse opposite Mike Garrison's headquarters. He peeled back the canvas covering over the roll bar. He needed the air all around him. He could drive, feel the breeze along his ears, and look for Joe's boat. Maybe his luck was changing.

He took a left at the intersection with Highway 11 and noticed the difference in the new pavement when he went across the bridge. At least the fire had accomplished something. They had resurfaced the entire length of the bridge. The big tires of the Jeep hummed along on the new, smooth surface. At first they thought they had corralled the young culprits who had started the fire. But then it turned out they had perfect alibis. It was just as well. They should have received medals rather than be prosecuted.

To his right, the river stretched toward Knoxville and the next dam ten miles upstream. To his left, the river disappeared around Siler's Bend. He would begin his search for Joe the last place he saw him. Joe's house had new occupants. Palk could see from the road that the houseboat was gone. He knew Joe didn't like to go toward Knoxville, so he probably headed downstream toward the wider lake and the island areas where the fishing was better.

There were three marinas along a ten-mile span of River Road. Palk stopped at each in turn and asked about Joe. No luck. The managers of all three knew Joe, but no one had seen him for months. One thought he saw the old houseboat go by over a month before. Palk figured that would be about the time he last saw Joe around the first of May.

Disappointed, he started back toward London but decided to stop by the river near where both bodies had been found. He had read about *visualization*. Perhaps he could sit and visualize the bodies being tossed into the river. He would see the killer or killers. He was ready to try anything. He might drive up to Knoxville and consult with a psychic.

Palk skidded the Jeep to a stop in the loose gravel of the river access where he had stood the morning the first body had been pulled from the water by Jake Rathborn. He walked to the edge of the river. The carcasses of dead willowflies lined the shore where the water lapped up to them. A swarm of shad minnows swam just beneath the surface and feathered the water's otherwise tranquil skin. No one was in sight.

He walked downstream to a huge rock that jutted out over the water. He sat down on the smooth boulder that had felt the soles of countless generations of humans. The rock was warm and felt good to the palms of his hands. It was calm. He closed his eyes and tried to imagine the bodies, the killers, the reasons.

After a minute, he opened his eyes and looked toward London. He liked it here on the rock. He was away from all the questions, all the criminals, and all the pressure of his job. He turned downstream and squinted, searching the river for as far as he could see. He envied Joe. It must be good and soothing to get away from business on the river. No red lights, no phones, no bodies. If Joe knew he needed him, he would come back. He was sure of it.

Time passed but no clue floated up to him. No vision materialized. Even when he thought back to the body he had seen, there was nothing new.

His beeper signaled. He looked at the number and walked back to the Jeep and his phone.

"Luann, what did you want?"

"You need to go down to the river."

"I am down at the river."

"Well, you need to go to where Deputy Ratliff and Jesse Putnam are. Old Mill Ferry Road where it dead-ends into the river." Luann was reading from her notes. "They've got another body there." She paused. "You hear me?"

"Yes," Palk mumbled and placed the phone back in the Jeep. He took out a pair of binoculars and trained them downstream and onto the opposite bank. He saw the blue flashing lights of a patrol car and several men standing near the bank. They were only a half mile away but on the far side. He would have to drive twelve miles to get to them.

He sat in the Jeep and started the engine. He felt a headache coming on. Another body. He was in no hurry to see it. The gods of missing bodies must be playing poker along the river banks and tossing their losings into the Tennessee. What had he done to deserve this?

After a twenty-minute leisurely drive, he was there. Ozzie had already taped off the area. A few curiosity seekers milled about near the line. News photographers clicked their cameras at him. It was a mistake for him to want to be one of the first to a murder scene. At least now when there was no one to arrest. Mike Garrison stood out of the way talking to a reporter.

Palk pushed the tape down and stepped over. If Putnam was already there, it meant the person was dead for sure. The ambulance's lights weren't flashing. He walked to the plastic-draped body near the riverbank.

"Was it in the river too?" Palk asked no one in particular.

"Yes, General Palk," Ratliff said, "and guess who found him?"

Palk looked around and saw the sallow-faced Jake Rathborn

sitting hunched against the base of a tree, his chin resting on his
knees. Expressionless, Rathborn tugged on the bill of his Red Man cap
and flicked his cigarette's ashes onto the root of the tree.

"Jake got another one, huh?" Palk said and nodded toward
Rathborn.

"Yep. Fishing again."

Palk and Ratliff walked over to the squat figure. "Don't bother
to get up, Jake. Looks like you hit the jackpot. Two out of three."
Palk smiled and hovered over the farmer. "Where did you catch this
one?"

"Charlie, this one was hung up in some tree limbs just a little
ways down the bank here," Rathborn said and pointed downriver. "I
thought it was just a passel of old rags when I first saw it. I was
fishing from the bank instead of from my boat. Just walking along.
I poked it with my fishing rod. That's when I seen it was a body." He
blew smoke from his nose and tossed the stub of the cigarette into the
river.

Palk looked toward the deputy. "Ozzie, is there anything
unusual about this one?" He walked toward the body.

"Well, I'd say we're lucky on this one. Doesn't have a face.
Looks like a shotgun blast got that. Athletic shoes. No fancy boots.
No rope. But it looks like he has a wallet in his back pocket. We
haven't removed it. Could be some I. D. there."

Palk raised his eyebrows at the news. He stepped nearer and
motioned for a deputy to take the black plastic away. The sickening
sight was not diffused by Ozzie's description. Palk turned away. He
didn't want to puke on camera. He looked back to the body and saw
in the right back pocket a piece of leather. He breathed deeply and
motioned to cover it back up.

"Get the body to Dr. Trout," he said and walked toward the
reporters.

Seventeen

T he late afternoon sun glinted off the Pyramid barely above the horizon making it appear like a huge gold javelin point tossed to Earth by ancient gods.

Joe was glad to see it. He glanced at the sun and knew, without having to check his watch, that he had two hours until sunset. Time on the river was measured in sunrises and sunsets. He made it a rule not to run his boat after dark. There were too many hazards on the Mississippi. He could be at the Mud Island Marina in Memphis within an hour.

Since Paducah, THE CARP had gone with the current past Cairo, Illinois, Caruthersville, Missouri, and Osceola, Arkansas. Memphis beckoned Joe like a lady of the night. She offered easy pleasure and no commitment. That was more than he had gotten from the other little towns along the way.

The Ohio and Mississippi had turned mean on him. Used to the snail-like flow of the Tennessee, he was rapped awake by the speedy current of the two brown rivers. In three days he had lost a pair of shoes, a spare gas tank, and a six-pack of beer—all washed overboard by unexpected waves. Whirlpools, eddies, and hidden stone and concrete walls that directed the water into the main channel had demanded all of his navigational skill to pull the boat through unscathed.

There were few other boats of his kind on the Mississippi. They knew better. Over four days, Joe had seen no more than the same number of pleasure craft. The river wasn't made for them. It was for the mammoth barges strapped six-abreast and eight deep and pushed by giant tugs. He had seen two casino boats on the Ohio, but after the Mississippi it was purely commercial. His little boat was a nuisance to the other craft although he always gave them a wide berth.

Twice he had run his gas tanks to near-empty. At Osceola, he looked for a dock and found none. He dropped anchor near a grain elevator, hefted two six-gallon auxiliary gas cans, and jumped onto the dark bank—only to sink ankle deep into the sludge-like sediment. It sucked his shoes off, and by the time he retrieved them, his arms were as covered as his legs. As he walked the miles to a gas station, the gray-brown mess dried to make him look like he had been plucked from a concrete mixer. He had the good sense to leave J. R. tied on board.

The day before, the engine of THE CARP had cut out in the middle of the river. Joe had changed the spark plugs and cranked it again before any river traffic came along. Floating only by the power of the river scared Joe. It was the first time on the trip that he had felt totally out of control.

The Harley had been lashed to the wall with no opportunity to ride. At Memphis, things would be different. He might even cycle over to Graceland. He was probably the only native-born Tennessean who had not made a pilgrimage to Elvis's home.

He checked his maps while the boat plodded along on the now-smooth water to where he could see bridges connecting Tennessee and Arkansas. Baton Rouge was probably just four or five days away considering the pace he had been keeping. He could use a night in Memphis. He'd listen to some Blues on Beale Street, eyeball some women, and eat the tangy barbecue.

Cathy had not visited him since before Paducah. He may have been right. She was just a Tennessee River apparition, a dream-induced phantom. Baton Rouge would tell him. He would stay the summer until he found her, the woman with perfect beauty.

He eyed the marina area as he pulled the boat off the main channel and beneath the bridges. The thing he wanted most—second only to Cathy—was a long hot shower. He felt his face. He needed to shave. Maybe Cathy wasn't into visiting a man who smelled worse than a pig and looked like a grizzly bear. His hair was growing to where he thought he had enough to brush back.

He pulled up beside the dock's gas pumps and felt the mild bump of boat against rubber fenders. He tied it down and looked for an attendant. There were plenty of boats docked behind the service area, but there was no one around. The tram was still running between the island and the city. He could see people on the far side.

"You okay there?"

The black man's voice took Joe by surprise. He turned and looked directly into the sun and then shaded his eyes with his hand.

"I want to fill it up."

"That's good. That what we be here for." The man grabbed the nozzle end of the gas hose and looked for the tank of Joe's boat.

"Way in the back," Joe said and stepped in that direction. "What's the chances of me leaving the boat around here for tonight? I want to go over to Beale Street, listen to a little music, eat a little barbecue."

"Not s'pose to," the man said and looked around. "But the boss man's not here. You'll be okay to leave it here. We cut the pumps off in another hour. Won't be nobody down here on a week night."

Joe looked around. "Can I get my cycle from here over to Beale?"

"Sure. Just follow that driveway around by our change house and over across that little bridge. Not s'pose to let people drive that way. But you tell Ernest that Willie said it's okay." The black man winked. "You want a woman? Willie knows where they's at. Take my card." Willie held the gas hose with one hand and with the other gave Joe his card.

"Thanks, Willie," Joe said and began to loosen the Harley.

"What's your name?" Willie asked.

"Carp."

"Like the fish?"

"And like the boat," Joe said and pointed to the name on the stern.

"Carp, do you mind I tell you something?"

"No. Go right ahead."

Willie looked around again. "You need a bath. You ripe, man. Ain't no woman going to get ten feet of you. You don't have enough money to pay them to." He paused. "But I can help you on that too. You can use our change house up there on the hill. Good showers. Anybody asks, just tell them Willie said it okay."

THE HOT SHOWER WAS the best thing that had happened to him in a week. He stood in the almost scalding water and let it beat off the top of his head. Shampoo suds ran to his feet. He opened the faucets to full blast and turned his back to the pulsing streams. The massage loosened his tired muscles.

He grabbed several towels and tied one around him. At the mirror, he rubbed some gel into his hair and brushed it straight back. It was at least an inch—maybe an inch and a half—long now. He shaved the five-day stubble from his face and admired himself. He was tanned and bright-eyed. Hadn't touched any liquor since Paducah. His shoulders, arms, and stomach were taking on the appearance of someone in good shape. He nodded. The pushups, running, pullups, and swimming were paying off. Cathy would want him.

THE HARLEY FELT NEW again under him. Its unmistakable rumble—like a giant's heartbeat—drew the attention of the pedestrians. They looked at him and his machine.

Dark now and he was just cruising. He knew where Beale Street was, but he wanted to see a little of the downtown area. He passed the city hall and the federal courthouse. The cycle spoke in slow rhythms as it circled through a Civil War park overlooking the river.

Two more blocks and Joe saw people standing in line. At first he thought it was a theatre, but then noticed it was a museum. These people didn't have a life. Then he caught a glimpse of the marquee that showed what they were waiting for. He throttled the Harley down and stopped.

The giant picture was in all shades of gold. It showed a princess being pulled through the streets of a distant city in a gold-encrusted carriage. He read the lines below. Items from the reign of Catherine the Great were on display. Fate had brought him here. He had to see what the other great Cathy looked like.

For over an hour, the line snaked its way through the halls of the museum until it finally arrived at the display of the Russian Czarist. He was most taken with the carriage. Rear spoked wheels as tall as Joe. The wheels and woodwork were all covered with gold as though they had been dipped in the liquid like candle wax. There was a detachable canopy. She could ride in splendor in good weather and bad.

A mannequin was supposed to represent Catherine in her prime. She had been the wife and successor to Peter the Great, according to the placards around the display. She ruled Russia in her own right from 1762 until 1796.

Joe thought back to what he knew of his own history. Tennessee became a state in 1796, the year of Catherine's death. His ancestors were homesteading in East Tennessee near the forks of the Powell and Clinch rivers. They had not seen anyone like Catherine in the frontier of that time. He doubted that they had even heard of her. Now, one of their descendents was struck by her beauty and possessions.

He was nudged on by those in line behind him. He moved to the portraits. Catherine with her husband when she was a young woman. Then the one of Catherine by herself on a throne. He had seen her before. It was not the hair, for it was dark. But the eyes. Yes, the burning coals behind the green eyes were there in the portrait just like on the river that first night when he had met his own Cathy.

He closed his eyes and imagined Catherine the Great being pulled through the streets of St. Petersburg in the royal carriage accompanied by servants running alongside, the horses snorting and their breath crystalizing in the cold air. Catherine was not cold though. She was wrapped in furs. There Joe was as a peasant on the streets of the Russian capital and the great lady looked at him. He could see it in her eyes. She wanted him.

"You got to move along, buddy." The guard was nice but firm.

JOE PARKED THE HARLEY along Beale Street near the place that had been recommended by Willie. "Good ribs and good music," he had said.

The cycle leaned near others, but it drew the most attention. Other bikers milled around while Joe fastened his helmet to the back.

"That's a great bike, man," a leather-clad young man said.

Joe looked at him. He had earrings, a nose-ring, and a Mohawk with the remaining hair dyed orange. A young woman, blonde with dark roots, stood next to the youth. She had on a fluorescent green tank top and leopard skin tights. Her bare midriff displayed a gold navel ring. Beneath her halter top a gold chain swung between her breasts. Joe imagined what the ends were connected to. She chewed gum while the guy talked.

"What year is it?"

"1972 Harley FX with a sissy bar," Joe said and looked toward the open air restaurant from where a soulful beat and aroma of smoked pork were flowing.

"Can I sit on it?" the youth asked.

Joe started to correct the youth's language but thought better of it. Every time the young man spoke, Joe focused only on the shiny stud that pierced the center of his tongue. What a place for a piece of jewelry. "Yes, you *may*. But just a bit. I've got to get something to eat."

Joe looked around while the young man tried out the feel of the Harley. There were a lot of weird people around. He was dressed conservatively compared to most. Then there were the tourists, cameras around their necks. The middle-aged couples walked with interlocked arms, the women clutching their purses close to their sides—scared, but wanting to see the wild side of Memphis. They had visited Graceland and couldn't leave without walking Beale Street.

"Real cool," the girl said when she got off the Harley.

"That's a real bike," the guy said.

They wandered off. Joe felt for his pistol and Bowie knife to be sure they were still in his belt beneath his jacket. He didn't know why he had brought them, but felt safer knowing they were there.

He took a table on the patio where he could keep an eye on his cycle, listen to the music from a distance, and enjoy his platter of ribs in solitude—more or less.

He amazed himself with his control. He had been off alcohol for a week. When the waiter asked what he wanted to drink, he had selected iced tea. He pulled Willie's card from his pocket. A woman. Did he want a woman? No. If he was going to exercise self-control and discipline he would beg off the women of easy virtue too. Cathy awaited him. He would withhold himself for her. He would enter a process of re-virginizing himself. No sex until Cathy agreed.

He reached into his leather jacket pocket and pulled out a thick cigar. He properly wet it with his tongue and then drew in deep breaths while the match flamed at the end. There were just so many pleasures he could give up at once. The music came tumbling out behind him until way past midnight. Smoke rose from his table but nobody cared.

THE HARLEY WAS TIED once again to the wall of *THE CARP*, and the taste of cigars and pork ribs were still on his tongue when Joe slipped into his bed in his boat beneath the copper-colored security lights of Mud Island. He laid the Mustang keys from Cathy's purse on his bare chest and rubbed them against his skin. He would connect.

The moon was full and shone through the window next to his bed. He looked at it and thought back more than two centuries to Catherine the Great and her carriage. The street on the other side of the inlet was clear of traffic. The water was calm and the sheen from the moon made it appear silvery and almost a part of the pavement. There were no serenades by crickets and frogs like he had enjoyed on the Tennessee. Here, the sounds of the night were the wails of sirens answering distant calls. He drifted off.

He knew he was dreaming. It was like when he was a child. He would realize he was dreaming but want to stay in it to see what happened. He was a spectator in his own dream as though he was not really there. It was just a movie he was enjoying.

She came down the street and across the water on a carriage pulled by four white horses. Instead of having her fur coats, she was adorned in the white gown he had seen before. Her hair hung down to the floor of the carriage. And, as he watched, the carriage's top was taken off and it changed into a red Ford Mustang convertible. Still there were the huge golden spoked wheels. Cathy stood up and then sat where the top had disappeared behind the rear seat and held a scepter in her hand.

She smiled and waved. When he looked closer, the scepter looked more like a twirler's baton. The queen alighted. She came and stood in the doorway of the boat. She held out an old key. Did she want him to take it? He waited. She stayed in the moonlight, its rays glittering off the gold of her scepter like specks of fire from a sparkler.

"See, see." She spoke and looked directly at him. If he answered back, would she vanish? Should he reach out for the key? No. He was afraid it would disappear. She turned and walked back toward her carriage where the horses stood on the water. A servant opened the door of the red convertible. She seated herself and looked back. He wanted to touch her. He wanted to kiss her. He raised his head and leaned against the cool stillness. His lips sought warmth but found only a glassy hard surface. Then as the Mustang turned, a great light struck him. It was like a huge fireball coming up out of the water and reflecting off the golden carriage.

Joe awoke to the sun piercing the window where his head rested. Willie was leaning down, looking in. Joe put his blanket around him and walked to the door.

The black man smiled, widely spaced teeth showing. "You shore was putting one on that window. Was it as good for you as it was for the window?" He laughed and looked toward the rising sun. "You should've called me last night. I knows where the women are," he said and thumped himself on the chest.

Eighteen

When he departed Memphis, Joe left Tennessee. He figured that was it. Cathy only appeared to him in Tennessee or on the Tennessee River. She had not shown her face and beauty in Kentucky, Ohio, Missouri, or Arkansas. In Alabama once, but that was on the Tennessee River. She definitely had a connection with the state and its namesake river.

He checked his maps. He would see no more of Tennessee or its river. Baton Rouge awaited. It was the home of Cathy. There he would find her and make his conquest. He knew more now since the last vision. Her Ford Mustang was red. It looked like a 1965 or 1966 model to him. The golden-spoked wheels were from Catherine the Great's carriage and not the car of Cathy of the River. He'd check it out in Baton Rouge.

The engine on *THE CARP* died again. He changed the plugs and looked at the wires. When they cooled down it ran fine. But the days were longer and hotter. By the time the sun reached to straight-up, the humidity and scorching heat made it feel like a sauna. He had to keep moving to have a hint of a breeze. At the next stop he would buy a set of plug wires and replace them. Must be a break in one or more of them that made itself known with the heat and expansion. He made the repairs while drifting downstream in slow circles. No power meant no control. He hadn't passed a barge in an hour and the river was clear of other traffic. The maintenance took less than five minutes, and he was back in business.

As the day drew on, barge traffic became heavier. He would move the boat to one side of the river or the other depending on the next curve ahead. He could cut nearer the banks than the barges since he needed less clearance for the 34-foot houseboat. He was shooting a course that would straighten the bends of the rivers and make it a shorter trip to Louisiana.

After a barge passed, Joe had to aim the boat into the waves created by the wake of the heavy carriers or else suffer the consequences of being rocked and rolled by the series of swells and following troughs. He did it by reflex now. It made for a longer course but a smoother and safer ride. He had experimented with not doing it and watched as boxes tumbled over, dishes fell out of cabinets, and loose items slid from one side of the cabin to the other. It would feel as though the boat was going to capsize in the big waves that hit broadside. He chose the safer method of hitting them head on.

ONLY A FEW SHOWERS that lasted less than ten minutes each had visited Joe on his odyssey so far. But when he looked to the west now, he saw huge anvil-head storm clouds coalescing to cover the entire horizon. Lightning shafts were visible coming from the dark, flat bottoms of the ominous covering. They struck distant targets. He listened but could hear no thunder. Perhaps it would end or blow itself out before reaching the river, the boat, and him.

The hot afternoon air became cooler. The wind picked up and created little whitecaps on the water. He saw rain falling in sheets just a few miles to his west. The water moved from the clouds to the ground in vertical layers that looked like serpentine drapes. Trees on the banks turned their leaves palm up to the wind showing a lighter shade of green.

Soon, clouds rolled in from the west, low like bunched up dirty steel wool scrubbing an iron skillet. The waves from the wind began to rock THE CARP like it was a toy in a bathtub. J. R. huddled at Joe's feet and with the first crash of thunder crawled to the farthest corner. Joe looked toward the banks of the river but saw no place to pull over that would be any safer than being on the river.

Lightning pulsed down in front, to the side, and behind. Now, the electrically charged air sizzled with each streak and thunder followed almost instantaneously. A vertical stroke flashed down to a tree directly to his right and knocked a limb off. Joe hoped the boat sat low enough in the water not to be an attractive target. But he looked around and saw nothing taller. Just downstream the river made a bend to his left. He steered the boat toward the middle of the river and the far side toward the bend.

The rain started in big drops and then came as though in buckets. Joe's palms began to sweat as he held tight to the wheel. This was going to be bad. He stood and stripped down to his shorts while maintaining his white-knuckled grip on the steering. He glanced around the cabin for the slim ski jacket. He reached and put it on.

The boat rocked from side to side and made a disaster out of his not-so-neat housekeeping. The crumpled up sheet and quilt on the bed fell off and covered the dog. J. R. didn't move.

The water came from all directions. Waves splashed over the sides and front. Rain blew in horizontal sheets against the side of the cabin and found ways to get in that Joe thought were sealed. He stepped through the cabin entrance and his body was buffeted by thousands of stinging drops of rain thrown at him by the wind like needles into a voodoo doll. He retreated to the steering wheel.

When the cool rain hit the warm river water, a fog arose like loosely spun cotton. It sprung up so suddenly that Joe could not see the far side of the river he was heading for by the time he reached the middle. He turned all his lights on and hoped that all barge traffic had dropped anchor. The lightning and thunder passed to the east but the rain was just beginning.

As soon as he came in sight of the far bank, he would find a place to tie up and wait out the rain, Joe promised J. R. The dog still hadn't moved. The cabin windows glazed over with the effects of the moisture too. Joe could not see beyond the glass. He walked the few steps to the cabin door again and opened it. The rain and water came in but he had to see. He tied it back with a rubber bungee cord. He would clean the mess and let it dry out later. He thought he saw the far bank just a couple of hundred yards away.

Then, within a minute, he felt the vibration of the engine cease. The steering wheel froze in his hand. He stepped quickly to the back window, wiped the moisture off with his hand, and looked toward the engine compartment. He couldn't believe his eyes. He had left the cover off after he changed the plugs. Cascades of water from the deck were running in and over the engine. When he heard the blast of a horn, he fell to the floor and began looking under the bed.

THE CAPTAIN OF THE tug signaled for another blast. The *MARY ANNE* was pushing thirty barges filled with corn and soybeans upstream. They were strapped five-wide and six deep. The tug and the barges occupied three hundred yards of length and a football field and a half of width just around the bend from *THE CARP*.

Nothing appeared in the captain's binoculars through the fog, but the radar showed something in the river about a mile ahead.

"Have we had any radio traffic?" he asked the one peering at the radar screen.

"No, sir. Not supposed to be any vessels for ten miles. Must be a fishing boat."

"Is it getting out of the way?"

"It was, sir. But now it seems to be stopped dead. It's in our path."

The captain laid the binoculars down. "You'd have to be crazy to be out in a fishing boat in this storm. Run eight of our men forward to the front barges. Tell them to take life rings and ropes. We may be fishing some people out of the river in a few minutes. There's no way to stop this thing for a mile and a half. They won't have a boat left if it's in our way. Tell the men to radio back as soon as they have a visual." He stared ahead.

WITHIN THIRTY SECONDS JOE had retrieved all the rope from beneath the bed and was now tying one end to another large coiled stack of thin trotline. He pushed the cover off J. R. and picked up a tennis ball from the bed.

"Come on, boy. We've got to go." He pulled the reluctant dog out of the cabin and onto the deck. Rain began to mat J. R.'s fur. He lay down while Joe secured the other end of the trotline to a ring in his collar.

From the bottom of the pile of the larger rope, Joe grabbed the free end, crawled to the bow of the boat, and tied it through an eye-bolt.

When the blast sounded again, Joe looked downstream but could see nothing. If they were blowing their horn, he knew they could see him on their radar and believed he was in their course.

The boat had continued to drift toward the eastern bank, but Joe figured they were still a good fifty yards away and the boat now was only going downstream with the flow of the river. He could barely see the outline of the shore through the fog. It was a ghostly silhouette. The only hope he saw was to swim to shore and find a tree to wrap the rope around. He couldn't swim with the rope, but he hoped J. R. could. The trotline would be light. If they made it to the bank, then they could pull the heavier, sturdier rope in and make it. If they stayed on the river without power, they would be crushed by these barges. And if not them, the next one down river.

He looked at the dog. J. R. made no move to enter the water. The horn sounded again. It was closer. Joe squinted through the fog and rain and thought he saw the pale needlepoint glare of a spotlight in the distance.

He stood and looked first at the river and then at his dog. "You never wanted to go into the water first, did you, J. R.?" He petted the dog under the chin, got him to his feet, and scooted him nearer the water. "We've got to go for a swim," he said, clapped his hands together, threw the tennis ball ahead of him, and dove into the brown water.

Joe turned onto his back and looked for the dog. J. R. had jumped right behind him. The tennis ball had been swallowed by the percolating river, but J. R. paddled toward his master.

"HOW FAR AWAY NOW?" the captain asked.

"Right at a half mile."

"Any word from the men up front?"

"They just radioed that they see a dim light in the distance. It's definitely a boat."

"Can we miss it on our present course?"

"Could have. But the radar shows that it's beginning to drift back out. There's no way we can move enough if it keeps drifting."

EVERY FEW YARDS, JOE would turn onto his back and check for his dog. His progress toward shore was slow. The current was pushing him downstream too fast. J. R. swam hard just a few yards behind. The trotline followed making a barely distinguishable line between them and the boat.

He first felt the bank with his hand. It oozed slime. Another stroke and both hands were grasping the silt. He tried to stand up and fell back down into the water. He pushed for a foothold and leaned forward as far as he could. He slid into the water again.

Joe looked back for his dog. J. R. was gone. Then he bubbled out of the frothy water. Joe looked toward the boat. The heavier rope was feeding off the pile and into the water. Its weight pulled J. R. under. The dog would come up and then go back down. His paws were thrashing the water when he came up.

Joe dove back into the water and toward J. R., just ten yards away. When he reached him, Joe put a hand under the dog's collar. Together they swam toward the bank.

J. R.'s feet had no more traction on the bank than Joe's. Neither could stand and walk. Joe rolled to the dog, undid the line and tied it around his wrist. He stood and fell again. And again.

Finally, Joe gave in. He spread his arms and legs into the form of a frog where he lay and slowly moved through the muck up the embankment. His chin scraped a line that his arms and legs followed. He became one with the mud. The dog followed, crawling on all fours.

Near the top, Joe dug his hands into the mire and finally was able to push himself up into a half-standing position. Each step he took toward the nearest tree was met by the water-soaked earth holding onto a foot that sunk ankle deep into the mud of the Mississippi's bank. The rope was heavy and pulled him back toward the water. He teetered, almost falling, but regained his balance.

When he fell down the next time, he rolled and dislodged himself from his ski jacket. It had lessened his ability to advance. Now it was him, the rope, and the slime. He crawled and almost swam in the muck. He glanced toward the boat and saw the barges for the first time. They were within a hundred yards of each other.

His hand met the beginning of the large rope when he was just five feet from the tree of life. His fingernails dug into the bark at the base of the tree, and he quickly began to wrap the rope around it. Bracing himself against the tree, he pulled the rope in until he felt it tighten. He looked and saw it was now out of the water and taut between the tree and *THE CARP*.

He laid a hand on the stretched rope and hoped it would be strong enough to hold. He listened to the creaking sound and plucked the rope like a large guitar string. It sang a low tone. All his possessions except for his dog depended on it not breaking. In the distance, *THE CARP* began to swing into shore like on a half arc of a pendulum propelled by the current and the rope tied to its bow. Joe tied the rope off and moved as fast as he could on all fours toward the point where the boat would meet the bank. J. R. followed.

THE MEN ON THE forward barges pushed by the *MARY ANNE* watched with relief as *THE CARP* swung away from them and toward the bank. They looked toward shore where they saw a mud-soaked man scrambling down the bank with what looked like a huge weasel or seal following him. The four men on that side of the barges turned toward Joe and made gestures with their hands.

WHEN JOE SLID TO near the water's edge and looked at the hulks of the barges passing by, he saw the four men with life rings and rope that had been prepared for his rescue. Two of them were giving him a thumbs-up signal while the other two gave him the finger.

He swam the few feet to *THE CARP* and retrieved another rope while J. R. stayed on shore. This one he tied to a support at the stern and threw it to the bank.

After he secured that rope to another tree farther up, Joe slid back down the bank to where his dog lay in the silt and panted. He stripped off his shorts and threw them into the Mississippi. He grabbed his dog in an embrace of joy and they rolled in the slime like the hogs in Goose Collins's pig lot.

After he exhausted himself with J. R., he propelled the dog ahead of him up the bank, turned, and sat nude on a log facing the river. He put his elbow on a knee, bowed his head, a clinched hand beneath his chin, and said a prayer of thanksgiving, the first prayer he could remember saying in years.

A streak of sunlight came through the dispersing clouds and reflected off what appeared to be a modern version of *The Thinker,* still dripping dark clay and ready for the oven.

Nineteen

From near its source in Minnesota, the Mississippi River serves as a boundary between states as it snakes its way south toward the Gulf of Mexico. It's part of the border for Minnesota and Wisconsin. The river then stands between Iowa and upper Illinois, then Missouri and lower Illinois. The same is true for Missouri and Kentucky, Missouri and Tennessee. Arkansas and Tennessee terminate at the river, as do Mississippi and the lower area of Arkansas. But when the United States' greatest artery leaves the corner of Mississippi near Fort Adams, Louisiana claims her for its own until she flows into the Gulf a hundred river miles southeast of New Orleans.

Joe's repairing and drying of THE CARP's engine wiring had not required a lot of work and was done swiftly. His own cleansing and that of his dog had taken longer and was still in progress when the boat entered its state of destination. Greenville, Vicksburg, and Natchez, Mississippi, had served merely as day markers since his near collision with the barge. In a different time and frame of mind, he would have liked to stop and tour the Civil War sites of these great southern Mississippi cities. But now his one goal had grown more possessive.

The wide river and the sunny weather afforded Joe the chance to sit at the bow of the boat with J. R. and a bucket of clear water. He cleaned the silt from beneath his fingernails and alternately unmatted his dog's coat with a currycomb. The carpet in the cabin was beginning to dry from the drenching of the storm. Joe left the door and windows open to assist.

When he was not cleaning his own body and his dog's, he unscrewed the caps on the bottles of his stock of Jack Daniel's and poured the smooth amber liquid into the muddy water of the river. Then he tossed the bottles into a trash can strapped to the cabin. He did the same with the last of his beer.

He glanced down river and shook his head. Forgetfulness. That was what had caused his near disaster. If he had closed the cover over the engine after the changing of the spark plugs south of

Memphis, the boat would have cruised through the storm with no
trouble. It had almost cost him all that he had left . . . his dog . . . and
his life.

The same character flaw had combined with others to cause
him his suspension from law practice. He thought about the girl, her
death, his responsibility to the estate, and his letting it slip away
because he forgot to follow-up on timing. *FORGOT.* It rang in his
head like a fire alarm. He could have blamed it on a new secretary
who was not familiar with his system of reminders about time limits
expiring and tickle card followups. But in the end, the responsibility
was his.

Joe figured there must be some portion of his brain that had
been destroyed by his drinking. It evidently was the power to keep
things in mind and recall them. And even though he had not touched
a drop of liquor since Paducah, he was making his vow even stronger
by getting rid of the bottles of temptation.

He would be clear-headed and alert when he found Cathy. He
would like to start a new life with her. If she would move back to
London with him, he could start his law practice over and have a nice
life. If she wanted to stay in Baton Rouge, he might be able to adjust
to another state's law practice in time or move on to something else.

She had not visited the last three nights. Joe had checked to
be sure that Cathy's possessions in the purse had not been washed
overboard in the storm. They were safe. He rubbed them against his
body at night, relaxed to what he believed was an almost hypnotic
state, and waited for her to appear. He laid a pad and pencil next to
the bed so that he could record his recollections of her as soon as she
vanished.   Words and views received in dreams or visions always
seemed to disappear so quickly. It was like the vapor from a cup of
coffee. It was there and then it wasn't. But she still had not appeared
since Memphis.

When he finished dumping the liquor and beer, he checked his
course and brought his three weapons onto the deck in the drying
sunshine. Moisture sat like drops of sweat on his Bowie knife, double-
barreled shotgun, and his .357 magnum. He could almost see rust
starting to grow. He found a dry cloth and some high quality oil he
used to clean and preserve them and set to work.

Between college and law school, he had considered joining the
FBI. In anticipation of applying, he had taken courses in police
procedure and weapons at a local community college. Somewhere, he
had certificates acknowledging his expertise and marksmanship with
several weapons. With a rifle, he was deadly at a hundred yards. But
he had sold his favorite Winchester when the divorce came along. He
was down to the pistol and shotgun. He hefted the pistol and felt its

balance. He liked the power. The shotgun he had used years before for hunting. He preferred the double-barrel although people he hunted with mostly used automatics and pumps. He wanted to give the ducks a chance. If he couldn't hit them in two blasts, they deserved to fly away. It had been a decade since his last duck hunting. He didn't care much for that now. But he was proud of his gun.

The knife he had purchased from some collector. He liked it because it was a true replica of the one that Jim Bowie had made famous. He wondered if the knife would have been as popular if Bowie, Crockett, Travis, and the bunch had surrendered at the Alamo instead of accepting death. Its shaft was as wide as a sword and the deep curve gave it almost the feel of a woman. He rubbed it against his whetstone in strong smooth strokes until sharpness returned to the blade. He touched some saliva from his tongue, to his finger, to his arm, wetting the hair there. When the knife had an edge that could shave, he covered it with a thin film of oil and laid it on a towel.

The steel of the guns glinted in the afternoon sun once the cleaning and drying were through. He retrieved some shells and cartridges from the cabin to test in the weapons to be sure none of the firing mechanisms had been altered by the wetness.

Joe put two shells in the shotgun, snapped it shut, and tossed an empty Jack Daniel's bottle high in the air to the side of the boat. It sprayed the water with splinters of glass after his first blast. J. R. cowered to the farthest corner of the cabin and lay down. Another bottle and another hit. Satisfied, Joe sat back down and cleaned it again.

With the revolver fully loaded, he looked for a target but found none to his liking until he saw they were approaching a red buoy that would come close enough to mimic a man standing and swaying in the water. As the boat floated by within thirty feet of the target, he aimed and emptied all chambers toward the buoy. He heard the dings as the bullets found their target. Five out of six. He blew smoke out of the barrel like he had seen in western movies and sat back down. He needed to practice more but he didn't know if the Corps of Engineers would appreciate him using the buoys for targets. He recleaned the handgun and then took all three weapons to their places in the cabin.

NEAR SUNSET, JOE CHECKED his maps once more. He must be near Baton Rouge but he could see nothing on the horizon to indicate the city was around the next bend. His destination and search for Cathy would have to await another day. He found a place where a creek entered the river and pulled into the calmer waters of the small stream for the night. He tied off to two trees and dropped anchors at the bow and stern.

After a dinner of fried Spam and the last of his green peppers and onions that he stir-fried with the meat, Joe brought out the Bible storybook that his mother had given him. He reread the story of Samson. He felt of his head where his hair had made a good start at growing out. He felt stronger now himself. His Delilahs were history. There would be no more bar maids, no more women of the night, no more Kellies and Roses. Cathy awaited him. And from her appearance always in a long gown, he imagined that she probably sang in a church choir. She would appreciate his Bible storybook and accept him. She was a lady of beauty and honor.

About the time the stars were in full view against a clear, black sky, the mosquitos also came out—as numerous as the stars—and drove Joe toward the cabin. But before he got to the door, he looked up at a meteor blazing across the sky from south to north. He took it for a sign. She was near.

By eleven, he laid the storybook aside, and pulled a sheet around him on his bed. His pad and pencil lay nearby where he could reach them when she spoke to him. The possessions of Cathy—almost icons to him now of his beloved—lay on and about him. By osmosis he would take her in and become one.

Every hour he awoke and looked toward the door where only darkness stood. He willed her to appear. At four he was startled awake by a sound of splashing. He walked to the door and shined his flashlight toward the creek's water. A school of fish were thrashing about. He went back to bed.

Before five, she was there.

Red hair. The white gown off the left shoulder. A scales of justice in her left hand and a red stick in her right. It was just like the first night. Except . . . except her back was turned to him. It *was* her though. The hair slid down her back all the way to her waist.

In his sleep, Joe saw but did not hear. Should he speak first? Yes. "Turn to me, Cathy," he mouthed aloud the words.

She stayed at the door, facing away. Did she hear? He spoke again.

"No," she said as softly as he ever imagined an angel speaking.

He jerked awake and sat bolt upright. She was gone. There was only a veil of fog lifting off the creek in the first hints of morning light.

Joe rushed to the door to see if she stood on the deck. When he looked in the direction that she had been facing, he saw them. Plumes of smoke and mist on the horizon that rose from the stacks of the refineries on the northern edge of Baton Rouge—her home town.

Twenty

S he hadn't looked at them in years. Now it was time. What she had preached to others, she would have to deal with once again herself. Who was her family? Carol Sent dumped out the box of family photographs onto her bed. This would require a full pot of coffee and maybe all of her Saturday. She went to the kitchen and retrieved her second cup. She took along a legal pad that she favored using to make diagrams.

GENOGRAM was what her profession termed it. A diagram of family. But more. Who did what? Who was addicted to alcohol or other drugs? How many divorces to an uncle or aunt that impacted on the remaining family members. It was Days of Our Lives in squares and ovals and connecting lines on a chart. The old pictures would be a source to remind her of those who played roles in her early and just past life. She had done it before. But not since her divorce.

Now it served a dual purpose. Her writing instructor wanted the class to tell a family story. They could either fictionalize it, or tell it just the way it happened. She was sure most would choose the side of fiction. People didn't want to believe that their families were too weird. But through her years of experience she had learned that if all the family weirdness could be compressed into a ball—it would be larger than the Earth.

Also, she wanted to see if she could understand her little sister. Was there a hope of salvation? Maybe the pictures and memories would help her to deal with someone she loved but didn't understand. Could she pull her back from the precipice? Should she care? Should she take a month off and search for the fleeting spirit of Cathy?

She sat cross-legged on the bed and smoothed the photos out into a layer across the quilt. She had promised herself to organize all of these into albums that accurately reflected a timely progression. It was another promise she had not kept. Here they mingled in a montage of old and new, family and friends, joy and death.

She pulled one of the newest ones from the quilt. It showed a grave marker and a lone rose. She had not known about the death of her father in time to even attend the funeral. She later visited the small cemetery in Wyoming and took the picture. She laid it to one side.

She picked up one of her mother and stepfather—Cathy's father—of ten years before. It was the last time she had visited them together. He still wore the cowboy outfit of the rodeo, although by health and injury he had been retired from the circuit. Her mother stood beside him looking toward the camera in the fading light of evening.

Carol's eyes fell on one of her and her former husband. She picked it up and reached for a pair of scissors. She carefully cut them apart. She had always wondered what it felt like to do that. Many of her clients had told her about destroying old photos of their spouses, in spite or rage. She hoped she was over her spite and rage and was severing the photographic bodies for clinical purposes only. But it did feel good.

She took up another Polaroid of her husband by himself in a bathing suit on the beach at Destin, Florida. She used the scissors again. This time she cut cross-wise below the waist. "Yeah," she said. "Take that you bastard." After two years she could take pleasure in his symbolic mutilation.

Carol threw the scissors down and wiped her eyes. This was not why she was here. She was searching for a story she could write about. She couldn't put pen to paper about her husband, nor her mother and her stepfather.

She uncovered a photo of Cathy sitting on a white horse that her mother and father had purchased for her sixteenth birthday. She had asked for a Ford Mustang, but they had surprised her with a real mustang, or at least a horse. Carol threw that picture to the top of the bed. She never had been given a horse.

Then her eyes settled on the one with her and her father scattering corn to the chickens in their back yard. Her mother must have taken it just before her parents split up. She couldn't have been more than four in the photo. But there she was. She held a bucket in her hand, wearing a billowy dress and slinging corn toward the scared chickens. That would be the story she would tell. Searching for eggs on a small farm. Her father gave her a nickel for every one she found. She later learned that was more than he could have bought them for at the store.

She grabbed her pad and began the diagram of her family. A father who disappeared after her mother chose another man. He loved his daughter, but he just couldn't bring himself to visit when her mother lived with another man. He had moved too far away for her mother to let her go to him. She grew up with a father she loved whom she could not see and a stepfather she hated because he had driven away her real father. She resented her mother marrying a rodeo rider who drank when he wasn't winning. And that was most of the time.

She added her half sister to the diagram. She was her only sibling. Her emotions had always tugged her back and forth with Cathy. Cathy had two parents at the house while Carol had only one. She wanted to be close to her because she was her sister. Carol had grown up as the older child and Cathy almost as an only child. It didn't make a lot of sense to think about but much of family dynamics was that way. It kept psychiatrists, psychologists, and marriage and family counselors in business. The building blocks of families were fraught with cracks—and crackpots for that matter.

Of her immediate family, only her half sister remained. Her stepfather died years before in a barroom brawl. Her mother, whom she never fully understood, died of cancer at fifty-six. Her father passed without reestablishing contact in Wyoming.

She penciled in the dates of birth, divorce, and death on the chart. Cathy had not been married. Just missing in action.

Twenty-one

DEA agent George Stephens sat across the desk from John Collins while they both looked closely at the drawings. The reconstruction artist had just delivered her renderings of the face of the body that was found a couple of weeks earlier in Clarke County, Alabama. It was bright and sunny outside their Mobile office, but the blinds were shut so they could peruse the drawings under artificial light that the artist had recommended.

"It's amazing what she can do with her computer and drawing skill," Collins said and traced his index finger across the cheek bone of the person depicted in the drawing.

"Yeah. There was just a little skin left on the guy's face when we last saw him resting on that parachute—pillow—out there in that field. She's put him back together. She could do a job on Humpty Dumpty that the king's men couldn't," the younger agent said and ran a hand through his slicked-back hair.

"I wonder, though," Collins said. He raised his eyebrows and stared at Stephens. "How much of this is accurate and how much is pure imagination? It sure doesn't look like what we saw out there in the middle of those piney woods."

"Maybe she visualized it. That's popular now. Let your mind flow. Touch a piece of evidence and imagine the perpetrator. I saw it on television," Stephens said and laughed.

They flipped through the three alternative drawings that had been prepared showing what the face would look like without any facial hair, with just a mustache, and with a mustache and beard.

"They've run him through a comparison with all the mug shots we have in the DEA and FBI, but nothing clicked. He might have a local record with someone who hasn't put him on the network yet. The plane was rented in Mississippi. We should run it by everyone in that state and all the surrounding ones." Collins looked at his map on the wall. "That's Tennessee, Arkansas, Louisiana, and Alabama. That'll be a start."

"What did the lab give us on the other items found at the

scene?" Stephens asked and laid the drawings back on Collins's desk.

Collins rose from his chair, lit a cigarette, walked to the window, and adjusted the blinds. He looked out toward the bay where boats were shining in the mid-morning sun. He squinted into the brightness and toward the direction where the modified Piper Navajo had gone down four months earlier. He blew smoke rings toward the ceiling, where they were scattered by the ventilation system, and turned over in his mind all that he knew.

"Not much really. All the equipment was high quality. Could be stolen military. Night vision goggles, gun, survival items. Serial numbers removed. Very good quality coke.

"A kilo of the coke would have brought thirty to forty thousand on the street. The markings, they think, say it is a certain processing facility we know of in Colombia. No ID on the body. No one missing that comes close to those drawings," Collins said and nodded toward his desk.

"So, three kilos of coke recovered—one on the plane, one a few miles from the body, and one near the body. That's ninety to a hundred grand. There had to be more, didn't there, John?"

Collins took his suit coat off, turned toward the window, and pointed his cigarette in the direction of the downed plane. "Yeah, strange, very strange. If that guy was the pilot, he may have been throwing the coke out to rendezvous with someone on the ground. In the hurry he could have left a package on board. Or it could have been intentional."

"Why?"

"He thought the plane would go down quicker when it hit the water and not crash near a fishing boat. If it was ever found, we'd just think that a drug smuggler crashed, drowned, and lost his cargo. Neither his body nor cargo would be found, but there would be traces of coke."

"You think he was going to meet someone on the ground and split the coke and disappear?"

"Could be."

"But what about the pillow?"

"Hard to figure," Collins said and stubbed out his cigarette in the ashtray. "Somebody set him up. His ground people or his supplier. He was apparently very inexperienced in using parachutes or he would have checked. You can bet this guy was not a member of the 101st Airborne.

"Let's go over to the locker and look at the plane again. Then I'm going to send you over to Jackson to talk with the airport manager where the plane was leased. Show him these drawings and see if he recognizes any of them as being the pilot."

THE STORAGE BUILDING TO which George Collins referred was a warehouse near Mobile Bay. It was home to all forfeitures from drug busts and housed a separate area that contained evidence on all cases that were in the pipeline. The FBI and IRS also stored seized goods there. After a certain length of time, the agencies held auctions where the public could buy cars, trucks, household furnishings, boats, and anything else that at one time may have had a hint of coke dust on it. The money went back into prosecution. They didn't sell the seized weapons as they had once done. There was something about putting weapons back on the street that might one day be trained on them in some alley.

Armed guards and electronic surveillance made sure no one entered without authorization. Collins had phoned ahead to get approval for their visit.

After showing the proper identification and being ushered into the climate controlled warehouse, John Collins and George Stephens were escorted past the rows and rows of motorcycles, cars, trucks, and a high-powered speedboat toward a back room. There the only plane in the warehouse lay in two pieces just as it had broken apart on impact in February.

"That's a nice little plane," Stephens said as they both walked around the aircraft. "It cracked open like an eggshell."

The plane gave the appearance that the giant hand that had cracked it against the water could just as well pick it up and put it back together. Except for bent props, the plane appeared in remarkably good shape.

"Does that plane have the fuel capacity to fly to Colombia and back without refueling?" Stephens asked.

"Oh, yeah. With the modifications. This Navajo with the wings, engine, and tanks it has could cover a good piece of ground. It could fly into small airports. It could go from Colombia to Tennessee without refueling. Some of the agencies down in the Caribbean use similar planes to fly interdiction and patrol the drug routes. It's popular with the good guys and the bad guys.

"Down in Central America, they use them legitimately on sugar and coffee farms. Then again, the drug dealers buy them," Collins said.

"Was this a legit plane or one that had been used all along for drugs?" Stephens asked.

"Legit as far as we can find out. This one belonged to the airport in Mississippi. They would lease it out. Their records are clean. No suspicion there. The one who leased it knew what it could do."

Collins leaned over and looked into the passenger area.

"I thought you said one time that the Coast Guard picked this plane up on radar in the Gulf out from New Orleans. What ever happened on that?" Stephens asked.

"They did pick up an unknown that morning. But they lost it. We just theorize that it was probably this one. Our office in New Orleans hasn't given us anything new on that. Could be that they weren't related," Collins said.

Stephens stepped closer to the plane and looked over Collins's shoulder. "What are you looking for now?"

"Nothing in particular. It's just that I learned a long time ago that you have to go back time and time again to look at evidence anew. You may see something you missed or something different on that second or tenth trip that you didn't see, or didn't see that way, the first time or the ninth time.

"This is the tenth time I've been out here. Plus our lab boys have been over it with a fine-tooth comb, you might say."

Stephens studied the frame and engine. "It could carry a thousand pounds or so, plus the pilot, couldn't it? About eight hundred pounds of coke—three hundred fifty kilos—at thirty thousand per kilo that's . . ." the younger agent's voice trailed off as he punched in the numbers in a hand-held calculator. "That's close to ten million in street value."

Collins smiled. "You ready to change sides?"

"No. It's just that that's a lot of money for one load. One trip to Colombia. You could retire on one load."

"You could. But they don't. It's just like a game to some of them. The more they get, the more they want. Just like those people who play the lotteries and win. You ever see one quit? No, they just keep on playing. It's a high. Gives them a thrill. Fast planes, fast women, and power. That's what it's all about. Money is just secondary. Now, money is important. I'm not saying it's not. And in this case, if that guy who had a pillow for a parachute was trying to run off with this much coke, he's lucky he died the way he did. Because if the big boys found him alive, it would be a lot more painful than falling from the sky into the red dirt of Alabama."

When agents Collins and Stephens concluded their inspection of the plane, they walked to the evidence room where the other items from the plane and from the dead man were laid out on two tables. There were the packages of coke from the plane, the one from ten miles north of the site of the body, and the one from the area of the body. They all had tags on them. All these items had to be inspected in the presence of a custodial agent in order to prevent any claim of tampering with evidence.

They turned to leave the windowless room. Agent Collins switched off the lights at the door while Stephens and the guard walked ahead. He looked back one last time toward the table that held the coke. He blinked his eyes when he saw a faint green glow from one of the packages. He turned the light on and the glow disappeared. Back off and it appeared again. He yelled at his companions, and they turned back to the room.

"We'd better have someone from the lab to look at the covering on that package again." He looked at the evidence label and saw that was the one that had been beside the body.

ON HIS DRIVE FROM Mobile to the airport in Jackson, Mississippi, Agent George Stephens had time to consider his role in this investigation. It was his first big case since joining the agency out of law school at the University of Alabama.

For the past year, he had been learning procedures and working with more experienced agents. During that time, he had always been around John Collins but had only recently been assigned to his direct supervision. He liked the gruff black man. The agency background check must have shown that George's father had once been a leader of a county division of the Ku Klux Klan. It had to be in his personnel file, but Collins had never mentioned it.

Collins had talked quite a bit about his father with his younger cohort. He had told him about a father who worked on the railroad and put his children through college, about a father who farmed when he wasn't railroading, and a father who cared enough about education to build his own library. Collins had even complimented Stephens for having a father who also cared about education enough to see that his sons went to college.

As Stephens saw it, the only real differences between Collins and him were the difference in age and the color of the skin. And after only this short period of time, the color of the skin was really no concern. They were both sons of Alabama who cared for their families, state, and nation. They both worked to make drugs less accessible to the youth.

This was his big opportunity to investigate on his own. He hoped he turned up something of interest.

The airport manager was out on an errand when Stephens arrived, but the receptionist said she would beep him. While he waited, Stephens watched a few small planes come and go on the one strip that was available. He saw two hangers that housed ten planes, according to his counting. The manager returned shortly.

"I'm Carl Balfort. What can I do for you all this time?"

"I'm George Stephens, agent with the Mobile office of the

DEA." He held his identification out to the airport manager who nodded and began to light a cigarette.

Balfort sat at his desk and opened a file folder that held less than ten sheets of paper.

"Mr. Balfort, I work with John Collins who spoke to you before about the Piper Navajo that was leased out of here and went down in Mobile Bay."

The manager nodded and blew smoke to the side.

"Now, I know that Agent Collins covered with you last time about the papers being forged with another pilot's name who turned out to be in Denver when all this happened. I just want to follow up and see if we can develop anything new."

Balfort leaned back and clasped his hands behind his head. "Okay, ask away."

"Here's three drawings that I want to show you to see if any of them look like the pilot." Stephens laid the sketches in front of Balfort.

Balfort wrinkled his forehead. "Is this the same man?"

"Yes. One with a mustache. One with beard and mustache. And one clean shaven. He may have changed his appearance." Stephens let Balfort look at the drawings. "Does any one of those look like the guy who leased the plane?"

"No. Can't say that they do." He studied the views and then looked toward the agent. "The ones that your people showed me last week looked a lot closer."

Stephens swallowed hard. He turned the response over in his mind. What was he talking about? They had only received these drawings today. Who was *your people*? He groped for a response while the manager bent nearer to the drawings and blew another puff of smoke from his mouth.

"Like I told your people from New Orleans, the mug shot they had looked quite a bit like the guy I remembered, but I couldn't say one hundred percent."

Mug shot. New Orleans. Stephens had been to the DEA office in New Orleans but thought the Mobile office was in control of this investigation. John had not told him that anyone from New Orleans was working the case except to say that the New Orleans office had reported the plane being picked up on radar by the Coast Guard. He just nodded as though he knew all about it.

"Mr. Balfort, could I get a copy of all those papers in your file? Mr. Collins may have obtained them before, but I'm not certain."

"Sure. All we have is the lease, flight plan, license verification. And then the papers where the bonding company paid off with the insurance company on the loss of the plane. Do you want all of that?"

"Yes. Might as well. Never hurts to have too much. We can throw away what we don't need. Did they already pay you for the plane?"

"Yes. And the bonding company came through on the confiscation. That was a nice plane. Two hundred thousand."

"Yes. I saw it this morning. Real nice. Built to take off on short strips, wasn't it?"

"Yeah, just like this one. That's why I bought it. Has great power, maneuverability, and take-off and landing ability."

"Said he was going to Daytona?"

"Yeah, that's what he said. Then ditched it in Mobile Bay. You haven't found him yet, huh? That picture last week sure did look like him."

Stephens nodded again. He put copies of all the papers in his briefcase. He reached down for the three drawings. Balfort suddenly pushed his hand aside.

"Wait a minute . . . . You know what? . . . This guy looks like the one who was in the car with the pilot the day he first asked about the plane. He never got out of the car. Nice older car. Probably an antique. A sixty-something red Ford Mustang. Convertible. But the top was up. Black top. He didn't say anything. I was mainly looking at the car. He didn't even look at the plane. It was like he was just along for the ride. I never saw him the next day when the other guy took the plane. But somebody had to bring him to the airport, huh?"

Stephens wrote all of it down. He asked a few more questions, but Balfort didn't know anything else. But now they had more. A car connected to the pilot who leased the plane. Before he left, Stephens decided to ask another question or two and try not to sound too stupid.

"Just one more thing, Mr. Balfort. Did you get the name of the agents you talked to last week."

"They probably told me. Flashed badges like you. I don't know one badge from another. My memory's getting bad as far as names. You're Agent . . . Stephens? Right?"

"Yes."

"I asked them the name of the guy in the mug shot. But they didn't tell me. Said it was still under investigation."

AS SOON AS GEORGE Stephens got back into his car, he phoned Mobile to talk with John Collins. Collins had already left for the day. He left a message on his voice mail suggesting they get together the first thing in the morning.

Twenty-two

London County Sheriff Arnold Scarboro had held the office for twelve years. Now, at sixty years of age, he had two years to go on his present term and wanted to be re-elected one more time to take him to retirement. He felt more at home in the clothes of a farmer or factory worker, but because of his office, he usually wore a navy blazer and contrasting color trousers. He didn't waste money on ties. His stock went back to the thin ones of the late sixties. His bow to the uniform of a law enforcement official was his Canadian Mounty type hat that he wore.

Sheriff Scarboro continued the tradition of an almost burr haircut from his military service with the Marines. His ramrod straight posture had deteriorated slightly over the years with bone problems. Light blue eyes stared out from a face that had little expression. Blond to gray eyebrows were thin and barely visible. No one could accurately recount ever seeing him laugh, cry, frown, or show any other emotion. His only hobby was poker.

"Luann, no phone calls, no interruption, no nothing while I'm with these folks," District Attorney General Charles Palk said. He escorted Sheriff Scarboro and the reconstruction artist into his office.

"Okay, General Palk," Luann said and went back to filing her nails. Deputy Osborn Ratliff sat beside her desk and chatted with Luann while his boss went into the attorney general's office.

The reconstruction artist worked full time at the forensic anthropology department at the University of Tennessee in Knoxville. Cory Wiggins had developed a computer program that helped to draw and make appear human what had earlier been skull and bone fragments. Wiggins, a short young man with dark stringy hair that tended to fall over his left eye, knew computers. His sole interest appeared to combine his job and hobby. He loved helping law enforcement agencies identify unknown bodies.

Palk had given Wiggins authority to go to Johnson City and meet with Dr. Linus Trout to look at the bodies and to measure, photograph, and analyze every facet of the mystery in order to identify what were now three bodies that had washed up in the Tennessee River. Wiggins loved it. He carried his laptop with him into the office.

"Arnold, you realize the problem you and I have in these dead bodies showing up here in the county?" Palk looked at the sheriff. "Sort of a mutual problem for both of us."

"It's probably more of one for you than for me, Charlie, since I don't have to run this year. But I understand what you're saying," the sheriff said matter-of-factly while rotating his hat in his lap. He thumbed the gold braid that decorated the brim.

"Yeah, but if Mike Garrison gets elected, he's going to put it into your lap for the next two years."

"Maybe. But he and I get along all right."

Palk coughed. "Well, anyway, I have Mr. Wiggins here, and he's made some drawings of what he thinks these three men looked like before they spent a couple of months in our river." He nodded for Wiggins to lay out the drawings.

"I'm going to keep these here in my office, Arnold, and just release them as we get possibilities. But what I need from you is to have all the manpower we can get to search along the river banks to see if we can come up with some more evidence—clothing, a weapon, anything to help tie these bodies to a name."

"At least we're sure they're all men, right, Charlie?"

"Yes. Autopsy said that." Palk took a map from in front of him and showed it to the sheriff. He had marked the location where each body had been found. "I want a two-mile search on each side of the river. I'm going to put divers in to see if we can find something near the sites where they were found. I need some good luck."

"Yep, I'd say you do."

"Now, Mr. Wiggins," Palk continued, "how accurate do you think these drawings are?"

"Well, sir," he began, brushed the hair back from his eye, uncrossed his legs, and sat up, "we never know until we get an actual photo of the victim. But from my past experience, I'd say these are close. They're young men which makes it easier. Fewer wrinkles, scars, nose and ear elongation to worry about. I've had real good luck. Out of about a hundred I've done, authorities have identified about a third."

"A third?" Palk said and frowned. "That means two-thirds remained unidentified."

"Yes, sir. But a third is a good batting average."

"Yeah, but a third of the votes isn't worth a jar of warm spit."

Palk escorted them both to his door and made a request of the sheriff to start the search as soon as possible. "Keep the drawings a secret for the time being. I'll take care of releasing them at the proper time."

Palk turned to the papers on his desk and pulled the three files to the top. A file for each body. He had lost count of how many times he had gone through them. Time and time again he had read the autopsy reports and drug screens, seen the photographs of the bodies before they were moved and during the autopsy, and reviewed his notes and those of Dr. Trout. Only one body—the one with a wallet in the back pocket— could they put a name to, and he was not sure about it.

Again he reviewed the known facts and compared them to missing person reports from across the country for the past six months. All three had been killed by gunshots to the head. The first two had a single .22 caliber wound. Both bullets were useless for ballistic tests. The third and most recent body had a redundancy of killing. Another single .22 shot to the head but also a shotgun blast to the face. Dr. Trout was unable to say which had come first.

While each of the first two bodies had an expensive cowboy style boot on one foot, the third body wore moderate priced athletic shoes. The first two had remnants of the same type of rope tied to a leg and the third didn't. No possessions, aside from the clothing, were found on the first two bodies but the third had the wallet and a small package of marijuana.

The TVA would be lowering the level of the Tennessee River by two feet over the next two days, and Charlie Palk planned the riverbank search for that time. The lower water level might leave a piece of evidence stranded along shore or in an overhanging limb. Putting divers into the river was an almost hopeless proposition. The likelihood of finding anything was less than the proverbial needle in a haystack.

THE SUN WAS JUST edging above the eastern horizon when John Collins turned into the parking garage of his office building. As usual, he came to the Mobile office early. From six-thirty to eight-thirty in the morning, he could accomplish more than most agents did in the whole day. It was a quiet time. The secretaries were not there yet. The phone rarely rang. Few interruptions. He habitually dictated his reports, letters, and memos early in the morning.

His life had always been one of early risings. His railroader father left the chores to him and his brothers and sisters when he was gone. John Collins liked the farm, but sometimes it seemed it had been too much when he was young. Feeding the cows and slopping the hogs came before his preparation for school. But he could not forsake one for the other. His father saw to that. He just had to be more efficient.

The enforced routine served him well later. In college he often annoyed his dormmate with his early awakenings. He had become a morning person. While everyone else was avoiding 8 a.m. classes, he relished them. He was more alert than his professors. He would lead any class discussions. It impressed them so that they gave him extra points, and he kept a B+ average.

Now, as a DEA agent, he was often given superior ratings for his aggressiveness and willingness to work long hours. He was never in bed when the sun rose. It was a sin in his family. The compensatory time he had built up was rarely used. Soon, he would take the Fourth of July off and drive up to see his parents. His visits tended to occur around holidays and birthdays.

The light filtering through his window shaded the surroundings in pastels when he reached for his phone and listened to his voice mail. George Stephens's tone had a ring of urgency to it. He wanted to meet early. Collins smiled. His younger colleague's eagerness reminded him of his own just a few years before. The young man was full of energy and bored ahead at full throttle, although he was a little naive.

He punched the button and listened to the message again. "Must meet on airplane deal first thing in the morning."

"Well, I'm here when you are," Collins said aloud and began to move papers around on his desk. He knew Stephens was an early riser too and would probably be there within the half hour.

Collins looked up when there was a knock on his door and then looked at his watch. Stephens was even earlier. He walked in and sat down, a bit out of breath.

"Any luck on those drawings?" Collins asked.

"That's why I wanted to see you first thing this morning," Stephens said and opened the folder. "The airport manager couldn't put a name to them, but he finally said they looked like a man who was with the pilot the day before he took the plane. He said the man never got out of the car or said anything. He didn't see him on the day the airplane was taken."

"Hmm, that's interesting," Collins said and leaned back in his chair. He closed his eyes. "These drawings look like a man with the pilot but not the pilot. I guess we either had two men on the plane or the one who leased it turned it over to this man to fly." He rocked back down and opened his eyes. "Two . . . or more."

"Yes, but that's not the strangest thing I found out."

"It's not? What else?"

"This guy, Balfort, said he ID'd a mug shot of the pilot last week for a couple of our agents from New Orleans."

"What? The hell you say!" Collins stood up and scattered the files on the desk with his hand. He walked to the window and looked out over the bay where streaks of pinkish orange were unmasking the ships in the early light. "New Orleans? What are they doing in this case?"

"That's what I was going to ask you. I hadn't heard you say anything about them except in regard to the report on the airplane that first morning."

Collins lit a cigarette and took a long draw. Stephens sat motionless, his hands clasped beneath his chin and his eyes fixed on Collins.

"This is our case. If things have changed, I need to know," Collins said and pointed to the phone. "When their office opens, I'm going to call over there and remind them that we're the same agency. If they have some information on this plane and the pilot, they'd better tell me about it or have a very good reason not to. This kind of bullshit really ticks me off."

"If this guy wasn't the pilot," Stephens said and pointed toward the drawing he had shown the airport manager, "where is the pilot?"

"This guy could've still been the pilot. The guy the airport manager said he ID'd last week for New Orleans could've been a front. Just rented the plane and turned it over to our man. Or they could have been on there together. I don't know. I'm pretty sure our man was on there. He died from the fall. That's for sure."

Collins thumbed through the file. He stopped at one of the papers and pulled it out. "New Orleans. This damn bond was made in New Orleans. Wait a minute. Now I recognize this." He took a key from his desk and went to a file cabinet in the corner. After looking through a few files, he took out an armload and handed them to Stephens. "Take these and go through each one until you find the bond company's name. I know it's here, but I just can't remember which file."

Stephens stood, took the files, and started toward his own office.

"Wait. Don't go yet. Sit back down."

Collins went to his desk and looked under several sheets of reports and wire dispatches from law enforcement agencies throughout the southeast. After a few minutes of frantic searching, he held aloft two sheets of paper.

"See this? There've been three bodies found in the Tennessee River about forty miles southwest of Knoxville. Three. All unidentified. That's our territory. There may be no connection, but I'm going up there next week, after the Fourth, and take our book of known drug dealers in this area and see if any of them match up. I talked to their prosecuting attorney there . . . let's see . . . his name is Palk. He has drawings but didn't want to circulate them yet. He'll let me look at them in person. Said he's anxious to identify them himself."

"You think they're connected with this?"

"I don't know, but it's worth a trip. This is smelling more and more like a drug deal gone bad. Someone dead where they did the drop. A crashed plane. Three bodies in Tennessee. Somebody didn't have a smooth operation.

"George, you did a great job. New Orleans has a mug shot of the one who leased the plane—the one we thought was the pilot. Now get your ass into your office with those files and find me that bonding company's name in one of them." Collins glanced at his watch. It was only seven-thirty. He would wait another hour before he called New Orleans.

WHEN CHARLES PALK RECEIVED the call from Agent John Collins of the DEA, he thought it was the best news he'd had in weeks. If those bodies were drug runners and Collins could identify them, his job would be almost complete. They were involved in interstate smuggling and it would be a federal problem. So they had three fewer drug pushers. They were all dead. Who would care who killed them? Good riddance.

The next best news was that no new body had floated to the surface of the river in over two weeks. Maybe this was the end of it.

Palk flipped open the file folder that had the information on the last body. The contents of the wallet were encased in a plastic snap-lock bag. Palk opened the container and removed the two one dollar bills and the driver's license. He looked at the photo on the license and compared it to the reconstruction artist's depiction of the face of the last victim. Palk had not shown the license to Wiggins in order not to influence the artist. He also wanted to see how accurate he actually was when he compared the drawing to the photograph.

"Close, very close," Palk mumbled as he held them side by side. "Could be."

It was time to call the corresponding attorney general in the state and county on the driver's license. He would see if there was a missing person report on the subject. He had checked all the recent wire reports and could not find this person's name listed as missing. It took them time to get the information on the wire sometimes though. He buzzed Luann to track down the attorney general he wanted.

He swiveled his chair around and watched the people on the sidewalk while he waited. He glanced over at the headquarters of Mike Garrison and saw someone entering. He looked over his shoulder at the wall calendar. It was just ten days until the primary when they both would be officially nominated. Then the main event was the general election in September.

He turned and flipped through his mail. He wanted a card or letter from Joe Chapman. There was none. He needed Joe. Too many things were piling up. Too many bodies. He faced an inevitable defeat by Mike Garrison if things did not start turning around soon.

Luann buzzed back. "General Palk, I have an assistant attorney general by the name of Lou Fontaine on the phone. He says he may be able to help you."

"Thanks, I'll take it."

Palk pressed the button with the flashing light. "General Fontaine. This is District Attorney General Charles Palk in London County, Tennessee. We're near Knoxville. How are you today?"

"Fine, General. And things in Tennessee?"

"Not so well. I've had three bodies turn up in the Tennessee River in my district over the past couple of months. We're having difficulty putting names to them. They are murders. But we don't know who, why, or where."

"Sounds bad. I'm glad they're in Tennessee and not here in Baton Rouge. How can I help you?"

"Well, the last one we found did have a wallet with a driver's license that gave a Baton Rouge address. I wanted to see if you know anything about him or have a missing person report."

"Okay, I'll try to be of service. What's the name on the license?"

"Kent Bartley."

AT PRECISELY EIGHT-THIRTY John Collins was on the phone with Agent-in-charge Charles Jackson in the New Orleans DEA office.

"I don't care that they thought it had nothing to do with us. When you're asking the airport manager whether someone is involved with a plane that went down in my territory, I think I should be notified. I know you say it pertained to another incident, but it made my man look foolish not to know you guys had interviewed this guy and showed him a mug shot."

George Stephens had returned to Collins's office and sat in silence while his boss let New Orleans have it.

"I'll tell you what I'm going to do," Collins said, "I'm going to send George Stephens over to Baton Rouge to check out this man whose mug shot you've been showing around. I hope your people in Baton Rouge will cooperate with George. Else, we'll get it straightened out in D. C.

"Now, what is that guy's name again?" Collins wrote the name on a scratch pad. "Yes, and send us a copy of his mug shot and anything else you have on him."

Collins hung up the phone and turned to Stephens. "Go down to the secure fax room and get what New Orleans is sending us. Then you drive over to Baton Rouge and see what you can find out on this guy. New Orleans says they already have two agents up there, so you might run into them. The bonding company thing can wait." He tore off the piece of paper with the name and handed it to Stephens.

"Kent Bartley," Stephens read aloud.

Twenty-three

J ust below the Interstate 10 bridge and on the east side of the Mississippi, Joe Chapman persuaded the watchman at an empty Baton Rouge warehouse to allow him to moor *THE CARP* for his stay in the Louisiana city.

Joe slipped the guard a hundred dollar bill and asked about an extension cord he could run to some electrical service. For the next two hours he busied himself with getting the boat secured for an extended stay. He ran a hose to an outside faucet for fresh water. Inside the warehouse, the guard showed him where he could shower and use a bathroom.

Joe introduced J. R. to the guard, and the dog went about a sniffing expedition around the building.

By noon Joe had showered, had the Harley off the boat, and was ready to begin the search for Cathy. He walked around the boat another time to be sure everything was secure. He would leave his weapons and his dog on board while he drove through the streets of Baton Rouge.

Joe looked at the boat and shook his head. She had done quite admirably for a craft that was only meant to cruise around the lake near his home. The navigation maps showed they had traveled over fourteen hundred miles. Throw in an encounter with a sand bar in

Alabama and a near disaster during the storm in Mississippi and it
was an extraordinary trip. Now the craft would serve as his home for
however long it took him to track down his quest.

Joe was anxious, yet hesitant, about straddling the cycle and
taking off into town. Doubts resurfaced. Was this just a chasing of
rainbows where she would always be beyond his grasp or would she
turn out to be receptive toward him? Rejection bothered him more
than the frustration there would be in not finding her at all.

From her purse, he only had two real clues that he could follow
up immediately. One was the post office box key with the other being
the key chain from Deb's Balloonery.

After tying J. R. to a long rope on the boat and being sure he
had plenty of food and water, Joe kicked the Harley to life and headed
out in search of a barber shop. His hair was in need of a little shaping
and trimming up after seven weeks, and he always liked an old
fashioned straight razor-shave that he could only get at a barber shop.

After lunch at a hamburger joint, he found a barber shop a few
blocks from the main campus area of LSU. The few old men who sat
around talking had not heard of a Deb's Balloonery but made
recommendations as to flower shops. The shave and hair cut were
refreshing, but he was after a last name, an address, and telephone
number for Cathy.

His next stop was at a local library. There he found the
volume of the national Zip code directory that contained Baton Rouge's
listings and began making notes of the addresses for the main and
branch post offices. He calculated the number of post office boxes for
the whole city and found there were near fifty thousand, and the city
had at least thirty-five Zip codes. He shook his head. This was going
to take a while. He had the whole summer and longer. Maybe the key
fit one of the fifty thousand.

He took the local telephone book and looked up Deb's
Balloonery. There was no listing. He phoned the other balloon shops
listed and no one knew of a Deb's Balloonery or remembered any
Cathy as a customer or employee.

He bought a city map and began the testing of the post office
box key at various branches. He kept track. He started at the highest
number, believing that the lower numbers would have been used by
long-time customers, and tried the key on as many as he could without
being too obvious or causing suspicion. A post office box that opened
to the key would give him a last name and perhaps a street address
for his Cathy if there was mail in it.

After he finished at one branch, he would cycle to another,
keeping an eye out for balloon shops along the way. When he saw one,
he went in and looked around for Cathy, or at least his vision of Cathy.

At the main post office, he willed up enough courage to talk with a postal employee.

"Is there any way to tell what post office box a key fits by just looking at it?" Joe asked.

The employee frowned, reached under the counter, and brought out a box. He shook it. "These are lost keys that people have turned in. There's no way to match them up unless the patron has marked them in some way. We keep these for a while in case somebody inquires. They may have put a scratch or attached a plastic label to one so that they could recognize it. Otherwise, it's just a flat piece of metal. If they lose a key to a particular box, then we can give them another key to that box or redo the lock."

Joe nodded his head in recognition of the bad news.

"You lose a key or find one?"

Joe winced. If he admitted finding one, they would probably want it back. "Lost one. But I have an extra. Just didn't want someone else getting my mail," he said and walked away.

FOR THE NEXT TWO days he spent every waking moment cycling from one post office to another and trying the key. Thousands of tries and thousands of failures. He noticed an employee or two who cast a suspicious eye toward him after he had visited the same branch five times in one day.

When he went back to the boat, he took J. R. running along the wharf and up onto the levee where the city had made a park. As he ran along the well-maintained paths, Joe kept an eye out for Cathy. She was athletic and was probably out walking or running. He saw no one with the long hair and beautiful body of the one he had seen in the visions and dreams on the boat.

He tossed the tennis ball for J. R. to retrieve, had him snatch sticks from his grasp, and exercised on an outdoor gym setup in the park. He swung from metal rung to metal rung across a space of twenty-five feet with kids who watched him with admiration. They wanted to play with J. R. Joe let a few throw the ball and watch the big yellow dog retrieve it. A few young mothers cast glances toward him.

Early one morning, as soon as it opened, he went back to the library and checked the old telephone books for the past five years to see if a Deb's Balloonery was listed. The palm of his right hand started to feel clammy when the index finger stopped on a listing for Deb's Balloonery that was three years old.

He wrote down the telephone number and address. He tried the phone first. The number had been disconnected a message told him. When he rode over, there was no balloonery at the address. Now the building housed an antique shop. It was within five blocks of the LSU campus and within eyesight of the barber shop where he had stopped on his first day in the city. The owners of the shop knew nothing about the balloonery except that it preceded them in the building.

At nine the next morning, Joe dressed in his lawyer suit and drove his Harley to city hall. He walked to the window of the clerk who was in charge of business licenses. After talking with three different clerks, he persuaded one to check the archives to see if Deb's Balloonery was among the businesses that once had a license but were now out of business. The clerk brought him a copy of the license application with the information about the owner. He beamed a smile. Now he had a name, telephone number, and address for a person who might have had contact with Cathy.

The number had been disconnected. The people who lived at the address listed were not the same ones. They had bought the house from the owners of Deb's Balloonery. They believed the owners still to be in the city. Directory assistance listed no number for them.

He went to the nearest branch post office and filled out a form under the Freedom of Information Act and handed the clerk the required fee. If the owners of the balloonery were still in the area and had an address, they would tell him. The clerk returned in five minutes with a new address for the ones he was seeking.

Joe grabbed his map and went to his Harley. The building was a combination shop on the lower floor and an apartment on the top. It was a balloon, gift, and flower shop that he had missed in his travels around the city. However, he recognized the name of the shop as being one that he had already called on the phone. The manager had disclaimed any knowledge of a Cathy. He propped the Harley up and went in. He was here and might as well give it another try.

A lady carrying an arrangement of balloons for a birthday party opened the door and exited as Joe entered. A middle aged man with thinning, grayish hair was on a stepladder rearranging a display behind the counter. He did not notice Joe.

When the man turned, he was startled to see Joe. He grabbed his chest. "I'm sorry. I didn't notice you come in. You must have come in when my wife went out—on the same ding."

"On the same ding?"

"Yeah. The door dings whenever anybody opens it. But I thought the ding was my wife going out. You came in at the same time, I guess."

Joe gave a blank stare.

"Well, never mind. What can I do for you?"

"Yes. Are you George Potter?" Joe asked while he looked at the sheets of information about the business license and the postal form.

The man hesitated a minute when he saw the papers in Joe's hands. "That depends. Why are you asking?"

"Oh, I'm not government or anything. I was just looking for a Mr. Potter to ask about a person I'm looking for."

"Okay. Then, I'm George Potter." He stuck out his hand to shake. "Who are you, and who're you looking for?"

Joe fished the key chain from his pocket and held it up. "I'm Joe Chapman from Tennessee. I'm looking for the person who had this key chain."

Potter took the black piece of plastic and held it close to his glasses. He smiled. "We haven't given these out for two or three years," he said and handed it back to Joe. "We used to be Deb's Balloonery. Key chains were a kind of promotion when we were down the street. We closed up there, expanded our business to flowers and gifts, and reopened here."

Joe turned the key chain to where it showed the name of Cathy. "Do you remember a Cathy?"

"My wife mainly ran the shop back then until I had my heart attack. Now I help some around. Back then I just helped in the evening.

"I can't remember any Cathy who was a customer. We only had some part-time help. Mainly ran it ourselves. Lot of work. Little money. We had a Barbara working for us a while." He looked at the key chain again. "Why are you looking for her?"

"I found her purse and just wanted to return it."

"Didn't she have a driver's license or something?"

"No, that's the problem. I don't know where she lives or what her last name is."

"Where did you find it?"

"Tennessee."

"Tennessee? And you came all the way here to look her up? You sure you're not the law or something?"

"No. Just curious." Joe noticed the man edging away from him. It probably did sound crazy to come all the way from Tennessee with the trinkets he found in the purse. "You don't remember any customers or employees by that name?"

"No, just Barbara. And Cat worked a little."

"Cat? Who's Cat?"

"That's all I ever knew her by. My wife wouldn't let me around the shop much when Cat was here. She caught me watching her climb that ladder I just came down from, and I didn't hear the end of it for a week."

Joe rubbed the plastic between his thumb and index finger. He leaned over the counter toward George Potter. He whispered, "Do you reckon that *Cat* could be short for Cathy? What did she look like?"

"I don't know. Could be. My wife kept the personnel records. You could ask her when she gets back."

"What did she look like?"

"Cat?"

"Yeah. Did she have red hair?"

"Red, shit. It was the brightest red that I've ever seen. She usually wore it up in a bun. But when she let it down, it came down to her ass. I tell you, between her red hair, fair complexion, and that . . . pretty ass—prettiest ass in Louisiana—she was a knock out."

Joe noticed beads of sweat popping out on George Potter's forehead at the same time he wiped perspiration from his own.

Potter continued. "We never lacked for customers when Cat worked a few hours at night. She would come in from the gym still wearing a black leotard outfit that fit like . . . well . . . like it was a second skin. She'd let her hair down. It'd sway along her back as she moved between displays. I'd tell her to work in the window. Walk-in customers streamed into the shop. She'd be stretching and turning.

"I don't know whether she really knew how attractive she was. Cat was responsible for more wives, girlfriends, secretaries, and daughters getting balloons than all the advertising we ever did. They'd walk in to watch her work and end up ordering something."

Joe said nothing as he listened to a person who knew Cathy describe her. The woman of his visions was taking on a reality. The similarity was eerie. "That sounds like her," he finally said. "What else do you know?"

"Not much. She was real popular with the children. She could make animals and things out of those long balloons. She'd do almost like a puppet show with them.

"I heard a few people refer to her as *Cat Red* because of her red hair. But for the life of me, I can't think of her last name. I'm thinking it had something to do with an animal. Fur . . . skin . . . coat . . . something, but I can't remember what.

"Oh, I do remember hearing . . . ," he leaned down and whispered again, "that she had another night time job at a strip joint somewhere around here. I never did see her there because I didn't go. But I thought about it a lot. Even I would probably have paid a few dollars to see that."

"A strip joint?" Joe repeated the words and frowned. He had thought about her more with a choir robe on. She was pure and holy—everything that he wasn't. She could not be a female Joe Chapman. "You sure about that?"

"No. I'm not sure. Like I said, I never saw her there. But the name—*Cat Red*—sounds like it fits, doesn't it?"

"Do you think your wife could find the employment records for me if I come back tomorrow? All I need is a name and an address. Maybe a Social Security number if you have it."

Potter looked toward the door. "I'll ask her. If my wife thinks I'm trying to look her up, I'm in trouble. Come back by in the morning."

Back on the Harley, Joe thought more about what Potter said about Cathy working at a strip joint. If it was true, she could still be doing it. How many topless bars or exotic dancing clubs could there be in Baton Rouge? He went to a phone book again. Ten. He slammed the phone book shut after writing down the addresses. He looked up and down the street. Louisiana's capital must have more strip joints, video stores, tanning salons, and beauty parlors per capita than any city its size in the United States. Where were the theaters, museums, libraries, and the cultural hotspots? He knew where one library was.

For the remainder of the afternoon, he focused his attention on the post offices in the vicinity. Night would be a better time for the nudie clubs. They would require money. His cash was stashed on the boat.

Five hundred post office boxes later, Joe headed for *THE CARP*. The key had not slid into any opening. He was feeling guilty about his neglect of J. R. The dog spent his days lying in the shade of the cabin while Joe checked post offices and followed up any leads. Cars sped by on the I-10 bridge above and just a short distance away, their drivers unaware of Joe's search and vision.

He ran along the levee again with J. R. leading and sometimes following. His mind rushed ahead. He didn't want Cathy to be a stripper—a druggie—a hooker. She had to be more than that. He hadn't spent the better part of the spring searching for someone he would not want.

He thought about the children that George Potter had mentioned. They liked Cathy. Children were good judges of character. She performed for them. Balloons and shows. He would like to have children of his own. His and Cathy's. Her body would be for him alone—not on display for anyone who would pay a five or ten dollar cover charge to watch her peel to the skin. If she was doing that, he would rescue her. There had to be some Bible story about that—a prophet and a prostitute—but he couldn't remember the names. He only remembered Samson and Delilah.

When the sun dipped below the horizon, Joe returned to the boat. He pulled out three hundred dollar bills, several twenties and tens. He put a wad of ones in another pocket. They were good for stuffing in garters of dancers. They might buy information about *Cat Red*.

From eight until two-thirty in the morning, Joe made the rounds of four exotic clubs. He blew fifty dollars on cover charges, another fifty for Cokes that cost the same as mixed drinks, and at least a hundred on the girls who danced. He was interested more in information than their bodies. It was a first for him. He remembered the times in Knoxville at the Mouse's Ear and Katch One where he was more interested in skin and sin than enlightenment and information.

All the girls denied knowledge of Cat Red. Turnover in the business was rapid. Some of the ones he quizzed had worked Dallas and Seattle just a week before. They traveled from city to city. If they could move rhythmically to popular music and if their bodies were not too pock-marked by needles and if they retained a somewhat slender appearance, they would get a job. They would make a circuit of the underbelly of America, supporting a coke habit or looking for the perfect love.

Passion. Passion was what he noticed was missing. They didn't seem to care. Their bodies moved, but their minds were blank, void, gone. He saw it in their eyes. They looked straight through the men, and when he looked into their eyes, all he could see were the backs of their heads. Occasionally a new one, a young one, would take the stage who evoked some passion. It was rare. He hoped that Cathy was not burnt out. He needed passion in his life. And love too, if that were possible.

Then she sat down beside him. Joe had not noticed her dancing. She put a hand on his thigh and squeezed.

"Buy me a drink," she said and lit a cigarette.

"What do you want?"

"What're you having?"

"Dr. Pepper."

"That's okay. It costs the same. That's what the boss is worried about. We can't chat with you without making money for him."

Another dancer serving as a waitress brought the two drinks.

"I hear you're looking for Cat Red."

Joe leaned down and spoke into her ear. "I can't hear you. Too much music and noise here. Let's move to that corner," he said and pointed.

"I hear you're looking for Cat Red," she said again when they had moved. This time he heard.

He nodded. "You know her?"

"Could be. What's it worth to you to find her?"

Joe felt of his pocket. He had less than half of what he started with left. He would bargain with her but not for long. "A hundred if you can get me to her apartment or home."

She blew out a long stream of smoke and started to stand. "I get more than that for a hand job. I thought you really wanted to find her."

Joe grabbed her arm and smiled. "I was just kidding. How much will it take?"

She started to open her mouth when the announcer said, "And now welcome to the stage Dee . . .li . . . laahhh . . . straight from the French Quarter and Big D."

"I gotta dance. Hang around. I'll be back."

"You're Delilah?" Joe asked. She nodded and laid the remains of her cigarette in the ashtray in front of him.

Joe concentrated on Delilah's eyes as she danced. His attention would from time to time slide down her body, but he wanted to see if he could read her eyes. Did she know Cathy's whereabouts, or was she just taking him for a sucker who would throw money at her for information that proved useless? The more he watched, the more he found his attention drifting to her movement rather than her eyes. She was watching him. It was as though her whole show was for him.

She was taller than he had imagined Cathy being. Delilah had black hair and an olive complexion like her namesake's picture in his Bible storybook. Her skin was smooth and the curves gentle. He did not detect any drug use by needle evidenced on her body. Except for the thoughts of Cathy, he would have wanted to bed her down for the night. He would do what it took with Delilah to find Cathy. He was sure of that.

She was the last act of the evening. It was 3 a.m. and time for the place to close. When she walked back to his table, she was dressed all in black leather—boots, slacks, and jacket.

"We can talk more about Cat Red at your place or mine . . . for the right price," she said and leaned closer. "Are you interested?" she whispered with extra breath into his ear.

He handed her the hundred. "I have more at my boat on the river. Can you go?"

She didn't seem to care that he didn't have the extra motorcycle helmet with him. She let her long hair blow out behind while she ran her hands up and down between his chest and abdomen. The Harley puffed out low bass notes through the city's deserted streets and rolled toward THE CARP.

J. R. sniffed at her boots when she walked onto the boat. "Oh, he smells my dog," she said and reached down and patted his head. She looked around and over to the river. "You live here . . . ? I'm sorry, I didn't even get your name."

"Carp. Joe 'Carp' Chapman. My boat's *THE CARP*."

"Carp? That's good. Not many mommas name their boys Carp."

"Nor do they name their girls Delilah. What's your real name?"

"That's it. Delilah. My mother had a sense of humor. She thought Delilah got a bad rap. What girl wouldn't turn her man in when she was under that type of pressure? Live to fight another day, as they say. Besides, Delilah didn't know they were going to do all those bad things to Samson."

"I thought she sold him out for silver," Joe said.

"Silver is a lot of pressure, honey."

Joe brought another chair out to the deck of the boat and poured them a Dr. Pepper into glasses with ice. He took off his jacket and leaned back, looking at the moon that was already three quarters of the way to the western horizon.

"Why are you looking for Cat Red?" she asked. She peeled her leather jacket off and had nothing on beneath.

Joe looked at her breasts. She must have wanted him to. They were nice. Their sag was hardly noticeable. Implants, but nice.

"I found her purse where I live in Tennessee. It just floated into me. I thought she was giving me a sign. Maybe she would fulfill my fantasies. I've been near two months coming down this river on the boat with my dog and Harley. I'm here and I want to see her."

"Fulfilling your fantasies?" She held one leg out to him. "Would you pull my boot off?" He did. "And the other one?" She stood and unzipped the leather pants at the side and slid them off. Joe sat and watched. "Men always have fantasies? Why is that? Why did you say you wanted to fulfill your fantasies with Cat Red? Why not fulfill your desire for love, truth, and the American way?"

She was deeper than Joe had thought or else she was stoned and he hadn't noticed.

"Women have fantasies too," he said and turned up his glass of soft drink. "I do want a woman I can love."

"Love? Or make love to? Sex? Or a relationship?" she asked and stood. "Do you have any music here, Carp? It's nice out tonight. I want to dance . . . with you. Nude. Under the moonlight."

Joe stepped through the door of the cabin and retrieved a radio. He brought it back out and handed it to Delilah. "See if you can tune in the kind of music you like."

She fiddled with the dial and finally settled on a slow, mournful tune. "Let's dance," she said. Joe stepped toward her. She put her hand out, palm out, like a policeman. "No, no. You have to be nude too. It wouldn't be right otherwise."

Joe started to strip. "I really just wanted to find out about Cat Red, Delilah. I didn't bring you out here to have sex. I took a vow to be true to Cathy." He was nude now.

She looked him up and down and smiled. "A vow? To someone you've never met? Carp, you are one crazy man. I'll tell you what. You dance with me real good, lay your head in my lap later on and let me run my fingers through your hair, and if you don't want sex, that'll be okay. And for another five hundred, I'll tell you where you can find Cat Red." She looked at his arms and saw the scars. "What happened to your arms? It looks like a machine tried to pull them off and partly succeeded."

"No questions and no scissors allowed," he said and moved into her arms.

From where the glow of the moon met the muddy water of the Mississippi, an orange rope of reflective light ran across the water to the boat where Joe and Delilah swayed softly together to the music of the portable radio. Her body felt good against his. He ran his hand down the small of her back, across her buttocks, to the back of her legs. She gently prodded a thigh between his and rubbed him the right way. He gazed up at the half-moon. Lunatics: those who stare at the moon and lose their minds.

"What is the difference in dancing nude with a woman and having sex with her as far as your vow to Cathy's concerned?" she whispered in his ear.

He didn't answer while he thought. It was as bad but it was better. He must be on the edge of insanity one way or the other. Three months before, he would have known exactly what to do. But now, he felt he was tied to Cathy by vows of marriage that had not yet been spoken. Yet, he was dancing naked on his boat in front of his dog with a woman he had only met an hour before. The purse had led him to a fixation on a vision, to obsession with its discovery, to compulsiveness, to . . . insanity.

WHEN JOE AWOKE THE next day to J. R. licking his face, he was alone on his bed. He rubbed his eyes and looked out the window. The sun was high in the sky. He checked his watch. Noon. He threw his pillow at the door and lay on his back.

His memory was fuzzy. It was like the fog that had come up while he and Delilah were dancing. He could remember that. They had come inside to the cabin. He had lain in her lap as he had promised. He didn't remember any scissors, but he reached for his head and ran his hand across his scalp. His hair was in tact.

He remembered a few words. He had talked to her about his bouts with Cathy's vision. He closed his eyes and could see Delilah's face and breasts looming above him. He had given her the five hundred dollar bills. They didn't have sex, did they? He looked down his body. He was still nude. He didn't recall. If he had had sex, he would have known. He had never forgotten that with any woman, at least for a day. But he couldn't say for sure.

What had Delilah told him about Cat Red—his Cathy? She had danced with her at a joint in Baton Rouge. She wrote the name down on a piece of paper and folded it. He remembered that. He sat up and began to look around. He brushed the sheets off and reached for the pillow where Delilah had propped her back against the wall at the head of the bed. He smelled her perfume on the pillow, and there on the bed where the pillow had lain was the paper. He opened it up.

"The Classy Kitty Cat."

He started to step through the door to go to his Harley and on to the club. This would be his day to see Cathy face to face. Then he remembered he was naked. He sat down and began to dress.

Another thought intruded on his search for his shoes. He had told George Potter he would return to his shop this morning to retrieve the personnel records on Cathy. It was already past noon, and he had not kept his appointment.

GEORGE POTTER EXTENDED THE card toward Joe.

"I told you her name had something to do with an animal," he said and smiled.

Joe looked at the card. "Pelton, Catherine L., age 23, place of birth: Louisiana, marital status: single, address: 2211 Washington Place, No. 3, no dependents for income tax purposes."

"Cathy Pelton," Joe mouthed aloud the name he had only known partly until now.

"Pelton. Fur, skin, pelt. Get it?" Potter asked.

"Oh, yeah. I see, " Joe said and looked around the shop. "Did your wife say anything else? Has she seen Cathy lately? Is this a current address? There's no phone number."

"That's it."

"Thanks," Joe said and started out the door.

"Oh, Joe, my wife did say she thought Cathy worked from time to time at the Classy Kitty Cat. It's not far away."

Joe nodded and slammed his hand against the door facing. He had given six hundred dollars to Delilah to get the same information that George Potter had given to him as an aside. He looked back at Potter. It was just as well. He would rather remember dancing nude with Delilah than picture himself doing the same with Potter.

Twenty–four

In five minutes Joe was at the front door of the Classy Kitty Cat. It was mid-afternoon, but the club was open. He didn't really expect Cathy to dance the early shift. She had to be the main attraction. But just on the chance that he could see her and check her out before he approached her, he would go into the place and act like any other customer. If she was not there, he had her address. But how would he make his move on her? It was hard to believe and remember that she had not actually seen him before. The visions were one-way experiences. Unless she had been having visions of him too. If she had, a mere glance and she would know that he was there to take her. She would rush into his arms.

The club was like the others he had visited. Dark, loud music, the smell of smoke, sparkling lights near the stage, and a girl on stage doing slow turns, bends, and stretches that passed as dancing. A few men sat on stools and at a couple of tables near the dancer. Some were acting like they were having conversation, but they were watching the girl. Joe took a seat in the back. He only wanted to see Cathy.

He asked the waitress about Cathy as soon as she took his drink order for another Dr. Pepper. She gave him a puzzled look and shook her head at the mention of Cathy Pelton or Cat Red. The waitress had only worked there a month. For the next hour he asked each girl who came to his table the same thing. "Where was Cat Red?" None had heard of her. All had been dancing for less than a month at the club.

Fifty dollars later, one of the girls told him the owner was in. Joe could ask him. She led him up steps beside the stage and to a mirrored door. She knocked on the door, a gruff voice barked from within, and an electric lock was disengaged.

"This is the gentleman who was asking about Cat, sir," the girl said before she turned and left Joe and the owner alone.

Joe stood in the cool room where a blue light embedded in the ceiling gave out the only illumination. The owner was highlighted by the reddish-orange glow of the cigar he puffed on. He sat behind a small desk. Behind Joe was a leather couch and a wooden chair on either side. Around the walls were what appeared to be portraits of some of the dancers. Cigar smoke clung to the ceiling like a fog that could not escape. Behind the manager was a window that looked out onto the stage. Joe knew he had not seen it from outside. It had all appeared to be a big mirror.

"My name's Carp," he said while the owner studied him from his chair. There was no invitation to sit and no hand extended to shake.

"Carp? What the hell kind of name is that?" He spat a piece of cigar that had broken loose into a nearby trash can. He sat squat in the chair like he was welded to it. His hair was slicked back and revealed a bald crown, but he had long sideburns that reminded Joe of pictures he had seen of Elvis. As Joe's eyes became accustomed to the light he could see the owner's jowly face. A bulbous nose showed a lace-work of tiny burst blood vessels. He either drank too much or had high blood pressure—or both.

"Just like the fish," Joe said and scooted one of the wooden chairs in front of the desk to where he was facing the owner.

The owner finally smiled and extended a rather limp hand. Joe shook and thought it was like holding a dead fish. "Why're you looking for Cat?"

"Just curious, Mr. . . . " Joe hesitated waiting for the man to tell him his name.

"If I'm going to call you Carp, you can call me Sir," he said with a throaty hoarseness and blew out rings of smoke.

"Yes, Sir."

"I haven't seen Cat since New Year's Eve. Wish I would. She's a crowd drawer," he continued and swiveled in his chair to where he was looking out onto the stage. "When Cat danced, this place was full. She's worked here off and on for the last two years.

"I interviewed her myself. Of course, I interview them all myself," he said and nodded toward the leather couch. He turned toward the window where a dancer was putting her breasts against it from the stage side. She then turned, bent over, and backed up to it. The owner smiled. "All the girls know I have this glass here where I can watch. Sometimes they go out of their way to try to entertain me."

"You interviewed Cat? What kind of interview do you do with a dancer?"

"With all the others except Cat, I screw them before they work here. Right there on that couch. Not Cat. She's special. She was good enough to dance without me getting the fringe benefits. Now why did you say you're looking for her?"

"I found her purse up in Tennessee. I wanted to return it and meet her."

Sir smiled again. "Yeah, meet her. Or meat her? Tennessee, huh? She travels a lot, but I never knew her to go to Tennessee. Anything valuable in the purse?"

"No."

"You could just leave it with me then. I'll give it to her when she shows back up."

Joe looked down and twisted a bit in his chair. "I really want to meet her. And give back the purse in person. I've come a long way."

"Did you have a picture of her in the purse?"

"No. I've been told she's good looking."

"Good looking? Shit. She's the most gorgeous woman in Baton Rouge. Perfect ass. Golden red hair. Not that fuzzy red frizzy stuff, but smooth sunrise red like spun gold that was a bit more red than gold."

"Yeah, that's what I imagined."

"She has the grace of a ballerina and the body needed for a place like this. Small breasts like most ballerinas. But no one marked her down for that here."

"Do you know anything about her? Like her family or education or anything?" Joe asked.

"She didn't talk much. Seems she doesn't have much family. Maybe a sister—and a shiftless boyfriend she runs off with occasionally."

"Do you have a phone number and address?"

"Sure I do. But I don't give them out. Every pervert in the state would be stalking our girls. Phone number's been disconnected. I tried it a week ago. She'll show up when she needs some money. She's probably gone on a little trip. Maybe even to Tennessee. Did you look there?"

"No." Joe looked out to where one girl was finishing her routine and another was taking the stage. "You pay them pretty good?"

"No. They pay me twenty-five dollars a week. We split the tips. Most of them can make a couple of hundred a night. Cat could make five hundred any night she worked. I could put up on the marquee out front that Cat Red is back and this place would be full in an hour."

"Why is she different? You've got a lot of good looking women out there," Joe said and nodded toward the stage where a blond was doing the splits while holding onto the shiny metal pole.

"Cat is educated and cultivated. She'd have them screaming before she took one thing off. Why she'd arrange to have a piano and black piano player on stage with her sometimes. She'd dance to

Chopin, Mozart, or some of those other classical dudes. You ever see anyone strip to classical music?" Joe shook his head. "I didn't think so. The piano player just kept on playing. Never looked at her. Now that's concentration.

"Cat saved us from being closed down for obscenity. One of those do-good committees started trying to close down all the nude clubs until they got to us. A judge looked at a video of Cat dancing to Chopin and refused to do anything. He said it was art." Sir pressed the cigar into the ashtray and glanced at the dancer behind him.

He looked back at Joe. "You might check with the local ballet club. She danced there and did performances until they found out she moonlighted for us. Some of the sponsoring *ladies* threatened to cut their donations if they let her dance." He paused while Joe digested what he had just told him. "Oh, yeah. I almost forgot. She was almost the winner of the local beauty and talent contest until they found out she worked some here too. Threw her out. I told her she should sue. But she's not that type. She just quietly dropped out.

"Carp, Cat Red is the perfect example of a phrase I heard a few years ago—*contradiction in terms.* She is educated, bright, and talented. But she loves to dance and show her erotic, sensual, sexy side. She's rather aloof though. Never dated any of the patrons. Just that free-loading boyfriend."

"Do you know his name?" Joe asked.

"Naw. Seems like it might be Barton. Ken or Keith or something. He had his picture in the paper a few months ago—was arrested for selling some marijuana or something."

"Thanks for the information," Joe said and began to get up.

"You know you're the fifth person to be looking for her during the last month. FBI and DEA were here about a week a part. At least that's who they said they were. Showed me some badges. Who am I to argue?"

"FBI and DEA?" Joe asked more to himself than to Sir.

"Yeah. FBI first, then the DEA. I asked the DEA boys why they didn't talk to the FBI. DEA guys just looked at each other funny."

Joe reached for the door.

"Wait. I'll walk you out. You want to see a portrait of Cat Red?"

Joe's heart began to pound. A portrait? He would finally get to see the woman of his visions. Yes! He said to himself but only gave a slight nod of the head to Sir.

"I call it my Wall of Fame. Pictures of all of my best dancers."

They walked back out, past the stage, and into a corridor that led to a video game room. The walls were lined with life-sized framed color photos. Sir stopped and pointed to the one of Cat Red. Unlike the nude photos of the other dancers, the one of Cat Red showed a fully clothed young woman.

Joe leaned for support against one wall and stared at the picture of the woman he had been seeking.

She stood there in a white gown with a red long-stemmed rose in her right hand. The gown swooped down from her right shoulder past a bare left shoulder. Her hair was up with a single white silk ribbon tied at the crown. She was looking into the camera. There was just a hint of a smile on her lips, but her pale green eyes reflected the flash of the camera as if there were coals afire in their depths.

"That was her when she was in the Miss Baton Rouge pageant," Sir whispered to Joe who had slumped wide-eyed against the wall.

IT WASN'T QUITE DARK when Joe throttled his Harley onto Washington Place and began to look for Cathy's street number. He rode up and down the narrow way several times, steeling his nerves for the knock at her door. If what Sir said was true, she probably wasn't home. But she might be. He had to make a good first impression. He looked down at himself and leaned over to look in the handlebar mirror. He could do better than that. He took a sideways glance at her house and headed the cycle back out onto the main street and toward his boat.

The muffled throbbing of the engine and the air blowing in around the helmet soothed him almost like the river. His mind was on Cathy. Her portrait looked so much like his vision. It was as though the photo had been thrown into the Tennessee River and then walked onto the bow of *THE CARP*. He couldn't have drawn one that was a closer resemblance to what he had seen on the river than the one on the wall at the club.

What did the news that the FBI and DEA were looking for her mean? The way Sir had described her was exactly what he was looking for—except for the fact that she worked as a stripper. Intelligent, talented, beautiful, and sexy. Throw in the fact that she liked kids, according to George Potter, and he had the perfect prospect for a wife. He had not seen any flaw in her as he always had in any other woman. She was misled to be dancing and showing her body to other men, and she was misled to be running with that guy, but those were minor corrections that he could take care of.

After a shower, shave, and change to his lawyer suit, Joe was back on his Harley headed for Cathy's. He felt refreshed and smelled heavily of cologne. He hoped Cathy liked the fragrance. He stopped at George Potter's shop and had him to wrap a single long-stemmed red rose and make a balloon that said "Cathy" on it. Potter had smiled when he saw Joe dressed up for his possible first date. "Good luck," he had said.

This time he would go straight to the door without riding up and down the street so many times.

Darkness had wrapped Cathy's house by the time the Harley's headlight shone back and forth on the circular drive. Joe leaned the cycle over onto its stand, put his helmet near the back bar, and brushed his hair one last time. He swallowed and walked gently up the three steps. He could not see beyond the black shutters that were trimmed in gold. There was no light emanating from within.

He took a deep breath and knocked with the hand which held the balloon. No response. He knocked again, louder.

"She ain't there," a loud, brassy voice from his side said. Joe squinted over his left shoulder and saw a silhouette on the porch next door. He stepped back down from Cathy's porch and walked toward the next house and the voice. The five small brick houses were in a semi-circle off the main street. They were of similar construction with the only difference being the way that each occupant decorated the front. Cathy's was the only one with black shutters trimmed in gold.

He looked up toward the corpulent figure that stood above him on the concrete porch. She said nothing at first. Just stood there.

As Joe's eyes adjusted to the light, he could see it was an older woman. She stood like a tree stump or partial totem pole. There was little differentiation in circumference from head to knee. Her head sprouted hair that frizzed to about four inches in length before it fell in dirty cascades around her ears. She had the eyebrows of John L. Lewis and a nose that would make bookends with the one of Sir.

The only makeup she wore was bright red lipstick, apparently applied without the aid of a mirror as the fluorescent grease did not end with the lines of her lips but extended above and below, as though she might have been interrupted on her way to audition at the circus. A protruding lower abdomen served as a shelf upon which lay ponderous breasts which could not be contained by any regular size bra. It would have taken puptents.

"I'm the owner," she said while Joe stood below her like a subject before a monarch.

He still didn't speak. His voice would not come. He had expected to see his lady of beauty next door and now he was confront- ed with the opposite. He had previously believed that the braless look was sexy, but now, on further observation, was convinced that some women should keep them covered under several layers of clothing. She unscrewed the cap of a Skoal tin and put a pinch in her mouth. "You want some?" she asked. Joe shook his head.

"Cathy's not home," she said and sat down on a wooden bench on the porch. It creaked under her weight. Her knees spread wide as the dress rode up. Joe could see she was wearing old Converse All-Stars like he wore in elementary school. They were black but her socks were pink. As her knees splayed open, he saw layers of fat move like waves of the ocean until they settled to stillness. He couldn't see if she was wearing panties. He didn't want to. He took a step to the side and noticed the odor of urine, cheap perfume, and cigarette smoke that clung to her body, trapped apparently by the force of gravity. He stepped toward her other side, hoping to be upwind from her.

"Cathy left the first of March and I ain't heard hide nor hair from her since. I'm her landlord," she said and spat into a paper cup. "Are you one of her boyfriends?"

"No, ma'am," Joe said, surprised that he had his voice back. "I wanted to return a purse." He explained his mission in Baton Rouge for the third time in a few brief statements.

"Don't surprise me none. Cathy's been all over the country. She just ups and takes off. Then comes back in a few months. Just like I told those other fellers who've been looking for her."

"Who?"

"The law. Damn FBI, DEA, city. Lawsy, I don't know who all. They're looking for her and that no good boyfriend of hers."

"Yes, I heard about that. What's her boyfriend's name? Ken or Keith Barton?"

"Bartley!" she shouted. "Kent Bartley. He's out on bond on some drug charge. Disappeared. They think she might be with him. Took her Mustang and drove off."

"Took the red convertible?" Joe asked, thinking of the one he had seen in the dream in Memphis.

"That's the only one she's got." The landlady spit again. "You've met her then? You know she has a red Mustang."

"Only in my dreams," Joe said.

The landlady laughed. "Yeah, that's the only chance you'd have with her. *Only in your dreams.*"

"Did the police act like they knew where she was headed?" Joe asked.

"No. They didn't tell me anything. Just wanted information. They didn't give any out. I just told them she'd left. She gave me enough money to cover some rent and keep the power and telephone on. But that started running out. The phone's already off. They'll cut the power off in another week. Her rent's good for another month."

"Can I go in and look around?"

"Hell, no. Can't let you do that. Nothing there much anyway. She's a little weird. Burns a lot of candles. Don't even think she's

Catholic. She goes down to New Orleans and buys books about voodoo and such."

"The police take anything?"

"No. Acted disgusted when they couldn't find anything."

Joe turned and looked back toward Cathy's house. He bet he had a key to her door among the ones from her purse in his cycle's saddlebag. He'd come back later. He had to see inside. The landlady took another pinch of Skoal.

"What about family? Does she have any family I could talk to and turn her purse over to?"

"She has a sister. She was by a while back. I have her name and address on a card she gave me." The landlady labored to get up. She shuffled through the doorway and returned with the card. She handed it to Joe. "I want it back. You can write down the name and address and telephone number."

Joe reached for his wallet, took one of his attorney cards, and wrote the information on the back. "Carol Sent, Plaza Professional Building, Suite 105" and the telephone number. He wouldn't call, though. He would go.

"The feds get this information on her sister?" he asked as he handed the card back.

"No. They might have already known. Or . . . they might not be as smart as you," she said and winked. "You're kinda cute. Would you like to come in for a beer? Looks like you're all dressed up for a date. No need to let it go to waste."

Joe took a half step backward. "No. I have to do some other checking. Maybe some other time . . . but," he looked down at the rose in his hand, "you take the rose. I appreciate the information."

"You're not married are you?" she asked.

"No."

"Me neither. We could make some beautiful music together."

Joe was silent for a moment while his imagination took over. He could hear the squeaking of bed springs and see himself in a ghastly naked clinch with the landlady.

"I'm sure," he said, "but not tonight." He began to walk toward the Harley.

"Hey, wait."

He turned around.

"What about the balloon? Can I have the balloon?"

Joe looked at the balloon that had Cathy's name on it. "Sure. Hope you enjoy it," he said and handed it to her.

"It'll brighten up the place," she said and took it from his hand. "Goodbye, Sweetie," she said and blew him a kiss.

Joe kicked the cycle to life, took one last look at the landlady, and remembered what he and Charles Palk used to say about some of the girls in high school: "Beauty is skin deep, but ugly is to the bone."

IN AN HOUR, HE was back at the rear door of Cathy's house. His Harley was parked a block away and he had changed from his suit to an all black outfit. The rings of keys were in his hand. He stepped quietly onto the back stoop, holding the keys in both hands so they would make no noise. He brought them near his eyes and picked out the two that looked like door keys. The first one didn't fit but the second one did.

Inside, he was met with the musty smell of a house closed up for several months. There had been no cooling air, and the heat was still a bit stifling. He turned on the pen light he had brought and shined its beam around the room where he was standing—the kitchen. While most of the windows were shuttered and dark, the ones in the kitchen let the moonlight sift through the gauze curtains.

He eased open the refrigerator, and the light startled him. Power was still on. It was bare except for a head of lettuce that had collapsed in on itself, a small opened package of sandwich meat that had grown a beard of mold, and a clear plastic jug of milk that had curdled. He looked at the expiration date on the side label—March 3.

He closed the refrigerator door and began to crawl around the other rooms. The house was neat but small. It appeared the occupant had just stepped out for a late evening walk. He smiled. Cathy was a good housekeeper. And she wasn't used to luxury. She would be at home with him now that he had no luxuries.

When he got to the end of the hallway, he took a handkerchief from his pocket to open the bedroom door. He would wipe his fingerprints off the refrigerator before he left. He turned the knob and pushed the door gently open to a slight squeak. Hinges needed oiling. Darkness spilled out of the room. If there were any windows, they were shuttered and draped.

He turned the flashlight back on and circled its shaft of yellow light around the edges of the room. The bed was made and had a quilt draped over the foot. He aimed the light at the walls and found two windows that wore thick drapes. He remembered seeing the black, gold-trimmed shutters on the outside. He felt it safe to stand now and got to his feet.

Then he saw what the landlady had mentioned. From the baseboard near the door, all around the circumference of the room, stood small, stubby candles. They looked to him like a legion of miniature soldiers marching around the room, guarding both window sills, the table, and the dresser. Most had tasted fire and had given up part of their tallow to illuminate this room for his Cathy. They were of all shapes—plain candles, candles in holders, the ones that had been lit, others that had never seen a match—and they all stood as immobile witnesses that Cathy would rather light one than curse the darkness. They were potential light in a darkened sepulcher. Joe remembered the candle shop in Gatlinburg and vowed they would go there on their honeymoon.

Beside and beneath her bed, Joe found stacks of books. The landlady was correct again. Most dealt with voodoo and witchcraft. He leafed through some and saw passages underlined and notes beside paragraphs. The flyleaf showed most had been purchased at a shop in New Orleans on St. Philip Street. He put one book in his pocket.

On a dresser to the side of the bed and against the wall, surrounded by the marching line of candles, were four framed photographs. One was a smaller version of the one he had seen at the Classy Kitty Cat. He picked each one up and held the pen light near. The soft glow gave Cathy the same appearance she had had on the boat when the pale moonlight had highlighted her features.

The second photo was of a bit younger Cathy with her arm around another woman who wore a graduation gown. Maybe this was the sister that the landlady had mentioned. He studied them. They didn't look all that much alike. His woman was much prettier.

The third photo was of Cathy in a high school majorette's uniform leading a band in a parade. The red hair was falling across the purple and white trimmed uniform. There were the strutting legs and a wide smile below burning eyes looking directly at the camera.

He lifted the fourth picture slowly. It showed a young man standing in front of a 1965 red Ford Mustang. For some reason, Joe knew he hated him. It had to be Kent Bartley. He was slight of build with long hair, a thin mustache, and an expression of slight agitation or anger. He didn't really want to be photographed. Joe held the photo up near his eyes and stared at it. This was the one he would have to contend with for the affections of Cathy. Joe burned the image of his rival into the retina of his memory.

When he set it back down, he laid the flashlight on top of the dresser and his hands moved to the pulls on the top drawer. He took a deep breath in the warm room and felt his hands begin to sweat. He was going to open the containers of Cathy's most intimate apparel. He didn't know whether he should be doing this. He would never tell her if she asked. His curiosity and wanting to become one with Cathy drove him.

He slid the top drawer open and pulled the delicate underclothes of Cathy from the darkness into his hands and raised them to the ray of light. The coolness of the silky slips and panties met the hotness of his hands. He felt the thin layers between his thumb and

index finger. He crushed the material in his hands and imagined
Cathy being there. He held them to his chest and shut his eyes. He
saw her on the boat. He saw her in Memphis. He was as close to her
body as he was going to get that evening.

Each drawer contained new treasures. If she left all these
behind, what did she take on her trip with the criminal Bartley? He
brought a pair of black panties with red lace trim to his face. He could
almost smell Cathy—and taste her—as he felt the silk against his
tongue.

He threw a few of the garments onto the bed and walked to a
closet. He slid the door open and shined the light on the row of
clothes. Apparently they were some of the garments she wore at the
Classy Kitty Cat. He picked up and then hung back a pink and black
set of bra and panties, black lacy panties, a black leather mini-skirt,
scarves, garters, crotchless panties, and puffy boas. On the floor
beneath sat high heeled boots and pairs of shoes in three rows.

He stepped to the other side of the closet where more conventional clothing hung—blouses, jackets, slacks, and at least twenty pairs
of jeans. The jeans were all shades of blue with a few black ones
sprinkled in. He could imagine Cathy moving to the old country music
hit— "Baby's Got Her Blue Jeans On."

He took a few pairs from the hangers and held them beside his
legs. She was probably at least five-foot-seven. They were good
brands. He looked at them front and back, trying to imagine Cathy's
legs and bottom filling them out. She liked all brands and styles, but
there was one thing in common about the jeans—none of them had
back pockets. He went back to the closet and examined some of the
other slacks. No back pockets. Then he remembered what George
Potter and Sir had agreed on. Cathy had the "prettiest ass" in
Louisiana.

She knew it. She was not about to let the lines of the pockets
interfere with the curves of her derriere. He wondered if she wore
panties beneath the jeans? Would the panty lines ruin the effect of
her perfectly shaped buttocks?

He stepped back to the dresser and stacked up the things he
wanted to take with him. There was a high school annual, a program
from the local ballet, a horse farm brochure, the photo of her in the
majorette uniform, and the picture of Bartley. He would add these to
his collection. And a pair of panties.

He turned the pen light off, went to the bed, and lay among the
heap of Cathy's panties and slips. He opened his shirt and felt the
garments against his skin. He closed his eyes and imagined her
there.

Twenty-five

J oe Chapman awoke the next morning when he heard traffic on the street in front of Cathy's house. Her underclothes were bunched in piles on his body. The only light was the faint glow that came down the hallway from the kitchen. He sat up and squinted at his watch. He hadn't intended to spend the night. He grabbed the short stack of possessions and crawled down the hallway toward the back door. He didn't need another confrontation with the landlady. He eased down the back steps, into the alley, and toward his cycle.

Back on *THE CARP*, his stomach rejected any thought of breakfast. He brewed some strong coffee, sat, and put his feet up on the rail facing the Mississippi. J. R. stretched in the sun at his feet. He considered what he had found out about Cathy and contemplated the next place to look. He laid the articles he had taken one by one in the sun. The ballet company might have some information. The horse farm outside of Baton Rouge may have been frequented by Cathy. If anyone knew her whereabouts, it would be her sister. He looked at the card—Carol Sent. Carol and Cathy. Sent and Pelton. Cathy wasn't married. Carol must be married to some Sent fellow.

Then his eyes focused on the picture of Bartley. He let his mind wander. Bartley had been arrested. There would be a record. Court appearances. A mug shot. Maybe a prior conviction and a parole or probation report. Public records. He could play lawyer and find out as much about his adversary as possible. He put away his card that had Carol Sent's address on the back. He would see her too—while he had his lawyer's suit on. Getting on the good side of a sister wouldn't hurt.

His muscles ached from the strange bed. He changed into some shorts and athletic shoes, picked up the tennis ball, and called

J. R. onto the asphalt beside the warehouse. He started in a slow trot, throwing the ball ahead of him for the dog to retrieve. They both needed the exercise. Sweat came soon in the hot morning air. He pulled off his shirt, bunched it into a ball, and put it down where he would pick it up on his return. His chest glistened with moisture. He burst into a sprint and J. R. leaped to follow. He pumped his arms. A block, two, and three. He slowed and turned in the direction of the boat. His heart raced and his breath came in great heaves. Gradually his heart returned to its normal beat and the air came easier.

He stopped and positioned himself on the hot pavement to do pushups. The dog brought the ball to him. "In a minute, J. R.," he said and began to count. At a hundred, he stood, threw the ball farther toward the boat, and raced the dog to it. He stopped where the boat was and looked over the edge of the dock at the river. The Mississippi had a deceptive flow. Even here, where boats were docked, there was a treacherous backwash. He could handle it, he decided, and jumped in. He swam beside the boat, back and forth, for fifteen minutes while J. R. watched. When he pulled himself up to the deck of the boat, he could feel a layer of gritty dirt covering his body. He took two large towels and called J. R. to go shower with him.

Washed, shaved, and refreshed, he put on the suit and cycle helmet and took off toward the courthouse, leaving a clean J. R. drying on his back on the deck of the boat.

He had not lost his legal research ability. He went quickly to the correct office and received the file from the clerk. It contained not only the basic charges and papers but also a questionnaire Kent Bartley filled out to request court appointed counsel as an indigent. He looked at mug shots in profile and facing him. Bartley was still irritated at having his picture made. There was nothing really prominent about his features. His hair was a little longer and the same for his mustache. He appeared a little emaciated. Too many drugs. Bartley was five-foot-eight, a hundred and sixty pounds.

Joe compared himself to Bartley. He was six-foot-two, a hundred and ninety pounds. He knew he was more handsome. Even if his hair hadn't grown completely out, it looked better than Bartley's. The only advantage Bartley had was that he was younger—30 to 39. Joe smiled. The only other advantage was that Bartley knew where Cathy was and was with her.

Bartley had made bond. Joe looked at the amount. How could a person too poor to hire his own lawyer make a hundred thousand dollar bond? And why was it so high for such a petty offense? One ounce of coke. Why were two federal agencies involved with this? He took the bondsman's name and address and went to see him.

Ace Bonding was just two blocks from the jail, convenient for business. Wives, mothers, sisters, and sometimes fathers would mortgage their houses and draw out any savings to pay ten per cent of the bond's face amount to secure freedom for their loved ones until the trial. Who did Bartley know with ten thousand dollars?

Ace Bonding was Sean Bodine. Bodine was Ace. When Joe entered the store-front office, Bodine motioned him to a metal chair while he finished a phone conversation. Bodine scowled and tapped the end of his pen against the desk. He laid it down and took up his cigarette. He drew deeply and blew out a horizontal column of smoke that rose into a ceiling fan just before it hit Joe in the face.

Bodine spoke in staccato phrases. "Yes, I know. No, you don't. He'd better be there. It's his ass." He slammed down the receiver and buried the cigarette in an ashtray that flowed onto the desk. He eyed Joe before he spoke.

"You need a bond?"

"No, I'm here about one you have on bond. Kent Bartley."

Bodine raised his eyebrows and tapped another cigarette from the package on his desk. He lit it, and this time directed the stream of smoke upward. "You know Bartley?"

"No. I don't know him. Only what I read in his police and court file. I'm looking for his girlfriend—"

"Cat Red. Cathy Pelton. Dancer. Ballerina. Horse woman. Hot piece of ass. Yeah, I know of her."

Joe put his hands together and squeezed his fingers into a webbed vault. He didn't like someone talking about his future wife that way, at least the last phrase.

Joe explained his quixotic quest for the hand of Cathy to the fourth person in Baton Rouge and received the same type response. They looked away, grinned, or studied their watches. Bodine looked at his watch.

"Tennessee to Baton Rouge. Fourteen hundred miles in a boat. A lawyer on a summer holiday. Shit. You're a work in progress, Mr. . . . , what did you say your name was?"

"I didn't. They call me Carp."

Bodine laughed, opening his mouth and showing discolored teeth. He lit another cigarette although his other one rested on the lip of the ashtray, barely a half inch of ash showing and sending out a small plume of smoke.

"You must be crazy, Carp. You'd fit in good here. You want a job looking for Bartley? You find him, you find your hot piece of ass."

Joe leaned forward. Bodine probably didn't mean anything, but he was a bit too crude in his references to Cathy. The bondsman was all laughs—an easygoing Cajun, maybe. The accent betrayed him.

"How did Bartley make bond in the first place. About ten thousand, right?"

"Twelve-five. I said he was a high risk. He was arrested in January. Had his prelim postponed until March 15. Skipped on me. He had half the money and a guy by the name of George Hipshire had the rest." Bodine was looking at his file. "I have until the middle of August to bring him in or I forfeit a hundred big ones. I can't find him. This Tennessee angle may be our last shot. If Pelton's purse was in Tennessee, you can bet Bartley was nearby. I'd venture he liked her purse better than her ass."

"Listen, Mr. Bodine, you're going to have to quit referring to Cathy's ass." Joe stood and slammed his fist down on the desk.

"Sorry. I didn't know." Bodine raised both hands, palms out. He shuffled through some papers and opened Bartley's file. "We can work together on this. You like this Lady Catherine, and I want Bartley's ass." He looked up. "See, I said *Bartley*." He smiled at Joe. "You're a lawyer. You look smooth, bright. You could open doors that my other goons . . .," he looked back up at Joe, "my goons couldn't. See, you bring Bartley to me and you keep your lady. Kill two birds with one stone. Eliminate the competition. And I'll pay you a little for your trouble."

"How little?"

"Ten thousand to you or anybody who brings Bartley through that door." He motioned to the front door. "You have a gun—a pistol?"

"A .357 magnum," Joe said.

"Not as good as a forty-five," Bodine said and slid his desk drawer open. "More knock-down power. You get in a fire fight with a thug, you don't want him shooting at you after you've shot him. Dangerous. You kill him. It's just the same to me. Bring his hide through that door. You heard of *Taylor versus Taintor*? It's an 1873 Supreme Court case." Bodine took a printed copy and handed it to Joe with the forty-five.

"The Supremes gave bondsmen more power than the police. We can go anywhere and do anything to take back the body of the one we made bail for. There's none of that due process shit. If you find him anywhere in the country, you can haul his ass back, handcuffed or whatever."

Joe felt the weight of the gun and glanced at the court decision. "This is all I need?"

"A little more. We'll get you a certified copy of the bail bond, the warrant for his arrest, a paper showing that you're my employee," Bodine said. He squeezed a metal seal onto documents he was going through. "With these, you can break into any place that you find Bartley, and no one can do anything. It's a good idea to tell the local police what you're doing so that you don't get shot for kidnapping or something."

"If they're not in Tennessee, and they're in Louisiana, where do you think they are?" Joe asked.

"Probably New Orleans." Bodine looked at the papers he was writing on. "Now, give me your real name so I can fill this in. You'll be official. I'll give you a copy of my whole file. It's all I have on him. I have others looking for him. I don't care who finds him first. I just want him back."

"Joe Chapman. Why New Orleans?"

Bodine continued to write. "Both into experimenting with voodoo or some kind of cult stuff. Those kind of people can hide out their friends for a long time. I'd look there first."

Joe thought back to the books he had seen at Cathy's house. He had taken one with the New Orleans address. "Bodine, do you think it's peculiar that Bartley was able to come up with twelve-five for his bond when he couldn't afford a lawyer?"

"This whole case is strange. They caught him with two bales of marijuana and a little cocaine. He was never charged with the pot, just the little bit of coke. Maybe they were waiting to charge him separately. But where is it? The police act like they don't even know it exists. But Bartley told me himself."

"What was George Hipshire's relationship with Bartley?"

"Beats me. He had the money. I took it. Should've asked more questions, huh?"

"I've been told there're FBI and DEA looking for Bartley. What do you know about that?" Joe asked.

"DEA, yes. FBI don't have anything to do with it. I'm not sure why the DEA is interested on such a small amount. Could be that they smell something bigger. They won't tell you anything. I told them what I knew because I don't care who finds him, as long as he's found." Bodine looked around the room. "Joe, my copier's down. I'll give you part of these today. You'll need to stop by tomorrow to pick up the rest."

"Does this authorize me to carry a gun?"

"Sure does, as long as you carry that certified bail bond and warrant with you."

Joe folded the papers and put them in an inside pocket of his jacket. He felt official. He had a job. He was someone. He was on a man hunt—part of a *posse comitatus*. In his law practice, he had always represented the defendant. Now, his former partner, Charles Palk, would be proud of him. He was after the bad guy. Maybe he should give his friend a call. He had been gone two months.

First things first though. He kicked off the Harley and headed toward Carol Sent's office. He had learned as much about Cathy and Kent as he was going to without talking with a relative. Kent had none listed. Carol Sent was the only relative of Cathy's that he knew about. According to the map, he was less than five minutes from her office. The late afternoon air, scented with the aroma of magnolia blossoms, felt good against his face.

He pulled into the office complex and circled the parking area. It was nice. A brick building that looked more like a large, sprawling house sat among large oaks veiled with Spanish moss. There was a stream that ran between the main parking area and the building. A small dam made a pond where ducks swam and the water tumbled over a two-foot high ledge of old, mossy river rock. There were benches and tables beneath the trees in the shade.

He looked at the sign. "Family Care Center of Central Baton Rouge." Below it were listed the names of twelve professionals. Doctors, psychologists, physical therapists, and then, Carol Sent, M. S., Marriage and Family Therapist, Suite 105. He shook his head. His wife had been after him for years to see one of those. Now he was, although it was too late for them. He was after the therapist's sister.

"Could I help you?" the receptionist asked.

"Is it possible that I could see Carol Sent?" Joe asked.

"Did you have an appointment?" the receptionist asked and looked down at the daily calendar.

Joe smiled. "No. I'm not here to see her on a professional basis. I wanted to ask her about a sister, Cathy Pelton."

"And your name, sir?"

"Carp," Joe said reflexively. He noticed the raised eyebrows on the young lady. "Oh, well, that's what some people call me. But you can tell her it's Joe Chapman."

The receptionist was writing it down. "Does Ms. Sent know you?" She looked up and Joe shook his head. She continued to write. "Very well. Have a seat. I'll see if Ms. Sent can see you. She's a very busy person, you know." The receptionist watched Joe as he found a seat near a table that held some magazines. She then turned and walked down the hallway.

Carol Sent was busy working on her latest writing assignment and between appointments when the receptionist tapped on her door.

She looked up. "Yes?"

The receptionist stepped through the doorway. She handed the note to Carol Sent. "This guy wants to see you, Carol. Says he wants to ask you about Cathy."

Carol looked at the piece of paper. "Joe Chapman. *Carp*. What does that mean?"

"Carp is his nickname."

"I don't know any Joe Chapman. What does he know about Cathy?"

"I don't know. But, Carol, you ought to see him. He's a real hunk. And . . . no wedding ring. You know I check those things out. He said it's not a professional call. So maybe you can make it *recreational*."

Carol smiled slightly at her receptionist who had been trying for two years to set her up with a new man.

"Dot, I've told you before, I don't need a man in my life. I'm through with men and love and . . ." she looked at the note again. "Well, show him in . . . in five minutes. I'll buzz you. Make him think I'm real busy."

Dot nodded. "You'll like him. Has a great smile. Good teeth. Tanned."

Carol waved her away. When the door closed, she looked at the name again. Maybe she could do a role reversal. Before, Cathy had stolen away her guys. If this man was a past acquaintance of Cathy, it would be fair for her to steal him away. Then she shook her head. No, she didn't need the bother. She was happy with her career and her new hobby of writing. Then she stood, walked to the mirror on the wall, checked her makeup, and brushed a stray hair back in place.

"It'll be a few minutes, Mr. Chapman. She's real busy, but she's going to try to squeeze you in before her next appointment."

Joe nodded and picked up a copy of *Southern Living*. He noticed it was the same issue that he had looked through at Goose's house. Then a thought struck him. He reached for his wallet and pulled out the business card of Goose's son, John Collins, DEA, Mobile, Alabama. Maybe he would call John Collins and find out why the DEA was looking for Kent Bartley.

In a few minutes, Carol buzzed Dot's machine. "She'll see you now. Let me show you to her office." Dot watched Joe get up and allowed him to precede her down the hallway. "Third door on the right," she said. She appraised his backside and nodded her head.

Dot caught up with him when he reached the door and squeezed ahead, barely brushing Joe's leg. She knocked on the door again.

"Ms. Sent, this is Joe *Carp* Chapman. He wants to talk with you about Cathy," Dot said and winked at Carol where Joe couldn't see. Dot turned and left the room, closing the door behind her. Carol had stood at the side of her desk but returned to the chair behind it.

"Yes. Well, sit down, Mr. Chapman," she said and pointed to one of three matching comfortable well-stuffed chairs. She leaned on the desk and brought her hands together beneath her chin. She looked to Joe to make the first conversation.

Joe had studied her from the first moment he had entered the room. He was curious as to the appearance of the sister of Cathy. She was pleasant looking enough. More business than social—dressed in a navy suit and blouse with a single wide, flat gold chain adorning her neck. Large golden tear-drop shaped earrings and a gold bracelet. Her pale white complexion could be the same as Cathy's. She must work a lot and not get much sun.

Her hair was much different. Not nearly as long, pulled back and fastened with a navy-colored cloth clasp at the back. It was not the golden red of Cathy's but a dark auburn. But when she had turned to sit down and the sun from the window had reflected off it, Joe had noticed a streak that reminded him of Cathy. She had nice legs, calves that had not seen the climbing of many hills.

He looked into her darker eyes for burning coals but saw none. He noticed the dark red of her fingernails was the same as her lipstick. Nice cheek bones, but a slightly Roman nose. And breasts? His eyes bore into the chest of Carol Sent. Smallness must run in the family.

"May I help you, Mr. Chapman?" The sound of her voice brought Joe back to the purpose of his mission. "I only have a few minutes before my next appointment." She smiled slightly and there was an almost imperceptible raising of her eyebrows.

"Oh, yes. Please call me Joe." He looked around the room searching in his mind for the correct way to approach the subject. Then he just blurted it out. "I'm looking for your sister, Cathy."

"Cathy? Why're you looking for her?"

Joe shifted in his chair, cleared his throat, and looked out the window while he tried to think of the most appropriate way to tell a mental health professional that he had developed an insane obsession with her sister who was reputed to have the most beautiful ass in Louisiana. His eyes skimmed across the dark green papered walls to the plaqued degrees and certificates of Carol Sent. The dark paneled wood that covered the lower third of the walls and the matching carpet told Joe that he was in the office of someone who probably would not put up with much nonsense.

"I found your sister's purse in Tennessee. I'm trying to return it."

"How odd. You found it in Tennessee? You're from Tennessee?"

Joe nodded.

"Do you have it with you?"

"No. It's back on *THE CARP* with J. R."

"*THE CARP*? J. R.?"

"Yes, *THE CARP* is my houseboat and J. R. is my dog. I came downriver fourteen hundred miles with her purse."

"I see," she said and looked at her watch. "I thought you were Carp." She looked again at the note that Dot had given her.

For the next five minutes, Joe gave Carol Sent an abbreviated version of his search for Cathy. At points she would smile politely. At others, she raised her eyebrows. The visions brought responses of "I see."

While Joe jabbered on, Carol looked into his eyes, watched his expressions, and studied his hand movements. His hazel eyes were almost hypnotic. He was tanned and his neck gave way to wide shoulders. When he gestured about the way Cathy appeared to him, his arms swept the air with force and passion. He spoke in the language of an educated man who was well-read when he likened her sister to Catherine the Great and told about the carriage. He was a work in progress, a diamond in the rough, an unwashed pearl. He just needed a little polishing by the right woman. She felt a warmth enveloping her. This man was looking for Cathy, but she felt a magnetism drawing her in toward him. Did he feel the same way? Or worse, did he detect her feelings and not have the same? His story was strange, but her impulsive desire was stranger. Dot was right. He was a hunk. She had to get hold of herself. She brought her hands down as he finished his monologue and held on to the sides of her chair.

"There wasn't much in the purse of value," he concluded.

"What do you do for a living, Mr. Chapman?"

"You can call me Joe. I'm a lawyer."

Carol glanced at his left hand. Dot was right. There was no wedding ring. But many married men didn't wear them.

"I take it that you have more than a passing interest in my sister. Are you married?"

"No. Divorced really. A few months ago."

Good. Carol smiled to herself, but continued on as though she was looking out for Cathy. "And without ever having even met Cathy, you want to marry her?"

"Yes. That sounds a little crazy, doesn't it?"

"A little. But I've heard stranger tales. That's my business."

"Yes, I noticed. There are several professional types in this building. What's the deal?"

"Yes. We have a medical doctor, a psychiatrist, psychologist, and a couple of marriage and family therapists. It's a unique center. We deal with the whole person. We can refer between or among us or to others as we help to deal with problems that beset the individual or family."

"Which kind do you think I need? Where's the couch?" Joe turned his head and looked at the other chairs.

"Well, you're here on a personal mission and not a professional one, I was told. Is that correct?"

Joe nodded his head. Carol was glad. Her profession had strict rules about mixing personal and professional business. No dual relationships. No dating clients. No sex with clients. No business dealings with clients. She wanted to keep Joe on a personal rather than a professional level.

"I can't advise you as to what kind of help you need, but you won't find any couches in any of our offices. There's no need for one. You see, I'm usually seeing a couple or family. So we just sit in chairs. If I had a couch, who would I let be on it? Or would they just take turns? Your view of the mental health field is rather stereotyped. Besides, when you told me you were from Tennessee, I didn't look over my desk to see if you were wearing shoes, did I?"

Joe sat silent. His foray had been repulsed. He had met his match. He hoped Cathy's intellect matched her sister's. He noticed the photos on the credenza behind Carol.

"Is that a photo of Cathy?"

"Yes. That's her with the Miss Baton Rouge crown," Carol said, stood, and walked to the end where the photo was.

"She won?" Joe asked.

"No, she didn't win. But they made a photo of each finalist before the pageant was over to have ready for the winner. Cathy withdrew from the pageant before it was over. But I thought it was one of the best pictures she ever had made. That's why I keep it." She looked at Joe. "She is a beauty, isn't she?"

Joe nodded. "When was the last time you saw her?"

Carol thought for a moment. "Near Christmas."

"Christmas? That's over six months ago. Aren't you worried?"

"Joe, Cathy and I aren't close. I see her about three times a year." She paused and stared at Joe. "You look at me as though I'm an uncaring sister. But, it's not that. You don't know Cathy. I do.

"It's not unusual for her to be gone months at a time. She just disappears. She's done it since she was sixteen. She'd be gone for two or three months and then turn back up. I might get a card or a note. Sometimes nothing.

"You see, Cathy can go anywhere and get by on her looks. Beautiful, charming, sexy. Have you heard that she has the most gorgeous ass in Louisiana?"

Joe shook his head and frowned.

"Well, that's what they say at that exotic dance club where she works off and on—or I might say on and off. Can you imagine a woman doing that?"

Joe opened his eyes wide but said nothing.

"But I'm also not too worried because I've received two cards this time."

Here was news. Joe sat up straighter. "Where were they from?" he asked.

"She didn't say where she was?"

"No. Where were the cards mailed from?"

"Oh, that doesn't matter. Cathy always plays these little games. She picks up a card in one town, goes to another, gives it to some truck driver to mail from some place else. The cards and postmarks mean absolutely nothing."

"Well, I'm just curious. Did you keep them?"

Carol slid open her desk drawer and pulled out the two cards. "I used this Kentucky horse farm one for a writing project. Let's see, it was mailed from Denver. This other one is from Birmingham. It was mailed from Pensacola. Mailed a week apart. May 20 and May 27. They got here the same day though. How's that for the U. S. Mail?"

"Did she say anything that would tell you where she was?"

"Let's see. She says, 'We are traveling north.' So that means they were probably going south." She flipped over the other one. "It says to water her flower bed if I get the chance." She handed them to Joe.

The intercom buzzed and Dot's voice came through. "Ms. Sent, the Smiths are here for their four-thirty appointment."

"Thank you. I'll be right with them."

She turned back to Joe. "I'm sorry, Mr. Chapman . . . Joe. I'm going to have to get back on my appointment schedule. I wish you well in finding Cathy, but I'm afraid you're going to be disappointed. She likes younger men. Not that you're old or anything. She just likes someone she can mother, like that Kent hoodlum she's been seeing." She stood and started walking toward the door.

Joe started to get up. "Well, Carol—may I call you Carol?"

Carol nodded.

"Could I talk with you a little more tomorrow?"

Carol leaned over her desk and looked at her calendar book. "I'm sorry, Joe. I'm all booked." She paused for a moment and then turned to face him. "I'll tell you what. How about dinner tomorrow? We can talk while we eat." She picked up one of her business cards and wrote on the back. "This is the name of the place and the address. Is seven okay?"

Joe took the card and noticed Carol wasn't wearing a wedding ring. "Sure, that's great."

"This is not a date. Just talk. Got it? Dutch treat?"

"Yes. That'll help a lot. Thank you for your time."

Carol smiled. "Yeah, I want to help you find my sister—the girl with the perfect ass."

Joe nodded and walked out the doorway just as Dot was bringing in the Smiths, an unsmiling fiftyish couple.

Carol sat down and made a note on her daily calendar. She smiled when she wrote, "Meet Carp for dinner." Joe "Carp" Chapman—a handsome lawyer from Tennessee in search of her sister. Her mind went back to the many times in the past when she had brought a date home only to have him stolen away by Cathy's beauty and "perfect ass." If she heard that term one more time, she was going to explode. Maybe this time the tables would be turned. The knight who came looking for Cathy might be spirited away by Carol.

"A perfect ass," Mrs. Smith said, and Carol was brought back to the problems of the couple sitting across from her.

"What did you say?" Carol asked.

"I said my husband made a perfect ass of himself yesterday," Mrs. Smith said and pointed an accusing finger at her husband.

Twenty-six

J oe was back to *THE CARP* by six. The sun was two hours from setting and hung hotly over the river. He undressed and lounged in the sun on the deck of the boat, wearing only a pair of swimming trunks. J. R. eased up and lay beside him in his shade. He brought the contents of Cathy's purse back out to go over one more time along with what he had taken from her house.

He was getting close. George Potter at the balloon shop, Sean Bodine at Ace Bonding, Sir at the Classy Kitty Cat, the landlady,—oh, the ugly landlady—Cathy's house, and finally Carol Sent had inspired him on. All had been helpful in their own ways. There was more to come from Carol. She was a bit of a mystery herself.

He fingered the post office box key and felt the sharp serrated teeth. Now that he had an address, he would go to the nearest post offices and fill out the official form requesting a mailing address on her. There were two post offices about equi-distance from her house. He looked at the Saint Christopher's medal and hoped that the saint of travel had kept her safe in her journeys. Maybe her trip with Bartley was about over and she was heading home to Baton Rouge. Or, perhaps, as Bodine alluded to, she was in New Orleans and he would have to go there.

Would Carol go with him and help find her sister? He looked over toward the cabin. He would have to clean it up more. A woman of her dignity and standing would require more than he was used to.

He did not notice the two men who stepped onto the boat behind him until J. R. turned and growled.

"Are you Joe Chapman?" the taller one asked.

"Yes," Joe said and began to get to his feet. He patted J. R. "It's okay, boy. Sit," he told the dog. He turned to the men. "Who are you?"

"FBI. I'm Agent Florentine and he's Agent Rodriguez," the taller one said. They both flipped open wallets that displayed some type of badge. They closed them before Joe had time to look closer.

"What can I do for you?" Joe asked.

The shorter man kept his eyes trained on J. R. while the taller one did the talking. "We hear that you're looking for Cathy Pelton. We're after Kent Bartley. They're traveling together. We don't need anyone interfering with our investigation."

Joe felt his heart begin to beat faster. He clinched his jaw muscles. These two men were invading his space without invitation. He didn't believe they were FBI. "Oh, I see. My puny efforts at finding Cathy Pelton are going to hurt your investigation," he said and then spit toward the river.

"Some people get spooked as soon as they hear one person's looking for them, let alone several," Rodriguez said. "We just need to keep the search within law enforcement. Understand?" The tone was more threatening than questioning.

"I've been employed by the bondsman to bring Bartley back. I have papers. And I have a right to do it. Do you understand that? And let me see your badges again so I can write down your names and numbers. I'll check with the head of your office," Joe said in the same tone of voice that Rodriguez had used.

The short one lunged forward, grabbed Joe under the chin at the throat and pushed him to the cabin wall.

"Listen, you hillbilly bastard," he said and brought a pistol up to Joe's head with his free hand, "this is the only badge you're going to see. If we find out you're still snooping, you'll end up as alligator bait."

The taller man had also drawn his pistol but stayed where he was. He held his gun down to his side while Joe's adversary put his away. Then the shorter one slugged Joe in the stomach. Joe slid down the wall until he was sitting on the deck. J. R. growled and bared his teeth toward the men, while the hair on the back of his neck stood out. Joe weakly motioned the dog over to him. He tried to suck air into his deflated lungs. He was not anywhere near his weapons.

"I understand. I get the message," he said hoarsely and slumped over toward his knees.

"You better get the message, hick. Else we'll blow this piece of crap out of the water. I could just about kill that dog now," the shorter one said and took his pistol back out.

"No need for that," the taller one said and smiled. "He understands." They walked off the boat and didn't look back.

Joe reached out and wrapped his arm around J. R. Joe's knees shook and his breath came in short gasps. He looked toward the cabin door. He would never be without his pistol and Bowie knife again. He hadn't expected the sudden attack and wasn't ready. He'd be prepared the next time. And there would be a next time. Nobody threatened his dog and got away with it. Rodriguez and Florentine—or whoever they were—would pay.

Twenty–seven

J oe was up early with the rising sun the next morning. His sleep
had been spasmodic. He had killed the two men over and over in
different ways. They had questioned his Tennessee heritage and
threatened everything that belonged to him. They would not keep him
from his mission. If they were after Bartley, Cathy stood to get hurt
if she was in the way.

He looked in the mirror and saw slight bruising where his
throat had been clutched. There was a discoloration on his abdomen
where he had been hit. His eyes were puffy. He had let a punk about
half his age slam him into his own cabin's wall. Leverage. The short
guy had come up under him and taken him backwards. The punk
knew what he was doing. He would have to be more careful and
prepared. The .357 magnum fit snugly inside a light jogging jacket.

He looked at his calendar. Independence Day—July Fourth—
was the following Monday. He wanted Cathy on his boat by then. But
today he had things to do. He brought the card close to his eyes that
Carol had given him with the name of the restaurant. He could smell
the perfume where her hand had touched it.

While he jogged with J. R., he made a mental list of things to do before his dinner date. He needed holsters for his knife, his gun and the one Bodine had given him, and he would go to the post offices.

On his return to the boat, Joe fell onto the deck and did his pushups. At the warehouse, he found a heavy metal bar and did bench presses with it. The short guy was strong as a bull—he would give him that.

At a nearby gun shop, he bought holsters for both guns and his knife. He splurged and took ones that would have the guns at his side, on his chest, or at the base of his spine on his back. He bought three boxes of cartridges for each gun and practiced on the indoor firing range. He quickly got the feel for the .45 that Bodine had given him. By the time he returned to the Harley, the .357 was on his chest and the Bowie on his belt.

It was at the second branch post office that he struck gold. His request under the Freedom of Information Act was met with a reply that Cathy had a box just a few feet away—number 254. Joe looked at his lists of boxes he had already tried and saw it would have been another week before he would have found that box in his routine searches.

He didn't go immediately to it. He waited ten minutes and came back in when another clerk was near the counter. He had no authority to go into someone else's post office box even if he had the key. He didn't know how many laws he would be breaking, but they would be sufficient to keep him off the streets for quite some time.

He placed the key into the slot and pushed. It slid in like it was made for it, and when he turned it, the box popped open. It was stuffed with mail, and he could barely pry the mass out. When the box was empty, he took all the cards and envelopes to a table near a window and waste can. He began to discard ads, mailers addressed to "occupant," and announcements that Cathy was already a "winner" of some sweepstakes or the other.

Among all that was left were two yellow cards that were notices from the post office that other mail was being held that would not fit into the box. He glanced toward the counter. He couldn't take the chance of asking the clerk who had just given him Cathy's box number for her mail. That could wait. He turned back to what was left.

The dates on the postmarks showed that Cathy's box had filled before the middle of March and no other mail had been placed inside since. Then he noticed an envelope from the book shop in New Orleans where Cathy had shopped. He opened it. There was a book waiting for her that she had ordered. He looked back at the remaining mail. There was very little. A couple of credit card bills which showed only routine purchases in the Baton Rouge area before March.

Then another bill caught his eye. "U-Store-It," a company that rented self-storage units, was billing her for the months of April, May, and June for unit 124. Joe looked at the address. He had the urge to open her storage unit. He checked the remaining keys from her purse and noticed the same numerals scratched on one of them—a Yale brand.

He glanced back toward the main area of the post office and saw the clerk he dealt with leaving through the main door. This was his chance. He walked to the counter with the two notices.

He handed them to a clerk he had not seen before. "Box 254. My wife and I have been out of town for a while. Need to pick up her mail," he said and smiled. The worst that could happen would be that the clerk would tell him she would have to come back herself. But if he looked like he knew what he was doing—perhaps he could bluff them and get the mail.

The clerk didn't hesitate. He walked back to the metal shelving where they stored mail and brought out a box load. "You've must've been gone a while," the clerk said.

"Yeah, since the first of March. Thanks for holding it. If I can borrow your box, I'll bring it back in as soon as I empty it into my car." The clerk nodded. Joe carried the box to his Harley and poured the contents into the saddlebags. He would go through it later. He wanted to make his escape before the clerk became suspicious.

After he took the box back in, he kicked the Harley into a full throaty roar and was off to the storage unit before the door of the post office had time to fully close behind him. He hoped the unit had not been repossessed for non-payment of the rent.

When he eased up to the U-Store-It address, the gate was open. A sign indicated that unit holders had access anytime between 8 a.m. and 8 p.m. There were five rows of one-story block-type construction buildings. Each storage compartment opened onto a driveway area. Green numbers were attached to the centers of orange garage-type doors. The manager was located at the end of one row in a unit that had been converted from storage to office. Joe put his legs out as his Harley slowed. He scanned the doors for number 124.

When he found it, he leaned the cycle over on its stand near the door and felt for the keys. He looked all around the door for any signs of sealing. There were none. A single copper-colored Yale lock kept the contents safe, and he had the key. It, too, responded to his solicitation and popped open on the first turn. He took the lock off, pulled the hasp back, and slid the door upward.

The eight by ten foot compartment was not half full. He looked around first from outside. The heat that flooded out was worse than the bright sun where he stood. Joe shaded his eyes. There were a few pieces of old furniture, and at the back, a blue plastic tarp covered some bulky items that came halfway up the wall. Along the right wall a more conventional brown canvas tarpaulin hid some other objects. An oily, smoky aroma emanated from the canvas.

Joe walked in toward the back and lifted one corner of the blue plastic. Below were books. Cathy could start a library of her own or donate them to Goose Collins for his. He picked up a few and looked. There were old college books, ones on ballet, voodoo, and witchcraft. There was a whole stack on horses. More and more of what he had seen at her house.

When he pulled the tarp completely off, boxes of her other precious possessions came to light. Candle boxes. He stepped near and opened one. Cathy had forgotten about the heat of summer. She must have stored them in the winter, figuring to use them by summer. Candles that had once stood like stanchions of protection had been reduced to puddles of tallow or flaccid reminders of their firm past.

He sat down and went through all the boxes. Books and candles and magazines. Then there were two boxes of Girl Scout chocolate mint cookies. He shook his head and imagined what the contents would look like after a summer in Baton Rouge. He reached to pick one up and found it stuck to the book beneath—or at least it seemed glued to the book. But it was just unusually heavy. It was as though the cookies had been transformed by petrification into stone. Finally, he lifted one and set it on his knee.

When he opened the flap of the lid, the sparkle of gold met his eyes instead of dark chocolate. At first he thought they were play coins, but when he took one from the row, he saw that it was the approximate size of a U. S. silver dollar but was actually a South African Krugerrand. He took them out one by one and laid them in his hand. Thirty in one box and another thirty in the box beneath. Sixty pieces of gold.

His heart began to beat as fast as when he was attacked by the scoundrel the day before. He took the boxes and went to sit on the canvas tarp nearer the door where he could get some cooler air. No one was near, but he took caution to leave the coins on his side that would shield them from view.

The vision of Cathy in Memphis flashed through his mind. He took four of the coins and turned them on edge in the palm of one hand, holding them with the other. They looked like the wheels of the carriage she had ridden in and shined like they were newly made. He placed all but the four in his hand back into the boxes, put them where he found them, and recovered them with the blue tarp. He sat on the other tarp and considered what to do with them. He could give them to Carol . . . or place them on his boat . . . or turn them into cash. No, he would leave them. He had four. He'd take one to a coin shop and find out what they were worth.

He stood to leave. The oil of the tarp clung to one hand. He tried to wipe it off on his pants when he remembered he had not checked under that tarp. In the rush of finding gold, he cared little for what remained unless it was another box of Girl Scout gold.

He turned the tarp back and was struck by the sight of two bales. He leaned down and sniffed. It wasn't alfalfa. He broke some dried leaf off and looked at it in the sunshine. He was sure it was marijuana but not certain it was the same two bales that Bodine had mentioned Bartley was caught with. He knew one thing—Bartley had a key to Cathy's storage unit and had stored it without her knowledge. Maybe the gold was his too. Proceeds from his illegal trade.

Why hadn't the FBI or DEA found this already? Did they have the unit under surveillance, waiting to see who showed up to retrieve the pot or gold? Joe covered the bales back up with the tarp and walked to the door. He looked up and down along the rows of storage units. He saw no one. But if they were good, he didn't expect to see anyone. If they came in now, he would probably be charged with being in possession of the bales and sent away for a long time. He closed the door, relocked it, got on his cycle, and rolled slowly to the office at the end of the row.

"Can I help you?" the older lady behind the desk asked.

"Yes, I'm a friend of Cathy Pelton's. She has storage unit 124. She's still out of town and wanted me to check to see if she owes you anything for her space. When's it paid through?" Joe didn't feel he was lying by saying he was Cathy's friend. He had stretched the truth so often lately that his heart didn't flutter at the deception.

The lady raised her eyebrows and turned to a ledger book. "Well, let me check. Just a minute." Her index finger with bright red nail polish slid down two pages until she found the entry. "No, she's okay. Paid through October. We received her payment for six months' rent on the twenty-eighth of March."

Joe repeated the words. "Six months. March twenty-eighth."

"Yes." The lady smiled and closed the book. "I mailed her a receipt to her post office box. Didn't she receive it?"

"Probably not. She was out of town. She just called me to check . . . uh, to be sure you got it. How did she pay?"

The lady gave Joe a glare. "I would think she'd know how she paid." She looked back to the book. "Money order."

Joe bit his lip. No help. He couldn't trace a negotiated money order. He pushed it. "Did you keep the envelope it came in?"

The woman laughed. "Why?"

Joe knew the question sounded strange. He was grasping. He

turned and walked to the door. He looked back and smiled. "Thanks, ma'am. That's a nice dress you have on."

Two blocks before he reached Ace Bonding, Joe pulled into the parking lot of a coin and stamp shop.

"A friend of mine wanted to give me this coin to pay a debt," he told the man behind the glass counter and handed him the Krugerrand. "I don't know anything about coins. He owes me three hundred. Is this coin genuine and what's it worth?"

The man took the coin, rubbed his thumbnail across it, held it up to a chart on the wall behind him, and then handed it back to Joe. "Yep, it's a real Krugerrand. Prices fluctuate. Right now they're going for about three seventy-five. I prefer the Canadian Maple Leaf for gold. It's purer. Krugerrand has been as high as four fifty during the past year. If he owes you three hundred, it's a good deal."

"It is real though?"

"Oh, yeah. It's a goodun."

Joe's mind began to do the calculations as he walked back to the Harley. Sixty Krugerrands at four hundred, give or take a few dollars. Twenty-four thousand dollars in Girl Scout cookie boxes in Cathy's storage unit. And two bales of marijuana. No wonder they paid the rent in advance.

SEAN BODINE STUBBED OUT his Winston in the ashtray and lit another one immediately. He listened to the DEA agent from Mobile. He never felt at ease with the feds even though they usually wanted the same thing he did—the return of some bail jumper. He was more comfortable with the locals with whom he could have a beer. These DEA and FBI agents were all business. They didn't seem to have a sense of humor.

He looked at the card while the agent talked. George Stephens, DEA, Mobile, Alabama, had an interest in Kent Bartley. That was interesting since the crime he jumped on was a state and not a federal charge.

"We're anxious to help you find Bartley, Mr. Bodine, because we have some questions to ask him about other incidents." Stephens looked into the file that Bodine had handed across to him.

"Yeah. You must think he's done something bigger than this little caper."

"I came to you first because I know you're concerned about Bartley's return. I'm going to chat with the D. A. next. Does Bartley have any family around here?"

Bodine shook his head. "No. That's the problem. He's an orphan. Raised in a group home. Usually I can just sit around mom's or pop's and they show up after they get tired of Daytona or Galveston.

These runners usually come home to get money or food. And I can remind the relative what they have to lose if they've signed the bond or if they're harboring a fugitive.

"They say blood's thicker than water. But I can tell you money's thicker than blood. A mother will turn her son back in if she's going to lose her house. She believes he's innocent and will be set free just as soon as there's a trial." Bodine laughed. "I've hired someone to look for Bartley full time. Lawyer from Tennessee. He's out checking now."

Joe Chapman stepped through the doorway just as Bodine was mentioning him.

"Hell. Here he is now. He's a damn good investigator." He waved Joe over. "Joe Chapman, I want you to meet George Stephens. Stephens is with the DEA out of Mobile. He's looking for Bartley too."

Stephens stood to shake hands with Joe. He looked down at the back of the motorcycle helmet that Joe held in the crook of his left arm. "Good to meet you. What does that *Carp* mean on the back of your helmet?"

Joe glanced down at the gold lettered name that Keith had painted on his helmet in Paducah. "Oh, that's my nickname. A friend—an artist—did that."

"Have any luck, Joe?" Bodine asked. They all sat down.

Joe eyed the agent and then looked at Bodine. He shook his head. "No. Seems Bartley just vanished. Maybe it's like you said. He could've headed for New Orleans."

"What about the girl?" Bodine asked.

"No. Nothing there either. Just gone."

Joe opened his wallet and removed a card. "You're from Mobile, Agent Stephens?"

Stephens nodded.

"Do you know a John Collins?"

Stephens's jaw dropped only slightly. He took the card from Joe and looked at it. "Yes. John Collins is my partner. He's the one who asked me to come over. How do you know him?"

Joe smiled, took the card, and put it back into his wallet. "Met him at his father's farm in Alabama. They rescued my boat from a sand bar. Nice family. But don't ever let his dad invite you to church unless you know a song you can sing."

"So you know some DEA in Mobile, Joe. You've got to tell me more," Bodine said.

"Did you all ever find out about that plane that went down out in Mobile Bay that his father mentioned?"

Stephens's mouth came open a little wider. "No. That's pretty stale." He handed the file back to Bodine and stood to leave. "I have to go to some other places. Keep us informed on Bartley. Be careful. We don't know what he's up to. We need to talk with him." He handed Joe a business card. "I'll tell Agent Collins that I ran into you, Mr. Chapman. I'm sure he'll be happy to hear that you think so highly of his family."

Bodine and Joe watched Stephens get into his car and pull away from the curb.

"Now tell me what you really found out, Joe." Bodine lit another cigarette.

Joe gave a five-minute run down of his discoveries of the past day and a half. The post office, the storage compartment, the gold, the marijuana, and the attack by the two goons were all laid before the hawk-nosed bondsman as though he would have an answer. Instead, Bodine rolled his eyes to the ceiling, put the half-smoked cigarette in the ashtray, and lit another.

"Twenty-four thousand in gold and two bales of pot? That Bartley and your queen, Cathy, sure are up to no good if you ask me." He stood, walked to the door, locked it, pulled the shade down over the glass, and walked back to Joe. "You know with the DEA and those two guys you ran into looking for him, Bartley must be into more than my bond covers him for."

"Look at what I'm wearing now," Joe said, stood, and pulled his jacket up. "I'm packing. I'm not going to take any shit from anybody again." He held the Bowie up to Bodine's eyes. "This is a nut cutter."

Bodine went back to his chair. "You'd better be careful. I don't know who we're playing against or who Bartley has made mad at him."

Joe put his knife away and sat down across from Bodine. "I have a date with Cathy's sister tonight—not really a date, just dinner. She's not bad looking. Kind of interesting to talk with. But I've got to stay focused on Cathy and find your Bartley in the process."

"A date?" Bodine smiled and his long eyelashes flickered. He got up and paced the floor and then sat near the shaded window next to the door. He motioned Joe to come over and whispered, "New Orleans is a good bet. The French Quarter. You ought to go down there to that book store you mentioned had sent the note. She might have picked the book up or they may have seen her."

"Well, maybe after I find out all I can from Cathy's sister. If I could take her with me—if she would go—it could make it easier to track down Cathy. Someone might tell a sister something a lot sooner than they would me."

"Right. You can persuade her. You're tall, dark, and . . . a good talker," Bodine said and laughed. "She might like to go to New Orleans with you for the weekend, if you get my drift."

"No, I'm not interested in that. I want her sister. I've sworn off women until I find Cathy."

Bodine shook his head. "Any port in a storm."

"What else do you know about Bartley?" Joe asked.

Bodine leaned near Joe, almost knee to knee. "He's a streetwise, creative kid. Not much formal education. But he knows how to get things done. He knows how to disappear. I've had him on a few minor things before.

"He can create a new identity. He talked to me one time about checking cemeteries and obituaries for dead people's names. He'd go to a college and take a student's Social Security number off some posted test score. He would just buy someone's driver's license.

"He can drive anything. Cars, boats, cycles, airplanes. He took up flying last year at a little airport out here. Gave them a bad check is how I know.

"If you find him, Joe, be careful. He's never been charged with anything more violent than a fist fight. But he looks to me like somebody who wouldn't blink if he wanted to shoot you. He has no emotion. No guilt. No sense of right and wrong. Probably a good candidate for an insanity plea."

Joe stood and stretched. He looked at his watch. "I've got to get ready for dinner, Bodine. Bartley sounds pretty crazy. I wonder what my Cathy sees in him?"

Bodine turned and peeked behind the shade out the window. "He's an outlaw. Lots of women are attracted to that type. Living on the edge. Excitement. Don't make good sense. But that's why folks like you and me have jobs."

Joe nodded his head. "I guess."

"Why were you asking that agent about a plane in Mobile Bay?"

"Oh. His partner's father mentioned it when I was visiting. Agent Collins didn't want to talk about it then. And did you see how this guy's face turned pale when he heard me ask about it? I just wanted him to know . . . that I knew. He's going to have to go into training if he wants to be a poker player."

Twenty–eight

O akwood Plantation House and Restaurant was a recently constructed building that resembled on the outside the type of house that its name suggested and for which Louisiana is famous. Wide verandas swept around the front and sides of the white boarded structure where patrons sat in rocking chairs or swings waiting for their names to be called for seating. There they could sip iced tea or mint juleps below the slowly turning electric ceiling fans that stirred the air enough to make it bearable.

The front approach to the restaurant was by way of a bricklined path that serpentined its way beneath a canopy of moss-draped oak trees. It ended at steps that ascended to the porch between white brick columns.

Joe Chapman's Harley looked out of place parked among the Volvos, Porches, Jaguars, and Cadillacs. He looked around and decided to chain his helmet to the sissy bar anyway. There was no telling who'd want to try on his helmet and sit on his cycle just to get the "feel of the road." He stooped down and brushed his hair back by his reflection in the side window of a Corvette. He adjusted his jacket collar, smoothed down his windswept eyebrows, and made his way across the parking lot, along the brick path, and up the steps.

Carol Sent awaited him, sipping iced tea in a swing on the veranda. "Mr. Chapman . . . Joe, I mean," she said and waved when he reached the top.

"This is nice, Carol," Joe said and looked around. The vantage point of the elevated porch gave him a view of the manicured lawn where dark greens were highlighted with the bright colors of giant marigolds and a scattering of what appeared to be wild roses. A small pond to the side was occupied by ducks and fish that could be thrown scraps of bread from the porch by youngsters. He sat in the swing beside her, careful not to touch, and looked around at the other diners. They were talking quietly or sipping their favorite drinks. Occasional giggles or low laughter rose and fell like ocean waves on a calm day as stories were told or the day's accomplishments recounted.

"They said it would be about a half hour before we could be seated. Would you care for some tea or something stronger? They have a young man who makes the rounds."

"Tea will be fine," Joe said. He looked at Carol. She was more relaxed and dressed more casually than the day before. A cool yellow sundress showed more of her arms, and a slightly scooping neckline indicated that she did indeed have breasts. Her lipstick and fingernail polish were of a softer hue. Carol dressed for the occasion. Here she wasn't in the office atmosphere where she had to appear in charge. Here she was just another young woman ready for a pleasant dinner.

"How are you able to take a whole summer off and look for my sister? You said you were a lawyer, didn't you?" she asked.

The young waiter handed Joe a glass of iced tea. He squeezed the lemon wedge and watched the droplets filter down through the amber liquid while he pondered his answer. He didn't like hard questions. The truth was embarrassing. He did as he had always done. He deflected with humor. "I'm on a sabbatical." He smiled and watched her face for a reaction.

"A sabbatical? I thought that was something professors or men of the cloth took."

"Yes. That was the original intent. I just expanded it. Take one year off after every six years of working. I'm entitled to two from my law practice, but I'm just taking one."

Carol looked toward the yard. "That's an interesting concept. I only have four years in practice, so I couldn't take one for another couple of years."

"Yeah. But you need to work up to it. You should take a week or two or a month off soon, so that you'd know what to do with a year when it gets here. We could look for Cathy together." There, he had said it. He had laid the groundwork. Maybe she would go to New Orleans with him. She needed to find her sister as much as he did.

"I haven't had any time off since I started counseling. I've thought about it. But I have to look out for my clients. If I'm gone, they still need care. We have someone else at the clinic and someone else across town that I could refer to, but then my clients might decide they like the other therapists better."

She had ignored his reference to looking for Cathy together. At least she had not said "No." For the next half hour until they were seated for dinner, Joe and Carol never again mentioned Cathy by name or implication. Light and non-specific conversation was the tone for the veranda. Joe preferred it.

"I hope you like Cajun cooking. That's about all they have here."

"It'll be fine. I like to try different dishes. What do you recommend?" He looked down at the words on the menu that meant very little to him.

"Crawfish jambalaya with a bowl of their special gumbo would be good for a beginner," Carol said.

"I'll take your word for it," he said and closed the menu. The waiter took their orders with Carol having the same thing she had recommended. Joe took another sip of his tea and looked across the table at Carol. "Can you tell me more about Cathy?"

"Cathy? Oh, yes, Cathy. I almost forgot why we're here. You're still looking for my little sister, the beautiful redhead with the perfect . . ." Carol waited for Joe to finish the phrase. He just looked at her and smiled. "Did you find out much today?"

"No. Practically nothing," Joe said and glanced at his hands to see if any of the gold from the coins had rubbed off.

"We're not full sisters. We had the same mother but different fathers."

"Okay, that explains your different last names."

"Not altogether. I've been married. Sent is my married name. I've been divorced for two years."

The waiter brought the gumbo and a loaf of bread which he sliced for them at the table. Joe stirred and looked deep into the liquid.

Carol watched his eyes. "I know what you're thinking. 'How can she be a marriage and family counselor and be divorced herself?' Well, it's simple. Lawyers don't win all their cases and sometimes get sued themselves. Doctors get sick. And some counselors have failed marriages. The fact that the marriage failed doesn't mean that the person is a failure." She said it as though she had practiced it a hundred times and was almost convinced of its truth.

"Very well put. But that wasn't what I was thinking. I was wondering why you didn't take your name back. Do you have children by your former husband?"

"No. I just retained the name because I was already professionally known as Carol Sent and it would be confusing to change it. I don't intend to get married again, so I'll always be Carol Sent."

"You've given up on marriage . . . and love?" Joe took a spoonful of gumbo.

"Marriage for me, yes. Love . . . I'm not sure if I'd know it if it infected me again."

Joe laughed. "You have a way with words."

"Thanks. I've just joined a writing class at LSU where I go once a week. I'm trying to express myself better."

"You're having success."

They finished their bowls of gumbo and the waiter arrived with the heaping plates of jambalaya. Joe leaned over to smell the aroma wafting up from the brown rice layered with crawfish. A bowl of red sauce waited at the side of the plate. The waiter put down another loaf of bread.

"Do you like crawfish?" she asked and poured a little sauce over a portion of hers.

"I do . . . as fish bait," Joe said and lifted one of the creatures from the mass of rice.

"Just think of them as inland shrimp with a little earthy taste. Your nickname is Carp, so you know how some things get a bad name."

"Carp deserve it," Joe answered and took a mouthful of rice and a portion of crawfish. He chewed and swallowed. "I used to catch crawfish back home in drainpipes to use for bait. They're fast little devils. I never thought of eating them though."

"These are more domesticated. They feed them and fatten them up on farms. Aren't carp a type of catfish?"

"They don't have whiskers like catfish. They're not closely related. Very lowly esteemed. I wouldn't put them in the same family, but a biologist might. I'm not sure."

"Lowly esteemed, huh?" Carol said and pushed the bread plate toward Joe. "You need more bread?"

He nibbled around the plate, picking up the fleshy parts of the crawfish with helpings of rice that would neutralize any foreign tastes.

"I am to Cathy what carp are to catfish," Carol said.

"Welcome aboard, but I might warn you that the title is already taken."

"Cathy is the talented child. I was the one who had to work twice as hard to achieve. She seemed to have a natural talent for dance, the piano, just about anything she wanted to do.

"Once she got to be twelve years old, all the guys started to hang around her. I became a nobody. Her beauty is notorious. You might want to talk to the people at the city ballet. Maybe somebody at the beauty pageant office. Who knows, she might keep in touch with them. She doesn't with me. She got into horses during the last year. Went to some horse farm outside the city."

"What about this Bartley fellow? How'd she hook up with him?"

"She's trying to be a mother without giving birth. When we were home, everyone she dragged home was some pathetic case. They were either going to or coming from a juvenile detention center—or on work release if an adult."

"Have you ever met Kent Bartley?" Joe asked, tore off a piece of bread, and dabbed at the sauce.

"Once. He didn't speak to me, and I didn't speak to him, if you call that meeting. I could tell at first sight that he was no good. That's a lousy way to judge people, but it works as often as not. Can't tell Cathy anything. She thinks these imbeciles are angels that everybody's mistreated."

There were periods of silence over the next few minutes while Joe digested what Carol told him about Cathy. He also thought about what she was saying about Carol. He found little that would aid him in locating his Cathy, but he was developing a nagging need to bring Carol into the search with him. She was becoming comfortable to be around. She didn't put on airs of a psychiatrist or psychologist. Of course, she wasn't.

Then she turned the conversation toward him and became more of an inquisitor. He told her about his divorce, bankruptcy, and *sabbatical* that was not voluntary but had been recommended by the lawyers' board. He didn't give all the details, just the general drift of how things had gone.

Carol smiled. "Well, if you were ten years younger, I'm sure you would be a perfect candidate to be latched onto by Cathy. You're about as down and out as you can get without a criminal record, if you don't mind me saying so. You have no criminal record, do you?"

Joe shook his head while cataloguing in his mind all the offenses he had committed that could have led to a criminal record. He had told her things that he wouldn't have thought about telling somebody else over dinner. She was smooth. She had a way of setting him at ease. She must be good at what she did.

Carol took the paper placemat, turned it over, and started drawing on it, doing blocks and ovals. She connected them with lines and turned back to Joe to get more information.

"What are you doing?"

"It's a diagram of your family history from what you've told me. It's called a genogram. This one is very rudimentary. You can go back several generations to see what forces account for what you are, to an extent—how different people in your family and what they did and didn't do affected you in the long run. You are at least partly a product of your family history." She looked up and turned the placemat around. "I don't have all of yours, but this is a start."

"It doesn't look like much."

"Well, it will once I fill in the details. I need to put in all the divorces, incestuous relations, alcoholics, drug abusers, anything that might have impacted on you."

"You think I have all that in my family history?"

"Most people do to some degree or other. Or else they've done a real good job at denial. I do this for all my clients."

"I'm not your client though."

"Right. It'd be unethical to go out . . . to engage in a social occasion . . . to have dinner with a client." A slight tinge of crimson began to move up her neck. She folded the placemat and put it in her purse. "I'll finish this later. I'll tell you about Cathy, but you have to tell me about you. I can't turn my sister over to someone I don't know anything about even if your intentions are honorable."

They finished the jambalaya and the waiter came and took their plates. "Would you care for any dessert?"

"Just a small bowl of orange sherbet. You want some too, Joe?"

Joe nodded.

"Did you always want to be a lawyer?"

"No. I wanted to be a spy or work with the FBI or CIA. I was an electronics whiz in high school. Majored in electrical engineering in college. Thought I'd combine it with law. Then I saw that I might be able to do some good in my home town and started a small law firm with my friend. I still dabble in electronics. I put in a security and monitoring system for my friend who is now the attorney general. I could have left a bug at your office yesterday. They're so small, you know."

"You wouldn't do that, would you?"

"Not to Cathy's sister." The waiter placed their bowls of sherbet in front of them. "Did you always want to be a marriage and family therapist?"

"No. I wanted to be an astronaut. But I was too out of shape and too old when I decided."

"Too old? When did you decide?"

"Last week."

Joe smiled. "Anything else?"

"Yes. I counseled the dying. I studied a lot about it and worked in a hospital setting for a while. It turned out it wasn't for me. I lost all my clients. I wasn't sure I was doing any good."

"I'm sure you were."

Carol nodded. "Maybe. I hope so. Death is something we all have to face. Have you ever been close to dying, Joe?"

It wasn't something he liked to think about. He wanted to live forever. Samson died heroically. He brought down the Philistines' temple and killed more in his death than his life. Joe looked down at the orange mound of sherbet and studied the little rivulet of liquid that edged down the side.

"One time," he said, "I had a real bad case of food poisoning. I puked my guts out for five hours. I thought I was going to die. Then after barfing for three more hours, I was afraid I wasn't going to die." He looked up. Had his attempt at humor swayed her from her question?

"No. I mean have you ever been really in fear of dying? You're always trying to make a joke."

Joe let his mind wander back over the years. He knew where

he was going but he didn't want to walk those paths. He had tried to bury them deep inside his subconscious because they still frightened him. Until his nighttime visions had been replaced with Cathy, he often dreamed about them. He had looked death in the jaws and seen the flames of mortality leap about him and survived. He would recount one for the therapist. Maybe she could help him exorcise it from his memory. And if that one, then he would tell her the other. If she could find a place for them on the diagram of ovals and squares, maybe she could point him toward the source of evil spirits that occupied his thirty-nine year old body from time to time.

"Okay. You sure you want to hear this?" He looked her in the eyes. She nodded.

"In London County where I live, there are some bootleggers still selling homebrew. Ten years ago, I was defending a man accused of attempted murder. One of these bootleggers was supposed to be a witness, and I drove my old pickup truck out to see him. He lived in a little shack back up a hollow. There were no nearby neighbors, no electricity, no telephones— just out in nowhere."

Joe looked at Carol to see if she was listening. "You want me to continue?" She nodded and took a spoonful of sherbet.

"Well, there was this sign on the old rickety gate that said 'Beware of Dog.' I didn't pay any attention because half the people in the county have a sign like that. Anyway, I went in the yard and yelled out for the old man I was looking for. He didn't answer.

"Then, all of a sudden, I saw this blur flying through the air to my left. There was no barking, no growling, no nothing. Just this slick-haired beast coming through the air toward my neck. I instinctively raised by left arm to block him from my neck, and he latched onto it in mid-air. When he fell toward the ground, he still had my arm and almost took me with him. He wouldn't turn loose, and I could feel and hear my skin being ripped and what sounded like a bone popping."

Joe looked around the room and leaned closer to Carol. He continued in a loud whisper.

"But I knew better than to go to the ground with a pit bull. All they want is a chance to get you by the throat. I struggled to stay on my feet. We were doing this dance of death, him and me. He wouldn't let go of my arm, and I wouldn't fall down. Every time his back feet hit the ground, he'd try to jump toward my neck, but he wouldn't exchange the grip on my arm unless he was sure he was going to get my throat. His gigantic jaws were clamping down on my arm like a vice and he kept increasing the pressure.

"I tried to swing him off by turning around quickly. But he just loved that. He was probably trained on an old tire chained to a tree that I noticed while we were doing this. Anyway, I kept swinging and hitting him with my right fist. He didn't even seem to notice. It was no more than a feather duster to him. Blood was running down my arm to the ground. I looked for a rock or big stick nearby but there was nothing. I gouged him in the eyes with my fingers. That didn't work. At that point I knew one of us was going to have to die to give the other one some relief."

Joe paused and took a bite of orange sherbet.

"Go on. What happened? Did the owner come?"

"I started to have this crazy thought. I could see me in a casket with the other lawyers filing by. They were pointing and saying I had been killed by a dog.

"About that time the old bootlegger came around the corner of his shack and just stood there watching his dog chew on my arm. He leaned against a tree and started to smoke a cigarette. He didn't say a damn word, and I was there pleading for my life. That really made me angry.

"Finally, in desperation, I took the only thing I had on me, a Bic pen, from my shirt pocket. I took the top off with my teeth and held it like an ice pick in my right hand. I stabbed that old dog with it, and it took about ten times before I hit him in the eye. It stuck, and I pushed it all the way in until it punctured his brain.

"All kinds of gore came out of his eye socket, but he was still holding onto my arm. His body quivered a little, and I could tell he was gone. But even in death, he didn't release. I had to go to the ground and pry his jaws apart to get my arm out.

"Then I thought the dog might have rabies. So I carried him to my truck and threw his carcass in the back. I came back inside the gate and backhanded the old man and dragged him to the truck too. I threw him in the back with his dead dog and headed off to the emergency room with blood running down my arm into my shoe.

"My arm was broken. I had nerve damage and went through six months' rehabilitation. The dog didn't have rabies. I had his head mounted and gave it to my friend, Charlie Palk, who I always thought looked like a bulldog.

"That's as close as I've come to death. What do you think? Do you want the rest of your sherbet?"

Carol's lipstick looked brighter now against her paler face. She shook her head slowly from side to side.

"I still carry a Bic pen," Joe said and took one from his shirt pocket.

"Excuse me. I need to go to the restroom," Carol said and hurriedly left the table. She put a hand to her mouth.

When she returned, Joe had finished his sherbet. "I hope that story didn't bother you. You said you wanted me to be frank, right?"

"No, no, it didn't bother me. And, yes, you have to be truthful. I appreciate it."

"You know what I learned from that incident?"

"No. Do I want to know?"

"First, you can't fight fair when you're fighting with a mad dog. And, secondly, never be without a Bic pen. Medium point. I bought five shares of stock in the company and sent them a note about what happened. I thought they might could use it. But I guess it wasn't the type of endorsement story they wanted. They did send me a package of pens though. Free."

The waiter brought separate checks. Carol picked hers up.

"Carol," Joe began in a low whisper, "could we do this again tomorrow? I promise I won't tell any dog stories. I'll give you some more information for my genogram, and you tell me more about Cathy. Could you go to New Orleans with me to look for Cathy? She *is* your sister. I think I might have a lead on her there."

"New Orleans? I don't think so. When? This is all happening too fast. She is my sister, but she probably doesn't care for me looking for her." She reached in her purse, took another card, and wrote a name of another restaurant on it. "This place has barbecue and a live band. Tomorrow at the same time. I'll think about New Orleans. When are you going?"

"Maybe tomorrow night after dinner. We could take the boat."

They walked out together to where Joe's Harley was parked.

"That's a nice machine," Carol said and rubbed the seat. "Very nice color."

"Come ready to ride tomorrow night. Pack a bag and we'll go down the river on the boat. You'll be safe and be back after the Monday holiday."

Carol smiled and barely shook her head. Joe walked her to her Volvo. He opened the door, and she got in. "I'll see you tomorrow at the restaurant," she said and closed the door.

She started the engine and turned on the air conditioner to full power. She watched Joe kick the Harley to life and listened to the low growl when the cycle passed by. He waved.

She hated the term "falling in love." How many times had she rolled her eyes to the ceiling when clients used the phrase. But now her hands were trembling and it wasn't because of the heat that the cooling was just now overcoming. She had felt the fire of this strange lawyer from Tennessee who was searching for her sister. His wit, charm, and smile, overcame his crudeness.

What was she going to do?

Twenty–nine

T wo men stood on the bow of *THE CARP* the next morning when Joe awoke to a chorus of barking from J. R. He saw them sweating in the early morning heat of riverside Baton Rouge despite the light colored suits they wore. Joe pushed the curtain back across the small window and reached for the .45 Bodine had loaned him. He rolled out of bed and went to the cabin door.

They weren't Rodriguez and Florentine.

When they saw the gun that he held to his side, the two men flashed open their suit coats and displayed their own weaponry. "We're DEA!" they shouted simultaneously. "We're here to ask a few questions. You don't need that gun. Put it down."

"I need to see some I. D." Joe said and kept the gun at his side. They walked toward him and flashed their badges. Joe examined them closely. They looked legit. He laid his .45 on the chair next to the door but kept his back to them where, at the base of his spine, was holstered the .357 magnum.

"You know Agent George Stephens?"

"Yes. Out of Mobile."

"John Collins?"

"The same. Mobile."

"FBI agents Rodriguez and Florentine?"

The DEA men looked at each other and shook their heads.

"That's okay. They probably weren't real agents. What do you want?" He didn't feel comfortable with them but had no reason to believe they weren't who they said they were. He wanted them to get their business over and get off his boat. He was tired of uninvited guests. The boat had to be made ready for Carol.

He listened to them. It was the same story. They were looking for Kent Bartley, and it would be a good idea to limit the search to federal officers. They didn't need any bounty hunters getting in their way. Joe showed them his papers from Bodine, but they ended up where they had begun—a stalemate.

"You say you're from the New Orleans office. Why are New

Orleans and Mobile both interested in Bartley?"

"Two different crimes. Mobile has an interest in something that went down over there. We're covering the charges here."

"Seems a mighty petty crime for the DEA to be that interested. Is there more? What happened to that marijuana he was supposed to have had when he was arrested?"

"Wasn't any. The report was wrong," the shorter one said.

Joe looked him in the eye. Something was up. He knew where the pot was. "Leave me your cards, and I'll let you know if I find him."

They obliged. His DEA cards were growing into a small collection. He added Floyd Miles and Mike Constanzo to the ones in his wallet of George Stephens and John Collins. Maybe someday they would be worth something like baseball cards—depending on what these agents scored.

Joe got into his morning exercise routine as soon as the agents left. He and J. R. ran along the levee. He stopped and did pull-ups on the gym set, ran some more, did his push-ups, bench pressed the heavy metal bar, and fell exhausted onto the deck of the boat. J. R. came up and gave him a wet lick across the nose.

"She did a wonderful job for us," the slender old lady with a face like a walnut told Joe at the office of the city ballet. She slowly rotated a large marking pen in her hand while she considered her next words. "Of course, we had to request her departure when we learned of her avocation. Our sponsors did not approve."

"You mean her dancing at the Classy Kitty Cat?"

She acted like she didn't hear. "She had such graceful and beautiful movements for a girl of her proportions. It was quite unusual."

"Proportions?" Joe asked.

The lady leaned forward and whispered. "Most ballerinas are practically flat-chested. Cathy isn't. But she was never encumbered or handicapped by that. I suppose it is a matter of balance and movement," she continued and put a curled index finger to her mouth. She appeared to be thinking out loud. "Large breasts probably are not ideal because of inertia."

"Large breasts?" Joe thought back to what Sir at the club had told him about Cathy's breasts. He said they were small. It was probably a matter of comparison. For a stripper they were small. For a ballerina they were large. Just right for Joe Chapman.

An older gentleman walked in. He was dressed in a suit with a vest, held an unlit pipe between his teeth, just below a mustache that tended toward a handlebar.

"This young man is asking about Cathy. You remember Cathy, don't you, Horace?"

"Indeed. Are you a relative?"

"No. Just a friend of her sister's. Cathy's disappeared and no one's heard from her for several months."

The old man puffed on the unlit pipe. "Awful. I'll walk you out."

When they were outside, the old man turned to Joe. "I hope you find her. I was against them making her leave. She's a wonderful girl . . . and has legs and an ass that just won't quit." He winked at Joe. "When she performed we had standing room only. Now we're lucky to get a hundred old turds and turdettes out for a show. If you find her, tell her that Horace was asking about her."

At the Miss Baton Rouge office the story was the same. It had come as a shock that the nice little Cathy worked at the Classy Kitty Cat. She had been ahead on the preliminary judging when word got to the officials.

"We have a morals clause in our contract. That covers things like the girls having posed nude for magazines, having been convicted of some crime, or in this case dancing at the Classy Kitty Cat. When we learned of it, we had no choice.

"I must say though, Cathy took it like a real lady. She didn't want to embarrass the organization. She admitted it and stepped down without raising a ruckus," the dark haired lady told Joe while she busied herself arranging a display of stand-up posters of former winners. "This is a year-round job. We'll be choosing this year's winner next month."

"Would you happen to have any photos of Cathy?"

"Well, it's been three years." She went to a filing cabinet and started looking in folders. "This is her. We take photos of them in their evening gowns, bathing suits, and at their talent. She played the piano. Would you like one?" She laid them on the desk in front of Joe.

"Could I have one of each?"

"I suppose so. We shouldn't have any need for them."

TWO O'CLOCK IN THE afternoon was a slow time at the horse farm. All the rentable horses except one were in the stable, out of the hot afternoon sunshine. There they munched on grain and hay and swatted flies with their tails.

"Cathy Pelton? Sure, I remember Cathy. Anybody who saw her would remember her," the manager said and chewed on a stem from a piece of hay. He tilted the large straw hat back and took a ledger book from where it hung by one of the stable doors. "It doesn't seem like that long since she was here. Here it is. Well, it's longer than I thought. December fifteenth. She rode Diablo. That's her favorite," he said, pointing to a chestnut colored horse two stalls down that had a blaze down its nose.

"Did she ride often?" Joe asked.

"Quite a bit once she got into it. She would come out here in her tight beige riding pants, calf-high boots, a riding jacket, and even a rider's cap. She did it up right. I had to warn her the first time she rode about the Absalom Syndrome, as I call it."

"What is that?"

"Remember Absalom? He was King David's son who rebelled against him. He had real long hair, and when he was riding through the forest, his hair caught in a tree. His father's soldiers came along and found him just swinging there by the hair of his head. They killed him. So, I call that the Absalom Syndrome in the horse business.

"Cathy has such pretty long hair. The first time she came out here it was hanging down to her waist. I told her she couldn't ride that way. It might get caught in something and pull her off the horse. Or break her neck. Anyway, she was quite appreciative, and after that she always wore it in a bun when she rode."

"Did she ever ride with anybody?" Joe asked.

"No, always alone. Some men followed her around. But she never took up with any of them."

THE LITTLE AIRPORT OUTSIDE Baton Rouge hangered twenty planes, mainly single-engine low powered models, for local residents who flew as a hobby. A twin engine Bonanza and a twin engine Piper sat away from the others and nearer the office and maintenance area.

"Kent Bartley? I haven't seen Kent since December," the paunchy old man with thin white hair told Joe. He leaned down and tried to light a cherrywood pipe. "Kent is a wheeler-dealer in his own mind. He told me he was going to start a charter flight business as soon as he became instrument proficient on multi-engines. Said he was going to buy a Bonanza twin engine and fly between here and the Bahamas."

"Did he ever buy one?" Joe asked and watched a pilot practicing touch and go on the runway.

"Naw. Kent couldn't afford the proverbial 'pot to piss in,' " the manager said and took a deep draw on the pipe. "I don't know how he afforded flight lessons. He shot a good line of bull."

"Could he fly?"

"Oh, yes. He was a quick learner. He got his multi-engine instrument rating in December. He could fly that Bonanza or Piper, either one. He couldn't afford to buy one though."

"And you haven't seen him since December?"

"Yep, that's right. Except in the newspaper. I saw where he was arrested for having a little coke—back in January, I believe."

CAROL SENT PACKED HER bags. She would have them in her car just in case. She would have to feel safe, very safe, to take off to New Orleans with Joe Chapman. He seemed harmless enough. But even a serial killer could seem harmless enough on a couple of occasions. And that was all she had to measure him by. A visit in her office and the dinner of jambalaya. This evening she would know. She packed enough clothes for a three day stay. She had talked to Dot, her receptionist, about it. She had been all for it. Dot was a romantic at heart. She had looked at her schedule for the following week. It was slow. A lot of people gone for the holiday. The other therapist would cover for her if she had to stay longer than the weekend.

It felt like the right thing to do. Cathy had been gone longer than usual. She was the only family Carol had left. They had to look out for each other. She was her sister's keeper whether she wanted the job or not. And there was the bonus. Maybe this Joe Chapman wouldn't be so bad to get to know.

TONIGHT JOE WOULD BE leaving for New Orleans. There was nothing to gain by staying in Baton Rouge. He knew more about Cathy now, but nothing he had learned pointed to where she was. He would revisit three places before he left, starting with the landlady.

"Any word from Cathy?" Joe asked and stood back from the door.

"No. Nothing new," the landlady said. She took a drink from a beer can and smiled. "You want to come in?"

"Did you see her leave?"

"Yeah. Her and Bartley. They took her Mustang and were pulling a U-Haul trailer. I didn't see her load very much. Just one suitcase and her baton from high school. I don't know why they needed a trailer."

JOE CYCLED OVER TO the storage unit and retrieved the remaining gold Krugerrands. He put them in the saddlebags over Cathy's mail he had not yet sorted. If he found Cathy, she might need some cash. It would be just as safe on *THE CARP* as it would at the storage building.

SEAN BODINE WAS INTO his second pack of Winstons by the time Joe came to the office.

"The trail's dead around here. I'm boating down to New Orleans tonight. I believe you're right. She's probably hiding out there with Bartley. Plenty of agents checking into it. Have you heard anything?"

"No." Bodine blew smoke rings toward the ceiling. "An assistant D. A. downtown called me this morning. Said they had heard some rumor about Bartley. Wouldn't say anything else."

"Did you get his name?"

"Fontaine," Bodine said and slid a note pad over to Joe.

"That's good. My best friend is the district attorney up where I'm from. I might call him and ask a favor. He probably could get some information through the Baton Rouge D. A. I need to call him anyway."

"How're you doing with Cathy's sister?"

"Depends on what you mean. Lots of information. No sex." Joe looked at his watch. "I've got to go. I'll keep in touch. Let's hope for the best."

"Be careful, my friend," Bodine said and bowed deeply at the waist.

BACK ON THE BOAT, Joe emptied the saddlebags of the gold coins and stored them beneath his bed. He took out all the mail and sorted through it—all junk, except for a credit card bill. He tore it open and ran his finger down the list of charges. There were only two and they were both made in March. The first one was for a hotel in Birmingham and the second one was for the book store in New Orleans. They were a week apart.

Joe opened a drawer and took out a Rand McNally road map of the southeast. He popped the top off a large black marker and drew a deep line down I-75 from Lexington, Kentucky, to I-59 at Chattanooga, then to Birmingham, through Mississippi, to I-10 in Louisiana, to New Orleans. For some reason, Cathy and Kent had gone to Lexington and then returned to New Orleans to hide out. The postcard with the Lexington scene, the one with the Birmingham skyline, and the credit card charges proved it.

The route would have taken her within two miles of his home in London County, Tennessee. It was probably there at a gas stop or rest area that someone had stolen her purse and thrown it into the river. She had to be in New Orleans.

"J. R., we're going to New Orleans. I hope you like to party." The dog jumped up to Joe's waist and opened his mouth.

Joe scrubbed and cleaned the interior of the boat. He changed the sheets on the bed and swept the carpet. He folded his clothes that had accumulated around the walls, making the cabin area presentable and attractive enough for Carol. She had to go with him.

SHE WAS WEARING JEANS, a light denim blouse with two buttons open at the top, and had her hair tied back with a red bandana when she got out of her white Volvo. Her bags were hidden away in the trunk. Joe was sitting on his Harley waiting.

"You're dressed for a ride," Joe said and stood up beside her.

"Maybe." She smiled. "We'll see after dinner. You like the sound of this place?"

Joe looked at the neon sign. "Hog Heaven." He patted the seat of the cycle. "Yeah, just right for a country boy and Harley-Davidson man."

They walked along the path toward the riverside barbecue roadhouse. Joe put his hand lightly on her waist and guided her around a slightly akimbo decorative tree. She didn't flinch at his touch.

Rough-hewn timbers and a polished brick floor set the tone for the home style restaurant that specialized in racks of barbecued pork ribs. Joe ordered the specialty and Carol some chicken. Homemade bread, slaw, and baked beans were served with all meals. They sat on the porch beneath a slow-turning fan with the river in the background. As day faded away, kerosene lanterns on the walls gave dancing light to their features.

"Tell me about Cathy."

"Tell me about Joe Chapman."

For the next hour they swapped information. Joe got the history of Cathy and Carol, of the different fathers, of the mother who was a mystery. Carol added notes to Joe's genogram. He confessed about the tires he burned and his shaved head. With each incident, Carol wrote a brief phrase beneath his box. Joe told her about his divorce and bankruptcy. He had left London on the first day of May with a shaved head, a case of Spam, Cathy's soaked purse, and a dog that could ride a motorcycle. He mentioned the case of the girl but gave no details.

"You shaved your head? That's very interesting."

"I didn't shave it. The bar maid shaved it. I lost a bet."

"Yes, but you allowed it. Subliminally, you were making a statement." She looked into his eyes and lifted the pencil from the paper.

"What statement?"

"Well, from what you're telling me, you were divorced, bankrupt, and suspended from your law practice when you started this trip in May. I'd say you had some depression. You were looking for a fresh start—a new beginning—the hope of the phoenix.

"When a man goes into the military, what are the first things they do to him?"

"I don't know. Give him orders?"

"Close. They take his civilian clothes and shave his head. They take away one identity and give him another—a military one. He's now a private—a nobody. And by the time he completes his military service, they've made him into a new personality—military style.

"So, I see your head shaving as a subliminal impulse. It was a recognition that you would have to start over. You'd have to be somebody new. And the trip you planned for the river for the summer was your attempt to find who you'd be. Your finding Cathy's purse gave you an excuse to hunt for something. You know what that is?"

"No, I can't say that I do." He wiped the grease from the pork ribs onto a napkin. "You seem to be on a roll. Tell me what I'm hunting for."

"You say you're in *pursuit of happiness* like Jefferson talked about in the Declaration of Independence. But you're really seeking perfection. The perfect woman. You imagined Cathy to have perfect beauty. You're only partly right. She has physical beauty, but she has flaws as we all do. You won't find the perfect woman in Cathy. You'll be disappointed. Happiness and perfection are not connected. Rarely are happiness and joy.

"Remember, you told me about burning those tires when you left in May?"

Joe nodded. It was one of the crimes he had confessed to over the past hour.

"Don't you see what that was?"

"Yeah. I was mad as hell, and I wasn't going to take it any more."

"No. It was redirected aggression. You were showing your disgust that those things weren't perfect. The courthouse was justice. The judge's birdbath was a relationship gone bad. I don't know what the bridge was. Maybe you just didn't like it creating a bottleneck. Right? Am I getting close? Mr. Chapman? Joe?"

Joe wiped his hands and looked toward the river. "You may be right. I do get annoyed when things don't turn out perfectly, when people don't do what is expected of them, when the laws of nature seem to act against me. But how do you know all that because I shaved my head?"

"It's not just that. I could tell from the start that you always tend to judge people as imperfect. I bet you've even picked out something about me that you think is less than perfect."

Joe looked up. "I don't think so. What would I pick?"

Carol thought for a minute and then smiled. "Will you tell me the truth if I guess it?"

"Sure. If I've found an imperfection in you, tell me what it is and I'll confess."

"My nose."

"What?"

"My nose. You're such a visual person when it comes to women. I bet the first time you saw me you thought something like, 'She's not bad looking—except for that Roman nose.' Right?"

Joe felt the heat rushing up his neck to his forehead. His color betrayed him even in the dim light of kerosene.

"You have a beautiful nose. Just like my grandmother's."

"Thanks. That's just what every woman wants to hear. 'You look like my grandmother.' That's what you thought, though, isn't it?"

Joe nodded. "You've got my number. Can we go listen to the band for a while? You're telling me more about me than I want to know."

They sat on a bench and leaned against a wall while they listened to the band. There was a small dance floor and some were dancing. But they sat, listened, and talked some more.

"You know that I haven't spoken to my best friend in two months. I thought about that today. I need to call him."

"I didn't even know you had a best friend. The way you've been whining, I thought that you didn't like anyone and no one liked you. Except that you were obsessed with my sister."

"That's about true. But I do have one friend, Monkey Palk."

"Monkey? You guys have strange nicknames. Carp, Monkey, and your dog . . . what is it, J. R.?"

"No. His name is J. R. Monkey got his nickname a few years ago." Joe told Carol the story about the orangutan.

She laughed. "That's cruel. Poor Mr. Palk is doing his job as a prosecutor, and you saddle him with a name like that. An orangutan isn't a monkey anyway."

Joe nodded. "Only ten people in our county could say orangutan, and nobody could spell it. So, 'Monkey' stuck."

"I listened to your dog story last night. Now you're going to have to listen to my primate story since you brought up monkeys," Carol said. She paused and waited for the band to finish a number.

"Okay," Joe said and took a drink of iced tea.

"I went to a conference last year where I heard this psychiatrist compare men and women with four other primates—gibbons, orangutans, gorillas, and chimpanzees.

"Well, gibbons are pretty well monogamous. They bond for life and will fight off anything that comes around—including their own offspring. As soon as their children are old enough, they kick them out of the tree and won't have anything further to do with them."

"Pretty smart," Joe said.

"Orangutans are too big to share the same tree. The males are grouchy. They only come down from their trees to mate. Then after that they go back to their separate trees. The females just about raise their babies by themselves. The orangutans are very shy and don't form close bonds."

"I know the type," Joe said.

"Gorillas are polygamous. The males sometimes have harems of females. The males compete like moose or elk to be the dominant male in a group. The dominant male has control of the harem. The females are very friendly and get along well with each other. Their bonds with the males are not very personal. The males are just a source of impregnation."

"Sort of like a singles bar," Joe said.

"Chimpanzees," Carol continued, "are in some ways most like humans. The female chimps bond together to form a child rearing cooperative with no males. The males leave home at puberty and go live with other males. These males sometimes form raiding parties on the females where they rape and pillage. Chimpanzees will kill any babies, including their own, who stand between them and the females when they go on the raping raids."

"Sounds like a military academy," Joe said.

"Which one sounds like you?" Carol asked and squeezed a lemon wedge above her iced tea. She looked back at Joe who was watching the band. "Did you hear me?"

Joe had heard. Was this a story that she told all her dates? Would his answer forever mark him in her sight? What was the right answer? Or was there one?

"I have some of the bad qualities of all . . . and some of the good. I'm grouchy sometimes. I've thought about having a harem. And like the chimps, I left home at puberty. But I have never raped. Made a few raids on an all girls dorm in college but only collected underwear."

Carol looked at him. "You are probably more orangutan than anything else."

AT THE PARKING LOT, Carol agreed to ride the Harley over to Joe's boat to check it out. The extra helmet fit her just fine. She complained that she had to look at "Carp" on the back of Joe's helmet. She was one of the best novice riders that Joe had ever had behind him. She leaned when he leaned. She held lightly to his belt at both sides of his waist without a hint of tenseness.

He took her on the scenic route. They motored through the downtown streets of Baton Rouge and along the nearly deserted refinery roads where the piping was lit up like Christmas lights. A narrow ribbon of asphalt ran along the top of the levee for a way. There Joe slowed the Harley to a speed just fast enough to keep it from dropping over. The moon's soft glow was punctuated by the stabbing beam of the headlight. To their right the Mississippi flowed toward New Orleans and eventually the Gulf.

Carol leaned farther toward Joe's back. How could she be swept away in just three days? Here she was a professional woman with a college degree riding on a Harley in the dark of night with a man she had never met until he wandered into her office looking for her sister. And she had decided she would go to New Orleans with him to find Cathy if he still wanted her to go along. Reason had deserted her. She could blame it on her instinct to find her sister. But was it more a search to find love? Perhaps a couple of days in New Orleans with Joe "Carp" Chapman would be good for her. She could gain a new perspective on life in general and why people did compulsive things in particular. He seemed harmless enough.

He stopped when he got to the part of the levee that angled off toward the wharf where the boat was moored. He killed the engine.
"You ready to go on the boat now?"
"No."
"No? I thought you could just check it out. I won't attack you."
"No. I know you won't. You need to take me back to my car."
"Why?"
"I've got to take it back to my apartment. I have suitcases in the trunk. I'm ready to go to New Orleans with you."

IN AN HOUR THE boat had been made ready for its night run to New Orleans. For the first time on the trip, Joe turned on the four headlights and the two overhead spotlights that also aimed forward. With the bright moonlight, he needed them more to be seen than to see when he pulled back onto the river. He sat at the controls with Carol beside him. J. R. paid them little attention and slept near the back of the cabin. Joe slid the cabin windows open and let the night air wash over them.
As the lights of Baton Rouge disappeared behind them, the levees enclosed them on both sides to where little was visible except the ribbon of river.
"Tell me more about your dreams of Cathy," Carol said when midnight passed. She handed him a cup of coffee.

Joe related every detail he could remember. He told of her first appearance, how she only appeared when he was on the river and alone. With the darkness, sounds of the river, and the late hour, a shiver ran up his spine when he told the stories.

"Dreams are very interesting—and strange," Carol said. She watched Joe concentrate on the river ahead. "Some psychiatrists think they understand them. Some psychics think they can interpret them. But to me—I don't know—they can't be understood."

Joe turned. "But some of these didn't really seem like dreams. It was like she was actually there."

"I know. Some of the ones I have are very vivid at the time—then I can't remember them at all after I've been up for an hour. Some deal with things in the past. Some with things I've thought of or talked about that day. Then, the really strange ones seem to have nothing to do with any of that.

"We don't understand sleep. So, I guess it's not unreasonable to know that we don't understand dreams either."

"But they were so real. It was just like she was standing right there at the cabin door," Joe said. He put his hand on her knee and pointed to where Cathy had stood the first night.

"Have you noticed, Joe, that in dreams past, present, and future blend into one? They just sort of freely merge into the vision of whatever the dream is about."

Joe was silent for a minute. He had never analyzed dreams before. He had heard about books that interpreted dreams but had not read any. He couldn't explain his encounters with Cathy adequately to anybody, but they were more than dreams. She was there—her spirit, her being, or whatever.

Carol stood and walked to the front of the boat. Joe watched her through the window while he kept his hand on the steering wheel. She tilted her head toward the moon, stretched her arms upward, and yawned. Her hair and the bandana blew in the wind. She clutched her arms to her as though she was cold. She turned, came back in, and sat beside Joe.

"It's just as well that I took off a few days now," she said and pointed toward the moon visible through the screen.

"Why's that?" He looked at the moon and then back to Carol.

"Don't repeat this, but people go loony during the week of the full moon. I know it sounds crazy coming from a mental health professional. But I've noticed the cycle. I've documented it. There's more craziness around a full moon than any other time."

"Maybe there's just more light."

"No."

"So, you believe in the power of the moon? That's beautifully

weird. What about a person changing to a werewolf during a full
moon?" He turned toward her, bared his teeth, and with one hand
pushed up the hair on his scalp.

"No. Not werewolves. Just loonys." She reached over and
smoothed his hair back down with her hand.

"What about Cathy? Is she really into astrology? The occult?
Maybe voodoo or witchcraft? Do you think that she might be mixed up
with any groups that are into those weird rituals?"

Carol slowly shook her head, stood, and walked to the door in
front of Joe. She leaned against the door facing and looked at him.
"As I've said before, we haven't been close for some time. She was
always experimenting with this and that. There were Eastern
religions, meditation, yoga—you name it. If she's into anything you
named, it's probably just a passing fancy. There're no witches in our
family—to my knowledge. What makes you ask?"

"Nothing much. Her landlady mentioned some books and
candles. That's all."

"Landlady? That old heifer is as much a lady as J. R. lying
there." The dog raised his head at the mention of his name.

"I agree," Joe said and grinned. "But hand me that little book
there that I bought. It's about witchcraft."

Carol handed him the book. He flipped through the pages until
he found a picture of a supposed witch and read the caption beneath.

"Rich, abundant red-gold hair seems to manifest itself in most
witch families." He closed it, handed it back, and they were silent for
a good five minutes.

They looked at each other and then out the window. In the
distance a long-legged heron lifted out of the water near the bank and
flew upward, cutting directly across the face of the moon and making
a witchlike silhouette in black and white.

Thirty

A ttorney General Charles Palk pounded his desk. "Dammit, dammit, dammit."

A fourth body had been found the day before. TVA had lowered the water along the banks of the river, and his search team had found it among the brush within a half mile of where the others had floated to the surface. This one was a woman.

She now lay with the others beneath the thirty yard line of the East Tennessee State University football field where Dr. Linus Trout maintained his house of horrors. Altogether, the doctor had accumulated over a hundred bodies—or parts of bodies—from throughout the state. They lay in cold storage in the cavernous basement awaiting identification—and perhaps prosecution of their murderers.

Palk held the photos of the bloated body of the female near his eyes and examined them in the early morning light near his third floor office window. Like the third victim, her face had been blown away by a shotgun blast. But even with that, he saw that she was young, had an athletic body and very long hair. He could not determine the color of the hair until it was cleaned at Dr. Trout's facilities. She still wore sneakers, jeans, and a sweater.

JOHN COLLINS SMILED WHEN George Stephens told him about seeing Joe Chapman in Baton Rouge.

"He told me to tell you, 'Hi.' It's strange that he's looking for
Bartley too."

"He hooked up with a bondsman, huh? Chapman sings a
beautiful 'Amazing Grace.' "

Collins flipped through a file and then looked back to his
younger associate. "You didn't meet up with our brothers from New
Orleans, did you?"

"Just one time. They were a little hesitant to talk. They still
thought it was their ball game. Not yours. But they didn't want to
ruffle your feathers."

"And Bartley may be dead up in Tennessee. That's interesting—if it's true. I can't get up there until the day after the Fourth.
I'd like you to go to Tennessee with me. I'm going to call that attorney
general and remind him I'll be there."

THE LIGHT LIT UP on Palk's telephone console. Luann
wasn't in yet. He pushed the button and brought the receiver to his
ear.

"This is Agent John Collins, General Palk. I thought you might
be an early riser. I just wanted to remind you I'll be up there on
Tuesday. I'm going to meet another agent, George Stephens, at your
office."

"That's fine, Agent Collins. The sooner the better."

"Why's that?"

"Another body was discovered yesterday. A woman."

"Uh oh. Was she young? Maybe twenty-five, twenty-six?"

"Could be. She seemed to have a nice body. Of course she's
been in the river a while too."

"Long hair?"

"Yes, definitely. How do you know?"

"We had a report of a young woman—a dancer—with long red
hair traveling with Bartley. Did she have any identification?"

"There was supposed to be a wallet with her. I don't know
what it had, if anything. I'll know by the time you get here."

"Thanks."

Palk returned to his desk. He sat down and began to write a
few notes for the speech he would give at the county park on the
Fourth about the blessings of independence.

FLORENTINE AND RODRIGUEZ DROVE along I-10 near La
Place, Louisiana, early the morning after Joe and Carol left Baton
Rouge.

"Do you think they'll head for the witchcraft shop or the
bookstore first?" Rodriguez asked his taller friend.

"From what we heard on our bug in Bodine's office, I'd say it's an even shot either way. Chapman thinks the girl and Bartley are in New Orleans. He'll go to one of those places first."

"It's too bad about Cathy's sister being with him. I hate to kill women," Rodriguez said and screwed the silencer onto his pistol. "We should be there about the same time his boat arrives. We told that Tennessee hick to leave the looking for Bartley to us. So, it's his own fault that he's going to spend the last day of his life in New Orleans."

AGENT FLOYD MILES AND Agent Mike Constanzo stood in the warehouse parking lot and looked toward the Mississippi to where *THE CARP* had been moored.

"No wonder we lost the signal on the bug we put on the boat. It's gone. They must have done like they were talking about and headed to New Orleans," Miles said to his younger colleague.

"Are we going back down there or stay here?" Constanzo asked.

"We'll just call in and tell the office to have someone tail them in New Orleans. They won't be hard to find with that old boat he has. If they happen onto Bartley and Pelton, the agents there can take over.

"We need to check out that body in Tennessee to see if it's really Bartley. The D. A. up there called Fontaine and said they had a wallet and driver's license with Bartley's name," Miles said and turned to walk back to their car.

"What if it is Bartley?"

"If Bartley's dead, we're up shit creek—or shit bayou. We'll have some heavy explaining to do to the bosses. Of course, I have my twenty years in. I can retire. But you, Constanzo, they'll transfer to Colombia and put a DEA placard on your back."

"They might as well put a bulls-eye."

JACKSON SQUARE WAS STILL practically deserted when Joe and Carol sat down outside the Cafe DuMond. They had made good time and moored the boat near a warehouse a block from the French Market. The sidewalk artists were setting up, and a few tourists were stirring. But those present on the morning of the third of July were nothing compared to what would congregate on the evening of the Fourth when crowds would jam Jackson Square and watch the fireworks along the river.

Joe had slept two hours while Carol had taken over the helm of the boat on some of the less dangerous sections of the river. She had slept four. Now they both looked at each other through eyes they could barely hold open. Maybe the French coffee would perk them up. When they had finished a beignet and their first cup of coffee, they took another cup to go and walked into the square that was enclosed by a black wrought-iron fence. They sat on a bench near the statue of General Andrew Jackson that stood guard over the park on the end near the St. Louis Cathedral.

"There's one great Tennessean," Joe said and nodded to the statue.

"Bull," Carol said.

"Why did you say that about the savior of New Orleans? Jackson beat the British here in the War of 1812."

"The war was over. That battle was useless. He got a lot of publicity for something that didn't matter. Then he went on to be President and drove the Cherokees out of Tennessee, Georgia, and North Carolina. The trail of tears. One of my ancestors was in that. I'm part Cherokee. Something like one sixty-fourth or near that."

"I didn't know."

"We haven't forgiven that Tennessean."

"Obviously."

"He was just another male Tennessean in New Orleans in pursuit of glory. Maybe in pursuit of the *perfect* battle."

Joe sat silent for a minute. It was good to know that Carol, and probably Cathy, could trace their ancestry back to a Tennessee Cherokee. They would have more in common with him. He may have walked along the river near one of their ancestral homesites, or perhaps he had picked up an arrowhead that had been made by their great-grandfather several generations removed. Cathy's purse appearing in Tennessee was just another artifact.

"Nobody's perfect, Carol. Isn't that what you told me? Give Old Hickory a break. He just did what the majority of people wanted. That's democracy. I agree that in his time your Cherokee ancestors were not treated fairly.

"I didn't know you had Cherokee blood in you. But I had noticed you have nice cheekbones."

Carol bit her lip and then looked at Joe. "Cheekbones? Is that the only saving grace of Indians? What about the minds of Indians? Hearts and souls? I'm tired of hearing about cheekbones. Praising cheekbones is the white chauvinistic attempt to find some redeeming value in those who aren't white. It has to be physical—not mental or spiritual."

It was time to change the subject. "Where are all the pigeons? When I was here fifteen years ago, there were pigeons all over the place," Joe said.

"Ah, another white man's decision. They said the pigeons were too dirty. They got rid of them. Made it against the law to feed them. The pigeons dropped too much shit on General Jackson. Pigeons are good judges of character," Carol said.

Joe stood up and searched his mind for a safe topic of conversation. "Let's go to the witchcraft shop and the bookstore to see if we can get a lead on Cathy." It was now ten-thirty and more people were populating the square. The shops had opened. They walked toward St. Philip Street in silence.

The witchcraft shop was off the main tourist beat but close enough that some wandered in and others stood and pointed from the sidewalk. Joe had taken along a couple of the eight-by-tens of Cathy from the Miss Baton Rouge pageant to show to anyone who might have seen her. He chose the one of her in the evening gown.

Once inside the shop, Joe and Carol acted like other tourists. They looked at the items on display—a combination of the occult and sex bondage toys. Cathy was brought to mind when Joe saw rows and rows of candles. Leather and blackness predominated. Masks, handcuffs, and whips hung from the walls. He didn't look Carol in the eye. Then in one corner of the shop, there were books on voodoo and witchcraft along with short to mid-length knives and daggers. Six-pointed wax stars lay inside a display cabinet next to containers of incense.

The lone clerk, a pale young emaciated man with a ponytail, sat by a desk putting information onto a form from a younger man.

"You have to be sincere!" the clerk shouted at the youth. He stood and tore up the form. "Witchcraft and the wiccan religion are not something you enter into just because you want to put a hex on somebody." He threw the pieces into a waste can. "Come back when you've studied more. And are sincere." The scolded youth walked hurriedly out the front door.

"Ah, the youth of today," the clerk said as he approached Joe and Carol. "They all want instant gratification. He wants to be a witch so he can place a hex on his professor. How stupid! No one wants to study. Instant witches. What do they think this is? They are not sincere about the old religion. Pardon me for rambling on. What can I do for you or help you find?"

Carol grasped Joe's arm and let him speak. "We're looking for this girl," Joe said and laid the photo of Cathy on the display case.

The clerk eyed it. "She's beautiful. And what gorgeous hair. Would it be golden-red?" he asked and looked closer at the black and white image.

"Yes," Carol answered.

"Is she a witch?" the clerk asked.

"No. I don't think so. But she may have checked into it. That's why we're here. She's my sister. She's disappeared. Do you recognize her?"

"No, but I've only been here a short time. Let me show it to Claudine in the back." He took the photo and turned to walk toward the back.

"May I talk to Claudine?" Joe asked and started to walk after the clerk.

The clerk turned and placed his hand in the center of Joe's chest. "No offense, but no one talks to Claudine unless she invites them." Joe stepped back and the young man disappeared around a thick curtain.

While the clerk was in the back with Claudine, two young women who looked almost like twins with long blond hair, short black leather skirts, knee high black leather boots, and sleeveless tight-fitting gray pullover shirts walked in and began to examine all the leather items. Joe followed them with his eyes. Carol elbowed Joe. The clerk returned and rushed to the two young women and hugged them. They each bought a pair of handcuffs and a short leather whip and left the store.

The clerk watched Joe's eyes. "They're just street girls. They have a passing interest in the wiccan, but they're mainly interested in sex toys. They tell me they have a large clientele."

Joe smiled. "I thought we were going to see a virgin sacrifice."

"They wouldn't qualify," the clerk said seriously. He looked first at Joe and then at Carol. "Claudine says the girl looks familiar, but she will have to ask some of the other witches in the coven before she can tell you. She wants to know why you're looking for her? If you're trying to kidnap her out of our religion and deprogram her, Claudine will be of no help. A lot of parents come by thinking we have brainwashed their children or made slaves or something out of them. Bunch of nonsense."

"No. We just want to make sure she's okay. If she's in a coven and wants to stay, that's fine," Carol said.

"Very well. Leave the photo and return at six this evening. I will relay your concern to Claudine, and perhaps by then we can tell you something."

Carol and Joe looked at their watches, thanked the clerk, and walked out the door. From behind the heavy curtain of the back room passageway stepped the short, stout Rodriguez. He counted off five one hundred dollar bills and handed them to the clerk. "You did well, my friend. I will be back before six to provide you with the message for our searching guests." He picked up Cathy's picture, drew an X with his fingers across it, and laid it back down.

"Joe, I'm tired. How about if I go back to the boat and sleep a while before we come back up here at six?"

It was past eleven. Joe wanted to check out the bookstore where Cathy had ordered the book. He escorted Carol back to the boat and then returned to the French Quarter for his visit to the bookstore.

The store was three blocks over from the witchcraft shop. Joe could imagine Cathy walking from one to the other. She could be here this day. He would recognize her now if he saw her. The noontime heat that rose from the concrete and asphalt with the intensity of a sauna had driven most of the tourists off the streets and into their hotels or to the coolness of shops and restaurants.

He stopped by a novelty store on the way to the bookstore and made two purchases. One was an authentic looking police badge and the other was a little leather wallet that would accommodate the badge on one side and one of the DEA cards on the other. If need be, he could flash the wallet and display a badge and a business card. To the casual observer, he would appear official.

Proud of his work, he closed the wallet and slipped it inside his jacket pocket next to the credit card bill that showed the book purchase. He stopped long enough to listen to a sidewalk band and threw a dollar bill in the box at the conclusion of an upbeat version of "When the Saints Go Marching In." He thought it ironic since he was anything but a saint. He was getting ready to walk in and commit another crime if necessary—the impersonation of a federal officer. He patted the pistol beneath his jacket and felt for the papers Bodine had given him that allowed him free rein in searching for Bartley.

Three browsers and two clerks were the only ones in the bookstore when Joe walked in. It was a small shop with a high ceiling. A metal ladder that moved along a rail at the top of the last shelf allowed the clerks to find books that were more than ten feet from the floor. The musty smell of old books and mold mixed with the street odors to give the store a unique aroma. Three ceiling fans stirred the air enough to make it bearable at noon.

Joe walked to the counter behind which one of the clerks was marking off books from a computer generated list. Technology had made its way to an out-of-the-way bookstore in the French Quarter.

"May I help you?" she asked and looked up from her work. She brushed a stray lock of hair from her forehead and looked at Joe with tired but attentive eyes.

"Yes, I'm George Stephens with the DEA," Joe said and unfolded the fake credentials. She gazed at the official appearing badge and card for about two seconds before looking back at Joe.

"We don't sell drugs," she said and smiled weakly.

Joe folded the wallet and replaced it into his pocket. "Oh, I'm not here for anything like that," he said in a soft voice as though he was in a library. He smiled. "I'm just trying to locate someone who may have been a customer of yours."

"My goodness. I didn't know we dealt with drug pushers," she said and wrinkled her forehead. She put a finger to her lips. "Oh, I bet you're looking for Ralph. He looks suspicious."

"No."

"Well, who're you looking for? What's his name?"

"It's not a him. It's a her. Cathy Pelton's her name," Joe said and slid another copy of Cathy's photo onto the counter.

"My, she's a lovely girl," the clerk said and studied the photo. "Why would she be involved in running drugs?"

"She may not be. Just a witness. I just need to talk with her. Do you recognize her?"

The woman looked from the photo to Joe and then back to the photo. "No, I can't say that I do."

Joe took the picture back. He showed her the charge card bill that indicated the purchase in March. After a bit of scurrying around the back office, the clerk was able to locate a sales slip for the day in question.

"That was a phone order," she said, pointing to a line on a computer printout and a corresponding sales slip. "The girl who took this is no longer with us. We usually get the telephone number, but there's not one on here. That's why we had to let that girl go. She wasn't good at details—always leaving something out."

"Do you show where the book was shipped, or was it picked up?"

The clerk scanned another sheet. "Neither. It's paid for. But it's still here." She looked in a box beneath the counter and pulled a book out. Attached to it was a note with Cathy's name. It was a horse book. She wanted something about her new passion.

"If she calls in for this book or stops by, try to get an address or phone number. I'll check back in a few days to see what you've learned." Joe turned to leave.

"May I have one of your cards? Then I'll just call you if she stops by," the clerk said.

Joe began to sweat. He looked into his wallet. There were no cards. "Sorry, I gave out my last card earlier today. I'll just check back." He stepped through the open doorway before any more questions could be asked.

Carol was still sleeping when he arrived back at THE CARP. J. R. was unusually frisky for that time of day. Joe and the dog played their old games. Joe threw the tennis ball and J. R. retrieved. For an hour they romped along the riverside. When the dog tired, Joe went to the boat and found some of the rib bones he had saved from his dinner the night before and gave the special treat to J. R.

Carol had awakened and stood in the doorway watching Joe and the dog without their knowledge.

"You love that old dog more than anything in the world, don't you, Joe?" she asked, stepped through the cabin opening, and sat beside the two. J. R. nuzzled her leg with his nose. She scratched him behind the ears.

"He loves me more than anything in the world," Joe said and smiled while he watched Carol pet the dog. "That's good enough for me. I haven't been giving him enough attention the last few days."

"I haven't seen him ride on the cycle." She nodded toward the cherry-red Harley that was strapped to the side of the cabin. "Why don't we see if we can all ride on it through the French Quarter?"

"You'll have to sit real close to me. Think you can do that?"

Carol nodded.

"Some places we'd look awfully strange, but I bet we hardly get noticed through the streets here. They're used to everything. I saw a woman here who raised ducks. The babies, just hatched out, would follow her wherever she went. Strange."

"That's known as bonding. The first thing the young duckling sees, it bonds to. I studied a little in college about that."

"Bonding," Joe repeated and patted his jacket pocket where Bartley's bond papers were that had been given him by Bodine.

Through the streets of New Orleans rode the trio. They all had helmets. Carol was tightly pinioned between Joe and J. R. They rumbled slowly down Canal, Poydras, St. Ann and the other streets of the French Quarter where two-story buildings and houses clung to the streets with over-shadowing balconies of decorative wrought-iron. Bourbon Street was barricaded to motor traffic because of the pre-holiday rush, but on the other streets, tourists did turn and point to the odd sight of a dog riding a Harley. It was something that even New Orleans had rarely seen.

They stopped near the end of Jackson Square where drivers of mule-drawn carriages waited for tourists to take them up on their promises of scenic tours. J. R. was especially attracted to the flower-covered sun bonnets that the mules wore. Then he sniffed behind them and looked at the diapers they wore. When the dog walked too near to the hind legs of the mules, Joe pulled him aside.

Back inside the square, Joe and J. R. lay in the grass and wrestled while Carol bought an ice cream bar for each from a street vendor. There they lounged, rested, and awaited the six o'clock appointment at the witchcraft shop.

When it was near time, they returned to the boat and left J. R. tied inside the cabin. Joe and Carol walked back to St. Phillip Street. Only the clerk who was there earlier and a young couple were in the front of the shop. The clerk saw Joe and Carol and rushed to them, his ponytail flapping behind.

"Claudine was of great help. She spoke to a witch who has met your sister. She has arranged for you to meet with a man tomorrow evening who knows where your sister is. His name is Papa Legba."

"Why tomorrow?" Joe asked. "Who is this Papa Legba? Is he a witch?"

"No, no. He's more into voodoo. It seems this Cathy has tried both. Papa Legba knows where she is. Claudine doesn't. Tomorrow's the soonest. He has business today. Here's the address," he said and handed a piece of paper to Joe. "It's a warehouse, but nobody will be there except for you and Papa. He doesn't like to be seen in public. Go to the side door. It's the only one that will be unlocked and open. Will you go?"

"Is it far from here?"

"Just a few blocks."

"And we're supposed to meet him at ten o'clock at night? On the Fourth of July?"

"Right."

Without asking Carol, Joe replied. "We'll be there." He took the note, grabbed Carol's suddenly cold hand, and walked back out of the shop.

The clerk returned to his chair behind the counter. Rodriguez came around the curtain.

"Good, very good, my friend." He handed the clerk two more hundred dollar bills. "What are a couple of more little pops on the night when all the big fireworks go off?"

Thirty-one

T he next morning Joe decided it was time to level with Carol. He
had to tell her more—that he was a bounty hunter looking for
Kent Bartley. He still did not feel at ease in telling her he had
broken into Cathy's house, had seen the candles, had felt the underwear, and had even looked into her refrigerator. He would break it to
her a little at a time.   He would not yet mention the sixty
Krugerrands—most of which were in a box beneath the bed in which
Carol slept.

However, Carol would know something was up when she awoke
and saw him sitting there in the morning sun—slowly cutting off a foot
and a half from the barrels of his shotgun and sawing the stock into
a pistol grip. He thought about how to tell her while the hacksaw
blade whined through the tempered blue steel of the barrels.

"What are you doing?" Carol asked. She was standing at the
cabin door rubbing sleep from her eyes.

"Making a sawed-off shotgun," Joe said and glanced toward
her. It was probably not the answer she wanted to hear.

She sat next to him with a cup of coffee and listened to his
explanation. He told her about Bodine and the bounty on Bartley. He
explained that Bartley was being sought by the DEA and two other
men who identified themselves as FBI but weren't. He told of his fear
when Rodriguez had pinned him to the cabin wall and stuck a pistol
to his throat.

Joe pulled his jacket back and showed Carol the pistol he
always carried now on his chest and his Bowie knife on his belt. He
read her the official papers he had received from Bodine but didn't
show her his fake DEA identification.

"Why this now?" Carol asked. "Are you nervous about the
meeting tonight?"

"I don't know. This may be our big chance to find Cathy.
Some of the people she's been running with are less than friendly. I
want to have some hidden firepower."

"You already have a pistol. Why do you need a sawed-off shotgun? Aren't they illegal?"

"Actually, I have two pistols." He stood and showed her the one at the base of his spine. "But the shotgun isn't for me. It's for you." He laid it in her lap.

Carol raised her hands and looked down at the gun wide-eyed. "I can't use this. I can't even carry it. It might go off and blow my legs off." She picked it up and gingerly handed it back to Joe.

"We're going to sew you a little holster-like thing in the back of your rain jacket. It'll be concealed when we go to the warehouse tonight. If everything goes okay, that Papa Legba we're supposed to meet won't even know we're carrying. If something goes wrong, it'll be your ticket out of there while I'm keeping Papa busy with this." Joe patted his gun at his chest.

Carol shook her head. "I'm not trained. I've never shot a gun. I think it's time for me to go home." She looked at Joe. "How can you be so calm about it?"

"Preparation. I wasn't prepared before for that little bully. I'm prepared this time and you will be too. It's easy to use a shotgun. You don't have to be real accurate. It'll spray a wide pattern. And you can be sure it'll scare the . . . hell out of anyone you point it at. I'm going to give you a little lesson on using it."

"I don't know."

"You want to find Cathy as much as I do, don't you?"

"Yes, I want to find her. But I don't want to die trying. And I don't want to shoot anyone."

"We won't have to . . . if we're prepared. This is all for self-defense."

After Joe gave Carol an hour of instruction on using the shotgun—loading and unloading, aiming and shooting, bringing the gun to shoulder height and holding it—they decided to take a break and go to some of the shops. J. R. stayed on the boat while Joe and Carol rode the trolley from the French Quarter to the Riverwalk. Carol window shopped while Joe scanned every passing woman to see if Cathy might be out shopping too. They sat near the window overlooking the Mississippi, ate beignets, and drank more French coffee.

"Right there is where that freighter ran into this place back in 1996," Joe said and pointed down the way about fifty yards. "That would have been scary."

"Not half as scary as what we're going to do."

They took the trolley back to Jackson Square, listened to some of the street bands, and walked over to where the riverboat *Natchez* was docked. "That's the size boat I'm going to take down the river next time," Joe said.

"What're you going to buy it with? You got some gold stashed away that I don't know about?"

Joe smiled but said nothing.

By eight o'clock they were back on THE CARP. The sun was going down behind the levee and the heat was easing. Carol brewed some tea and they sat and listened to the city sounds while waiting for the time of their appointment. Firecrackers began to pop all up and down the river area. Children with Roman candles didn't wait for darkness to shoot their fiery volleys toward the river. Joe watched, listened, checked, and rechecked his weaponry. He threw a large bottle into the river and fired off five rounds from his .357, hitting it on the last shot.

"You try the shotgun," Joe said to Carol. "Nobody's going to notice that we're doing anything with all the noise of the firecrackers." He pulled her up and took her to the edge of the boat. He stood behind her and brought her arms up with the gun and showed her again how to aim.

"I'm going to throw another bottle in and see how good a shot you are." He tossed the bottle just a few feet from the boat and watched it start to flow with the current. He brought Carol's arm and the gun up, urged her to look down the barrels toward the bottle, and put his hand on hers as she pulled the trigger. The gun roared, the barrels recoiled upward, and Carol stumbled backward, but Joe was there to catch her. The bottle burst and disappeared beneath the brown water.

"See how easy it is? You got it with the first shot. You had another shell left if you'd missed."

"That thing is as hard on the shooter as it is on the thing being shot at. I almost fell down."

"Yeah. Well, it's a twelve gauge. Has a lot of recoil. But you won't even notice if you're shooting at some game . . . or somebody. You'll be too concerned about what's happening."

Carol shook her head. She watched Joe reload the shotgun and place it in the lining of her coat where she would be able to grasp it through a hole he had made in the pocket. He reloaded his pistol and put several extra rounds in his jacket pocket. He put two extra shotgun shells in Carol's jacket pocket that didn't have the hole in it.

"We're packin', baby. How does it feel?"

Carol put her hand through the pocket hole and gripped the barrel of the gun. "It's the hardest thing I've had my hand on in a long time." Joe briefly smiled and turned away toward J. R.

At nine-thirty darkness was nearly complete. They began their half mile walk toward the warehouse. Carol moved in short steps, holding the shotgun beneath her jacket. Joe slowed his pace to match Carol's and constantly looked over his shoulder toward the row of empty warehouses. J. R. followed behind, wandering off and sniffing the ground from time to time before he caught back up with Joe and Carol.

Joe checked the address on the piece of paper one last time. He glanced up and saw the number above the door of the next warehouse. Behind them toward downtown, the sky was lighting up as fireworks arched above the lower buildings. Only security lights provided any illumination in the warehouse district.

When they neared the open door, Joe bent to J. R. and told him to sit. They started in, but when Joe looked back, J. R. was standing. Joe pointed. "Stay. Sit." The dog looked in but stayed outside.

Inside, the huge building was darker than the outside. Rows of barrels were stacked three high throughout with aisles wide enough for forklifts to move them from one location to another. After about fifty feet, a crossway led between other rows of barrels—black and gray metal used in the petro-chemical business.

When they reached the crosswalk, Joe noticed a slight bluish-fluorescent glow a little to the right. They turned in that direction and walked toward the light. Fifty yards ahead, a dark figure sat at a lone table. They walked closer.

"Hi, I'm Papa Legba," the solitary figure at the four-legged card table said and motioned them nearer. In a circle on the floor surrounding the table, at least a hundred short, stubby candles burned with weak flames. On the bare table sat two candelabra, holding seven candles each. There were two wax six-pointed stars and a knife as big as Joe's Bowie lying on the table before Papa Legba. He sat beneath a hooded cloak that reached to the floor. He rested his hands on the table, clasping within them an old leather draw-string bag about the size of a baby's bonnet.

Joe and Carol reached the edge of the circled candles.

"Stop," Legba said in a firm voice. He raised his head up and looked at Joe. The candles on the table reflected off the deep set eyes of the voodoo priest making it almost appear that light came from within. "Do not transgress the circle." Legba looked down at the feet of Joe and Carol. "You must stay on the outside of the circle. The spirits decree it. Sit down."

"Where?" Joe asked and looked for a chair or cushion.

"On the floor," Legba said and pointed to the concrete. When they had positioned themselves crosslegged on the floor, Legba continued. "You are seeking Cathy Pelton," he stated while massaging the leather bag. "I need something that belongs to her. Did you bring anything?"

Joe got to his knees and took Cathy's St. Christopher's medal from his pocket.

"Toss it to me," Legba said.

Joe obliged and then sat back down next to Carol.

Legba rubbed the medal between the thumb and forefinger of his right hand. A hint of a smile grew on his lips. "St. Christopher has been recalled. De-sainted. He is no longer an official source of protection in travels. The spirits laughed when you gave me this." He laid the medal on the table and undid the strings of the draw-bag. He loosened it and dumped the contents on the table. There was an assortment of small bone fragments, old and yellowed. "We must roll the bones to determine Cathy's whereabouts."

"I thought you knew where she was," Joe said.

"I know how to determine where she is." He looked down at Joe. "Have you ever heard the expression 'rolling the bones'?"

"Only in connection with dice," Joe said. He reached out and put his hand in Carol's jacket pocket and felt her hand against the shotgun. Both were cold.

"That's right," Legba said, "but misapplied. This is really rolling the bones. It goes back many, many years to my ancestors in Africa then to the Caribbean and now to me here in New Orleans. The spirits speak through the bones." He then took the bones up into his two huge hands, shook them, and threw them out onto the table top. They came to rest around the candelabra. Legba stared at the bones, pressed the palms of his hands to his temples, looked upward, and started a guttural chant.

Carol turned loose of the gun and squeezed Joe's hand while the old man continued his connection to the spirits.

Finally, he stopped the sounds but kept pressing his palms to his head. He looked across the table and now at Carol.

"I feel pain for Cathy. She is hurt in her head. I see her spirit loping along a creek, a river. She is troubled. It is as though her spirit is torn from her body by the hair of her head."

Joe looked at Carol and then at Legba. "But where is she? Where is she loping along a river or creek?" Joe asked, wanting a specific location. He, too, had seen her along a river. He needed more.

Legba pressed harder against the sides of his head.

"I see black and white. I see blue and green. There's a latticework of black, of white—there's a carpet of green and of blue. Cathy's spirit moves in great strides. She is seeking beside the river."

Joe shook his head. It didn't make sense. He wanted a clue, a telephone number, a street address. Legba lacked in substance. He started to ask for something more specific when he saw two shadowy figures move from one row of barrels to the next.

Rodriguez and Florentine stepped behind Papa Legba. Their pistols were already drawn and aimed at Joe and Carol.

"Papa, it's time for you to leave. We'll take care of your visitors."

"You must not harm them. It would be against the spirits. They came peacefully and must be permitted to leave peacefully."

Rodriguez stuck the barrel of his pistol to the back of Legba's neck. "Can you feel that through the cloth?"

Legba nodded.

"You can leave with or without your brains. The choice is yours."

Legba arose from the table, put the bones back into the bag, looked briefly at Joe and Carol, turned, and walked slowly down the aisle.

Carol's hand was colder. Joe whispered, "Don't do anything, yet."

"I can't do anything," she whispered back.

"What do you want?" Joe asked. He put his hands flat on the floor.

"What we wanted was for you to do what we asked of you in Baton Rouge. You should've left the hunt for Bartley and the girl to us. Now you've brought death to your door and to the door of your friend," Rodriguez said and moved a step closer. "Now I want you to stand and walk toward the door." He nodded in the direction from which Joe and Carol had come.

Joe started to his knees. He looked at the guns the two were aiming toward him and Carol. They hadn't asked him to drop any weapon. They didn't know he was carrying. This was not a good time to try to get the drop on them. He wasn't that fast. He would have a chance by the time he walked to the door. They apparently wanted to kill them outside. He got to his feet and put out his hand for Carol.

From the cross-legged position, she leaned forward, but when she was almost up, a foot slipped on the concrete floor. She accidentally squeezed the trigger on the shotgun as she stumbled.

The blast from the twelve-gauge propelled her backwards and away from Joe and the other two. The pellets struck the floor in front of her and ricocheted to strike the table, knocking it over and spilling the candelabra onto the floor.

Rodriguez and Florentine, momentarily stunned by the thunderous blast, dove for cover behind the nearest row of barrels. Joe did the same across the walkway from where Carol ended up. She scrambled behind another row of barrels and brought the shotgun up to shoulder height. Joe pulled out his .357 magnum.

"Stay down, Carol!" Joe shouted. "Don't move. Just stay

where you are."

The two would-be killers began firing in the direction of Joe's voice. The bullets pinged off the barrels or plunged harmlessly into their depths.

Joe saw the fire from the muzzles of their guns and returned round for round as he had opportunity. He had no good target, and his offerings also found barrels instead of bodies. He emptied the .357, put it into his pocket, not having time to reload, and reached for the .45 in the holster at his back. He heard footsteps going down one aisle. One or both were trying to circle him to get an angle on him. He fired toward where they had been and in the direction where he heard the footfalls. Each blast was deafening and echoed in the valley of barrels. He fired more rounds and left his position. He darted toward the row of barrels that was ahead of him and nearer where the men had been. At least, he would be between them and Carol.

When he had heard no sound for a full minute, he stepped out to go back toward Carol. Florentine appeared in the dim candlelight just across the aisle. Joe pivoted to fire but squeezed off the round too soon and missed. He pulled the trigger again, but the chambers were empty. Florentine smiled and took one step toward Joe and raised his pistol.

Joe felt the wind along the back of his neck when the second barrel of the shotgun emptied and caught Florentine in the shoulder. The gun flew from his hand but away from Joe. Florentine crawled away and behind another row of barrels. Joe looked behind him and saw Carol was again on the floor, a result of the recoil of the shotgun. He smiled.

"Watch out, Joe!" she screamed and pointed.

Rodriguez was less than ten feet away. He was smiling and walking slowly toward Joe.

Joe moved his pistol toward Rodriguez. No more than six feet separated them. Joe squeezed again hoping that the first sign that the gun was empty was just a misfire. It clicked.

"You're out, hick. This is not the movies. Your gun is empty. The shotgun is too. Don't even think about reloading, whore," he said toward Carol and alternated pointing his gun at Carol and then Joe.

Joe kept holding his pistol out. They were now gun barrel to gun barrel. Rodriguez stopped. All the reverberations of the shots had died to nothingness. In the distance was the sound of firecrackers. In the warehouse it was quiet. The only sound that remained was that of the fire of the candles sizzling on the floor against a liquid coming from the barrels. Joe could also hear his own labored breathing and his heart beating so hard that the blood coursing through his head sounded like rushing water.

Then in the quiet, he heard a different noise. Carol heard it too and turned toward the aisle. Rodriguez was the last to notice, but then he turned his pistol toward the new sound.

There was no bark, no growl—just the sound of galloping padded paws against the concrete floor. Joe turned just in time to see J. R. running faster than he had ever seen him. He was gasping in air as he came down the aisle like an airplane on a runway.

J. R. became airborne when he neared Carol, and then with his next bound leapt toward Rodriguez, showing glistening white teeth set in widely opened jaws.

The shot from Rodriguez's pistol caught J. R. directly in the underside of the neck. The impact somersaulted the dog backwards and to the floor. He slid to a stop near the shooter's feet. J. R. lay there and didn't move, except for his brown eyes that found Joe's. Blood started to pool and run from beneath him.

Joe dropped his gun and bent toward his dog. Rodriguez turned, aimed at Joe, and pulled the trigger. This time he only got a click. He reached in his pocket for another magazine of bullets.

Joe rushed toward him in the crouch of a football player. He buried his shoulder into the stomach of Rodriguez. The killer bent slightly but did not fall backwards. Joe brought a knee up with all the force he had into the groin of Rodriguez. The gun went flying and Rodriguez doubled over while all air left him like a tire that had been slashed.

In one swift move, Joe straddled him and jerked his head back by the hair with his left hand. He drew the Bowie with his right and in the same motion sliced the throat of Rodriguez. The knife's work was done in one stroke, and Rodriguez slumped to the floor. There was a gurgling sound but no words. His blood ran toward the candle wax and sizzled when they met.

Joe resheathed his knife and bent to pick up his dog. He cradled J. R. in his arms and motioned for Carol to run ahead of him toward the door. Just as they reached the opening, the liquid from the perforated barrels caught fire against the flame of the candles and quickly spread from barrel to barrel.

Joe breathed heavily against the fur of J. R. on the run back toward the boat. Carol struggled to keep up.

Near *THE CARP* and beneath a street light, Joe looked down, bent his head to nuzzle against J. R.'s, and felt him give one last lick to Joe's nose. When Joe knew that J. R. was dead, he laid him down, stood, and cried over him on the side of the levee. Blood and tears mingled.

Thirty-two

T here was no sleep for Joe and Carol that night, and the next morning Joe dug a grave for his dog while Carol sat nearby. From time to time, Joe would move a few steps away, bend, and make sounds as though he was vomiting. But nothing came out. All fluids and solids had been emptied from his system during the night. But his thoughts of killing a man and having his best friend killed continued to send him into dry heaves. He alternated between that and crying.

A dark smoke still came from the warehouse rubble a half mile away. Fire engines on shore and fire department boats on the river continued to shoot plumes of water onto the smoldering ruins. The warehouse had been practically leveled. The walls had caved in and the roof had fallen down. The intensity of the chemical-propelled fire assured the cremation of Rodriguez's body and the scattering of his ashes over the river area of New Orleans. Joe had reloaded his guns and kept them on him, not knowing whether Florentine had escaped or not.

While he dug into the soil on the levee, Joe wrestled with what to do. Should he report the death to authorities in New Orleans? There would be no body. No one would know. What would they do? Was he responsible for burning down a warehouse? He couldn't pay for that. The more he thought about it, the more confused he became.

"Just call your friend, the attorney general in Tennessee. What's his name? Monkey?" Carol said and rubbed his shoulders while he took a break. "It was self-defense."

"Was it self-defense? His gun was empty. Did I have to kill him? I know I wanted to when I saw what he'd done to J. R."

"Yes, it was self-defense. He had already shot at both of us. They were going to take us out and execute us. He was trying to reload when you hit him . . . and killed him."

When the hole was dug, Joe placed J. R.'s body into a plastic bag, inside a wooden crate he had found, and then into the grave. He said a prayer and shoveled dirt back into the hole. He replaced squares of sod on the surface. Then he took a metal railroad spike and drove it through a tennis ball and into the ground at the head of the dog's grave to mark the spot.

"This is just temporary, J. R. I'm going to take you home to Tennessee when it's time."

He and Carol walked back to the boat and sat for an hour while he thought.

"You're right. I need to call Charlie Palk and get his advice. Walk with me up to Jackson Square. I'll find a phone and call him. He usually gets to the office early."

Luann answered at Palk's office in London. "A collect call? Who? Joe Chapman? Yes, we'll take it, operator."

"Luann, is Charlie in?"

"Joe Chapman. You've been a stranger for so long. Why haven't you called before? Poor Mr. Palk has been looking all over for you. You should be ashamed of yourself."

"Why's he been looking for me?"

"All hell . . . oops . . . well, all heck has broken loose since you left, but I'll let him tell you about it. Hold on."

Joe listened to the local country music station through the receiver while he was on hold. His life over the last year had been a country music song.

"Joe? Where are you? I need you here. I've been trying to find you almost since you left."

"I'm in New Orleans and I have a little problem, Charlie."

"New Orleans? I thought you were on your houseboat. What are you doing in New Orleans?"

"I took my houseboat all the way down the Tennessee, Ohio, and Mississippi rivers. It's here with me. I want to tell you about my problem."

"I don't have time for little problems. I've got big ones right here."

For the next fifteen minutes, Palk explained his problems to Joe. Palk told him about the bodies that had begun to surface as soon as Joe had left in May. The campaign for reelection had put Palk into the political fight of his life.

"Now, how does your problem compare to these?" Palk asked.

"Charlie, I'm talking to you as my attorney on this. It will remain confidential."

"Sure. Shoot."

"I just killed someone last night."

"What?"

For the next ten minutes, Joe explained his recent odyssey, his search for Cathy and Bartley, his hooking up with Cathy's sister, and their trip to New Orleans.

"Tell me that name again. Who's the guy you're looking for?"

"Kent Bartley," Joe said.

"Shit. You're not going to believe this. We're working on the same case." Palk went on to explain the body that had surfaced with Bartley's identification. "I can't officially tell you not to call the police. But between you and me, I need you up here a lot worse. There's no body. No one's going to know. It sounds like it would be considered self-defense in every state in the Union."

Joe looked at Carol who was standing at his elbow. He motioned for her to sit on one of the nearby benches.

Joe turned back to the phone. "Were there any female bodies among those found?"

"Yes. The most recent. No identification yet."

"Was she young?"

"Yes."

"Long hair?"

"Yes."

"Charlie, I'm going to unstrap my Harley from the boat and head out immediately. That female might be Cathy Pelton. I'll bring her sister with me. That's the girl I've been looking for since I left. I hope it's not her. Could be just someone else Bartley hooked up with. Don't leave tonight until I get there. We'll be late. Get me everything you have on the female and Bartley by that time."

"Joe, I have a meeting later this morning with a fellow from the DEA in Mobile who's coming up here to check out this Bartley angle."

"John Collins?" Joe asked.

"How'd you know?"

"I've met him too."

DURING THE NEXT HOUR, Joe explained as best he could to Carol why they both should go to Tennessee. He talked and packed his saddlebags. He put one box of Krugerrands in each. He was having a difficult time persuading her that she should straddle the cycle and go nearly seven hundred miles with him to Tennessee. He told her about the body that might be Bartley, but he didn't mention the one that might be Cathy. Finally, he urged her to go for her own safety. If Florentine survived and escaped the fire, he and whoever he was connected with knew where to find her in Baton Rouge. She would be safe with him in Tennessee.

She finally agreed and stuffed some clothes into one saddlebag.

Joe handed the night watchman at the warehouse wharf where he had moored THE CARP another wad of money and asked him to keep an eye on the boat. Joe took his name, address, and phone number in case he needed him while he was away. He told the watchman he would pay him extra if he was gone more than a week.

Every two hours they would take a break from the cycle and stretch and walk at the rest areas along I-59 through Louisiana, Mississippi, and Alabama. The Harley roared northeast, but Joe was afraid to push the speed faster than sixty on the antique 1972 FX. At each stop it was a struggle for Carol to dismount. Her legs were not accustomed to straddling the cycle on a long ride. She bent, squatted, ran, and did anything else to rub the numbness from her legs.

By three o'clock in the afternoon, they were to Birmingham. Joe made an excuse to stop by the hotel that he remembered from Cathy's credit card bill. She had either been going to or coming from Louisiana when she stayed here. He had first assumed she was headed back for Baton Rouge, but now he realized she could have been on her way with Bartley toward Tennessee.

While Carol ate a sandwich at a nearby restaurant, Joe took his fake DEA identification and spoke to the manager of the hotel. After a brief search of computer records, the manager told him a person identifying herself as Cathy Pelton did stay at the hotel one night during the first week of March with one other unidentified person.

Cathy had not left much of a paper trail on her travels with Bartley. The hotel and bookstore charges were all that Joe had. After the first week of March he had nothing except for the postcards that Carol had received and the payment on her storage unit. They had been postmarked from Pensacola and Denver. It seemed she had disappeared into thin air—unless the body that Palk mentioned was Cathy. If it was true, it meant her body had been there the whole time. His trip to Baton Rouge and New Orleans had all been in vain. The only things he had accomplished were to violate federal laws and kill a man. He had lost.

Joe found Carol slumped over in a booth in the restaurant when he returned. She was asleep. She needed it; he did too. They had been traveling on adrenaline since their appointment at the warehouse had turned bad. They had to press on. They could rest in London. If Carol knew what he knew, she would want to get there as fast as she could. But now, she argued for sleep.

"Just a few hours, Joe. I don't think I can hold on any longer."

Joe looked at his watch. "We can be there in four and a half hours. We'll get a motel room for you and you can crash. I told Charlie not to go home until I got there."

"What's the hurry? If that body is Bartley, it's still going to be there in the morning." She looked him in the eyes. He turned away. "Do you think . . . do you have . . . do you know something that you're not telling me? Is Cathy dead?"

"I hope not."

"Did Palk tell you something?"

"There was a female body. They haven't gotten a positive identification on it."

"But you think it might be Cathy, don't you?"

"Like I said, I hope not. But if Cathy was with Bartley, there's that possibility. That's why I want to get there as soon as possible."

"Let's go."

ALL THE INFORMATION ON the bodies that had washed up in London County was laid out on the long walnut table in Charles Palk's conference room except for the wallet found on the female. The final autopsy reports were not done on her. But everything on the three men was there for John Collins and George Stephens to see.

In neat stacks were photos of the bodies, a list of items found on or near the bodies, photos of the sites where they were found, officers' notes, pathology, autopsy, and toxicology reports. The reconstruction artist's drawing lay beside the information on each body.

Collins and Stephens were mainly interested in matching photos of known drug runners with the sketches of these bodies. Collins had brought his own drawings of the man who landed in Alabama with the pillow. From memory and against the background of a large book that had mug shots of those who had been arrested in their area on drug offenses, Collins and Stephens examined each over and over.

"I don't recognize any of these gentlemen," Collins finally said and laid all the photos back onto the table. He took off his coat and stepped next to Charles Palk. "What's wrong with the cooling in here, General?"

Palk walked to the row of windows behind them and began to raise each of the three as high as he could. "Maybe we can get a bit of a breeze in here. The system shut down over the Fourth. The hottest time of the year, and the air conditioning goes out."

"Well, we wouldn't need it if it was the coolest time of the year," Collins said and smiled.

Palk, Collins, Stephens, and Sheriff Scarboro all huddled around the area of the table where the information on the body that had Kent Bartley's driver's license was laid out. They now had three depictions to look at—a blowup of the driver's license, the mug shot from Louisiana, and the artist's drawing.

"What do you think?" Collins asked and turned to Palk.

"Well, they're all three very close. But no two are perfect matches. There's even differences between the mug shot and the driver's license. The one by the artist with just the mustache looks more like the mug shot than it does the driver's license," Palk said and wiped his scalp with a handkerchief. "There's not much skin left on the fingers to do a print. We could do a DNA if we had some body material someplace that we knew was his. A tooth, hair, skin, or something. Of course, that's expensive and takes time. Do you know of anywhere he might have left part of his body?" Palk said and laughed.

"Not that I know of," Collins said and shook his head. "We might be able to sweep his girlfriend's house in Baton Rouge and come up with some hair. I don't know how we'd know if it was his or some other visitor. There may have been a hundred men in her house. If it wasn't for the ACLU, we could take a blood sample from everybody when they're born or from every criminal when they're charged with a crime and store it. Then we could do a DNA analysis anytime we needed it for identification."

"Yeah, it's a pity that a little thing like the Constitution stands between us and doing that." Palk laughed and they all joined in.

"I believe we'll do it in the next century though. We'll first start it on the basis of being able to identify people in a plane crash or some big disaster then work it down to police investigations," Collins said.

"Maybe," Palk said, "but it sounds too easy to me."

Luann knocked on the door and entered.

"General Palk, there's two more agents from the DEA out in the reception area who say they're looking into Kent Bartley's disappearance."

Palk turned to Collins. "Are they with you?" He looked at the note Luann had handed him. "Their names are Floyd Miles and Mike Constanzo."

Collins shook his head. "No, that's New Orleans. They're the ones in charge of the investigation over in Baton Rouge where Bartley was charged with possession of cocaine. I'm trying to see if he's connected to a crashed drug plane that went down in Mobile Bay. Frankly, we're not very friendly right now. But it's okay to show them in and have a look."

"You guys aren't going to fight, are you?" Palk asked and walked to the door.

When Miles and Constanzo came in, all six milled back around the table and went over the same information one more time. Then the four DEA agents decided they wanted to look at the actual bodies in Johnson City.

"What about the female?" Miles asked. "Bartley was traveling with a Cathy Pelton. Twenty-five or so years old, long red hair—real nice looking. Does that sound like her?"

"Long hair, yes. About the right age. But she wasn't very nice looking when we recovered her body," Palk said.

"Let's go take a look," Miles said. When they had shaken hands all around, the four agents left to see Dr. Trout's collection.

Palk sat back down with the sheriff.

"Joe Chapman is going to be here in a bit, Arnold. He's run into some info in Louisiana pertaining to this Bartley fellow. He's also bringing back the sister of the one Agent Miles named. I wanted to get his input before I told them we had the girl's wallet. If Joe needs anything, help him. He's working with me on this on a temporary assignment. Okay?"

The sheriff nodded his head.

JOE PEELED OFF TWO hundred dollar bills for the clerk at the Holiday Inn at Lanter City, Tennessee—just five miles from the London County Courthouse. Carol was exhausted. She leaned against the counter. The clerk handed them keys to adjoining rooms.

"You get some sleep," Joe said. "I'm going to Charlie's office and see what's up." He took a quick shower, changed into the only other clothes he had brought, and headed for his friend's office.

"DAMN, IT'S GOOD TO see you," Palk said and grabbed Joe in a bear hug. Luann stood nearby and smiled. Palk stepped back and looked at Joe. "You look in good shape. A little tired, huh? Didn't get any sleep last night?"

"No. I've been up . . . ," he looked at his watch, "thirty-six hours."

Palk ushered Joe into his office where the window toward Main Street stood open. The heat had not abated even at 8 P.M. He took Joe to the window and pointed down the street to where Mike Garrison's headquarters was lit up with people inside on telephones calling prospective voters.

"Joe, if I don't solve these murders, Mike is going to be our new D. A. come September."

Joe looked out the window and then back to Charlie. "I remember watching him as a quarterback. He's a great kid. He looks like a prosecutor should look," Joe said and stuck a finger into the soft belly of his friend and rubbed his smooth head. "If you weren't running, I'd vote for him."

"That's what I'm afraid everybody thinks." Palk walked to the table. "I have to identify these bodies, or I won't get ten percent of the vote. I believe I'm ready to release the name on that one—Bartley. But I'll let you take a look first."

Palk opened the files and showed Joe the photos and reports. Joe stood on one side of the table and Palk on the other and passed papers back and forth. "I found Cathy's purse the day before I left here in May. It didn't have any good identification in it. That's why I've spent two months looking for her. I had visions of her appearing on my boat." He looked up to see how his friend would react to the mention of visions.

"There are four DEA agents in Johnson City right now looking at the bodies. I don't think the ones from Mobile get along well with the one from New Orleans. Some kind of turf war, I gather."

Joe looked at the photos, newspaper stories, witness interviews with the ones who had found the bodies, and the notes from Dr. Trout. He noticed a sheet of legal pad on the table between them.

"Whose phone number is that?" Joe asked.

"What phone number?" Palk looked down at the paper and frowned.

"Right there," Joe said and pointed at the paper. "It says 222-8161."

Palk looked at the paper again. The scribbling was from his conversation with Dr. Trout about the etchings on the inside of the belts found on the first two bodies. He had written it down from Trout's words—1918-ZZZ, which meant nothing to him. He stepped around to Joe's side of the table and looked at the note again and saw what Joe had seen—a seven-digit telephone number.

"Shit." Palk hit the table. "I'm getting lazy, Joe. I should have gone and looked at those belts myself. Trout gave it to me like I wrote it. But when you look at it from this side, it does look like a phone number." Palk looked at the number again. "How many area codes are there? We should be able to check those numbers out in all the area codes in the U. S., Mexico, and Canada within a day or two."

"What about the girl's body? Did you get that wallet back?"

"Yeah, I got it. But I haven't even looked at it. I wanted to be able to deny to the DEA boys that I had any I.D. on her until I saw you." Palk walked into the adjoining room and brought back the wallet encased in a plastic bag. Palk opened an accompanying envelope. "The report says the wallet contained a driver's license, four ones, a five, and a Visa card."

Joe sat down and cupped his hands beneath his chin. He looked up at Palk. "What's the name on the license?"

Palk assumed a matter-of-fact voice and read as though it was a stock market report. "The driver's license is for a Cathy Pelton of Baton Rouge."

Joe's head dropped to the table. The surface was cold against his skin. His search had ended within a few miles of where it had begun. He took several deep breaths. He sniffed back tears. How could he have become so attached to a woman he had never met? For two months she had been the dominating aspect of his life. Looking for her had brought him out of despair and relighted a fire in him he had not felt in years. Now she had been pronounced dead. If her body had died in the river, perhaps her spirit lingered along the shore and attached itself to his boat—and to him. He couldn't take the losses of the last two days.

"Do you want to see the photos? We have a preliminary autopsy, but not the final."

Joe looked up. "Yes. I want to be reminded of how society treats a beautiful young girl. It's as though she is just a thing to be labeled, analyzed, and forgotten."

"I'm sorry, Joe. You may just want to see the black and whites before you decide you want to see the color. They're not pretty."

"I'll look at both. Hand me the black and whites first."

Joe studied them. He had seen gore before. Recently he had made some of his own. The first photos were not all that bad. They showed a body under some brush on the river bank. Vines and weeds were growing near the body. In the most pleasant view, he could not see that her face had been blown away. There was long hair matted with dirt and grime.

He picked up the color photos. The reddish tint of the hair showed through despite the muck. Blue jeans and a blue sweater still covered most of the body. He turned away from the photo of her face. He didn't want to remember that view. He searched his mind for the vision of the beauty pageant contestant. He'd seen enough. He handed the photos back to Palk.

"What was the cause of death? Gun shot?"

"Yes. Either the pistol shot to the head or the shotgun blast."

"Was the wallet in another purse or on the body?"

Palk looked back at his notes. "It was in the right rear jeans pocket."

Joe looked past Palk and out into the darkness. He thumped his fingers on the table. "I'll bring her sister in and break the news to her. I told her there was a female body. I'd better let her rest for a while. She hasn't had much sleep either. How about if I bring her in here in the morning?"

"Sure. That's fine. If it's her sister, I can release the names of her and Bartley. It'll help to at least have a break on knowing who two of the victims are. Who killed them, though, is another question. What do you think?" Palk asked.

"I haven't had time to think about it. I don't know who the other two could be. Maybe they're connected to that plane that Collins

is trying to track down. Looks like somebody killed all four of them
and dumped them in the river about the same time. They sure didn't
kill each other and jump in the water." Joe thought back to the gold
he had found in Cathy's storage unit. Maybe Bartley was skimming
and somebody caught up with him and his cronies. Cathy was just an
innocent victim.

"Not likely." Palk rubbed his chin. "By the way, Joe, your old
client and friend, Mattie Hensley, is in the hospital in Knoxville. She's
not very well. Kidney failure. I saw her two days ago and she asked
about you. You need to go by and see her. She's at Park West, room
263."

"I might as well go up there now. I still can't sleep. I'll go by
and see how Carol is doing. We'll see you in the morning." Joe
reached in his pocket and brought out the hairbrush that had been in
Cathy's purse. "If you do any DNA testing, this might be helpful. It
has Cathy's hair."

WHEN JOE GOT BACK, Carol was awake and sitting by the
pool in the jeans she had packed in the Harley's saddlebag. He sat
down beside her. He told her part of what he had learned at Palk's
office, but not all.

"My oldest client, a retired school teacher, is in a hospital in
Knoxville. I'm going to ride up and see her for a few minutes. It won't
take long. Visiting hours are probably over. I'll say I'm family. Want
to go?"

"Might as well. Can't sleep. Do you think we're safe here?
What about the one I shot? Do you think he's following us?"

"No. We took off so quickly, he'll have a hard time getting a
trail for a while. Besides, he may have died in the fire."

At the hospital, Joe decided he would tell Carol that one of the
bodies was probably that of Cathy. If she fainted or had some kind of
spell, there was plenty of medical help nearby. He would spare her the
gory details for now and just give her the basics. He'd wait until after
they saw Mattie.

It seemed like all he was getting lately was bad news. So, Joe
wasn't surprised when he walked into Mattie Hensley's room and saw
her. She had wasted away. Even with the medical help, the intrave-
nous solutions, and the other machines humming behind her, she
appeared gaunt and sallow. He remembered her as small but vibrant.
Now she was so frail that she reminded him of the baby opossums he
had found as a youth. Their bodies were barely opaque. If he held
Mattie up to the light now, he probably wouldn't need an X-ray to see
her bones. She was asleep, but her right hand twitched as though it
was searching for the bed railing.

Joe leaned over and placed a hand on top of her head and smoothed her gray hair. Carol stood by his side and watched. Mattie blinked open her eyes in what was an expressionless face until she saw Joe. Then her eyes widened. She opened her mouth to speak but it came out in a whisper. "Joe. I'm glad you came."

"I just learned you were sick."

Mattie looked past Joe to Carol. "Who's that pretty girl with you?"

"A friend from Louisiana."

Mattie motioned for Joe to bend down toward her mouth. "She's a keeper. Don't let her get away."

Joe smiled. "Get well, Mattie. We'll be back to see you in a few days."

"Don't wait long. This old lady with half a brain ain't going to be here much longer."

Joe squeezed her hand, said goodbye, and stepped quietly out the door with Carol.

When they got to the lobby, Joe asked Carol to sit down. She listened to the story about all the bodies. There were two unknown men, one thought to be Bartley, and the young woman. He told her about Cathy's wallet while he held her hand. He watched her eyes. They needed her to look at the photos and then the body to identify it. Could she do that in the morning?

Carol began to sob quietly into a handkerchief. "I should have known. If it wasn't this trip, it would have been some other. Cathy lived on the edge and traveled with people who were worse. I have readied myself for this day for years. I was the one who gave her the St. Christopher's medal that you found."

Joe put his arm around her shoulders.

"Joe, I don't want to wait until tomorrow. Call your friend and tell him I want to look at the photos tonight. If I think it's her, I'll go look at the body tomorrow."

AT ELEVEN THAT NIGHT, Joe and Carol were in Palk's office. Everybody else was long gone from the courthouse. Palk had removed everything from the conference table except what pertained to the female victim.

"All the DEA guys are at their hotels. They're going to come back by tomorrow. They want me to let them know if we get any identification on the girl," Palk said. He went to the windows and opened them again. It was still hot.

Carol started with the driver's license and Visa card. She forced herself to look at the black and white photos and then the color. She wept more into her handkerchief. She asked Palk the cause of

death and was told. Why the shotgun? Why the river? She had more
questions than Palk had answers. She didn't know who Cathy's
dentist was but probably could find out. She could not definitely
identify the body from the photos. She would go to Johnson City in
the morning. She looked closer at the pictures.

"Joe, come here. Quick. This is weird. Remember what Papa
Legba told us at the warehouse before all hell broke loose?"

Joe closed his eyes and rubbed his hair back. "I remember a
little of it. Something about colors. Green, blue, black, white . . .
Cathy's spirit loping along beside a river or creek."

"Yes. That's part. Look at these pictures. He hit it right on
the money. Remember, he said he saw a latticework of black and
white. See, this picture where Cathy was found. The brush and sticks
form a latticework of black and white over her body. He mentioned a
carpet of blue and green. She's lying on green grass wearing blue
jeans.

"And do you remember how he said she had a pain in her
head? That's where she was shot. Papa Legba was right."

"Who is Papa Legba?" Palk asked, looking first at Joe and then
Carol.

"He's the voodoo doctor we went to in New Orleans to help us
find Cathy," Joe said and watched his friend's face for his reaction to
the word *voodoo*. "What he told us about Cathy pretty well matches
up."

Carol turned back to the pictures and the rest of the file. "It's
really impossible to tell from the photos if that's Cathy. Everything
points to it. But when I was looking at one of the pictures something
went off in my head—like it was out of place or something. I don't
know what. I'll go and see the body."

IN THE DARK OF midnight, Joe and Carol sat in silence near
the pool at the motel, pondering the developments of the day. They
leaned their backs against the base of a wall that supported an
overhead walkway and stared at the water ten feet away. The pool
was officially closed for the night, but Joe had jumped over the low
fence and helped Carol over. They just wanted a place where they
could sit and think. The moon reflecting off the pool's surface
reminded Joe of the river.

He took Carol's hand. She had her sleeve rolled up and her
hand and arm felt cool to him while the night was hot. He started
massaging the muscles in her arm. She didn't object. He turned and
worked his way up to her shoulders and then down her back.

"That's good. I've been so tense the last twenty-four hours and
the motorcycle ride didn't help to relax me," Carol said. She turned

and bent slightly. Her blouse came out of her jeans at the back.

Joe brought his hands down and then beneath the cloth. Her lower back was warm. He kneaded the muscles along the spine and made his way up her back. When he reached the level where he expected a bra, he found none. He had resisted any sexual feeling toward Carol as long as he thought Cathy lived, but now he was experiencing a strange arousal. He should be mourning, but he was drawn to the warmth of Carol more and more. Then he thought of incest. Was it wrong to desire the sister of the woman he had wanted for the past two months?

What about Carol? She was in mourning too. She couldn't be thinking of anything physical—sexual—at this time. It wasn't right to think of his base needs when Carol was suffering.

"Joe, did you know that all emotions have a form of coalescing centrality or source?"

What was she saying? Was this some kind of mental health talk that he had missed? "What do you mean?"

"I mean if you take all the basic emotions—anger, love, mourning, happiness—and put them together, they overlap like circles drawn on a chalkboard. People cry when they're happy and when they're sad. Angry couples sometimes make the wildest kind of love." She looked at him for a response.

"I don't follow."

"Shut up and kiss me, stupid," Carol said, turned, and wrapped her arms around him. She began to kiss him, first on his cheeks, then his forehead, and then his lips. Joe didn't resist. He put his arms around her and pressed his fingertips into her lower back. He pushed her onto her back and lay beside her without ever taking his lips off hers. They began to roll around on the concrete apron of the pool.

Lost in each other's body, they moved on the hard surface until they rolled into the water, still entwined in arms and legs and lips that wouldn't let go. They separated at the bottom of the pool and sprang upward. They both laughed, rubbed the water from their eyes, and reached out for another touch.

"Let's go to my room," Carol said.

"What's wrong with my room?"

"I've seen how you keep your boat."

Joe helped her out of the water and carried her to the gate. He set her down, sprang over the fence, and held out his hand. She was over in a second. He carried her in his arms toward her room and reached down and opened the door. Inside, they fell together in a heap on the floor where moonlight angled through an opening in the drapes.

"That's all the light we need," Joe said.

He kissed her some more while their wet clothes made funny

noises against each other and the carpet began to blot up the water.

Within seconds, his fingers were on the buttons of her blouse. The wet cloth made it a greater task than he had experienced before. One by one they gave in to his entreaties. He peeled the cloth back and uncovered Carol's breasts. She closed her eyes when he started to run his tongue around one and then the other in circles that had her nipples as center points. He dallied there for a few seconds and then began to trace a trail between her breasts with his tongue and down toward her navel.

Her eyes remained closed, but her breath came in short gasps accompanied by moans. Her skin against his mouth was cool from the pool's water. He began to blow short bursts of hot air all up and down her stomach. Then she giggled.

"That feels like a miniature hair dryer," she said. "Keep it up."

Joe threw his jacket off, took out all the weapons he carried now, and peeled his own shirt off. He removed her blouse the remainder of the way and lay back down. He closed his eyes and pleasured himself with the sensation of her wet skin against his.

"My clothes are getting cold and soggy against me. Pull my jeans off," Carol said. Joe didn't hesitate, but the wet, tight denim clung to her hips and thighs as though her skin and the cloth had melded into one. She arched her back to no effect on the jeans.

"I'm not used to taking women's clothes off," Joe said while he worked the jeans down little by little.

"Oh, sure." She arched her back again. "Just put your hands in my back pockets and jerk them off!" she screamed.

Joe obeyed. "How's that?"

"No, no, no, no, no!" Carol screamed again when her jeans were down to her knees. She kicked out of his grasp, pulled her jeans back up, and got to her feet.

"It doesn't take you long to get out of the mood," Joe said and slumped to the floor in a rolled up ball.

"That's not Cathy!" she said while she was snapping her jeans. "That's what bothered me about those pictures. I just couldn't think what it was."

"What?" Joe whispered.

"Cathy. Her jeans. The wallet was in the back pocket. Cathy doesn't wear jeans that have back pockets. No back pockets for her. They would ruin the lines of her pretty little ass."

Joe sat up. He remembered all the jeans he had seen in Cathy's house. No back pockets.

"Cathy wouldn't be caught dead in a pair of jeans that had back pockets. That's not her. I'd bet my life."

Thirty–three

J oe Chapman found it difficult to persuade D. A. Charles Palk that
he was sure the female was not Cathy Pelton because of the kind
of jeans that she wore.

"No pockets. No back pockets. Monkey, you'd better wait for
the hair sample analysis and the dental records from Baton Rouge
before releasing any names," Joe said into the phone while Carol Sent
looked at the road atlas and the postcards she'd received from Cathy.

They sat together on the edge of the bed in her room.
Exhaustion had mixed with relief that the body might not be Cathy's.
They had slept until noon. Now they had begun to reexamine all the
notes, records, and the shreds of memory that would point to Cathy's
whereabouts. Joe was warning his friend that the bodies might not be
who they appeared to be.

Joe had told Carol the rest of what he had found out—the
Krugerrands in Cathy's storage compartment, the charge card bill, the
bookstore in New Orleans, and his stop at the hotel in Birmingham to
confirm Cathy's stay there.

"If that isn't Cathy, Charlie, I doubt that the one with Bartley's
wallet is him either. You don't want to have another orangutan affair
this close to the election."

Joe hung up and turned to Carol who was looking at the line
he had drawn on the atlas when he was in Baton Rouge. The dark
line marked with bold arrows showed Cathy and Kent going from
Lexington to Birmingham to New Orleans. Carol looked at the charge
card bill that Joe had stolen from Cathy's mailbox.

"Joe, you've been looking at things upside down."

"What do you mean?"

"Remember, I received cards from Cathy with Birmingham and
Lexington scenes on them. She had charges on her card for the
Birmingham hotel and the New Orleans bookstore. The one at the
bookstore was later. So you thought she had gone from Birmingham
to New Orleans. But what did they tell you at the bookstore? It was

a phone order. She was never in New Orleans after she left. And when did the lady at the storage unit tell you she received the payment?"

"Uh, late March. The twenty-sixth, I believe."

"What kind of card were the charges on?"

"Mastercard."

"What kind did they find on this body?"

"Visa."

"Cathy still has her Mastercard. There were no new charges on it after the bookstore purchase. Why?"

"Why?" Joe asked back.

"Bartley. He's crafty enough to have convinced Cathy that credit cards leave a paper trail that can be traced. Once they got to where they were going and got some money, they lived on cash. No checks. No credit cards. Does that sound reasonable?"

Joe looked at the atlas and cringed at the thought he had done the same thing as Palk—not looked at evidence from more than one direction. Carol was right. It was just as probable that Cathy and Kent had passed through Birmingham going northward rather than toward New Orleans. He had thought about it before but now it looked clearer. Where was she now if she wasn't in Dr. Trout's morgue in Johnson City? Birmingham or Lexington?

"Where do you think she went?" Joe asked.

"Where there're horses. Lexington, Kentucky."

"Lexington." It was obvious now that he thought about it. Cathy's new passion was horses. The book in New Orleans was about horses. Her house had horse books. She had been riding often in Baton Rouge. What place in the country is more famous for horses than Kentucky and the Bluegrass area of Lexington?

Carol cast her eyes downward. "Joe, I've got to get back to my clients in Baton Rouge. You should go on to Lexington without me. This is my fourth day to be gone. I need to get back."

Joe looked away from the atlas and toward Carol. It hadn't crossed his mind that she would leave before they found Cathy. He suddenly felt abandoned and lonely. He needed her to go on with him. She was smart. She had seen the clues when he hadn't. Even if he found Cathy, there was no assurance that she would even talk with him without her sister being there. She had to go. He liked her company. He would have to persuade her and do it quickly. Fear and guilt should be a deadly combination.

"What about the guy you shot? He's going to be waiting for you in Baton Rouge if he got out of that alive. It'd be dangerous, foolhardy to go back now. And Cathy must be in danger. She's your sister, Carol. Please go on with me. I need you.

"You can always help other people. We only have so many opportunities to help our family. This may be the last time you can help Cathy." He rubbed his temples. He thought of a Biblical illustration. "In the book of Esther, Esther's uncle asked her, 'Who knows whether you are come to the kingdom for such a time as this?' "

Carol reached for the phone and her purse. She pulled out her calling card and dialed in the numbers. "Don, I'm going to be gone for a few more days. Can you cover for me? I'll be in Lexington, Kentucky, looking for my sister. I'm with a . . . friend from Tennessee." She paused, listening to the response. "Thanks. I owe you one." She hung up but began to tremble and cry at the same time.

Joe moved closer and held her to him. He looked over her shoulder at the atlas and measured the distance to Lexington in his mind. "You did the right thing, Carol. It'll all turn out okay. Your clients would want you to take up for your sister. That's part of family."

He made one last call to Palk while Carol showered and packed. "Lexington, Kentucky. But keep it quiet. I'll keep you informed."

He then called Sean Bodine. "That's probably not Bartley that they found in Tennessee."

"I thought you were in New Orleans."

"I was. But things happened. It's a long story. I'm in Tennessee on my way to Lexington, Kentucky."

"Paper said there was a huge fire by the river. Did you see it?"

"Yes. Closer than I wanted to."

"Lexington, Kentucky, then. Call me soon. You know where you'll be staying?"

"No. I'll call you."

FLORENTINE SMILED WHEN HE listened to the tape recording of the telephone bug in Bodine's office. "I need somebody to go to Lexington, Kentucky, with me," he said to his two friends who sat with him in a Baton Rouge office three doors down from Bodine's. "The survivors are going to take us to Mr. Bartley and his lover. We also have a little unfinished business with Joe Chapman and Carol Sent. We must avenge Rodriguez." He lifted his bandaged left arm gently and removed the cigarette from his mouth. He blew out smoke and smiled again.

JOE PROMISED CAROL THEY would rent a car once they arrived in Lexington. She complained about her sore legs and back from the long ride to Tennessee. Now they were back on I-75 headed north passing Knoxville, Lake City, and Jellico. They stopped at the

Kentucky Welcome Center and relaxed with a Coke and Dr. Pepper. They lay in the grass near the Harley, taking in the sunshine. Two more hours and they would be in Lexington.

CHARLES PALK AND THE four DEA agents huddled in his conference room. "Can any of you tell me definitely who any of these people are?" Palk asked and pointed to each of the four files. None of the agents took the bait. "Now, I know we found drivers' licenses and wallets on two of the bodies that would tend to identify them as the two you're looking for from Baton Rouge. But that's not enough for me to go public with their names. Those items could've been planted on them—right?"

There was silence for a full minute, then John Collins nodded.

"That's right. Dr. Trout said he may be able to get enough finger tissue from the body that had Bartley's license to do a comparison on the prints we have from Baton Rouge. The girl didn't have a record, so there're no known prints. We could lift some from her house, but we still wouldn't be sure they were hers without comparing all we found in the house."

"Well, I have some of Cathy Pelton's hair. At least I think I do. We can start DNA testing with that. We'll be getting her dental records from Baton Rouge. It'll take a while," Palk said.

The four agents exchanged glances.

"Where did you get her hair?" Collins asked.

Palk looked down at the table. He had said too much. They didn't know his connection with Joe Chapman and didn't know he had been there.

"Y'all have met Joe Chapman. He's a friend of mine. He came through yesterday with Cathy Pelton's sister. They don't believe it's Cathy's body. But he had a hair brush he had found that he thought was Cathy's. That's what he left. He's gone to Lexington, Kentucky, to check out a lead there."

The agents nodded. "That's all you know, General Palk?" Collins asked.

"Yeah. He said he'd check in with me."

"Good. Keep us informed."

"Which office? Mobile or New Orleans?"

Collins and Miles looked at each other. "Both," they said together.

Collins caught up with Miles outside the London County Courthouse on the walkway where the sun-dried marigolds were attempting a comeback with the aid of a gardener's spraying of water.

"Just a minute, Miles," Collins said and took his counterpart by the arm. They stepped off the walkway. "Before you go back to Louisiana, I want to get one thing straight. You know or you have information that Kent Bartley was the pilot of that plane that went down in my territory in February. That's whose mug shot you showed to the airport manager in Jackson, Mississippi, isn't it?"

Miles nodded.

"And you either know or have a good idea who the body I have in Mobile is, don't you? The one that used a pillow for a parachute." Again Agent Miles nodded. "When are you going to tell me? We're working for the same agency. If I don't start getting some answers, I'm going to take it to Washington and see which office the shit falls on. You understand?" Collins asked in a forceful whisper.

"Sure, John, I understand," Miles said. Beads of perspiration gathered on his forehead. "But you've got to give me a few days. This operation is bigger than you or I. We'll have to get the authority from the head man in New Orleans, but I think we can identify your body for you. And, yes, Bartley is a key player in this. If that's Bartley up in the morgue, you won't have to worry about me. You'll be dealing with young Constanzo there because my ass will be canned. So, give me a few days, okay?" Miles asked and smiled. He put an arm around Collins.

"No more than a week," Collins said and turned back toward his younger partner.

JOE KNEW HE WOULD have to dip into the Krugerrands if the search for Cathy became more prolonged. He just gave the clerk at the Quality Inn on Newtown Pike in Lexington a hundred dollar bill to cover their first two nights. Carol still insisted on having a separate room. They were one mile from I-75 and two miles from Rupp Arena and downtown. It would be a good central location from which to coordinate their search for Cathy and Kent.

They met at Carol's room to look at the tourist guidebooks and maps he had taken from the motel's reception area.

He had asked the clerk how many horse farms there were around Lexington.

"Probably over a thousand," wasn't the answer he wanted.

He and Carol looked at the green map of Fayette County that showed many of the horse farm locations with little red horseshoes. There were at least a hundred on the map, and they were just the ones that paid to get on or were famous enough to be noted. Those with five or ten horses probably were not listed. He read the names, some of which he recognized: Spendthrift, Calumet, Hartfield, Overbrook, Cavehill, Terrebonne, Three Chimneys, Eclipse, Busby, and on and on and on.

It seemed hopeless. If Cathy, indeed, was living, working, or riding at one of the horse farms, it would be pure luck or coincidence if he found her. And there were other horse farms besides just in Fayette County. She could be in a surrounding county or not here at all. He wished he had another post office box key or one to another storage unit. All they had was the postcard with a Lexington horse farm scene.

The next morning they divided the county into squares. Each would go to all the horse farms in his or her box and see if anyone had heard of Cathy. Carol got the rental car while Joe stayed with the Harley.

Joe took a tour of Spendthrift in the morning to become acquainted with horse farms in general. It was strictly a breeding farm. Studs were boarded, waiting for mares to be brought in to breed. He noticed the farm employed very few women.

"Why?" Joe asked.

"It's too dangerous," his guide told him. "The horses can smell women during that time of the month. They go a little crazy. A month ago, one of the horses grabbed a visiting woman by the hair of her head as we were walking right along this fence. Horses have a very keen sense of smell."

Joe saw the breeding dock where, for a fee beginning at a thousand dollars, mares were bred in ninety seconds of fury.

He only told Carol part of what he learned.

"They bury the great horses and erect monuments to them. The near great, they bury a part of them. I didn't dare ask what part and how they do that—with a chain saw or whatever."

"Well, I visited ten farms, and nobody had heard of or seen Cathy. It was tiresome. There's a lot of horses around here."

Joe lay on the bed looking at the ceiling. "I wonder what they do with great horses' asses?"

Carol leaned over to look him right in the eye. "They name them Joe Chapman or Carp and send them to the Quality Inn."

"It's quite a life to be a horse at stud. They give you all the food you want, change your bed twice a day, and give you at least two rubdowns. Then they bring you a mare for a romp in the hay. If I believed in reincarnation, I'd want to come back as a retired race horse. A stud."

"Yeah, I've heard that joke. The guy wanted to come back as a stud and he ended up on a snow tire in Minnesota. That's where you'd be."

"There was one horse out there—a million dollar colt who broke a bone in his foot on his first race as a two-year-old. Been studding ever since. His potential as a race horse was great, but the little flaw in his foot ended it."

Carol took the photo of Cathy in the Baton Rouge pageant and looked at it.

"It's tragic when something as beautiful and talented as a Thoroughbred doesn't reach its potential," she said and still stared at Cathy. "That's what happened to my sister. Cathy's a Thoroughbred. She could be a great ballerina, or a great pianist, artist, or dancer. But that flaw . . . or whatever it is . . . of tagging after people like Kent Bartley is going to take her down just like that horse you saw at the farm." She turned again to Joe. "She's not the perfect woman you're looking for. Nobody is." She took a tissue and wiped at the corner of her eyes where tears had puddled.

"If I can find her, she'll change," Joe said and sat up. He put an arm around Carol. "If I can get her away from Bartley and with me, things will be different. She just needs a good man in her life."

Carol sobbed louder and buried her face in a pillow.

THE NEXT DAY THEY traveled together to the farms in Carol's rented car. A little way out Old Frankfort Pike, they pulled onto a narrow lane where, if two cars met, one had to take to the shoulder to allow passage. Joe pulled over at the crest of a small knoll where the shoulder of the road allowed a place to park. From that vantage point, they surveyed the miles of well-manicured pasture that lay on both sides of the road ahead and behind them as far as they could see.

The narrow way was lined on both sides by oak trees that in some places had grown into the remnants of stone fences that predated the days of Henry Clay. Joe and Carol stood in the shade of one of those trees and admired the neatly kept fields. There were no weeds, no scrubby undergrowth, just acre after acre of dark green Bluegrass. On one side of the road, the traditional white plank fences had taken the place of old stone ones. On the other side, black plank fences ran the borders of the pastures. A quarter mile to the right was a dirt workout area where three horses were gathered with their trainers.

The serenity of it all impressed Joe. The peace and freedom of the river had always encouraged him. Now the quiet pastures of Kentucky rekindled within him a desire to put the past aside and look to the future. Cathy must be a lot like him if this was where she wanted to be. All the great poets, writers, and philosophers had proclaimed the civility of nature. He had read many poems about trees, mountains, the moon, stars, rivers, and plains. Snowfall and gentle rain had also inspired those who put pen to paper. He could not remember a good essay or poem about a computer, typewriter, or even a finely tuned legal brief. If Cathy wanted to stay on a horse farm, he would gladly leave his world of word processors, docket soundings by judges, the reading of advance sheets of law cases, and research on the Internet to nestle here in the Bluegrass with the woman with the golden red hair and the heart and soul of an artist.

"Why are some fences black and some white?" Carol asked.

"They told me at the farm yesterday that horses can see the black fences better and don't run into them as often. The white fences are more traditional though, and many farm owners want to maintain the pristine appearance." Joe put a hand to his brow to shade his eyes, turned, and did a full circuit of the scene. "I suspect it also has something to do with maintenance. The dark fences don't have to be painted as often. White shows wear a lot sooner."

"Is that why only virgins wear white at weddings?"

"If that were the case, white would not be worn except on rare occasions."

Carol looked away and pointed. "Joe, do you see what I see?"

"What?" he asked.

"It's Papa Legba's words again," Carol said and turned completely around, looking at all the surroundings. "Remember what he said about where Cathy was?"

"I remember you thought it matched with the photos of that body we saw down in London County."

"No, I was wrong on that. But look here. He said she was near a latticework of black and white. Look at these fences around here. See?"

"Yes."

"He said there was a carpet of blue and green. See the green grass?"

"Yes."

"Bluegrass. And he said her spirit was loping along beside a creek or river. See just beyond the workout area?" She pointed toward the horses. "There's a creek or a river. Who's riding that horse? Can you see? Isn't it a girl?"

Joe squinted toward the mounted rider a quarter of a mile away. "It could be a girl. Let's go see." He hurried Carol to the car and drove toward the farm.

It wasn't Cathy. It was a girl riding the horse, but not the right one. How many farms in Fayette County had black and white fences with a creek or river flowing through their acres of Bluegrass? They took their map and pinpointed the ones that showed large creeks or rivers. When they drove near, they whittled them down further by choosing the ones that had both black and white fences in close proximity.

During the first week, they found nearly a hundred farms that met the description. No one at any of the farms had heard of a Cathy Pelton or acted as if they had seen the girl in the photo that Joe or Carol showed to them. Carol called Baton Rouge again and arranged for another week away from the office.

There were no good results the second week either. Carol called Baton Rouge again. This time she said it might be a month before she returned.

"Joe, if I don't go back soon, I won't have any clients left. After two weeks, they'll either want to stay with my associate or not come back at all."

"You're needed here. They can get by with someone else."

DURING THE DAY, THEY would check the farms in an endless tedium of the same questions and same answers. At night, Carol finished fleshing out Joe's genogram and practiced her profession by talking to him about his family, his background, and how he became who he was.

He had not mentioned his dog's death or that of Rodriguez since the day after they happened.

"Are you doing okay with losing J. R.?" Carol asked one evening while Joe was lying on the bed staring at the ceiling.

"I try not to think about him. But then I catch myself. If I see an old tennis ball, I start to pick it up and throw it for him. Or I turn around to see if he's there. Or I see a squirrel like he used to chase at home. Yeah, I miss him."

"Are you dealing okay with what happened to Rodriguez?"

"I think telling Charlie Palk helped me. I needed somebody who wasn't there to say it was okay. I still sometimes wake up after I've dreamed about him shooting J. R. I'm sweating and want to kill him again."

"That may last for a while."

"You were there, Carol. And I keep asking myself if I could have gotten away with you without killing Rodriguez. I didn't fight fair. But I knew who I was dealing with. He had threatened me before. He was strong and didn't seem to have a conscience."

"You did what you had to do. You're bound to remember it for a long while. You might feel better if you got yourself another dog."

Joe shook his head. "No. I had J. R. for seven years. I don't think I could get attached to another one this soon."

Carol handed him an apple and sat down beside him.

"Are you ready to tell me about what caused your bankruptcy and suspension from law practice?"

Joe's eyes narrowed. He didn't look at Carol. "No. It's simple but it haunts me. I can't talk about it."

"I know it involves a young girl. Right?"

"Yeah. I'll tell you sometime. Maybe you can help me through that. I can't now."

Carol rolled out the sheet of paper where she had been working on Joe's genogram. She started penciling in more notes.

"Joe, you said your father died when you were ten, but you didn't tell me how or I forgot to ask. That seems awfully young. What happened to him?"

"An accident."

"Automobile?"

"No."

"What then?"

Joe rolled up both sleeves of his shirt and alternated rubbing one arm and then the other.

"I showed you the scar from my fight with the dog." He held out his left arm.

"Yes, that was awful."

He held out his right arm, displaying skin from his wrist to his elbow that varied in color from a mottled pink to brown and looked like a grotesque patchwork quilt.

"What happened to that arm?"

"A fire." He closed his eyes.

"You want to tell me about it?"

"I was ten. We had a small dairy farm. I did the chores around the dairy barn where we processed milk from the cows into ten-gallon cans. We were pretty poor. We depended on the milk for a living when my dad wasn't working construction.

"One morning Dad was in a real foul mood about something. I don't remember what. I was goofing off with the cat that hung around the barn. She had just had kittens a week before. Anyway, I wasn't watching what I was doing and knocked over a fresh ten-gallon can of milk onto the floor of the dairy barn.

"My dad was furious when he saw it. He grabbed me by the back of my shirt, took his belt off, whipped me, took me over to the regular barn where we stored the hay, and threw me into a stable. I was crying and pleading for him to spare me any further punishment. He locked the door to the stable and told me I'd stay there until I learned to be responsible. He was cursing and going on.

"I couldn't get out, so I curled up in the corner. Then I smelled smoke. A fire had started near the next stall in some loose hay. I began to yell, but either he didn't hear or didn't pay any attention to me.

"The smoke got thicker and the fire was spreading from that stall to the entire barn. I banged my shoulder against the door, but it wouldn't budge. I tried to climb out, but I couldn't. I was trapped.

"It seemed like forever, but it was probably just five or ten minutes until everything around me was on fire. My stable was a little island that hadn't caught yet.

"I heard my dad yelling that he was coming after me. He told me to lie down on the floor. I did until I didn't hear him anymore. Then I started banging into the walls and door until I finally fell through to the stable next to mine. I fell into the fire. So I had to get up and run through the flames and out. My shirt caught on fire and the hair was burned off my head.

"There were other people outside by that time. They rolled me on the ground. But my dad . . . ," Joe wiped tears from the corners of his eyes, "my dad died when he went back to try to save me. He was a smoker and must have accidentally thrown a cigarette down when he threw me into the prison of the stable. Every time I look at my arm, I'm reminded of that. It was my fault that my dad died. If I hadn't been goofing off with that cat and playing around, none of it would've happened.

"I usually wear long-sleeved shirts all the time now. I don't like to think about either incident, and I don't like to explain to other people."

Carol dropped her pencil, scooted up to Joe, and hugged him. "Joe, you weren't responsible for your father's death. You didn't lock yourself up, and you didn't drop the cigarette."

"Maybe. But I did something that caused him to do that."

"You were just ten. Ten-year-olds play with cats."

"I still have a thing about fires. They scare me . . . but they enrage me, too. And it's odd, when I get really angry, I want to start one myself . . . or three like I did before I left in May."

"It's not so odd when you know that fear and anger are two sides of the same coin. When a person feels scared and helpless, he gets angry and tries to do something to regain control."

Joe didn't look her in the eye. He just nodded and bowed his head.

"How did you feel when you were in the stable and fire was all around you?" Carol asked.

"I felt scared and alone. I thought my dad had done it on purpose, that he wanted to get rid of me because I couldn't do anything right. I thought I was going to burn up and then burn in Hell."

Thirty-four

n the evenings after they had visited horse farms during the day,
Carol and Joe would split up and look for Cathy in downtown
Lexington. Carol hit the malls while Joe visited the more seedy
side of town. In taverns, strip joints, and clubs, he would show Cathy's
picture to anyone who would look. No one remembered seeing her.

Days turned into weeks with the first of August approaching.
The deadline for returning Bartley to Baton Rouge was nearing with
no sign of him. Joe called Sean Bodine.

"You'll have to ask the judge for an extension. Tell him you
have somebody in Kentucky working on it. We're hot on his trail."

"I'll ask him, my friend. I sure would hate to cough up a
hundred grand for him. Where are you if I need to get word to you?"

"Quality Inn on Newtown Pike in Lexington."

THREE DOORS DOWN FROM Bodine's office, a swarthy,
thick-set man with a mop of stringy black hair smiled. He wrote on
his note pad the words that Joe had just spoken. He took off his
headphones, laid his half-smoked cigar in his coffee cup, and dialed the
number of a Holiday Inn in Lexington, Kentucky. He asked for the
room number he knew by heart.

"Your friend, Joe Chapman, just checked in with Bodine. He's
at the Quality Inn on Newtown Pike. You know where that is?"

Florentine turned from the phone and looked at his companion
who was sitting in front of the television. "Yes, I know where that is.
We're within a mile. It's strange that I haven't seen him before this.

Keep listening to Bodine's phone. Bartley might accidentally check in."

He laid the phone back into its cradle, went to his suitcase, and removed two pistols—one already equipped with a silencer.

"I'm going to let you tail Joe Chapman for a few days. He may find Bartley for us. If he does or doesn't, he's dead this time next week."

"What about the girl with him?" the younger one asked.

Florentine looked past him and out the window. "Yeah, you can play with her. Then you have to kill her."

"With this?" the young man asked. He smiled as he ran the blade of a large knife teasingly against his own throat.

"Yes, with that. Joe Chapman will watch, and then you'll kill him with the same knife." Florentine took the knife. "It will be very satisfying for me."

CHARLES PALK LOOKED AT the lab reports on the hair comparisons from the dead female and the strands that Joe had given him from the hairbrush. "You were right, Joe. The dead girl isn't Cathy Pelton. The hair samples and dental records confirmed it. And we got enough tissue to compare the fingerprints of Bartley to the body that was carrying his wallet and driver's license. It's not him."

"Anything on the numbers from the belts? Were they telephone numbers?" Joe asked.

"No word yet. John Collins and his DEA office are helping me run those down all over the States, Mexico, Canada, and Central America. We'll have a list of everyone who's ever had that telephone number over the last five years in about a week. Then we'll see if the names match up with anything I have or they have. It's a long shot, but it's all we can do now."

"I'll keep trying on this end. We're not having any luck so far."

"Joe, before you go, I need to let you know that the two agents from New Orleans came back through here a week ago. They're headed to Lexington. You might run into them."

"Do they know I'm here?"

"Yeah, I let it slip. Sorry."

"Crap. I don't need any company up here. It's hard enough getting anybody to talk. Now with the feds in town, I may not find out shit."

"Settle down, Joe. They're on our side. I think."

Joe hung up and turned to Carol. "The feds are here looking for Cathy and Kent now. If we don't find them first, I'm afraid of what might happen. Kent might use Cathy as a hostage or shield against the DEA. We've got to work harder."

He fell onto the bed and began to rub his head. The search

was becoming so complicated and dangerous. He had been shot at, followed, assaulted, and no telling what else that he didn't know about. He thought back to May. If he could turn the clock back, he would have shoved the purse away instead of raking it in.

"I wish I was back on the river," he mumbled.

"That's pure escapism. You just want to be free of all obligations or responsibilities. You don't have a family, a job, or anything else. You want to seek happiness and perfection without paying the price. You have a problem with relationships, so you fantasize one. You don't want to be confined or restricted. That's why you like the river. You're in this search to stay, buddy. I'm going to see to that," Carol said and pointed a finger at him.

Joe looked her in the eye. "Is there any hope for me?"

"Sure. You're not that bad. You've got to work on relationships with humans. Your closest and most loving relationship was with your dog. You enjoyed that because J. R. made few demands on you. He had an unconditional love for you. You had him and your freedom.

"And you love your boat so much that you named yourself Carp for the boat. It was an alter ego. Carp wanted the wide and smooth course of the river rather than the narrow and bumpy road of life."

"Maybe you have me pegged right. But how does Cathy fit into this?"

"Fantasy, beauty, and perfection. Her presence doesn't threaten you because it's still just a fantasy. We're getting close, and you're ready to give up. If you do find her, you'll probably hope that she rejects you so you won't have to pursue that relationship any further. Or, you may think that Cathy, with her background of being a wild spirit herself, wouldn't be someone who'd restrict you to a straight and narrow course. She's your river. Wild and free. Hair of gold and feet of silver. Fun with no responsibility."

"Maybe," was all that Joe could say. He turned away from her and looked at the calendar. "I've got to call the man at the warehouse about my boat now that you've mentioned it."

He took the piece of paper from his wallet that had the telephone number. He punched it in without looking back at Carol.

"How's my boat doing?" he asked and listened to the response. "Who? When? . . . . Okay, just keep an eye on it. I'll pay you when I get back."

He hung up the phone, turned to Carol, and rubbed his eyes. "He said the DEA searched the boat. Didn't take anything. I can't imagine anything I left on there that they'd want."

AGENT FLOYD MILES SAT up when the phone rang in his

room at the Hyatt Regency Hotel adjacent to Rupp Arena in downtown Lexington. Agent Mike Constanzo beat him to it but handed it to Miles.

"Yes. We know that Joe Chapman and Pelton's sister are staying at the Quality Inn. We don't have their rooms bugged yet, but we're working on it. Bartley is bound to be around here from what we hear in Cincinnati and Louisville. . . . When will they be here? . . . Yeah. Thanks. We can use them."

Miles hung up the phone and turned to Constanzo who was reading the sports page of the *Lexington Herald-Leader*. "They're sending six more agents—two from New Orleans, two from Dallas, and two from Memphis. Bartley is so crazy that we'll need a show of force to take him. I want you to follow Chapman until we find Bartley. He may lead us to him. He's been here two weeks longer than we have. Don't let him see you. He might recognize you from Baton Rouge."

CAROL WAS TIRED, HOT, and sweaty the next afternoon when she reached her tenth horse farm of the day. It fit the description. There were both white and black fences encircling the farm and a large creek meandered through the pasture. For what seemed like the thousandth time, she held out the photo of Cathy toward the man at the stable.

He took his pipe out of his mouth, laid aside the rake he had been using to smooth out the bedding for the mares, and took the photo into his roughened hand. "Who did you say this was, young lady?" he asked and looked at it from various angles.

"Cathy Pelton. She's my sister."

He turned the picture one way and then the other. "Yep. I'd say that's Katy Gross. She started to work for us in April. Part time. She exercises the mares. It looks like Katy in the face, but I've never seen her in an evening gown."

A rush of adrenaline washed away all the weariness that Carol had felt. Maybe this was it. Cathy was here. She'd found her. Not Joe—her.

"Is she here now?"

"Nope. Only works three days. Rides the mares to exercise them. It's beautiful, just beautiful the way she rides. Like a queen. Just lopes along the trail down there by the creek like she's a part of the horse. A beautiful girl." He looked off toward the creek and trail as though Cathy was there now.

Carol wanted to be as sure as she could be before she told Joe and got their hopes up too high.

"Sir," she said and drew the older man's attention back to the here and now, "if I asked you to describe that girl's most outstanding physical characteristic, what would you say?"

He eyed her while he pushed back his soiled tan hat, scratched his head, and leaned for support onto the rake.

"If I were telling you her most outstanding feature, young lady, I'd say her hair. Like spun copper. But, if a man asked me and we weren't in the presence of ladies, I might say something else." He smiled and looked beyond Carol.

"She has the prettiest ass of anyone in Lexington?" Carol asked. It was like a bolt of lightning had hit the man. He jerked his hand to his hat and then smiled.

"Exactly. My sentiments precisely."

Carol's heart beat like a hummingbird in flight.

"When does she work next?"

"Day after tomorrow."

"Do you have an employment card that might have her home address and telephone number?"

"We should have," he said and looked at Carol. "I guess it'd be okay to give that to her sister. You are her sister, aren't you?"

Carol nodded and affirmed that she was. He stepped into a little office at the barn and came back out with a three-by-five card.

"Not much here. She didn't list a street address. Just a post office box. I don't guess she lives in that. It'd be too small. No phone. I guess whoever took the information in April was so caught up in looking at her that he forgot to get some of the detail." He handed the card to Carol.

She studied it. The name was different. The Social Security number wasn't Cathy's. Carol wrote them down. Joe was good at that. Maybe he could get a street address from the post office. She handed the card back to the man.

"Don't tell her I was here. I want it to be a surprise. What time will she work?"

"Seven to five."

Carol thanked him again and was off in her rental car to relay the good news to Joe at the motel. She looked at her watch. He should be there by now. She was just six miles away.

JOE LEFT HIS ROOM after returning early from his rounds of the horse farms. He'd had no more luck than usual. He left Carol a note on her door that he'd be downtown checking out the bars and clubs again. He would talk with her later that night. He left his Harley and walked the two miles along the streets to the Fayette County Courthouse and started his search of the downtown bars. He walked by the Mary Todd Lincoln house, Rupp Arena, and the Hyatt Regency before stepping into the first bar. He didn't notice Agent

Constanzo in the blue Buick pass him twice or the young, dark complected man who walked behind him.

CAROL READ JOE'S NOTE. She pounded her fists against the door. "Damn," she said under her breath. He would be gone until midnight or more likely two in the morning. She took the spare key to his room and went there to await his arrival. She showered and then lay on one of the beds. Now that she had good news, there was no one to tell. Then she heard a sound at the door.

"Joe? Is that you?" She ran to the window and looked out. Whoever it was had heard her voice and was quickly walking away. All she could see was the back of a man wearing a business suit and carrying what looked like a Walkie-talkie. She went to the door, snapped the other security lock, and then lay back down.

JOE CHAPMAN HAD NO luck at the first two bars he went to. By ten he was walking north on Mill Street when he stopped and read the historical marker at Henry Clay's old law office. He read in silence about the "Great Compromiser."

The sidewalks, lined by tall oak trees, were practically deserted. He continued his walk on this moonless night in the historical section of downtown Lexington. Wrought-iron fences on both sides of the narrow street protected the soft green turf from the tread of tourists and kept them directed on down the tour route. A cat screamed and ran after knocking over a trash can in an alley to Joe's right. He crossed Third Street and was at the entrance of Transylvania University. He put both hands to his throat in silence and walked on.

A left turn and another brought him back toward downtown on North Broadway. He was going around in circles—as was the search for Cathy. At some point he had to give up and go home to Tennessee. He'd have to admit defeat and go on with his life. He and Carol had tried every place they could imagine that Cathy or Kent would go—all to no avail. Joe didn't pay any attention to the Buick that passed him. Constanzo, in the car, had radioed Joe's location to Miles from early evening. Miles had attempted to plant a bug at Joe's motel room but was scared away by Carol's voice.

Joe's mind was on Cathy. He did not look behind him as much as he had in the past. The young man followed at a discreet distance and stepped into the shadows anytime that Joe stopped or turned.

The old Lexington Opera House loomed in front of him now. Joe stopped and read another historical marker. Al Jolsen and Will Rogers had performed there. It said that in 1906 a production of *Ben Hur* included an onstage chariot race.

The massive old building stood darkened now except for a faint light coming through a pane of glass at a side door. Joe imagined hearing soft piano music coming from the same direction as the light. He walked toward the side entrance, and as he approached, the music became louder.

He cupped his hands to his eyes and pressed his face to the glass pane of the door. Thirty feet in front of him, a solitary old black man straddled a straight back chair that had been turned to face him. He puffed on a pipe and stared straight ahead of him and to Joe's right toward an elevated stage. A janitor's push broom leaned against the chair's back. The old man was transfixed, looking toward the lone performer on stage. Joe looked to his right but could only glimpse a shadow.

A portable tape player was the source of the music. It sat at the edge of the stage while a blue spotlight was the sole source of illumination. Joe moved to a slightly different position. A dancer's foot merged with the shadow. Then she came into his sight doing perfect pirouettes ten feet from the music. She would step out and then back to where she would disappear from his sight.

Her hair was up in a bun, but there was no mistaking the golden red hue that he had seen so often, even in the blue of the spotlight. The apparitions and visions had taken on flesh. She was silent and beautiful. She flitted like a butterfly from blossom to blossom. Gravity appeared to have lost its grip on her. Her jumps and landings were like deer bounding through a forest.

Joe's heart pounded while he watched her kick her legs high and step about the stage on her toes. His hands began to fog up the window when he realized only the door stood between him and Cathy. He reached down and pulled at the handle. It was locked. He walked to the front entrance. It, too, was locked.

Beside the front doors in a glass enclosed case was a poster announcing the Lexington Ballet's next performance of *Swan Lake* featuring Katherine Gross. Joe gazed at the dancer on the black and purple background of the publicity piece. The eyes, hair, and body were those of Cathy Pelton—his Lady of the River. She had changed her name, but she couldn't disguise her beauty.

He walked a complete circuit of the building, trying every door in turn. None gave in to his pulling and pushing. When he arrived at the back parking lot there were only two cars there. One was an El Camino of 1970s vintage. The janitor's. The other was a red 1965 Ford Mustang. Any doubts were removed. It was Cathy's car.

A set of keys rested in his pocket. He reached in and fished out the key chain that bore the likeness of a Ford Mustang on one side and Libra on the other. He checked and the doors of the Mustang were locked. As the final test and confirmation that the young woman inside the opera house was Cathy, he slid the rounded Ford key into the driver's side door lock and turned it. The lock clicked and the button popped up when he rotated the key. He opened the door and put his head to the upper part of the driver's seat. He took in a long breath. He could smell Cathy.

For the next hour, he stood at the door where he had first seen the dancer and pressed his nose to the glass. He luxuriated in Cathy's form and the knowledge that he had finally found her.

When she finished her practice and bent down to turn off the music, Joe walked back to her car, opened the door gently, lay down in the back floorboard, and pulled the door silently closed behind him. He pulled the .357 from its holster. Adding kidnapping to his list of crimes would be no big deal. He prayed that she would be alone, would not see him, or hear him breathing when she entered the car.

Cathy Pelton picked up the tape player and smiled at the janitor who was praising her performance. She wrapped herself in a loose overcoat and headed toward the door. The janitor pushed the door open for her and then locked it behind her. He watched until she unlocked the car and sat in the front seat. He then turned to finish his sweeping of the stage floor.

When Cathy put the key into the ignition, Joe quickly reached around her neck with his left arm and brought the pistol up to her right ear. He could feel her trying to scream while she scratched at his scarred left arm.

"Don't be afraid. Don't scream. I'm here to protect you," he said and looked around the parking lot for any witnesses. He knew how ridiculous and incongruous the words must have sounded to her. She stopped her struggling when she saw the gun.

Thirty-five

S heriff Arnold Scarboro first rubbed his eyes and then ran his hand along his burr haircut. He fought to stay awake while listening to Attorney General Charles Palk. Only the prosecutor's request for this late night meeting would have kept the sheriff from already being home and in bed at this hour—ten till midnight on the next to last day of July.

Palk stood waiting for an answer to the question—or proposition—he had put to the sheriff. Would Arnold take more responsibility for the investigation concerning the four bodies that turned up from May to July in London County?

"Aren't you really asking me to take the blame?" Scarboro asked.

"Look, Arnold, you're not up for reelection until two years from now. Everything will be solved and smoothed over by then. I just want you to be a little more public. Instead of the reporters coming to me, they could go to you. This would help me, and then I'd be in a position to help you in two years. How about it?"

"You know it's been my habit to stay out of the limelight. I haven't talked to a reporter in two years. I'm a little skittish. I don't know a lot of big words, and I don't want to sound stupid. I've got a grandson looking up to me. Besides, you might lose, and then Mike Garrison would be pissed at me."

Palk slowly shook his head. "Well, at least think about it. Okay?"

"Yeah, I'll think about it." Sheriff Scarboro stood, put on his Mounty hat, and walked to the door. He turned. "Have you identified any of the bodies yet?"

Palk looked at the floor. "No."

The sheriff didn't change expression and the shaking of his head was barely noticeable. He walked out without another word.

"YOU THINK IT WAS the girl?" Agent Floyd Miles asked Agent Mike Constanzo. They faced each other over the small table in Miles's room at the Hyatt Regency.

"Yes. Chapman took her back to the Quality Inn. She drove.

It's a red '65 Mustang. The plates are Kentucky issued but not for that car."

"Shit," Miles said and slammed his hand against his knee. "If I had gotten that bug planted, we could be listening to them right now. She's probably telling Chapman where Bartley is. All we can do is wait and follow. You get your ass back out to the motel and let me know as soon as anything happens. If they leave, follow them."

FLORENTINE SAT IN THE Holiday Inn and listened to the same news from his younger associate.

"Good. Very good." He smiled, stood, and lifted his left arm above his head. He rubbed his upper arm and shoulder. "We know where three out of the four are. And they will take us to the skimmer. Go back out there and watch. Don't be seen. If Pelton leaves, follow her, or if either Chapman or Pelton's sister leaves with Pelton, follow them."

"Do I get to play with Pelton before I kill her too?" the younger one asked.

"Sure, just don't lose them, or somebody'll be playing with you."

JOE SAT AT THE desk in his room at the Quality Inn while Carol and Cathy hugged and cried in each other's arms. Then they would talk some, hug some more, and shed more tears. Joe listened, but they talked all around everything except what he wanted to know. He sat and stared at Cathy.

She had taken off the bulky overcoat. She sat on the bed still wearing her dance outfit of lavender leotard and white body stocking. Only her arms, neck, and face were bare. With nervous energy, she had fidgeted with her hair and taken it down from the bun. When she wasn't hugging Carol, she brushed her hair in long, soft strokes. She was everything in person that Joe had seen in visions. Yet, here she sat and practically ignored him—her rescuer—while she chatted away with her sister. Joe was a piece of furniture.

"I thought I was dead when he stuck that gun to my head," Cathy said and motioned toward Joe. Finally, he was noticed. "Then he started talking about things that only I could know—all kinds of weird things to assure me that he wasn't just a typical rapist or murderer." She smiled but looked at Carol.

Joe seized on the word *typical* while he sat silent. No he wasn't the *typical* rapist or murderer. Those were two things he had not done thus far on his summer away from the office.

"Then he has me drive out here. All the time, he's telling me that he's not going to hurt me. That my sister is waiting for me at the motel. Then he tells me about finding my purse in Tennessee and going on a three-month search for me. Then I thought this guy is *weirder* than your typical rapist or murderer. He's as goofy as I am."

For the next hour they all talked as though it was a family reunion. He told Cathy about the details of his quest but not the visions or his compulsive desire to have her as his wife. He would save that until they were alone. He longed for her. Maybe she could detect it in his eyes or from the story of how much he had put aside to find her. Intimacy was only hinted at, while the river odyssey came to life again.

Carol told about finding the farm—Barnaby Ridge—where Cathy worked. Cathy nodded. Joe and Carol waited for Cathy to volunteer information but little was forthcoming. Where is Kent Bartley? Where are you living? Why did you change your name? How did your purse end up in the Tennessee River and your wallet in a dead girl's hip pocket? Those were the questions Joe wanted to ask, but he skirted the issues, waiting for an opening.

"When . . . what's your name? Joe? When Joe finally pulled out that gold Krugerrand and my car keys from his pocket and stuck them in front of my eyes, I realized he knew who I was, and that he must be telling the truth about you being here." She started to cry again. "I'm glad it's over. I'm ready to go back and face the music."

Now she was ready to talk about what Joe wanted to know. He sat in rapt attention, vowing silently that she would know his name better before this was over.

Kent had been on a trip in mid-February just a short time after being released on bond on the cocaine possession charge. He didn't tell Cathy where he was going or how long he would be gone. When he got back to Baton Rouge a week later, he began to act stranger than usual. He wouldn't go out. He hid in Cathy's house until the first of March when he told her he had to leave and—if she loved him—she should go with him. They had to leave soon and not tell anyone where they were going. "Just grab a few things and throw them in the back of the car," he had told her.

Then he had appeared at her house with her car and a small U-Haul trailer hooked on behind. He would not tell her what was in the trailer. He told her it'd be better if she didn't know. Quickly and quietly they had driven out of Baton Rouge, into and through Mississippi, and on to Birmingham before stopping for the night at the hotel that Joe had found on the charge card account. Cathy had paid for the room with her card while Kent parked the car. He berated her in the room for using the plastic and told her not to use it again on their trip.

The next day, they slept late in Birmingham and spent the larger part of the afternoon sitting around the bus station and at the adjoining Hardee's. Kent watched the departing and arriving buses like he was expecting someone. Toward dark, he offered a ride to a young couple who had been in the bus station for several hours. Their bus to Ohio was overdue.

"That was all part of his plan, I learned later," Cathy told Joe and Carol who had not spoken a word since she had started her monologue. "They were about our age and build. The girl even had long red hair. All four of us rode in my Mustang up I-59 to near Chattanooga, then on I-24, and finally I-75. Kent was driving. He told the couple we were going to Ohio. That was the first I'd heard about it.

"About two in the morning, Kent pulled off the highway at the first exit after we'd passed over the Tennessee River. I woke up just long enough to see the river sign and stayed awake when he pulled off. I asked him where we were going, but he told me to shut up. He didn't want to wake the couple in the back.

"He turned right and then kept looking toward his right and drove slowly as though he wanted to pull over. He turned right onto another road that dead-ended at the river. He looked out, but turned back around and back onto the road. He went to the next road to the right about a mile farther down. It went to a bluff overlooking the river where a lot of garbage had been dumped. That's when he stopped and killed the engine."

"I know right where you're talking about. My house was less than two miles from there downstream," Joe said.

"It's hard to tell you what happened next," Cathy said and began to cry again.

"Let me get you a Coke," Joe said and went to the basin where there was a bucket of ice and a carton of drinks. He opened one and poured it over ice in a glass. When he got back to Cathy, she and Carol were entwined in arms with their heads on each other's shoulder, both crying. Joe handed the Coke to Cathy.

She sat back up, took a sip, and continued her story.

"I've had nightmares about this constantly. Kent got out and went to the trunk. He opened and shut it. When he came back around to the driver's side, he was carrying a shotgun and a pistol. Without saying a word, he opened the door, tilted the seat forward, grabbed the young man by the hair of his head, and dragged him out. He pushed him to the ground and shot him in the back of the head with the pistol.

"I jumped out on my side and fell to the ground. I screamed for the young woman to run. She was just waking up when Kent came around to my side of the car and yanked her out and did the same to her. She just fell in a heap and never moved.

"I started vomiting. I couldn't believe what was happening. I thought he was going to kill me too. Why had he brought me all the way from Louisiana to kill me here by the river? What had I done to make him so angry and crazy?"

She started to cry again. Carol handed her a handkerchief.

"What happened next?"

She sniffed. "Kent still never said a word. He went at it very businesslike. There was no emotion. He walked back to the U-Haul trailer, opened it, and carried a body back over his shoulder. I could smell a sickening odor as soon as he opened the door. He laid that body next to the young couple and went back to the trailer. He brought another body and laid him down there too. He was breathing heavily from all the lifting."

"Were both of those men?" Joe asked.

"Yes. I didn't know who or why."

Cathy blew her nose. Carol put a hand to her own stomach. Joe sat wide-eyed.

"On the third trip, he brought two concrete blocks and a length of rope. He cut it into two pieces. He tied a block to one leg of each of the bodies of the two men who had been in the U-Haul. He took anything they had in their pockets and put the things in a bag in the car.

"He carried one body with a block to the cliff, laid it down, and came back for the other. When he got them both over there, he checked the rope to the block, laid one block on the stomach of the first man, and threw him over the cliff. I counted to three before I heard a splash from below. He did the same with the next body.

"By that time I was sitting up with my back on the front tire of my car. I was crying, but I looked up occasionally. I was praying. I still thought he was going to kill me. When he finished throwing those bodies over, he came back toward me, kicked me, and told me to get my purse out of the car. He told me to get whatever money I had out but to leave my driver's license in my wallet. I sneaked out the credit card I had been using. The one I left in my wallet was maxed out.

"As soon as I stuck my head in the car, I heard a shotgun blast right behind me. I thought I was dead. Before I could turn around, he shot another time. When I looked, I saw that he had blasted the young man and woman in the face."

Carol got up and ran to the bathroom and closed the door behind her. The door didn't muffle the sound of her vomiting. Cathy stopped talking for a minute and gazed toward the door as though she could still see the results of the blasts. Carol came back holding a wet towel to her face.

"Weren't they already dead?" Joe asked.

"I thought so," Cathy said.

"I'm sorry," Carol said. "Go ahead and tell us the rest."

"He took my purse. He pulled the wallet out that had the driver's license and stuffed it in the back pocket of the girl's jeans. He took my calendar book and tore out some of the pages or tore them in half. He did the same with my notepad. He put the purse strap around her arm, put her cigarettes in my purse, carried her to the same spot, and threw her off the cliff. He took his wallet, took his money out except for a couple of ones, put it into the back pocket of the guy after taking the guy's wallet, and threw him off the cliff and into the river too. He dumped all four.

"By that time, I was sitting down with my head between my knees saying what I thought would be my last prayer.

"I must have fainted. The next thing I remember was dawn. The sun was coming up to my right. We were still on I-75 driving high on the spine of a mountain. When we started down, we came to a little town called Jellico, and then we were at the Kentucky border. He stopped for a few minutes at the welcome center and stashed the things from the bodies in different trash containers." Cathy looked at Joe and Carol. "Excuse me, it's my turn to throw up now." She clutched at her throat and walked briskly toward the bathroom.

Joe walked to the window and checked the drapes. Bartley was a sociopathic killer. He had no conscience, no remorse, no morals. He would as soon kill them all as give someone the time of day. If he thought they were taking Cathy back, he would kill them or die trying. Joe looked into the parking lot where the security lights drove some of the darkness away.

He turned to Carol and whispered. "We have to get her away. Soon. Now. In the morning. Bartley is dangerous. I hate to back out on Bodine, but I don't know if I want to tangle with this maniac."

"What if she won't go?"

"You can talk her into it. You're her sister."

"I don't know."

"We can kidnap her. I've done everything else. Taking her across state lines would be another federal offense, but I wouldn't think she'd turn us in."

Cathy came back out of the bathroom. Joe and Carol ceased their conversation and looked toward Cathy.

"Why did you stay with Kent?" Joe asked.

Cathy sat down beside Carol and rubbed her red eyes with a towel.

"He told me I was just as guilty as he was—that I was a murderer. He said if I ever tried to leave, he'd kill me. He said they couldn't convict him on just my testimony anyway. I was an accomplice." She looked first at Joe and then at Carol. "I've prayed for those two young people and their families every night. Carol, I'm sorry that you have me for a sister. Can you forgive me?"

"Cathy, you're only guilty of being stupid enough to stay with Kent. You didn't have anything to do with the killings. You tried to help the girl escape," Carol said.

"You'd only have a problem if you continued to try to shield Kent. You could be an accomplice after the fact, but that's all. I'm a lawyer, remember? Where is Kent?"

Cathy didn't look up. "He's either in Cincinnati or Louisville. Maybe upper Ohio. He makes a coke run every week. He sells five to ten kilos and comes back here. He'll be gone for another day."

They were all silent for a minute.

"Why don't you both try to get some sleep? Go to your room and think about this. Carol, you two need to talk," Joe said and emphasized the last word.

Cathy and Carol limped together toward the door which Joe opened for them. When Carol was in the doorway, she turned.

"I forgot to tell you. Someone tried to get in your room after I got over here this evening. He had a key or something. I heard it. When I asked who it was, he left. He was wearing a suit and carrying a phone or Walkie-talkie."

Joe walked to the bed and plunked down. "It's the DEA. Charlie said they were up here. Probably trying to plant something in here." He walked to the phone and unscrewed the earpiece and mouthpiece. He put it back together, stepped to the table lamp, looked under it, and then felt along the base of the bed. He looked at Carol and Cathy who were still standing at the door. He whispered. "Be careful in your room what you say. Don't mention any names or addresses. Get in the shower and turn the water on when you talk."

The women looked at each other and began to laugh. "You want Cathy and me to shower together? We haven't seen each other naked since we were kids, and I don't think we want to," Carol said.

"Well, just be careful. Your place might already be bugged. I'll go check it out."

When he did the sweep of their room, everything appeared to be in order.

"Don't go out for anything. Don't let anyone in. Don't answer your phone. I'll come over and check on you in the morning. Look out to be sure it's me. We can't be too safe," Joe said and left them to go back to his room.

He locked his door, double locked it, and triple locked it. He scooted a chair over and angled it against the door knob. He laid one gun on one side of the bed on the floor and the other on the opposite side on a night table. He put his Bowie knife beneath his pillow. He stripped to his underwear, turned all the lights off, and lay down. The bed felt as though it was turning beneath him. His mind whirled in the opposite direction. He opened and closed his eyes. It didn't stop. He had to get them out of Lexington without the DEA or Bartley knowing. Cathy had to be persuaded to go on her own.

Sleep eluded him. At the edge of dawn when the light started dripping through the bottoms of the room's drapes, he pulled on a shirt, pair of pants, and a light jacket that hid his weapons. He walked to the corner of the parking lot and called Charles Palk at home.

"She's alive and we have her. Bartley is on a drug run in Ohio," he told Palk as soon as he picked up.

"Who are these bodies then?" Palk asked.

"Go over to the Snyder Road dump area at Buzzard's Bluff. Look through everything, especially close to the cliff. That's where the bodies were tossed into the river. There might be some trace of clothes on the face of the cliff."

"Do you know who any of the bodies are?"

"The girl and guy with their faces missing are from Ohio. They were killed by Bartley at the dump. The other two he hauled up there all the way from Louisiana. I don't have any idea who they are. You might find a missing persons' report on the couple."

"When are you coming back?"

"As soon as I can persuade Cathy Pelton. I don't know if I want to tangle with Bartley. He's obviously deranged. If I have to get him to bring Cathy, I will."

"Be careful, Joe."

"Oh, yeah. If I see him and he even flinches, I'll empty my .45 in him before he can tell me he's scratching his balls."

"You might leave that to the DEA or the local police."

"Yeah, if Cathy'll come without him. Charlie, don't call me. I'll call you. The feds are trying to bug my room."

"Well, you're the expert in electronics. They don't know who they're dealing with."

"Don't tell them either."

Joe hung up and called Bodine.

"We should have Bartley back to you—dead or alive—by the fifteenth. We're close to having him. Either me or the local cops and DEA. I don't guess it matters except for the reward money."

"If you found him, you get it either way, Joe. Don't get hurt."

As Joe walked back toward his room, he noticed a man in a dark Buick with his head leaning against the car's window. Joe looked at his room's door and then back at the car. It was parked where his room could be watched. He drew his .45, held it to the side of his leg, and walked toward the car. He edged up behind the driver's side window and tapped on the glass with the barrel of the pistol.

Mike Constanzo jerked his head up and looked directly into the barrel of the .45. He put his hands on the steering wheel and attempted to tell Joe through the window that he was with the DEA.

"Speak louder," Joe said and leaned his head toward the window.

"I'm Agent Constanzo with the DEA. Remember? I met you in Baton Rouge with Agent Miles. On your boat—*THE CARP.*"

Joe put the pistol back down to his leg. "Roll down the window. What're you doing here?"

"I'm tailing you. Miles instructed me to. We're looking for the same person and thought you might lead us to him."

"Are you the one who tried to get into my room yesterday?"

Constanzo shook his head. "No."

Joe looked toward his room and then Carol's. "Well, I'm not here to help you. As far as I'm concerned, whoever catches up with Bartley first can have him."

"We know you have his girlfriend. I saw you take her from the opera house last night. There's no mistaking that red Mustang."

"She's the one I'm really after. You aren't going to arrest her, are you?"

"We'd like her to be a witness against Bartley."

"Her sister and I'll have more luck persuading her to than you and Miles."

"Maybe. Miles wants to meet with you to see if we can work out an accommodation. How about it?"

A meeting? Joe looked away. He'd like to find out why the DEA was so interested in Bartley. Did they know he was making coke runs to Ohio every week? Did that coke pass through Louisiana?

"Okay. I'll meet with him. Not today though. Tell him tomorrow at five in my room here. You know the number. Tell him not to follow me or try to bug my room. If I suspect that's happening, I won't cooperate. And . . . we'll exchange information. If he doesn't tell me why Bartley is so bad, I won't tell him what I know."

Constanzo started the car, drove out of the parking lot, and turned toward the Hyatt Regency.

In another corner of the parking lot, the young dark-complected man ran the edge of the long knife over the leg of his jeans while he observed Joe from an old Chevrolet. He smiled at what he had witnessed. Joe Chapman had berated a DEA agent. Chapman would not be so aggressive when he held the knife to his throat some day soon. He scooted down in his seat and pulled the baseball cap lower on his forehead. He laughed.

"Get ready for breakfast," Joe yelled through the door of Carol's and Cathy's room. He knocked loudly until he heard a groggy response. "I'll be back in a half hour. We'll go over to Denny's."

The Chevrolet eased out of the parking lot of the motel and pulled into the parking lot of Denny's while Joe returned to his room.

"TOMORROW AT FIVE? SURE, that's fine. We're still going to tail him today. We'll just use one of the other agents that he doesn't know. I'll meet alone with him, Mike. If he starts any funny stuff, I'll signal you. I'll have my Walkie-talkie and cell phone. He's found Bartley's whore. She'll lead us to Bartley. Then, we'll be out of here and back in New Orleans with little Kent within forty-eight hours."

HE WASN'T SURE, BUT Joe thought he had seen the young man on the far side of the room in the restaurant somewhere before. Joe chose a corner wrap-around booth for him and the two women. He could watch the door and be sure there was no one listening over their shoulders.

Over a breakfast of ham, grits, and eggs for Joe and a selection of fruit slices for Carol and Cathy, Joe listened to Cathy tell more of her story.

She didn't know where the cocaine came from. She just knew there was "oodles" of it. Every week Kent made a trip north to sell some. She figured he still had over half of what he had brought in the U-Haul at their rented house in the northwest section of Lexington. Kent would go on the selling trips alone. When he came back, Cathy helped him convert the hundred dollar bills to gold. Krugerrands were still her favorite.

Over the course of the almost five months they had been in Lexington, she had been to practically every coin shop in Kentucky and the southern part of Ohio. She would exchange a little less than five thousand dollars of currency for gold at a time. Kent didn't want to have the possibility of a coin dealer reporting a large cash transaction to the government.

Doing the small transactions took longer. Cathy figured her weekly visits to coin shops had now amassed over three thousand coins that were stored in ten metal boxes beneath the back steps of the house. Joe penciled in numbers on the paper napkin in front of him. Cathy had accumulated over a million dollars in gold coins.

"What about the gold Krugerrands and the two bales of

marijuana I found in your storage compartment in Baton Rouge? Where did they come from?"

"I don't know anything about two bales of marijuana. Kent had a key to my unit and sometimes stored things there.

"Each gold coin represented a night's work at the Classy Kitty Cat—give or take a few dollars. I just saved that for a rainy day. I felt bad about living off that kind of money, although I did sometimes. The rest I turned into coins and put them in wood-lined Girl Scout cookie boxes."

The waitress came back and refilled their cups with coffee. All conversation stopped until she was well out of earshot.

"Where did you get the name of Katy Gross?" Joe asked.

"Money can buy anything. Kent watched the papers every day once we got here. He said we had to have new identities. The way he did it was simple enough. He'd watch the obituaries to find a man about his age from another county who had died. He'd call up the funeral home and ask whether the family needed any help in paying for the funeral and burial.

"When he found a destitute family, he'd arrange to meet one of the family members. He'd dress up real businesslike and tell them he represented an organization that helped with the expenses in some cases like theirs. He told them he would need a copy of the birth certificate, the deceased driver's license, and social security card for the organization's records.

"Since the family wasn't going to need any of that, they would bring it to him. He told them he would get the originals back after the organization's headquarters made copies, but he never returned them. He paid for the funeral, and everybody was happy. He's now Frank Houser. Kent said it'd take the Social Security Administration years to figure out that some dead person was paying taxes—if he ever did get a legitimate job. But now he could open a bank account or get a credit card if the guy had good credit. From the birth certificate he knows the maiden name of the deceased's mother—which is what a lot of credit card companies ask for to help identify the person. He's clever and knows how to con."

The young man that Joe had noticed before got up from his booth, walked to a nearer one where he looked at a newspaper that had been left there, and sat down. He still wasn't close enough to hear unless he had some way to amplify their voices. Joe motioned for them to speak even lower.

"How did you come up with the name Katherine Gross?" Carol repeated Joe's question in a whisper.

Cathy bit into a piece of cantaloupe and then swallowed.

"I was particular about the name I wanted. I still wanted to be Cathy so I wouldn't have to remember a new first name. I also wanted one that fit me. I didn't want to be an Irene Crouch or Vada Blankenship. Katherine Gross died in Louisville in April, and it turned out her family needed help. So that's who I became. The last name isn't too great, but it'll do. Kent says we'll have to change names about every year to be sure we're not caught up with."

Joe shook his head. Had Cathy stepped across the line from being a victim to being an accomplice? He wanted to think he could get her out of all the charges that the law enforcement people might think up, but her story needed some fine-tuning by a lawyer. Could a jury believe that she had stopped being a victim and started her own life of crime when she started concealing the cash by turning it into gold? And it must be illegal to use someone else's name and identity under the circumstances that she was doing it. Had she done a Patty Hearst on them?

Looking across the table at her, all he could think about was her beauty. Even with little rest, using Carol's makeup, and wearing the bulky overcoat, she appeared just slightly less alluring. When he watched her take an oblong slice of cantaloupe into her mouth, he felt an urge to grab her and kiss her, but it passed quickly. Her lips and tongue moved in a sensual rhythm without her knowing it. The way she held her head, the finely carved nose with nostrils that could flare in moments of passion, and the green eyes that could pierce the darkness all combined to make him justify her actions. Her face was soft with slightly pouting lips. No one so beautiful could really be evil.

She would be much better off with him in London County than she would be if arrested in Kentucky or taken back to Baton Rouge. In London, he could depend on his friend, Charles Palk, to allow her to be a witness rather than a defendant. Perhaps, with a little fore-thought and planning, she would not even have to be a witness. If Kent confessed his misdeeds to someone else, the other physical evidence would be enough to send him away—either to prison for life or to the electric chair. Was Cathy ready for that step? If the DEA got their hands on her, they would play mind games with her until she was broken. She needed to go to Tennessee with him where friends awaited. He squeezed Carol's hand and continued to look at Cathy.

"Cathy, are you ready to start over? Ready to leave Kent? You don't really want a life on the run—a life of crime—do you?" Joe asked.

"I love Kent—or at least I did love the person I thought Kent was. But I don't know now. He killed those two kids without any thought. They hadn't done anything to him. Just plain cold blood. I've tried to put it out of my mind by going on with my dancing and horses—but I can't. It's the dreams that bother me."

"I know what you're talking about," Joe said.

"I know Kent'll kill me if I leave—and both of you too, probably. But I can't live with that anymore. I do . . . I do want to get it over with," Cathy said and blinked away tears.

Joe turned loose of Carol's hand and reached across and took Cathy's. "I have a plan. I thought about it all last night. I think we can get you out safely. I'll risk taking Kent myself, if need be, while you're away. I can help you with the prosecutor in Tennessee where the murders occurred. He's my best friend. He needs Kent a lot worse than he needs you. But I'll need your cooperation. Will you help? It won't be easy, but we can do it if we work together. How about it?"

Cathy. nodded.

"Let's go," Joe said, and they all left together.

The young man at the other booth went to a phone and called Florentine. "You want me to still follow them? . . . Okay. . . . You think they'll go to Bartley?"

Tonight was to be Cathy's debut at the Lexington Opera House in a performance of "Swan Lake." Joe and Carol told her they would be there. But first, they had a lot to do.

Carol drove the three of them on a circuitous route in her rental car as Joe instructed. To anyone following, it would appear they were going on a sight-seeing tour. In fact, Cathy was going to point out her house to Joe in the suburbs of Lexington. The drive took them by horse farm after horse farm, most of which Joe or Carol had already visited. Joe glanced behind them to see if there were any followers. He couldn't tell, but it didn't matter.

A slight nod by Cathy at her house was all anyone would have seen. Kent was still gone. His Ford Bronco was not behind the house as it would've been if he were there. The small house was on a long stretch of narrow road. At one time it had served as housing for farm workers but now stood in a row of four others—like remodeled sharecroppers quarters. Joe concentrated as he sized up the exact location and all the surroundings. He would be back shortly.

Back at the Quality Inn, Joe gave the women the plan—at least part of it. They would split up temporarily to confuse anyone watching them. He dropped Carol and Cathy off at a U-Haul truck rental center with instructions to rent a medium-sized truck for a week. They would say their destination was Dayton, Ohio. They would use Carol's driver's license and pay in cash, which he gave them. He borrowed Cathy's house key. They would meet back at the Quality Inn. He needed to make a trip to Radio Shack.

It worked. Both tailers continued to watch Cathy and Carol. It took Joe an hour to make nearly a thousand dollars in purchases at the electronics outlet. The DEA sent another agent to the Quality Inn area to await Joe's return. He didn't arrive back when they thought he would, and that was reported to Floyd Miles.

"What the shit is happening? He disappeared? And the women are at a truck rental place?"

Joe drove in Carol's rental car to Cathy and Kent's house. He had to move fast. Kent was due back tonight. He checked his pistols and knife before entering the driveway and parking behind the house where the car could not be seen from the road.

For an hour, he crawled around and over attic rafters, making holes with a portable drill, splicing wires together, and checking a battery pack.

He went to the bedroom and flipped the concealed switch at the base of the headboard and then retreated quickly up the ladder to the attic. He wiped the sweat off his forehead. It must have been over a hundred twenty degrees under the roof. He looked at the equipment he had stored there and was satisfied. He went back to the bedroom one more time, stood on a chair at the wall opposite the bed, and wiped a spot at the juncture of the wall and ceiling. This had to work or Cathy would be dead.

On his way out, Joe walked backwards to observe the rooms. He didn't want to leave anything to tip Bartley off that someone had been inside. On the table in the living area, he saw Cathy's horse books. On the floor and under each of the front windows were rows of candles like the ones she had in Baton Rouge. He made a mental note to buy her some as soon as they arrived in Tennessee. He accidentally kicked something over that was lying against the door facing as he opened the door to leave. He bent over and picked up the red-tipped silver baton that he had first seen in the photo of Cathy leading the band. He set it against the wall beside the door, turned, and walked down the steps of the small porch beneath which he knew there was over a million dollars in gold coins.

On the spur of the moment, he pulled out the loosened concrete blocks that concealed the ten metal boxes that Cathy had described. There was no need leaving the gold for Kent or the DEA. He would take it for Cathy. She could decide what to do with it.

He opened the trunk of the car and neatly stacked the ten boxes of gold coins inside. He distributed the boxes around so that the car would not look like a moonshiner's running whiskey. He would be careful not to park in tow-away zones until he transferred the gold to the truck. He started the car and drove very slowly out of the driveway and back toward the Quality Inn.

Thirty—six

A very diverse crowd mingled in the lobby of the Lexington Opera House for the opening night of "Swan Lake" produced by the Lexington Ballet Company. Carol and Joe were looking forward to Katy Gross's debut.

Among the crowd of five hundred that rubbed shoulders in the ornate entranceway and hall were eight agents from the DEA, Florentine, and his associate who always carried the long serrated bladed knife. None of them had seats as good as Joe and Carol—thanks to the star of the show.

Joe and Carol took their seats early. They walked in like a high school couple going to the prom. Joe had rented a tux, and Carol had purchased a flowing red satin evening dress. The off-the-shoulder affair had a low neckline and practically no back. Carol received many admiring glances on the way to her seat.

The DEA agents sat two by two in different parts of the expansive auditorium with Miles and Constanzo seated farthest from Joe and Carol. Unknowingly, Florentine and his youthful companion sat two rows in front of a pair of agents. This was the first time any of them had been to a ballet performance except for Carol.

She tried to explain to Joe what to expect. He didn't really care about the intricacies of the performance. He just knew that he would be in the presence of the two most important women in his life at this time.

"You look very nice in red," he whispered to Carol.

"Thanks. And I noticed a few women who gave you a sideways glance."

"It's only the third time in a year that I've had anything on resembling a suit or formal attire."

"You clean up really well," Carol said and smiled.

Joe stared away toward the stage. Beside the problem that he faced with Kent Bartley, he was troubled by some recent feelings.

Since May when he had first seen Cathy in his visions, his one goal had been to find her and be with her. His feelings of erotic desire and fascination with her beauty had been his driving force. There had been long hours of imagining and daydreaming about what their relationship would be like when he found her. Over those long hours on THE CARP, he had constructed the perfect life for him and Cathy. In Baton Rouge, he had seen his role expanding to that of rescuer. The final focal point had always been snatching her away to a mountain or lakeside retreat where he could make mad love to her for days on end. They would marry, have children, and live happily ever after.

Now that he had found her—from the moment he had shoved the gun to her head from the back seat of her car—he had experienced different emotions. What was the change? It was as though she was becoming like a sister or daughter. Even early this morning when he was aroused at her beauty at the restaurant, he had felt his desire to pull her over to him and kiss her passionately ebb noticeably within seconds. He was still awed by her beauty and grace, but now it was becoming more like an artist admiring a sunrise or sunset. Were his desire and lust doused by the reality of her presence, by her apparent lack of attraction to him, or by something deeper? He probably should talk to Carol about it. He glanced over at her and down to the line of where the dress barely met her breasts. Carol was not bad herself.

Carol pointed to the program and the names of the performers, with her sister at the top and in bold print. The lights lowered, and the production began. It seemed to Joe that all eyes were on Cathy. Twelve sets of eyes did follow her almost exclusively.

At an intermission, Joe and Carol walked out into the hall. Carol excused herself to the ladies' room while Joe scanned the crowd for any recognizable faces. He blinked and then squinted his eyes when he saw a man exit the bathroom across the foyer who looked like the DEA agent who was with Mike Constanzo in Baton Rouge. Floyd Miles. Wasn't that the name that Constanzo had mentioned this morning when they had talked in the parking lot?

Then he noticed someone who sent chills up his spine. He only saw him from the back as the man reentered the auditorium. But Joe would never forget that profile, that walk, that head. The man moved with a stiff left arm, bent and held to his chest. Florentine. He hadn't died in New Orleans. He was here. There was only one reason why he had followed them to Lexington. Florentine did not care for the ballet. Why would Miles and Florentine risk being seen? They must want him to know they were here.

It was time to leave. Joe wanted to grab Carol and Cathy and run. Forget Bartley. Forget Bodine. Forget the gold if necessary. Run. Run now. Run fast.

Carol took him by the elbow when she returned. "How is everything?"

He looked her in the eyes. "Fine. Let's go sit back down."

Carol was aglow. Her face radiated the pride and satisfaction that she had in the performance of her little sister.

"Are you envious?" Joe asked.

"No. Envy is negative. I admire her ability. I could never do it. She is talented. I just love to watch her perform."

Joe nodded his head. They'd stay and watch the full performance. If they left, they would be followed. He would lose their pursuers later. He would have to keep it from Carol that the one she had blasted with the shotgun was alive and within a hundred feet of them. He'd revise his plan and go forward.

"What do you think about her performance?" Carol asked.

"Beautiful. It's like she has escaped the force of gravity. Her movements are so fluid, the best I've ever seen."

"How many ballets have you been to?"

"This is the first one."

Carol nodded. "I thought so." She squeezed his hand and leaned over to him and whispered. "Do you still think she has the most beautiful ass in the country?"

"I think both sisters are pretty nice," Joe said and watched a blush move along Carol's neck. Or was it a reflection of her dress?

He paid little attention to the remainder of the performance. He was mentally mapping out a plan for their escape. Everything had to fall into place. He closed his eyes and prayed for their safety.

During the ten-minute standing ovation at the conclusion of the performance, and despite Carol's protestations to the contrary, Joe hurried them out to the entrance hallway and through the entrance to the performers' dressing area. Cathy had provided them with the passes to meet her backstage after the show, but they were the first ones there.

Miles motioned for one of the agents to follow them. Florentine told the same thing to his companion. Neither was allowed to the backstage area. As soon as the performers departed behind the curtains for the last time, eight DEA agents, along with Florentine's party, tried to look inconspicuous in the parking area where Cathy's

Mustang and Carol's rental car sat parked awaiting the eventual departure of the three targets.

An hour later when Joe and the Louisiana sisters made their way to the parking lot, fewer than twenty cars remained. Joe looked around the dark area where a light rain was beginning to fall. Which cars were the DEA's and which Florentine's?

"Can you do it, Carol?" he asked as they neared their cars that were parked side by side.

"Sure. Any woman driver can stall a car and block a drive-way," she said with a somewhat sarcastic tone.

Two sets of DEA agents waited in their cars on Broadway outside of the parking area. Miles, Constanzo, and two other pair were still in the parking lot. Florentine and his friend were in their car in the corner of the lot.

Joe entered the Mustang alone while Carol and Cathy sat in Carol's car beside him. The radios of the DEA cars were alive with word as to which car contained which occupants.

Joe eased the Mustang into gear, turned the lights on, and started as though he was going to exit in one direction when he noticed a set of headlights come on behind him. He turned sharply and went back beside Carol's car where Cathy quickly threw open her door and entered the passenger side of the Mustang. Carol put the rental car directly behind the Mustang, and they headed in tandem toward the narrow exit to Broadway. There she turned the car sideways across the drive while Joe spun the Mustang onto Broadway and headed in the opposite direction from Cathy's house.

Miles and Florentine could only curse in their separate cars in the parking lot while Joe and Cathy made their escape. They both looked for an alternate exit, but it was too late. Joe and Cathy were a mile down Broadway and out of sight before they reached the street. Miles had radioed the agents on the street, but only one car was able to give pursuit. The agent driving was finding it difficult to stay near the Mustang and yet drive safely in traffic. Joe was driving like a maniac, but there were no police cars in sight to slow him down. Within five minutes, he had lost them in the maze of downtown streets and alleys that he now knew by heart, thanks to all his wanderings about since he had been in Lexington.

In a minute, Carol restarted her car and headed toward the motel, followed by Florentine and a car load of DEA agents. They only watched when she parked and entered the room by herself. She triple-locked the door and sat on the edge of the bed with one of Joe's pistols trembling in her hands.

An hour later, after having driven over forty miles on the backroads and lanes of Fayette County, Joe arrived near Cathy's residence unnoticed by any of the agents.

"You know what you have to do?" Joe asked Cathy as he slowed close to her driveway. He looked at his watch. "I'll get a ride or call a cab to take me back to the motel. Remember where the switch is for the recording equipment. You have to get Kent to talk about all the murders and where he got the cocaine. If we can get that kind of confession on tape, they won't even need you to testify. They'll have enough to put him away for the rest of his life. You will have cooperated and can start your life over. You deserve it, Cathy." He took her hand and squeezed it. Was there any electricity? How did she feel? She was good about showing no emotion.

He stopped the car, opened the door, and quickly rolled into the grassy ditch. Cathy scooted beneath the steering wheel and continued down the graveled drive toward where her headlights illuminated a Ford Bronco that was parked behind the house.

After a two-mile walk, Joe arrived at a telephone booth. He called a cab and waited for his ride back to the motel.

CATHY PARKED THE MUSTANG behind the Bronco, out of sight from the road, and entered the back door to her house. Kent Bartley sat at the kitchen table with six empty beer bottles. He leaned down and snorted a line of coke from the table top.

He looked up when Cathy's footfalls stopped.

"Where the fuck have you been? You little whore. I know that ballet was over two hours ago. I read the poster," he said and threw a copy at her. He rose from the table and grabbed her by the wrist. He squeezed it harder and harder until she cried out.

"Stop it, Kent, you're going to break it."

"That's not all I'm going to break. You been giving it away to those queer stagehands?" He slapped her across the face with the other hand. "I told you to quit screwing with that ballet. Someone's going to recognize you and get us both sent to the chair!" he yelled and pushed her across the kitchen until she hit the refrigerator.

Cathy began to cry. "You know I can't just sit around the house while you're gone days at a time selling your coke. I'd go crazy. What kind of life is that? And you know I'm not out with anyone else. It's just that on opening night there's a lot of things to do afterwards."

"You expect me to believe that, you little bitch? Two hours? How many of them did you fuck in two hours? The whole cast?

"I'm tired of it, Cathy. You're not going back to that ballet. If I have to tie and chain you to the bed, I will. You can call them first thing in the morning and tell them your—what do you call it?—your understudy will have to take over. Because your little ass is going to be here tomorrow night when I get back from Cincinnati, or I'll break your neck and throw you in the river like those others."

"I thought you were back for a few days. Why do you have to go back tomorrow?"

"To sell five more kilos is why. You can keep your ass busy on the horse farm, but no ballet. Got it?" Cathy nodded. "Now, get into the bedroom. I haven't had any in three days," he said and finished the line on the table. "And I'm going to know if you've been giving it away."

In the bedroom Cathy steeled herself for the most important performance of her life. She had a talent for dancing, for the piano, and for most arts. The one thing she had never tried was real stage acting. The choreographed dance of the ballet was as close as she had ever been to acting. She had considered it but was afraid to try. Tonight, she would make her debut on video tape.

She ran her hand along the bed railing until she found the toggle switch hidden underneath that Joe told her would activate the tape machine in the attic. She looked around the room but could see no camera or microphone. Joe was good.

She rehearsed in her mind the line of questions that Joe wanted answered. Kent had always in the past refused to talk about the details. The less she knew the better had been the way he had put it. She could not be made to testify about things she didn't know. Joe had suggested a way to persuade Kent to talk. She would try it. She flipped the switch on.

She was crying softly when Kent entered the room. "What the hell is the matter with you? I didn't hit you that hard."

She pulled her knees up under her chin and sat back against the headboard of the bed. She pulled the sheet up to cover her body and to use as a handkerchief.

"I dream every night about that couple you killed in Tennessee. And you've never told me about those other two men and where you got all this cocaine. Maybe if you tell me, I can understand you a little better and we won't be fighting all the time. I can't continue to live this way." She sobbed into the sheet.

"I've told you before. The less I tell you, the better off we both are. Just leave it alone. Those two men and the coke don't concern you. It's bad enough that you saw me shoot those two kids. But I had to. They are us. We got some bad dudes looking for us. Those bodies will throw them off our trails. At least for a while."

Cathy wiped her eyes, blew her nose, and looked at Kent.

"I've got to know the other. You won't have to worry about me testifying. We'll get married. They can't make a husband or wife testify about the other one, can they?"

"Where the hell did you hear that?" he asked. "You been going to law school? Or talking to the cops?"

"I saw it on television or in a movie. There's a lot of good lawyer shows."

"It may be true. Jailhouse talk is it's changing. Besides, we ain't married. Getting married leaves records and stuff. I'm Frank Houser. You're Katherine Gross. I'm afraid two dead people getting married might show up some place."

"No.   There's bound to be a hundred Frank Housers and Katherine Grosses in the world. Just a ceremony in front of a justice of the peace. Tomorrow after you get back. Down at the courthouse. I can't rest until you tell me about this other stuff. I can't take it any longer. You'll just have to kill me like you did those other two kids. You know I didn't know you were going to do that, don't you?"

"Yeah, I know that. Hell, you couldn't kill a mosquito if it was sucking the blood out of you. Okay. We'll get married tomorrow. But no more ballet. Got it?" Cathy nodded.

"Listen. I'm just going to tell you this story one time. Don't ever ask me about it again. You'll just have to live with it," Kent began.

Cathy sat silent. She would speak up and ask a question only if she thought something wasn't clear.

THE TWO AGENTS IN the car at the Quality Inn were surprised when Joe returned in the cab and without Cathy. Florentine's anxiety and frustration rose with the development.

Joe and Carol sat quietly in her room and talked about Cathy's confrontation with Kent.

"Is she safe there with him?" Carol asked.

"As safe as she's been. She's smart. I don't think she's going to let anything slip. I just hope we know her. If she turns on us, we may be Kent's next targets."

"She wouldn't do that."

"I haven't had much luck with women lately."

"What about me? I've gone with you for a month now looking for Cathy. Don't you think that's quite a commitment?"

"Yeah. I should have said except for you. You've been great."

Joe walked to the window, eased the drapes back, and looked out. He paced the room. He rolled up the sleeves of his shirt and began to rub the scars on his arms.

"Do they hurt?" Carol asked.

"What?"

"Your arms."

"Oh. I do that sometimes without thinking. It's a nervous habit. But I do notice a tingle in them when I get agitated. More in the arm that was burned than the other one."

"Joe, we have a little time, and I know we can't sleep . . . do you want to—"

"No, I don't want to have sex. It wouldn't be right."

"I wasn't thinking about sex, but it must be on your mind. I wanted to know if you want to tell me about the girl—the reason you're suspended."

Joe sat down on the bed beside Carol. She began to massage his arms.

"It's not really all that complicated. There was a ten-year-old girl who was the daughter of an acquaintance of mine. She was killed in an automobile collision with a gas truck. It turned over and there was a fire. She and her aunt were killed. The truck driver escaped. It was his fault. He was speeding and had been drinking. It was a pretty cut and dry case of liability.

"The father and mother came to my office about a month later and hired me to represent them against the trucking company and the driver. It bothered me personally how she died. I could remember being caught in that stall in the barn when I was ten. I knew the parents were feeling guilty about it. They would never be able to replace that little girl or forget how she died.

"But that was during a time when I was drinking a lot and running here and there. I was over the line, as my wife said. Anyway, I started negotiating with the insurance companies. We had a year to file the lawsuit. They didn't want to go to court if we could get a reasonable settlement."

Carol pulled his sleeves down and buttoned them. "So, what happened?"

"I was so hateful to my last secretary that I ran her off. The new girl made a file on the case but dated the cards and our reminders for the date the couple came to see me instead of the date of the accident.

"The insurance company adjusters called me close to a year later and said they would make a final offer of two million to settle the case. I told them it wasn't enough. We needed at least three. Anyway, when I passed on their offer to my clients, they said to take it. I called the adjusters a few days later and told them we'd take it. There was a long silence on the other end. One of them finally said that the year had run and they were not legally obligated for anything. I didn't file the lawsuit in time. They paid the funeral bill out of the goodness of their heart, I guess.

"I left the next day and was gone for a week. I thought about killing myself. But instead, I did what had gotten me in the problem to start with. I got drunk.

"The couple went to Judge Harkness—the one whose birdbath I torched before I left on my trip. He turned me in to the board for gross negligence. The couple sued me. The insurance adjusters testified that they had offered me two million dollars before the time was up. That's what the jury awarded the couple against me. Of course, that bankrupted me. They got about fifty thousand. My wife divorced me—not for that but for my other craziness."

Carol reached around Joe and hugged him. "That's terrible."

"What's terrible was that I would wake up nights dreaming about the little girl dying that way. I knew the lawsuit and money wouldn't bring her back. But I let her parents down."

"So you accept responsibility for it now?"

"Oh, yes. I was totally out of control. I wish I could pay them. I didn't appreciate Judge Harkness turning me in, and that's why I burned his birdbath."

"But wasn't he obligated to? In my profession, if we know someone is violating ethical standards, we're obligated to report it."

"Yes, ours says that too. But he could've found a way not to."

"I know a counselor you can see to work on your problems."

"Is there hope for me?"

"Oh, yeah. You don't have half the problems I see in most people. Yours are big. But you still have a conscience."

"Samson still had a conscience after his eyes were put out and his hair grew back. He asked God to let him avenge the wrongs."

"Sometimes God gives you a way to make things right. You might make it up to somebody else."

"That's why I care so much about what happens to Cathy. I feel like I'm responsible now that I've given her a plan, and she's over there trying to get him on tape. I've got to get ready for my meeting with Miles tomorrow."

Joe got up, went to the bathroom, stood on the commode, and removed two of the ceiling tiles. Carol looked on from below. He climbed through the opening with the power drill he had used at Cathy's house. Here, the crawl space was cooler. He snaked his way over the ceiling until he reached a firewall that separated the spaces above the rooms. Pipes and cables passed through an opening, but there was no way he could get to the area above Carol's room from his.

He went back down and brought up his coil of cable. He ran it through the hole and pushed it toward Carol's room and then came back down with the other end.

"What are you doing?" Carol asked.

"I'm going to use the same camera that I have at Cathy's to tape Miles when he's talking to me. I want him on video and audio to make sure he can't deny anything later on if I need to use it. I'm going to put the recorder in your room and the eye of the camera in mine. This cable will connect them. I have to wait until Kent is gone to retrieve the camera and recorder from her house. You'll be able to watch Miles and me on your TV once I get the recorder set up."

"Do I want to?"

"Yeah. It should be a good show. Better than daytime television."

"When are you going to Cathy's to get the equipment and see if she got Bartley on tape."

Joe looked at his watch. "She is scheduled to work at the horse farm in the morning. So, she'll have an excuse to leave. She's supposed to come here and let us know how things went. I hope she'll know Bartley's schedule. I'll only need a few minutes to retrieve the camera and recorder."

"What are you finally going to do with Bartley? If we leave with Cathy, he'll find us."

"If Cathy got a confession on tape, I'm going to call Charlie Palk and get a warrant for his arrest and let the police up here handle it. If she didn't, we'll just leave and take our chances."

"So, you've given up on taking him back yourself?"

"Yep. He's too crazy to fool with. Reasonable criminals I could handle. Not Bartley."

"Good."

NEAR SUNRISE IN LONDON County, Charlie Palk drove to Buzzard's Bluff on Snyder Bend Road by himself in his Jeep. On that ground for the past fifty years, the environmentally challenged of London County had thrown household garbage that they were too lazy to take an extra two miles to the nearest trash collection point.

Strewn beside the gravel road and parking area were the artifacts of modern society. Beer cans and bottles, plastic covered diapers, discarded building materials, the dried skins of dead animals, old refrigerators, and washing machines competed in cascading waves for a view overlooking the Tennessee River.

According to Joe Chapman, this was where, in early March, four bodies were tossed into the river. They later surfaced to cause Palk a spring and summer of woes.

Dr. Linus Trout had told Palk that a dead body, without any weight attached, would begin to rise to the surface from seven to fourteen days after being thrown in. It all depended on the tempera-ture of the water, which in turn depended on its depth. Body tissues had to begin to decompose in order to gain the buoyancy of gases that would float them to the surface. A weighted body would take longer, but the weight would have to be at least the same or greater than the body to keep it down indefinitely. A dead body would eventually be able to float twice its own weight.

The two weighted bodies had surfaced after the unweighted ones. Dr. Trout surmised that they were found first simply because the other ones were caught in brush along the shore.

Palk walked to the bluff and looked over where four volunteers from the local National Guard rappelling unit were going up and down the face of the rock. They searched from the top to the water's surface for scraps of clothing that may have come from the bodies.

After two hours of scouring the limestone face, they found only a two-inch swath of blue denim cloth. Palk took it, put it in a clear plastic locking bag, and drove off toward his office. He'd send it to Dr. Trout to see if it matched the cloth from any of the clothes.

Thirty-seven

At nine that morning, Cathy knocked at her sister's door. Her presence was noted by the DEA and Florentine's associate. She came in and sat down beside Carol on the bed. Joe sat across from them.

"How'd it go?" Joe asked.

"If the machine worked, I think I did okay." She shrugged her shoulders and held her hands out palms up. "I felt bad about betraying him."

"You shouldn't," Carol said. "He's a killer."

"Where's Kent now?" Joe asked. He put a finger to his lips. "Whisper. Let's go into the bathroom where I can turn the shower on."

They walked the few steps to the bathroom. Joe turned it on and let the spraying water drown out their whispers.

"He said he had to make another run to Cincinnati."

"Great. I can go get the recorder and get set up here before Miles comes over at five."

"Who's Miles?" Cathy asked.

"Don't worry. You'll be in here in Carol's room. He's DEA."

"Oh, by the way, Kent and I are getting married tomorrow. I first said today, but he said it'd be better tomorrow. I don't want to."

"What?" Joe asked.

"That's the only way I could get him to talk. I prodded him into marrying me. I could never testify against him, like you told me."

"We'll be gone before that happens," Carol said.

"Where does Kent keep the stash of coke? I need a little to take back for evidence," Joe said.

"Look in the closet in the bedroom. There's a loose board in the floor. It's all down there wrapped in plastic and brown paper."

"Does he think you went to the horse farm?"

"Yeah. Hey, Joe."

"What?"

"When you get that tape, you're going to have to erase the last part of it."

"Why? I can't erase tape that might be evidence. That's what happened to Nixon and Watergate."

"What's Watergate?" Cathy asked.

Joe blinked and looked at Carol. "Oh, I forgot. You were probably in diapers when Nixon resigned. Never mind. Why should I erase part of the tape?"

Cathy leaned against the tiled wall and locked her arms across her chest. "The first hour we just talked," she whispered, "and that's where I got him to tell me about the coke and everything. But the second hour . . . may have some other stuff on there." She put her hands to her face.

"Like what?" Joe asked.

"I forgot to turn the switch off. We made love," Cathy said and looked at the floor.

"Well, I'm sure it would have been too dark when you turned the lights off and got under the cover to see anything. So don't worry."

Cathy looked up. "We didn't turn the lights off. This is August. We didn't get under any cover."

"Joe, you've got to do something about that part," Carol said.

"Okay, okay. I've got an X-rated confession tape that I'm sure General Palk would love to see." He looked at Cathy. Now he had to see the tape. Did she leave it on intentionally as a tease?

"You'll take care of it?" Cathy asked.

"Sure." He leaned nearer the shower and motioned for them to put their heads near his. "Ladies, this is our plan for today . . . " Joe began. He gave them a day's worth of instructions. By this time tomorrow they would be in Tennessee.

"What's the rental truck for?" Carol asked.

"I've got to put my Harley in there. I'd be too much of a target on it if somebody followed us. Also, if necessary, I can put you two in there out of sight and out of the line of gunfire."

"You got room for a few of my things from the house too, don't you, Joe?" Cathy asked. He nodded.

In two hours, they split up again. Carol and Cathy rode in

Cathy's Mustang to Lexington's largest shopping mall. Joe waited to see who followed before taking off in the rental car.

AT THE HYATT REGENCY, Floyd Miles paced back and forth across the room. He had begun when the agent phoned in that Cathy was back at the Quality Inn. Joe Chapman was playing games with them. If Chapman knew where Cathy lived, he knew where Bartley lived.

He turned to Agent Constanzo. "If he doesn't tell me at our five o'clock meeting, we'll have no alternative but to take the Pelton girl after the ballet tonight. We'll charge her with being an accessory. I think we can scare her into talking."

Then the phone rang. "Yes. Yes. Follow Pelton and her sister. I'll send another agent to watch Chapman." Miles turned to Constanzo. "They're splitting up again. Bishop and his partner are following the women. Call Jacobsen and tell him to get out to the Quality Inn and keep an eye on Chapman."

WHILE THE DEA AGENTS bit on Joe's ruse of sending Carol and Cathy out, Florentine's young friend waited for Joe. When he checked the parking lot from behind the window, Joe didn't see the young man in the phone booth at the corner. The lot was deserted of vehicles except for Carol's rental car and the U-Haul truck. Joe backed the car up to the truck and quickly unloaded the ten boxes of gold from the car's trunk to the truck.

Then he was off to the shopping mall where he switched cars. The Mustang would not look out of place behind Cathy's house. A strange car in the driveway would be an invitation to a bullet in the head if Bartley showed back up early from his trip to Cincinnati.

The DEA agents followed the women into the mall for five hours of leisurely shopping. Only the dark young man in the Chevrolet pulled out of the mall behind Joe when he turned toward Cathy's house.

In twenty minutes, Joe had disassembled the video recording equipment and loaded it into the trunk of the Mustang parked behind Cathy's house. For those twenty minutes, Florentine's accomplice had watched the house from a half mile down the road. He then decided to leave and tell the good news to his friend at the Holiday Inn that they had found the house where Cathy and Bartley lived. His Chevrolet passed the Ford Bronco of Kent Bartley a half mile from the house as they traveled in opposite directions.

Joe heard the sound of a car in the long gravel driveway coming from the road as he was making his last trip down from the attic. He set the box down and braced himself against a wall. His mouth went noticeably dry. His heart pounded to where it drowned out the sound of the car. He took to the floor and crawled to a back window. He knew it was Bartley as soon as he slammed the door of the Bronco. The Mustang was blocked in. He couldn't sneak out. He pulled his .357 from its holster and stood behind the door where Bartley would come in. Surprise would be his ally.

He listened to the key turning in the door. Bartley cursed and pushed it open.

"Damn it, Cathy. I've told you over and over to lock the door when you're here alone," he said and stepped inside.

It seemed like an eternity until Joe's eyes met Bartley's. He looked Satan eyeball to eyeball. Joe leveled the gun at Bartley's head, just out of an arm's reach. Bartley's eyes froze open and his mouth gaped but no words came out. Joe drew the hammer back on the revolver.

"Are you a burglar?" Bartley asked. "I'll give you money. Don't shoot me."

"I'm Joe Chapman and you're Kent Bartley. I'm here to arrest you in the name of Sean Bodine for Ace Bonding Company of Baton Rouge," Joe heard himself saying like it was a recording. "Don't move and you won't get hurt. You move and you're dead. I have a warrant and papers to return your body. Dead or alive. It's your choice."

Bartley offered no resistance. "I'm not Kent Bartley. Look in my wallet."

Joe cut him off. "Yeah, I know. You're Frank Houser. You're selling cocaine, and you've killed four people . . . that I know about. Don't try to pull any shit with me." Joe watched the blood drain from Bartley's face. He became more secure in his position. "Turn around and grab the door facing. Keep your hands up. If you even start to drop them, your brains are going to be wallpapering the wall in the next room." Joe frisked Bartley the best he could with one hand but found no weapon.

"How do you know who I am?"

Joe ignored him. There was no need to get friendly with a killer. "I want you to turn around and undress slowly. No sudden moves. I'm nervous. I want to see your hands at all times. Take everything off down to your underwear."

"What are you? Some kind of pervert?" Bartley asked but started slowly to undo his belt and unbutton his shirt.

"You shouldn't call somebody a pervert when they're aiming a .357 magnum at you. You ever see what one of these would do to your knee caps? Or your balls?" Joe asked and aimed the gun downward. "Don't say another word, or I'll drag you back out to the car with no legs and no nuts."

Bartley fell silent and finished undressing.

"Lie down on your stomach and put your hands behind your back." Joe grabbed a length of his cable and tied Bartley's hands with it. "Don't move."

Joe left Bartley in the kitchen while he walked to the bedroom and to the closet. He took the loose board up and began to load the remaining cocaine into the Mustang. Each time he walked by Bartley, he nudged him with his shoe and checked the binding. When the car's trunk was full, there was still a layer of coke left in the closet.

He walked Bartley out to the car and put him face down on the back seat.

Back at the motel parking lot, Joe backed up to the rental truck again. He had different cargo to load. He slid open the door, took Bartley out of the back seat of the car, and walked him into the far corner of the truck's bed. There he tied him to one of the rungs meant to secure furniture ties and let him sit on a box of gold. He unpacked the coke from the trunk of the car and repacked it in the other corner of the truck. He kick-started the Harley and rode it up the ramp. He parked it in the middle and tied a rope from the cycle to each side to keep it from falling when the truck was moving.

Bartley had not spoken since the house, but now he made a plea. "Please, sir. You can't leave me out here. This truck is hot as hell. I'll suffocate in here." He was almost crying.

"I don't know how hot Hell is, Bartley. But you better start getting used to it. But look . . . ," Joe swept his arm in a semi-circle pointing out the contents of the truck, "you have everything you could possibly want. You're sitting on a million in gold. There's more than that in cocaine in the other corner. And you have an antique Hog," Joe said and pointed to the cycle. "What else could a man want?"

"Water," Bartley said.

"There're no fountains or wells in Hell."

Joe slammed the sliding door down and locked it. Bartley wouldn't make any noise. He'd have a hard time explaining who he was and what he was doing there.

He took the video recording equipment into Carol's room and began to run the cable through the bathroom and overhead to his room. He was packed and ready to leave as soon as the women returned and he finished his bullshooting session with Miles. He needed a head start on the DEA and Florentine to return safely to Tennessee. Carol and Cathy could ride in the truck. He would drive the Mustang and cover them from behind. If his luck continued, he would be back in Tennessee by midnight.

When he finished the wiring and camera placement, he checked the screen in Carol's room. The angle of the camera on the

chair looked good. He slipped Cathy's video of her conversation with
Bartley into the video player and looked at his watch. He still had two
hours before the women would be back. He could watch the whole
tape in that time. He remembered what Cathy had said. His hands
began to sweat.

He relented, filled a quart squeeze bottle with ice and water,
and took it to Bartley in the truck. "You're going to have to make this
do for a few hours, Bartley," he said and stuck the flexible plastic
straw to the prisoner's mouth. Bartley drank half the water. Joe tied
the bottle to Bartley's waist where he could lean over and have a drink
when he wanted.

"Can't you untie me and still leave me in here?"

"No. You're lucky I gave you water. I'm too kind."

"What if I have to go to the bathroom."

"Piss on the floor. It won't hurt the gold . . . or the coke. Just
don't aim at the Harley or I'll come back and castrate you." He pulled
the Bowie from its holster and showed Bartley. Joe slammed the door
down again and locked it.

THE VIDEO WAS BETTER than he expected. Even in the low
light, the picture was clear and the color excellent. The auxiliary
microphone he had taped to the back top of the bed had picked up the
sound perfectly. His undergraduate education and hobby had come in
handy. He felt as though he was looking through the keyhole of a
honeymooning couple's bedroom. He sat back with a soft drink, turned
the room's lights off, adjusted the sound, and watched.

The story that Kent Bartley told Cathy was one of greed,
arrogance, stupidity, and violence. Bartley thought he could outsmart
both the DEA and Colombian coke suppliers.

He had been recruited by Floyd Miles in January to work
undercover in exchange for a promise of a dismissal of the prosecution
in Baton Rouge if he cooperated. Miles had an associate help make
the bond with Sean Bodine. Bartley's mission was to fly to Colombia
with a man Miles put him in contact with and buy as much cocaine as
he could for five hundred thousand dollars. He was to return to
Louisiana and help set up a wholesale sting operation. Miles saw it as
possibly the crowning accomplishment of his career that would put him
in place for a promotion.

Bartley and the man Miles introduced him to flew out of
Jackson, Mississippi, in the rented plane to Colombia on the twelfth of
February. Miles had also made the bond for the plane in Mississippi
through a company that the agency often used. Bartley and the other
man convinced someone in the Colombian drug hierarchy not only to
sell them a half million dollars of cocaine but to front them for another

million. They could easily retail it for over eight million. He and his new friend would have enough to live on the rest of their lives.

Bartley smiled and laughed when he told Cathy this part. "I conned the DEA and the Colombians. Man, I was smooth. I wore a suit and dark glasses. Strutted around. They were anxious to deal with me."

Bartley didn't want a partner or a witness. He bought two parachutes, and he and his partner received two hours of instructions on how to use them. But Bartley replaced the contents of one parachute casing with a pillow and marked it so that he wouldn't get the wrong one.

As he flew the plane across the border of Texas and Louisiana, he told his companion the rest of his plan. They would drop the shipment of coke, parachute out, send the plane on its way to the Gulf where it would run out of gas and crash. On the ground, the two would hike to the nearest town, either steal or rent a car, and return to load the cocaine. Both the DEA and Colombians would think they died in the plane crash.

Bartley had purchased enough sophisticated equipment—night vision goggles, two hand held altimeters, and other survival gear—to convince his companion that he knew what he was doing. They were going to be partners in a very big con.

Over southern Alabama in the early morning hours of Valentine's Day, Bartley watched while his companion jumped first, holding on to one kilo of coke dusted with fluorescent green powder to mark the drop spot on the ground. The man plummeted to the cold ground still clutching the precious cocaine when the parachute didn't open.

"I was too high even to hear him scream," Bartley said on the video and smiled. "There was no need to divide eight million in two when I didn't have to. I circled the plane over the drop spot marked by my buddy and pushed the rest of the coke out. When we opened the door the very first time, we accidentally knocked one loose package out a few miles from the main drop point. I wasn't going back for it. Some lucky hiker could have it. I had more than I needed. I left one package on board in case the plane was to crash and burn before it got to the Gulf. They would find remnants of coke but no bodies."

The trouble was, Bartley related on tape, Miles and the Colombians were smarter than he thought. Both recognized that it might be a scam and started to look for him. Bartley thought that the DEA might let it slide since the publicity that a two-bit criminal had scammed them would be too embarrassing. He surprised two would-be killers from Colombia in Baton Rouge and dispatched them with bullets to the head. Those were the two bodies in the U-Haul. That was when Bartley knew it would be too hot in Baton Rouge for him to sell the coke and took off with Cathy. She knew the rest of the story.

Joe shook his head. The DEA was, in a way, responsible for a load of cocaine being distributed in the heartland of America. No wonder Miles had such an interest in Bartley. He probably would rather see him dead than captured. Bartley on the witness stand would not tell a pretty story. And when Bartley confessed, he confessed good. The tape went on with a few more details when Cathy asked questions of her own.

When the talking on the tape ended, physical things began to happen. Joe reached to turn it off just as Cathy looked straight at the camera, turned, and let her nightgown fall to the floor. The prettiest ass in Louisiana, Kentucky, and Tennessee then got back into bed with Kent Bartley.

Joe pushed the rewind button and wondered whether he would ever watch the remaining hour of the tape. He stood there until it clicked off. He put in a new tape and set the timer to come on fifteen minutes before Miles was scheduled to arrive.

Thirty–eight

J oe decided not to tell Cathy or Carol that he had captured Kent
Bartley and that he now resided in one corner of the rental truck.
He would wait until after his meeting with Miles, and they were
ready to leave.

If Bartley's confession about the drug deal with the DEA was
in any way confirmed by Miles, it could mean a free ride to Tennessee
for Joe and his women companions. Miles would probably rather see
Bartley prosecuted for the murders than have him tried on the drug
charges.

At three-thirty, Joe walked to the pay phone across the street
and called Charles Palk.

"I'm coming home, and I have good news for you. I can't tell
you exactly what yet. Meet me at eight in the morning at the Holiday
Inn in Lanter City. Call John Collins in Mobile. Tell him I'll
guarantee it'll be worth his time to come up. It's okay to tell the press
that you'll have something to announce tomorrow. This may save your
ass."

"You caught Bartley?" Palk asked.

"I can't say. I'm going to need your help for a witness though.
You can help if we can explain those bodies and find the killer, can't
you?"

"As long as it's legal. You need any other help?"

"If I do, I'll call."

"Oh, Joe."

"Yeah?"

"Be sure you're not bringing an orangutan back, okay?"

Joe could hear the smile in Palk's voice. He hung up and dialed Sean Bodine's number.

"Bodine, you're going to make the deadline."

"How's that?"

"I've found our man, and he has been secured."

Bodine's Cajun yell was muffled little by the thousand miles of telephone wire. "I'll have the body for you tomorrow afternoon." Joe listened to Bodine dancing around his desk and hung up.

Florentine's Baton Rouge eavesdropper tried to call the room at the Lexington Holiday Inn but received no answer.

Joe was unlocking the door to Carol's room when the two women pulled into the parking lot and left the car near Cathy's Mustang.

The women lingered near the passenger door after they had unloaded their packages.

Carol nodded toward Joe who was going into the room. "What do you think about him, Cathy?"

"Joe?"

"Yes."

"Like I said before, he's a little weird, but I think he'd make you a good guy."

"Me? He came all this way to romance you."

"After I get away from Kent, I'm not going to think about another man for a while. I've learned my lesson. I'm going to concentrate on ballet and earning an honest living."

"You're not interested in Joe?"

"I've only known him for two days. We haven't bonded. He's a little too old for me. Did you notice when he mentioned Nixon and Watergate that he looked at me like I was a child? He's all yours, Carol."

Carol looked back toward the room. "He's going to be so disappointed."

"Not if he gets you. You're the sensible sister. You didn't run off with a murdering drug dealer."

"The tape was excellent," Joe said to Cathy when the women entered the room. "Bartley said the things we needed in order for you not to have to testify. That confession, with what we know, should be enough."

"Did you watch all the tape?" Cathy asked.

"No. I wouldn't do that. Just the confession."

"Good," Cathy said and lay crossways over Carol's bed. "I've got to get some rest before my performance tonight."

Joe looked at Carol and then Cathy. "You can't do that. It's too dangerous. Those Colombians and the DEA are following us. They're probably watching right now. You're going to have to call the ballet and let your understudy take over."

"You're just like Kent. He told me I couldn't perform either. How do you know there're Colombians following us?"

"Kent said he killed two. They won't stop until they've avenged that. That must have been who Rodriguez and Florentine were. I killed Rodriguez, but Florentine was at your performance last night."

"The other one from New Orleans?" Carol asked.

"Yeah, I didn't tell you. I didn't want you to worry."

"I thought we were just being followed by the DEA, which is bad enough. But you're saying the guy I shot is here?" Carol sat down on the bed and brought her hands to her mouth. "I'm scared, Joe."

"I'm going to take care of both of you. But we've got to stick together."

"Am I going to be on the run forever?" Cathy asked. "What good is living if I can't do what I want?"

"You'll be okay when we get back to Tennessee. You'll have police protection. I don't think the Colombians or the DEA will have any interest in you. They'd have more in Carol and me."

"Thanks a lot," Carol said.

"You girls stay here. I've got to go to my room for the meeting with Miles. Carol, be sure to check that it's recording. It's preset, but you can tell by the red light. If it goes off, push it back on."

MILES WAS ON TIME. He knocked at Joe's door precisely at five. Joe showed him to the chair at which the tiny camera lens at the juncture of the ceiling and wall was aimed. In the adjoining room, Carol looked at the screen and then the light indicating it was recording.

The heavyset agent wiped his forehead with a handkerchief and looked unsmilingly at Joe from eyes set above baggy underhangings.

Joe pushed the button on an audio cassette recorder in his pants pocket.

"Chapman, there's no need for me to beat around the bush. You know I'm after Bartley, and I know you know where he's living with that Pelton girl. We all had a very nice time at the ballet last night. You were clever enough to lose us when you took her home, but that can't go on forever. It's just a matter of days or hours until we locate their apartment or house.

"If I have to, I can just pick her up for questioning. I know she's next door with her sister now. I think she would eventually talk. Don't you?"

The women listened to the agent's threat through the audio on the monitor in the next room.

"I guess you two are right, Carol," Cathy said as she watched. "I need to go to Tennessee, or they'll never leave me alone."

Carol nodded but was paying more attention to the monitor than to Cathy.

"I need to get a few personal things from the house. Then I'll be ready to go. I'll be back within an hour," she said and turned to go.

"No. Joe doesn't want you to go anywhere. Whatever you need, we can buy in Tennessee. Just leave everything and wait for Joe to finish with this guy. It's too dangerous to go back out there," Carol pleaded.

"They're just a few personal items I can't replace. Photo albums and my high school baton and stuff like that. I'll be okay. Kent shouldn't be back until later tonight, and the DEA is in Joe's room. I'll just run out there and right back. Don't worry."

"Joe's going to be upset with me for letting you leave."

"Just tell him I wouldn't listen to you and went on my own."

The red Ford Mustang pulled slowly from the parking lot followed a few seconds later by two men in a dark late model Buick.

Joe listened while Miles talked. He appealed to Joe's patriotism and loyalty. He explained how the DEA works against drugs.

"As to Bartley, I've got a deal you can't refuse. Tell us where Bartley is and we'll see to it that you get paid by Bodine or by us. And if the girl cooperates, she can go on back with you temporarily. We may need her to testify . . . if Bartley is taken alive. He's not one to give up without a fight. We just need to recover the drugs that are left and any proceeds." Miles smiled, sat back, and waited for Joe's reply.

He was making it sound so good that Joe considered agreeing to the terms. He could be sure Cathy was safely returned, the DEA would have Bartley, and Bodine wouldn't have to forfeit the Bond. Would Miles keep his word? Would Bartley end up dead? Or worse, what would happen in the dark of the night to him, Carol, and Cathy? He wanted a few more answers to test his trustworthiness.

"What's the big deal with Bartley? He's just charged with possession with the intent to sell a small amount of coke. Why are you chasing him all over the country? Why didn't you leave it to the local authorities? If I had those questions answered, I might tell you where he is and get my ass out of here."

CATHY HAD NOT NOTICED the Buick following her a discreet distance behind. When she was halfway down the driveway, she saw Kent's Bronco parked behind the house. Her mind raced. She was too far down to turn around and go back. She would lie to Kent and say she had to go to the ballet for a few minutes to tell them in person of her inability to perform. Then she would escape with her few personal items. What if Kent had come home early so that they could marry like they had talked about last night? He had spoken of marriage before and never followed through. He wasn't likely to mention it.

She left the keys in the ignition and rushed up the steps to the back door. It was locked like Kent always kept it. As soon as she turned the key and opened the door, the muscled arm that felt like coiled steel wrapped around her neck and took her breath away. She struggled for breath as she had two nights before with Joe.

"Kent, stop it. You're scaring me to death," she rasped.

"My little one, this is not Kent. Shortly you'll be shouting my name in ecstacy. I am Manuel Torre," he said and shoved her through to the living room where Florentine was sitting on the couch. He held the long, silvery knife to her throat with one hand and let the other slide down to her breasts. She screamed. "You scream again, my little whore, and I'll cut your throat. Then I'll find out how it is to do it with a newly dead woman while her body is still warm."

Florentine puffed on his cigar and laughed.

Cathy turned to him and asked, "Where is Kent?"

"We were going to ask you the same thing."

"His Bronco is out back. I know you've done something with him. Where is he?" she asked.

"He must not have gone far if his car is still here. Where does he keep our coke?" Florentine asked.

"Your coke? Who are you?"

"He stole it from my boss. We want it back. You cooperate and you live. I can't say the same for Bartley."

"You can have your silly coke. I never wanted it in the first place. Just take it and go. You can have the gold too."

Florentine's eyes opened wide with the mention of gold. "Where is the gold and the coke?"

"The coke's under the closet floorboard in the bedroom. The gold's outside under the back steps in metal boxes."

AGENTS BISHOP AND STANSEL of the DEA had parked

their car at the next wide spot in the road's shoulder past Cathy's house and walked back along the fence rows out of sight. Through his high-powered binoculars, Agent Bishop could barely make out the movement of two persons in the house. He motioned for Stansel to retreat toward their car.

"CHAPMAN, I'M GOING TO tell you this just once. If it's ever repeated, I'll staunchly deny it.

"We leaned on Bartley after his arrest in Baton Rouge. We were planning a sting operation and we needed a heavy amount of coke. We made his bond and sent him to Colombia with a half million to buy some serious coke. We didn't care about his two bales of marijuana or the little coke he was caught with. That wasn't high profile enough to waste our time on. Coke and heroin is where it's at.

"We put him with another operative we thought we could trust who had contacts in Colombia. Our sting operation was called NOBRA for New Orleans-Baton Rouge Action.

"We shouldn't have trusted the little thief. He ran. He had never seen that much coke in his life. We lost a good operative. We had to pay a quarter million for the plane. Worse yet, we turned the little bastard loose with enough coke to supply mid-America for I don't know how long. That's why we're after him. That's damn plain.

"That's why we have eight agents in Lexington. If you cooperate, we'll find him a little bit sooner. If you don't, we'll still find him and make your life miserable the rest of your days," Miles said.

Joe listened silently, hoping the video was recording. He needed Miles a bit angrier. He would waste his backup audio recorder and pray for good results. He took it from his pocket.

Miles's complexion took on the tint of chalk, then reddened. "You been recording us? You bastard." Miles pulled his pistol from his shoulder holster and aimed it at Joe's head.

"TEN KILOS OF COKE. That's all there is under the floorboard," Torre said. He tossed the last of the bags onto the couch beside Cathy and Florentine. "We could find more than that in downtown Lexington any night."

"Check for the boxes of gold," Florentine told Torre. "We'll see if our little dancer is lying or not." He pulled a struggling Cathy to him and tried to kiss her. She bit his lip.

Torre returned carrying two concrete blocks. "This is all that's under the porch. No boxes of gold." He pulled out the knife. "Let me cut her left tit off, and she'll talk." He moved near Cathy.

"No. Wait. We'll wait for Bartley. He's probably lied to her too. He's cheated us and the DEA. He wouldn't mind cheating her."

Torre sat down in a chair across from Cathy and Florentine. "When can I play with her?"

TRAFFIC WAS REROUTED FROM the road in front of Cathy's house. Six DEA agents and a local SWAT unit converged on the area out of sight of anyone in the house.

"GIVE ME THAT DAMN recorder or I'll kill you right now," Miles said and continued to hold the gun toward Joe.

"How are you going to explain killing an innocent civilian in his motel room?" Joe asked while he held the recorder to his side.

"You're a partner with Bartley. I can make it look that way. You carry a gun, and one will be in your hand when they find you. I killed you in self-defense. I busted you for cocaine possession, and you tried to kill me. I got you first, thanks to my superior training."

"Cocaine? I don't have any cocaine."

"You'd have that too before anyone found you. I keep a package in the trunk for special occasions. Now, give me that recorder."

Joe handed it over. Miles punched the eject button, took out his cigarette lighter, and put a flame to the tape and plastic. It dripped onto the floor. He threw the recorder down and crushed it beneath his shoe. He looked at Joe. "Okay, that's good for starters. Now tell me where Bartley is or I'll do what I said I would."

Miles's mobile phone rang and he took it from his pocket. "Yes. . . . What? . . . Now? . . . Where? . . . Both of them? . . . Good."

Miles looked back to Joe. "I don't need your help. Your woman saved your ass. We know where Bartley is. When I'm through there, we'll come for you." He walked past Joe, out the door, and took off with Mike Constanzo who had been waiting in the parking lot.

Joe fell across the bed and smiled. They thought they had Bartley and Cathy. Bartley was in the U-Haul and Cathy was next door. He began to laugh until he heard Carol beating on the door and then saw her standing over him.

"She took off. I told her not to. She wanted to get a few personal things. She said she would come right back."

Joe rolled to a seated position and rubbed his temples. They throbbed. His arms ached. He began to rub them while he thought. He felt for his guns and his Bowie. His hands were shaking when he stood and took Carol by the shoulders.

"Load everything into the front of the truck. Put the video tape and equipment in the floorboard. Don't open the back door. Bartley's in there."

"What?"

"Check out of the motel. We'll meet at the mall parking lot near I-75. If something happens to me, you haul ass south until you get to London County. Go to Charlie's office."

"What?"

"I love you, but I've got to go save Cathy." Joe pulled Carol to him and kissed her hard on the lips.

"What?"

MANUEL TORRE LAY SPRAWLED on the floor, his eyes fixed in a stare at the ceiling where blood and brain matter clung in gray and red. The top of his head was missing as a result of Cathy having squeezed off a .45 magnum under his chin when he tried to pull her clothes off.

She had grabbed the gun from beneath the bed where she and Kent kept it for emergencies. Now she lay on her stomach facing the locked bedroom door. Beyond, in the living room, Florentine was cursing her. He fired through the door, and then fell to the floor himself when the first tear gas canister came through the window and exploded behind him.

BY THE TIME JOE arrived near the house, it was cordoned off by police. Nearby houses were evacuated. Television and print journalists aimed cameras toward the house and looked on through telephoto lenses.

"It's a 'Bonnie and Clyde' couple holed up in there. They've fired on the officers!" someone shouted near Joe.

Joe saw Miles a hundred yards away. He was with a group wearing bulletproof vests with DEA or SWAT unit jackets and attack hats. They huddled behind vehicles and peered over.

"Bartley's not in there!" Joe shouted toward Miles. He continued until Miles turned and waved him away.

Just then a shot did come through the living room window and slammed into one of the dark Buicks. The officers squatted nearer the ground. "Officers fired on! Shoot any threatening individual!" Miles ordered. "Put more tear gas in. Float the house away with it. The rats will come out."

Joe handed a bystander one of his last hundreds and grabbed the pair of binoculars from around his neck. He showed him one of his guns. "I need to borrow these. Official business."

He skirted the area where the officers were and began to crawl on his hands and knees toward the house. From time to time he would look at the windows. A crack of a high-powered rifle caused him to focus on the living room window where the shot missed Florentine.

Florentine crawled nearer the bedroom door and began to kick at it. Cathy's bedroom was the only one whose windows had not been broken by the tear gas shells. Flames flickered in the kitchen where an exploding canister had brought fire to the curtains.

When Florentine kicked in the door, a wall of gas came in too. Cathy could barely see the foggy figure when she pulled the trigger again. The last thing Florentine saw was Cathy aiming the .45 at him. He slumped to the floor dead from the wound to his chest.

She threw the gun down when she saw both of her attackers were now dead. She noticed the fire in the kitchen when she crawled past the door. She couldn't go out that way. Bullets were punching holes in the walls. She saw her baton by the door, grabbed it, and crawled back toward the bedroom and away from the living room where the gunfire seemed to be more concentrated.

She coughed, hacked, and rubbed at her burning eyes. Fresh air was all she wanted. Fire spread into the living room. She was trapped in the bedroom. She stood and neared the window.

"I don't have a gun! I give up!" she shouted. She raised her baton above her head to break the window.

Joe saw Cathy and the glint of the silver baton through his binoculars at the same time as a sharpshooter.

"There's a person in the window with a rifle!" Miles shouted. "Shoot!"

The marksman squeezed off one round from the rifle. It burst the window and went through Cathy's head. Joe saw it as though in slow motion. Cathy was holding the baton high, and then she tumbled to the floor.

Joe pounded his head on the ground where he lay. He beat his fists into the earth until the grass was worn away. Then he sat up, tore his sleeves up to his elbows, and began to rub his arms in a frenzy. He watched the house through tear-blurred eyes and couldn't believe his failure. Fire witnessed his defeat and would never leave his memory.

A volley of other shots tore holes in the house until the officers saw it was engulfed in flames. They held off then and waited for somebody to run out. No one did. The fire quickly consumed the frame house. It fell in on itself and onto the Bronco and Mustang parked at the rear. They burned too, sending a dark plume of smoke from the funeral pyre of Cathy Pelton into the evening sky. It lifted straight up a half mile toward the heavens before shifting southward.

Thirty–nine

I t wasn't an image that Joe would soon forget—Cathy standing at the window with her baton. It brought back all the visions. She was always just beyond his grasp. Miles would pay for his order to shoot. Who else died with Cathy? Joe wasn't sure. It was either Florentine or an associate. He could never be certain that Florentine was dead. Joe drove the rental car toward the rendezvous with Carol, but before he got there, he had to make one more call to Palk.

"I'm leaving now. I'll be in a U-Haul truck. If I don't show up, check every county jail between here and the state line. The DEA is after me, but I'll explain that to you when I get there."

Joe slid the rental car in beside the truck at the mall parking lot. He raised the rear door to check the contents. All was there. Bartley asked to be untied. Joe adjusted the rope but kept him bound. He hurriedly obtained containers of water from a nearby restaurant. He dumped one over Bartley to cool him and refilled the squeeze bottle with the other.

"What happened?" Carol asked when Joe scooted in beside her and the big truck lumbered forward.

Joe shook his head. Tears started again. "She's gone. It's too late for us to help her. We have to get out of here for our own safety."

Carol leaned into him and grabbed his arm. She put her head on his shoulder and began to cry. They were on I-75 headed south.

A HALF HOUR LATER, Floyd Miles talked to the press. The television cameras hummed and the power driven advances of the still cameras whined while in the background smoke still lifted into the air from the smoldering ruins of the house.

"This brings to a successful conclusion an investigation into a large drug ring headquartered in Louisiana and reaching to Ohio. Unfortunately, the couple decided to fight it out instead of giving up. We believe that both died by gunfire or were killed in the accidental fire. We will release their names shortly.

"We believe a very large cache of cocaine was also destroyed. There are two accomplices still at large in the Lexington area. As soon as they are arrested, we will have a more detailed statement." Miles gave a solemn little smile for the cameras and then turned toward the house.

At his car, Miles requested that the local police surround the Quality Inn and wait for his arrival. The two accomplices were there. They might surrender peacefully with a show of force.

When Miles arrived at the motel, the desk clerk told him about the suspects' recent departure. There was nothing left in either room.

Miles gave the local and state police the information he had on the rental car and truck. An agent phoned in from the truck rental that the truck was listed in Carol Sent's name with the destination given as St. Louis.

"Chapman will do the unexpected. He won't be going to St. Louis. He won't take the interstate. He won't head directly for Tennessee. He'll try to flank us. Keep an eye out for both vehicles. Have the patrol cars to be looking in a seventy mile radius. Concentrate on the less traveled highways with a presence also on the interstates just in case he gets careless. He's armed."

"I'M NOT STOPPING FOR anybody," Joe spoke as much to himself as to Carol. His hands gripped the steering wheel so tightly that his knuckles were white. They were just twenty miles now from the Tennessee border. His two guns and the Bowie lay beside him. "I could be put away for life with what I've got in this truck. You lie down if a police car tries to pull us over." He looked constantly between the road ahead and the scene in the rearview mirrors.

Ten minutes later, a Kentucky State Police car traveling north passed them on the far side of the highway. A few trees and bushes in the median may have hidden him from view. He looked into the rearview to see if the trooper braked or turned around. Nothing. The car disappeared over the hill behind him.

The mile markers showed that Tennessee was just six miles away when he noticed a green and white northbound sheriff's car pass in the far lanes. It braked and turned through the median to the southbound lanes. Blue lights came on a mile behind him. Joe put his foot to the floor, but the patrol car was quickly overtaking him. Other traffic moved to the side of the road. The officers turned on a spotlight when they were at his rear tailgate and flashed it back and forth.

Joe grabbed the .45 with his right hand. He would aim at a tire first if they tried to force him over. He didn't want to kill a police officer. When the car got even with his window, the officer on the passenger side rolled down his window and motioned Joe to do the same. Joe barely glanced sideways, but rolled the window down. It would be easier to shoot. When Joe looked over again, the spotlight flooded his face and almost blinded him.

"Is that you, Joe?" the whiny voice asked.

"Yeah, who're you?"

"Hell, Joe. It's me. Chief Deputy Ozzie Ratliff. Pull over when you get to the Tennessee Welcome Center. Me and Tom Trotter done come to escort you back to London." The cruiser fell in behind the truck and turned off its blue lights. Joe turned to Carol who was still lying in the seat. They both smiled. Joe took her hand and squeezed.

"Monkey and Sheriff Scarboro sent us up to meet you at the border," Ozzie told Joe when they talked at the welcome center. "But, heck, me and Tom wanted to see if our blue lights would work in Kentucky. We stopped three very unhappy couples in other U-Haul trucks until we found you. We have orders not to let anybody else take you. We'll escort you back to the Holiday Inn at Lanter City."

AT THE HOLIDAY INN, while the deputies went to pick up Palk, Joe unloaded the gold into his room, backed the Harley out of the bed of the truck, but left everything else as it was.

At eight o'clock the next morning, Palk brought Bartley before the press and announced that he was being charged with murder in connection with two of the bodies found earlier in the county. Other charges would follow. He displayed the mound of bagged cocaine that was found with Bartley in Kentucky.

Palk thumped one of the bags with his fist. "We've taken about four million dollars worth of drugs off the street."

Joe sat in the back of the room and read the front page story in the *Lexington Herald-Leader* where Miles was claiming Bartley died in the fire and the coke was destroyed.

Agent John Collins had already reviewed the tape of Miles's antics with Joe in Lexington before Miles was summoned to Tennessee. "This is terrible," Collins had told Palk and Joe before the news conference began. "He violated many of our standards and probably several laws. There'll be somebody here from headquarters to relieve him of his badge and weapons when he arrives. Is that okay with you?" he asked and looked first at Joe and then Palk.

"Sure," Joe said. "Whatever. He needs to be off the streets."

"General Palk, I think from the agency's standpoint, we'd rather you prosecute Bartley on the state murder charges than for us to do anything on the coke. You have a pretty strong case according to that other tape we saw. If Bartley's smart, he'll jump at two life sentences rather than wanting to go to a federal prison where we have a lot of Colombian drug dealers."

"That sounds good to me. What about the coke?" Palk asked.

"If that could be released to me, I could wrap up the plane investigation and move on to something else. I think the NOBRA escapade in New Orleans is going to backfire on a lot of folks over there. Who knows? I might be in line for a promotion."

JOE LEFT THE NEWS conference while Palk was still answering questions. Carol sat by the pool where they had rolled in nearly a month before. It seemed like so long ago. It was August now.

"I told you a month ago that Cathy's wanderings were bound to lead to no good—probably to her death. But now that it's finally happened, it's just so hard to accept. She really was my only family. The last two days were as close as we'd ever been. At least we had that." She looked away for a few seconds and then back to Joe. "Is there any sense of going back to Lexington to claim her body?"

Joe shook his head. "Palk has already contacted the D.A. up there. They're going to send her remains to you here in about a week." Joe wrapped his arm around Carol's shoulders. "Cathy lived her life the way she wanted. I thought we could save her, but it wasn't meant to be."

"Do you think Cathy died from the gunshot or from the fire?"

"Gunshot, definitely," Joe said. "I saw her holding the baton. She didn't know what hit her."

"Good. I'd hate to think she died in the fire."

"I would too. I think I'd go crazy if I thought that, because I would think I could have crawled in there and saved her."

"You're going to have to drop your Carp nickname and take on something different."

"What?"

"Phoenix. The mythical bird that rises from its ashes. You've had at least four fires that affected your life. When you were ten, the fire that the girl was in, the one in New Orleans, and the one in Lexington."

"Don't forget the ones I started the first day of May before I left here." Joe managed a small grin, the first in a while.

"Maybe you can come away from this fire to make a new start—a new life."

Then they noticed Charlie Palk at the gate to the pool.

"I thought you two might be relaxing out here," Palk said and sat down in a chair across from them. "Bartley's already talking about a plea deal. He's shooting a lot of bull. Quite a con artist. Says he could tell me where a million in gold is. Can you believe that?"

Joe shook his head. "Be careful what you believe from him, Charlie. Hey, I wanted to ask you something. Did you ever find out anything about those numbers on those guys' belts?"

"Oh, yeah. They were part-time strong arm enforcers. Otherwise they worked day jobs at a belt and boot company in Mexico City. They'd get drunk a lot. The owner said they were all the time calling him to bail them out of jail. Sometimes they were too drunk to remember his number—so they stenciled it in their belts. He said he had seen the belts himself."

Palk and Joe laughed. "So, you've identified them?"

"Yes."

"And the couple Bartley and Cathy picked up in Birmingham?"

"They were brother and sister from Dayton, Ohio. Their parents are on the way down to identify them and bring dental records."

"So, that's that. You don't need us any longer. We can take off to Louisiana when Cathy's ashes get here?"

Palk looked away and shook his head. He turned back to Joe. "I hate to give you any more bad news, but your old client Mattie Hensley died while you were in Kentucky. Kidney failure. There was nothing anyone could have done. The last time I saw her, she asked about you. I told her you were on a job for me in Kentucky."

"Just another place I should've been. Everybody's dying on me." He looked from Carol to Palk. "Where's she buried?"

"In her church cemetery. Oh, Joe, she mentioned you in her will."

"She did? I thought I drafted her last will."

"She had me to change it after you left. You know how persistent she could be. Can you come by the office in the morning—maybe about ten—to go over it?"

Joe nodded.

Forty

Luann Templeton sat applying polish to her fingernails and talking with Ozzie Ratliff when Joe walked into Palk's reception area the next morning.

"Ozzie, don't you have anything better to do than sit around here bothering Luann?" Joe asked and sat down.

"He's no bother," Luann said between breaths of drying air she was aiming at her nails.

"This is the place to get the hot-breaking news," Ozzie said.

"And that's why you're here?"

The deputy smiled and twirled his cap in his hand.

"Joe, are you going to be moving back? General Palk said you're staying at the Holiday Inn with that Louisiana woman. Anything to that? You two gettin' serious?" Luann asked.

"The way you said it makes it sound X-rated. We have separate rooms. Besides, you know that I don't know what *serious* is." Joe got up, walked to the window, and looked out at the dying marigolds. "We've had a hot, dry summer."

Luann looked at the phone console. "You can go in now. He's off the phone. Preacher Gallaher is already in there."

Joe stopped instantly. "What's that fat, greasy-haired asshole doing here?" he whispered loudly.

"I don't know. Something about Miss Mattie's will."

"You know Preacher Gallaher, don't you, Joe?" Palk asked.

Gallaher and Joe did not exchange eye contact or offer to shake one another's hand.

"Very well," Palk said when Joe sat down without answering his question.

"Gentlemen," Palk began and scooted his glasses down his nose. He peered over them at his guests. "Mattie Hensley thought highly of both of you. I don't know why." He coughed. "But be that as it may, she was aware of your disregard for each other. I revised her will in late May after her son was killed in New York in that car accident.

"Miss Mattie was a frugal teacher who made either wise or
lucky investments. In 1970 she bought eight hundred fifty shares of
Wal-Mart stock. It has had two-for-one splits at least nine times since
then. We've just received a quarter million as a result of her son's
death. All in all, she had an estate of nearly two and a half million.
    " 'Not bad for a woman with half a brain and a people greeter
at Wal-Mart,' I'm quoting here from the will," Palk said.
    "Anyway, I'm the executor. She directed me to put her money
into a trust fund with both of you to receive one-half of the income
each year."
    Preacher Gallaher sat up straighter at the news. He smiled
and started calculating on his stubby fingers.
    "There's just one condition."
    "What?" Gallaher asked.
    "Each of you will receive one-half of the income on Mother's
Day of each year if, and only if, Joe preaches the Mother's Day sermon
at the First Community Church where you are the pastor, Reverend
Gallaher, and Reverend Gallaher leads the song service."
    Joe stared straight ahead. The preacher's chin dropped to his
chest.
    "Mattie expected me to allow a disbarred lawyer to stand in *my*
pulpit in *my* church?"
    "If both of those provisions are not met, the money goes to a
New York charity for homeless artists."
    Joe and the preacher both left Palk's office without saying a
word.
    "Y'all have nine months to work on it!" Palk shouted after
them.
    "I don't need the money that bad," Joe told Carol when he got
back to the motel.
    "But doesn't it mean something to you that she wanted you to
preach the Mother's Day sermon? You have nine months to work on
one. You can use it every year. A tradition. If you preach it, I will
come."

    DURING THE WEEK THEY waited for Cathy's ashes, Joe and
Carol cycled all around the county, to the Smoky Mountains, and along
the lakeshores. Carol fell in love with the area. They took turns
crying and laughing. Mourning merged with relief. Joe took her to all
of his old haunts and to his former house where they walked out onto
the dock. He pointed to where he found the purse. They visited
Mattie Hensley's grave and laid a wreath of flowers near the head-
stone.
    When the ashes arrived, they did their own memorial service

by the river where Joe had seen Cathy as a vision that first night he anchored near Kinton. They walked out onto a rocky ledge over the river and scattered her ashes on the Tennessee just as the red lip of the sun was kissing the blue-green ridges of the Cumberlands to the west.

"Cathy was and always will be the Lady of the River," Joe said and hugged Carol to him. She nodded her head and wrapped her arms around his waist.

IN ANOTHER WEEK, BARTLEY pled guilty to two murders and was whisked away to Brushy Mountain Penitentiary to serve his time. Joe stored most of the gold in a rental unit when Carol told him to keep it. No one believed Bartley's wild claims of treasure except Agent Floyd Miles, and he was in Washington trying to explain his actions.

"The DEA owes it to you, Carol, for killing your sister. They shouldn't profit from their recklessness," Joe had argued. She finally agreed to take what Cathy had earned as a stripper but no more. She suggested that part of the remaining million in gold be used to set up a scholarship in Cathy's name at LSU for performing artists and part for a scholarship in Tennessee in honor of the girl who had died in the fiery crash that eventually caused Joe's suspension. He agreed.

THE NEXT DAY, THEY began a more leisurely return to Louisiana on the Harley. This time they stayed off the interstates and took the two-lane highways. They would see a little of the country and view the small towns.

In downtown Harriman, just a half hour after leaving their motel, a pickup truck's driver blew the horn at Joe when he was stopped for a traffic light. He looked in his rearview mirror and saw the two women occupants waving furiously. When the light turned, the truck eased up beside the cycle.

"Carp, Carp, is that you? Pull over," the driver insisted.

The voice sounded familiar and it was someone who knew his nickname, so Joe stopped the Harley in a nearby bank parking lot. He and Carol got off while the truck parked a short distance in front. When the women alighted from the truck, they both were wearing maternity blouses.

"Oh, shit," Joe said. "It's Kellie and Rose."

"Who're Kellie and Rose?" Carol asked.

"Never mind," Joe said. He saw eighteen years of child support staring him in the face.

"We saw 'Carp' on the back of your helmet," Kellie said. "We knew there couldn't be more than one 'Carp' around here."

Joe pointed to the bellies of the women and raised his eyebrows.

"No, no. These ain't your'n. We were two months along when we saw you back in May," Rose whispered in his ear.

"Carol, these are two friends of mine from way back."

"Come over to the truck, Carp, we want to show you something." They all walked over. "Look in there," Rose said.

Joe looked in at the women's big golden retriever who was lying down and being bombarded by pups from all around. Joe counted. There were eight fluffy balls of life trying to have dinner.

"How cute," Carol said when she looked over the tailgate.

"Remember your big dog and ours getting together out there on that island?" Kellie asked. "This is the result."

"You mean J. R. is the father of all these pups?" Joe asked.

"Yep. They're six weeks old. We were on our way to the Wal-Mart parking lot to give them away. The owner of the male dog gets first choice if you want one. It's tradition. Do you want one?"

Joe looked at Carol. She gazed back at the pups. "Does he want one? You bet. Which one do you want?"

Joe looked back over and leaned into the bed as far as he could. "I don't know. They're all so cute." The pups were darting here and there until one left his companions and ran over to Joe. It raised its head and licked Joe on the nose. Joe grabbed it and held it up to check its gender. "This is him," Joe said and smiled widely. "He's J. R., Jr."

They stopped every two hours to let the pup frolic in the roadside grass. While they rode, Carol held the pup like a new-born child against Joe's back.

CAROL AND JOE REVISITED the Plantation House restaurant the next evening. J. R., Jr. rested at Carol's apartment in the utility room. They ordered the same meal as the first one they shared together—crawfish jambalaya with a bowl of gumbo.

"Are you going to New Orleans with me to get *THE CARP?*" Joe asked.

"No, Joe, I've got to stay here. I'm going to Cathy's house and storage unit and clear everything out. I'll give some stuff away and keep a few things I think she'd want me to have."

"You might tell the local police about the two bales of marijuana before it gets smoked all over Baton Rouge."

When the orange sherbet was almost gone, Joe reached over and took Carol's hand. "Will you marry me?"

Carol dropped the spoon she held in her other hand. "Marry you?"

"Yes, I bought a ring one day in Tennessee. Here it is. I want to be with you forever. I love you."

"Joe, this is a surprise. I don't know what to say."

"If you're not going to say 'yes,' at least don't say 'no' until you've had time to think about it. I'll go to New Orleans and be back up in a couple of days. You can go back to Tennessee with me on the boat."

"The boat? I . . . I . . . I'll think it over. We've just known each other about six weeks. That's too short a time to really know somebody."

"The engagement can be as long as you say. I know what I want. I'm happy when I'm with you. My pursuit is over."

FOUR DAYS LATER WHEN Joe started upstream from Baton Rouge on *THE CARP*, he and the pup were the only passengers. The body of J. R. was in a large ice-packed cooler at the stern.

Four weeks later, after brief stops in Paducah to see Keith and in northern Alabama to visit Goose, *THE CARP* entered the inlet where London County Marina was located on the Tennessee. A sleek eighty-foot houseboat preceded it to the dock as it had all the way from Baton Rouge with Carol Sent at the helm. Keith had handlettered the name of the craft for Carol—*CARPE DIUM*—in gold letters shadowed by black. They docked side by side and began their eight-month engagement.

THE SERMON WAS SHORT as sermons go on Mother's Day at the First Community Church.

"As we remember Mother's Day," Joe said, "we must remember that all women may not be mothers. There are some women who have an influence on us like a mother. Such was Mattie Hensley. Some women rescue those who need help, as pharaoh's daughter did with the infant Moses. And some give their lives trying.

"For those everywhere who give that nurturing, loving, caring concern of a mother—this day is for you. By the Lord's grace we sometimes meet those women in our lives. 'And she called his name Moses; and she said, Because I drew him out of the water.'

"Now, Pastor Gallaher will lead us in a closing song—'Amazing Grace.' "

Pastor Gallaher wiped tears from his eyes when he stood to lead the song. Charles Palk, executor of Mattie Hensley's estate, duly noted the conditions had been fulfilled and slipped two cashiers checks from his pocket.

At the end of the service, Palk made his way to the front. "I have an announcement to make. As most of you know, Joe Chapman

and Carol Sent are to be married later this afternoon at the marina.
I will perform the service on her houseboat. You all are invited. Now
I'd like for Brother Gallaher to lead us in a stirring rendition of 'Shall
We Gather at the River?' "

THE SKY WAS A blue parasol with white cotton ball clouds
when Joe and Carol joined hands on the deck of the boat. Flowers
wrapped around the boat's railings. A light breeze lifted the fragrance
of lilac and honeysuckle from shore to the boat. Joe's suspension had
ended. He now stood with Carol before his new boss, Charles Palk,
who presided. The tuxedoed Joe looked into the eyes of his bride who
wore a white flowing gown. He adored her, even her slightly Roman
nose.

Joe's favorite people were there—Goose and Millie Collins,
John Collins, and Keith, who insisted on working, doing a sketch of the
scene while the vows were said. He would fill in the details later.
Ozzie was Joe's best man and Luann was the only bridesmaid. J.R.,
Jr., now ten months old and almost fully grown, yelped from the shore
where he was tied.

"I pronounce you husband and wife," Charles Palk said while
the women in the audience dabbed at their eyes and the men looked
away.

Joe and Carol kissed. Then he grabbed her around the waist,
hefted her high above, and pirouetted around the deck of the boat until
they both were dizzy.

"Put me down, you impetuous imp!" Carol shouted. He set her
down and kissed her again.

"Joe, stand back. I have to throw my bouquet over my
shoulder. It's traditional."

She turned her back to the people on the dock and tossed the
flowers in a great arc upward and backward. Luann, in all her
bridesmaid finery, jumped sideways and skyward at the same time in
a desperate attempt to snatch the bouquet from the air. She caught
it, but when she came down, her feet became entangled with Ozzie's.
They stumbled together a few feet until they flew off the deck and into
the shallow water.

Splashing wildly, Luann stood up, still clutching the flowers
with one hand and Ozzie with the other. Beside them a school of
startled fish thrashed the surface of the water.

"What is that?" Carol pointed and laughed.

"Carp, just carp," Joe said.

About the author:

Chris Cawood is a native Tennessean. He is a lawyer, journalist, and writer. He is a 1970 graduate of the University of Tennessee College of Law. He has served in the Tennessee General Assembly. He now lives in Kingston, Tennessee, with his wife, Sara. This is his fifth book and second in a series of Southern novels.

You may E-Mail Chris Cawood with comments about his books at:

booktalk@icx.net

Order other books by Chris Cawood

For autographed copies of any of the following titles, send $12 (includes postage and handling) to Magnolia Hill Press, P.O. Box 124, Kingston, Tennessee 37763

Tennessee's Coal Creek War (266 pages) a historical novel of the 1890s in East Tennessee.

1998: The Year of the Beast (312 pages) a political thriller set in 1998 in the South.

How to Live to 100 (and enjoy it!)—(120 pages) the stories of Tennessee Centenarians and their secrets to long life.

Legacy of the Swamp Rat—The story of the Tennessee versus Alabama football series.

Phone orders: 1-800-946-1967
Visa or Mastercard

You can read the first twenty pages of any of the above books and see the covers at no charge by visiting the author's home page at: HTTP://user.icx.net/~booktalk

Name:_____

Address:_____

_____

Titles Wanted:_____

At $12 each for a total of:_____

Autographed to:_____

Visa □ or Mastercard□ number:_____Exp:___

Mail to: MHP, P.O. Box 124, Kingston, Tn. 37763